Stand your Ground

Stand your Ground

kandi steiner

Kings of the Ice #5
by Kandi Steiner
Copyright
Copyright (C) 2025 Kandi Steiner
All rights reserved.

No part of this book may be used or reproduced in any form or by any means, electronic or mechanical, including photocopying, recording, or by any information storage and retrieval system without prior written consent of the author except where permitted by law.

The characters and events depicted in this book are fictitious. Any similarity to real persons, living or dead, is coincidental and not intended by the author.

Published by Kandi Steiner, LLC
Edited by Elaine York/Allusion Publishing, www.allusionpublishing.com
Cover Photography by Ren Saliba
Cover Design by Kandi Steiner
Formatting by Elaine York/Allusion Publishing, www.allusionpublishing.com

Author's Note

Hi, reader.

If you've read my books before, you know I always aim to deliver heart, angst, and steam. This story still has all of that — but I want to prepare you that it also turns the heat up higher than some of my past work. You'll find scenes here that are bolder, kinkier, and more exploratory in nature.

Because of that, I want you to feel safe as you read. At the back of this book, you'll find a complete list of content warnings and notes about some of the sexual elements that may be new or surprising, including Carter's group experience as a rookie and the role of The Manor in his journey. Please take a look if you'd like more detail before diving in.

At the end of the day, this is still a love story — one full of vulnerability, growth, and two people learning to trust each other in and out of the bedroom. I hope you enjoy the ride.

With love and gratitude,
Kandi

To the ones who rise from the wreckage
and turn pain into power.

This one's for you.

Chapter 1

Bark, Bark

Carter

"Did you take a pill before coming in?" Livia asked me, hanging one hand on her slim hip as the other pointed a very sharp tool in my direction. "Because that shot only numbs your jaw, and I *know* you gotta be high to say what you just said to me."

"Come on, Liv. Look—"

"Doctor Young," she corrected me, one dark brow sliding up into her hairline. "This isn't a barbecue at Daddy P's house. You're in my chair, at my job, and you will respect me and call me by my hard-earned title."

Fuck.

My cock hardened at her tone, at the way she snapped at me, at how she made me feel small and somehow made me buzz to life at the same time.

"Yes, Doctor," I breathed.

Livia narrowed her gaze, dropping it to my lap before she rolled her eyes. She was trying to keep her sassy attitude intact, but I saw the smile she was fighting. "Oh, my God, Carter, you don't seriously have a boner right now?"

"Can you blame me? That was fucking hot."

My words slurred a little as my jaw began to numb.

As a professional hockey player, I'd had my fair share of dental work. But somehow, I'd managed to avoid taking a high stick hard enough to break my tooth and send most of it flying onto the ice.

Until last night's game.

Which was why I was here now, in Dr. Livia Young's chair, shooting a shot that, until now, I'd been too afraid to shoot. And no, I wasn't just asking her to fix my tooth.

I was asking her to take me under her wing and train me to be better in bed — and in dating, period.

I'd known Livia for years. She was the dentist for the Tampa Bay Ospreys, the team I was now on a one-way contract with. She was also best friends with Maven Tanev, who was married to one of my teammates and closest friends. Because of that, we ran in the same circle — attended the same parties, went out to the same places, watched the same group of friends grow up and get married and move on while we played on the sidelines.

Maybe that was what had courage swelling up in my chest like a wave. It hadn't even been two months since we celebrated the wedding of our friends Aleks and Mia, and now, the whole friend group was preparing to celebrate Will and Chloe and *their* nuptials.

I had a sneaking suspicion Livia didn't care one way or another, but I was tired of watching everyone else find their happiness when I couldn't even find a fucking date.

Don't get me wrong — I loved my teammates, even when they ragged on me, and I was happy they were all finding their soulmates.

Stand *your* Ground

I was just also *unhappy* that my confidence had been eviscerated by an absolute hard ass of a coach when I was fifteen, and I had yet to recover it.

It pissed me off that something I should have been over by now had soiled not only my performance on the ice, but off it, too.

But that's how trauma works, as my therapist so often loved to remind me. We don't get to choose how long it sticks around and keeps its claws in us. We don't get to turn a dial and make it suck less. It's a part of us, like a mole or a scar, and we have to learn to live with it.

So, that's where I was now — acceptance.

My confidence was shit. I couldn't land a date to save my life, let alone a girlfriend.

But Livia Young was just the woman to help me change that.

She pinched the bridge of her nose, that sharp tool still dangling in her other hand. Her dental assistant stood by silently, a mask covering part of her shocked face, though I could see the young girl's eyes flicking between me and Livia. What I could see of her pale skin was flushed red. But I had no shame when it came to Livia Young, and she'd never been afraid to speak her mind, either.

That was just one of the many reasons I knew she was right for this job.

"Carter, you are in my chair because you were hit in the face and your two lower central incisors have been blown to bits like a mortar went off in your mouth."

"I love when you talk dentist to me."

"And the only lesson I will be giving you," she continued, waving that tool around like a wand. "Is to get a better mouth guard and learn how to dodge a high stick."

She was so gorgeous I could barely think straight as I listened to her threats, the corner of my mouth lifting helplessly. Deep brown skin, smooth and enticing, dark black hair pulled into a tight, professional bun. She wore little makeup today, and she was still stunning.

But I also knew that woman when she wasn't wearing a white coat.

I knew her in silky, body-hugging dresses and sky-high heels.

I knew her with red-painted lips and gold metal through every hole on her body.

And I knew, from the little comments she'd let slip over the years, that she owned more than a few leather outfits that had whips to match.

Which was exactly why I knew she was the right one to propose my hare-brained idea to. Any other woman would have already laughed in my face — if they'd even managed to hear me out.

What grown ass man asks a grown ass woman to teach him how to have swag in the bedroom — and out of it, too?

Me.

The kind of man who clams up or shoots off a corny pick-up line any time he's remotely attracted to a woman, all thanks to a bald, bastardly son-of-a-bitch who made him feel like the dirt beneath his feet years ago.

"Come on," I begged again, swinging my legs over the chair so I could sit up and face her. "Look at me, Li— er, Doctor Young," I amended when she cocked a brow. "I need help."

"I won't argue that."

"And who better to teach me than the master herself?"

I smirked a little with the use of the word *master* — well, as much as I could with half my jaw numb, anyway. If

I knew anything about Livia Young, it was that she loved a compliment. And damn if she didn't deserve every single one that had ever existed.

There were women, and then there were women like *her* — elegant without effort, sophisticated and composed, polished like a fine jewel. She didn't have to try to be beautiful or powerful or confident. All of it existed within her like the blood that ran through her veins.

She commanded attention from the second she walked into a room.

And from the first time I'd met her, she'd turned me to absolute putty any time we were within a foot of each other.

She was used to my antics, to my non-threatening grin and eye roll-inducing pickup lines. And even though she pretended to be annoyed by me (okay, she probably *was* slightly annoyed by me), she also laughed at my jokes. She smiled and tilted her head at me when I flirted with her, like she was just a little curious even if she pretended not to be.

I knew the woman saw my attraction for her, but this was the first time I was calling her on it — really bringing it to the surface.

And asking her to agree to the most ridiculous agreement anyone ever had, I was sure.

Livia watched me for a moment before she sighed, nodding to her assistant to take a break and leave us alone. I could hear the distant sound of drills and water picks from rooms down the hall as the door opened, the assistant left, and then it was just the two of us.

Liv crossed her arms, leaning a hip against the counter as she finally released the tool she'd been holding fast to. Even in the sharp and harsh light of the fluorescents above us, and even with a strange pair of magnifying goggle things strapped around her neck — she was still a knockout.

"What exactly are you proposing?"

I sat up straighter, hope ballooning in my chest. "Simple — I want you teach me how to break a woman's back in bed."

"There are magazines for this, you know," she shot back. "And YouTube."

"You think I haven't tried that?" I grabbed the back of my neck. "You think I'm not embarrassed as fuck to admit to anyone, least of all *you*, that I'm still a virgin?"

Something sparkled in her eyes at that.

"I mean, unless you count the one time a puck bunny let me stick it in her butt, which I don't, because it was in a room with three other guys getting to do the same thing."

Livia barked out a laugh. "Okay, I want that story someday, but while we're on limited time... why do you want this?"

My throat thickened a bit with her question, the truth churning in my gut. But I was too numb and too desperate to get into the real meat of it right now. I wasn't too proud to beg for help, but I was maybe a bit too proud to admit the source of my despair.

So I went for the shallow reason, instead.

"Isn't it obvious?" I shrugged. "I'm a professional athlete. I go out at least twice a week and have girls hanging all over me, but I can never land the deal. Either I run them off with my pathetic attempt at flirting or I get them home and fucking choke." I ran a hand through my hair, shaking my head as I looked at the ground. My jaw was really numb now, words slurring a bit, and I knew Livia needed to get to work doing whatever hellish things she needed to do to me before this numbness wore off. "I'm hopeless, alright? Somehow, I figured my shit out on the ice. I'm in the National League now, no longer being sent down to the A, and I've got a lot to offer someone. I just... I can't prove that if I can't get past first base."

Livia's gaze softened.

"Plus, I'm horny."

She laughed the sweetest, most genuine laugh at that.

I beamed with my broken-tooth grin, swallowing down the fact that the woman I'd *most* like to prove myself to was her. I liked Livia. I had for years. I knew it, she knew it, our whole fucking *crew* knew it — and they all teased me about it because they all saw the obvious.

She was entirely out of my league.

We were exact opposites; her dominant and me submissive, her confident and me insecure, her living carefree while I struggled to feel adequate every day I woke up.

Yes, I wanted her to teach me to be confident, to show me how to step into a room and take up space. But I also wanted to show her that I was more than the guy she'd immediately friend-zoned, that I could go toe-to-toe with her, that I could make her feel good.

I wanted her.

And maybe part of this hare-brained scheme was to show her that I deserved a shot at more than just friends.

But I couldn't admit all that just yet. Maybe one day she'd see me as more than an annoying fly buzzing around her, but for now, I just needed her to see enough to give me this.

"Okay," she conceded after a moment. "I can understand why you might want an arrangement like this. But... why me?"

I sucked my teeth. "Really, Liv? Come on. Look at you." I waved my hand like it was a magic wand covering her in golden fairy dust. "You're gorgeous, smart, savvy, driven as hell. I know you don't need to hear me say it to know I've had it bad for you for years. Besides, don't act like this doesn't intrigue you." I leaned forward, elbows on my knees. "I've heard your stories. I know you like to exercise control in more places than just this office, and you'd have *full* control in this situation."

"Don't act like you know me," she shot back immediately, but again, I saw the sparkle in her eyes, the curl of her lips she was fighting. "Also, that little bit about you having it bad for me makes me want to say no. Feelings like that make arrangements like this messy."

Holy shit.

Is she actually considering this?

I tried to tamp down the quickening of my heart, keeping my face level as I shrugged. "I said I like you, not that I'm delusional. I know you're not into me." That admission made my gut sour, but I ignored it and pressed on. "That doesn't change the fact that I know you're the perfect person to help me. And I think we're good enough friends that I can ask that of you."

She softened again at that, making it hard for me not to float away on that pesky cloud of hope.

"What's in it for me?" she asked after a moment.

"Besides the fact that you get to boss me around and make me do whatever you want in the bedroom?"

She flattened her lips, arched a brow, and waited.

Okay... so clearly that isn't enough.

"What do you want?"

"A million dollars."

I laughed heartily, but then coughed and choked a little when I realized she was serious.

"You're kidding," I tried.

"Not even a little bit."

I blinked at her.

I wasn't sure what I'd been expecting her to ask for in return, but it wasn't that. Livia seemed perfectly fine on her own financially. She co-owned a boutique dental practice that serviced high-profile clients and offered cosmetic procedures. I was fairly certain I'd never seen the woman wear anything that wasn't designer, save for her white coat, and she drove a Jaguar F-Type Coupe that made our car-crazy friend, Jaxson, nearly lose his mind the first time she pulled up in it.

"Listen, I make good money," she said, reading my mind and blank stare, no doubt. "I do veneers for half the celebrities in Tampa. But at this point, all of my best friends are married to, or seriously dating, a multi-millionaire. And then there's Mia, who will probably hit a billion soon on her own. And judge me if you want to, but I'm a bad bitch just like the rest of them. I deserve to jet set around the world, dress myself in diamonds, and buy myself a bougie ass car on a man's dime just because."

"Done."

The word was out of me even before her little speech finished. I thought I saw something vulnerable beneath her statement, something she was hiding, but I knew better than to press. I wasn't telling *her* the whole truth right now — why should I expect different?

It seemed we both had things we were running from, things we were fighting, things we were working through. If I could help her in some way, it would make the whole deal feel even.

And the truth was she didn't need to convince me, even if there wasn't another reason underneath the one she'd provided. I already agreed with her. She *did* deserve to be spoiled.

If she'd let me, I'd happily give her the passwords to all my accounts and watch her drain every single one.

Besides, I just signed a new contract with the team over the summer, one that guaranteed me more money in the coming seasons. I was no longer on a two-way contract, which was a vote of confidence that the team didn't expect to send me down to their AHL affiliate — like they'd done for the first three years. No, now I was firmly in a one-way contract. I was a Tampa Bay Osprey — for good.

I was also who they'd bet on to take the place of our veteran center who'd retired. I was the player they felt was up to the task.

No pressure, the weak little teenage boy inside me murmured.

That fucker always lived with me, though I'd learned through therapy how to snuff him out most of the time. Even with my fuck ups — and there were plenty — I was still playing at my best this season, proving to Coach and our general manager and everyone else on the team that they hadn't made a mistake by signing me.

But I still wondered sometimes.

I still worried I'd hit a wall and would bounce back to reality, to the place where I couldn't quite hang.

For now, though, I had the contract — and the money to go with it. I also still had a signing bonus from when I was younger that had done nothing but sit in a high-yield money market accruing interest.

What the hell was I going to spend that money on that would be better than bedroom lessons from Livia fucking Young?

Liv tilted her head like she didn't believe me, or like she didn't think I realized she was dead serious.

"You'll give me a million dollars," she said, deadpan.

"I'll give you two."

Her eyes shot wide at that. "*Two*-million dollars, and all I have to do is help you unleash your freak?"

"See?" I waved my hand toward the space between us. "Tell me this isn't a deal you can't refuse."

She should have laughed in my face. *I* should have been embarrassed by what I was asking, by how quickly I doubled her offer. But the yearning in my chest for what and who I could become if she actually agreed completely outweighed the shame I carried for asking in the first place.

I wanted to be the man who knew what he was doing. I wanted to be the man who didn't flinch when the pressure was on. I wanted to settle down, to find someone to share my life with, someone to go home to.

Maybe if I could pull this off — if she said yes — I could stop feeling like I was one mistake away from blowing it all.

She tapped her chin with one long, dark red nail, and I wondered what it would feel like to have those nails digging into the flesh on my back. I longed to know firsthand what it felt like to be under her spell. This wasn't the kind of woman who flirted and made you court her before she let you take her home after three dates and lay her down missionary-style in a dark room.

This was the kind of woman who had you on your knees before the first date, hands bound, a ball gag in your throat as she assessed if you were even worth the time she'd have to give you to let you take her to dinner.

I didn't know why, but that thought had me salivating.

I was sure my therapist would have something to say on the subject.

"No one else knows," Livia said.

That hope that had ballooned inside of me surged so quickly I thought my chest would pop, and I was practically panting as I leaned forward in my seat, nodding. "I won't tell a soul."

Is she actually agreeing to this?

"I'll teach you, but I also get to use you," she said. "Whenever and wherever I want. If I send a text, you come running."

"Faster than I ever have in my life."

Oh, my fucking God, she is. She's agreeing.

"You don't get to say no to anything until you try it at least once."

My heart skipped with a mixture of fear and curiosity. "No backing down."

"I mean it. No matter what I propose, you hear me out and try before saying yes or no."

"Use me, Liv. I'm yours."

She chuckled at that, one brow inching up like she wasn't so sure I knew what I was signing up for. Then, she opened the door and called for her assistant to come back in.

"We're drawing up a contract, too," she said, waving her finger at me. "And you're going to take this seriously or I'll drop the whole thing and still take your money — which you will pay a big portion of up front, by the way."

"Yes, Mommy."

"Jesus," she muttered. "You're more eager than that puppy dog you adopted."

"Bark, bark." I panted, too, for good measure, tongue flopping out before Liv shot me in the eye with the water pick.

"That's enough. Now, lie back and open your mouth."

"Wow, we're getting started already, huh?" I rubbed my hands together as I did what she said.

Liv ignored me, firing up the drill as soon as her assistant rejoined us, but her mouth quirked up into a grin.

I thought it kind of looked like she had a little too much fun causing me pain.

I thought I kind of liked it, too.

Chapter 2

Safe Word

Livia

Head Bitch in Charge.

That was the name of the shade of deep red lipstick I smoothed over my top lip, careful to inch it up into the swells perfectly before I dragged it along my bottom lip next. It was also the persona I was embodying for the evening, the one I wore so effortlessly.

Carter Fabri, center for the Tampa Bay Ospreys, was coming over to sign contracts that would bind us — in more ways than one.

And I was asserting my dominance in this situation immediately.

Not that I *needed* to, considering that boy was about as dominant as a kitten. But I never did anything half-assed. If we were going to do this, we were going to do it *right* — legally, financially, and consensually.

I tucked my lipstick away before exiting the bathroom and crossing to the full-length mirror in my bedroom. With one manicured brow cresting into my hairline and a slow smirk climbing on my freshly colored lips, I assessed the full outfit, reveling in the power it sent running through me.

I didn't care what anyone said — clothing, makeup, and jewelry were just as important as armor going into war. A woman could create her destiny with the right outfit. She could tell the whole world not to fuck with her with a perfectly curated ensemble.

Tonight, I was playing the part of businesswoman, teacher, and psuedo-Domme at once, which was why I'd chosen a tailored blood-red suit that hugged every curve like it had been sewn straight onto my skin. The blazer was sharply cut, cinched at the waist to accentuate my long, sculpted frame, with sleeves that flared slightly at the wrists and shimmered with a delicate gold-threaded pattern. Underneath, a deep-V silk blouse as black as midnight framed the soft swells of my breasts and the elegant dip of my chest bone. I didn't wear a bra. I didn't have a need to.

My pants were high-waisted and wide-legged, elongating my frame and pooling just enough over the pointed toes of my black stiletto heels — the bottom of them the same crimson shade as my lips.

I wore my hair in a sleek, low ponytail, edges laid, the length falling straight and glossy down my back like a whip. My gold jewelry gleamed against my deep brown skin — thick hoops, a stack of bangles, and a chain necklace that dipped between my breasts and disappeared beneath it at the apex, inviting curiosity. My eye makeup was smoky and bold but precise, my highlighter sharp as a tiger claw and my expression completely unbothered.

I looked like I could sign a million-dollar deal, ruin a man's life, and ride him into repentance — all without breaking a sweat.

Satisfied, I let the familiar sound of my heels clacking against my marble floor soothe me as I walked to the kitchen island, pouring myself a glass of red wine from the decanter I'd situated earlier. Tampa Bay stretched out in all its glory outside the floor-to-ceiling windows of my high-rise condo, and I tipped my glass toward the city I loved so much before taking a sip.

My stomach was a mess.

I didn't know if it was butterflies or cockroaches causing the fluttering sensation, didn't know if I was more excited or nervous or regretful.

It was an absolutely ludicrous arrangement to agree to — being Carter Fabri's *teacher* in exchange for two-million dollars.

But it was also absolutely genius.

Part of me longed to call my best friend, Maven, and tell her the predicament I'd found myself in. We'd known each other since we attended college together — her in undergrad, me in dental school — and we'd been thick as thieves since. I knew she'd laugh with me, knew she'd make jokes and have the tension coiled in my gut relaxing within sixty seconds on the phone with her.

But the bigger part of me was thankful Carter and I had agreed not to share this arrangement with anyone, friend or otherwise.

Because it was fairly easy to explain my willingness to participate to Carter, but my best friend would have called me on the bullshit immediately.

Sure, it made sense to the puppy dog rookie that I would say yes to teaching him to be a proficient lover in exchange for a nice payday. There weren't very many sane people in the world who would say no to an offer for that amount of cash. And I did mean what I'd said to him when he was halfway numb in my chair earlier this week.

I *did* deserve to be spoiled.

I worked my ass off. I had since the day my family cut me off and made me figure out how to do dental school — and life — on my own. Nothing had held me back, not the realization that reputation meant more to my family than my well-being, nor the mountain of trials I'd had to survive in order to gain my degree. I didn't just open a basic practice in the suburbs somewhere, either. I found the perfect partner to go into business with, one who had the same big dreams I did. We wouldn't just be dentists; we'd be artists. We'd serve the highest clientele with the most complicated requests. We'd fix the shattered teeth of hockey players and also sculpt diamond-studded grills for rap stars.

And we'd succeeded.

Full-mouth reconstructions, anti-aging bite lifts, luxury sedation suites — our office wasn't just a dental practice, it was a status symbol.

Years and years of hard work meant I had a lot to show for my efforts.

But it also meant I was *tired*.

Not just the kind of tired a vacation fixes. Bone-tired. Soul-tired.

Alone-tired.

I was over being everything for everyone and having no one to catch me when I collapsed.

Yes, like any hard-working woman, I wanted private airfare and bungalows over crystal-clear water. I wanted Michelin-starred dinners and luxurious massages on the beach. I wanted shopping sprees in Positano and yacht charters in the Seychelles.

But more than any of that, I wanted something I wasn't ready to admit to my best friend or anyone else.

A child.

My throat went dry even as the thought passed through me, chills breaking over my arms as I took another sip of wine to conjure my power back. This wasn't the time to get in my head, but I couldn't help but ruminate on the *real* reason I'd said yes to Carter's proposal.

To everyone around me, I was a powerhouse — Doctor by title and co-owner of *the* boutique dental practice in Tampa. I lived a life of luxury, from my clothes and shoes to my car and condo.

But in reality, even making the high salary that I did, I wasn't the kind of rich who never had to worry about anything. Between the cost of living the lifestyle I'd chosen and paying off my half-a-million dollars in student loans, what I had left to put away for savings was good, but not good *enough* — not for where I wished to be in the next five years, anyway.

Two-million dollars would be the equivalent of more than two decades of the *best* savings scenario for me, and I was about to make it in the snap of my fingers.

With Carter's offer and the means it provided, I could finally do what I'd been sitting on for years.

I was going to freeze my eggs.

I was going to start a family on my own time, without a man, whenever I felt ready.

Single mom — by choice.

I knew it wouldn't make sense to anyone, not even those closest to me, which was exactly why I'd never chosen to share it. Because I needed control — over my life, my timeline, my body. And admitting I wanted a child, especially as a single woman, cracked open too many doors. There would be questions I didn't know I could answer, risk of someone as logical as my best friend trying to talk me out of it and possibly succeeding, and an ocean of vulnerability I wasn't ready to swim in.

When I was ready — truly ready — I'd tell Maven and the rest of the girls.

But for now, this was just for me to know.

I was giddy at the fact that I wouldn't have to wait any longer. I was only thirty-two, but the last time I'd had my levels tested, my Anti-Müllerian hormone was lower than it should have been for someone my age. My doctor said not to panic, but the whisper was there — *'sooner is better.'*

Part of the reason I'd stalled was that I knew the financial burden I'd have to undertake, and I didn't want to take it lightly — not on top of the student debt I already had. I wanted this, a family, but I also didn't want to give up my life of luxury — or my autonomy.

But now, I'd have the financial backing for everything: the medical procedures, the pregnancy, the delivery, the cost of caring for a child, and the paid help I'd need to do it *my way.*

My daughter and I wouldn't want for anything.

Okay, so I didn't know the gender of my future child, but in my mind, it was always a little mini me. It was always me and my baby girl taking on the world together.

And I'd always keep her safe.

I'd never abandon her.

Unlike my own parents.

The next swig of wine tasted a bit sour with my mind going down that path. Fortunately, I didn't have time to wander too far down it before my phone rang.

"Miss Young, I have a Carter Fabri for you," Rolando said. He was one of the employees who ran the front desk in my condominium building.

"Send him up, please."

I was surprised to find the butterflies winning the battle in my belly as I ended the call, the anticipation of what was to come finally surpassing the anxiety I felt over my hidden reasons to agree in the first place.

I was going to play teacher and pseudo-Domme to Carter Fabri.

I couldn't help the smirk that spread on my lips at the thought. I'd been a Domme to my fair share of men, but I'd never served as a full-on teacher. It excited me, the thought of training him to please me. It also sent a strong wave of power through me to think he'd please *other* women with what I taught him, that they'd be unknowingly thanking *me* when they called out his name in bed.

But perhaps what intrigued me most of all was his confession that he was a virgin.

That was an experience I hadn't had since I was in high school, when I didn't know anything either, and the boy who'd chosen to lose his v-card to me had been a fumbling mess. The whole ordeal had lasted all of four seconds, and he'd been the only one to leave satisfied.

Then again, I was used to sex being a disappointment back then.

That was before I flipped the script, before I took control over my body and my pleasure and never let it go again. I'd learned a lot since then.

Now, I would get to share it with Carter.

To anyone who didn't know me well, anyone who watched my interactions with Carter on the outside, they'd likely think I was a mega bitch. They'd think I was mean and nasty, that I hated the man.

But it wasn't anything like that.

I adored Carter — in the way I adored all of my friends. It was wild, how life had landed me in this group of hockey players and bad ass women they called significant others, but they'd become my family.

They were my *only* family.

I loved each of them fiercely, and I knew them well — which was why I liked to fuck with Carter. He was like a labrador slobbering at my feet and begging for pets, and I knew after the first few jokes we'd shared that he *liked* when I sassed him. His eyes lit up every time. His lips always curved.

It was our own little game — him throwing every corny pickup line in the book at me without shame, me pretending to be annoyed when we both knew I found it entertaining.

This agreement, of course, would complicate that friendship a bit, but Carter assured me he understood what we were and what we were not, what we never would be. I had to take him at his word for that, and part of me was nervous, but the other part trusted that he was getting what he wanted out of this deal, and he wouldn't press his luck.

He said he knew I wasn't into him, and while I hated that he wrote himself off so quickly, he was right.

But it wasn't *just* him.

It was any man.

I didn't trust any of them enough to do much more than tie them up in bed and make them beg for mercy, and at thirty-two years old, I didn't see that changing.

A knock at my door had me setting down my wine glass on the kitchen island before I crossed my expansive living area to the foyer. It was January in Tampa, which meant it was just cool enough to have the gas fireplace going. It gave my condo a rich, alluring, and somewhat cozy vibe — the flames dancing in the stone frame, the cityscape serving as moving art, the beat-heavy sound of trip hop ticking up my anticipation.

Once again, I found comfort in the click of my heels against the hard floor before I swung the door open to reveal my victim.

I had to admit, I expected him to show up in his usual attire — some sort of athletic wear, whether it be joggers and a hoodie, or basketball shorts and a long-sleeve Dri-FIT tee. Instead, Carter surprised me by arriving to my condo like he was arriving to the arena before a game.

He wore a tailored navy suit with a subtle checkered pattern that only revealed itself under the light. The crisp white dress shirt beneath was open at the collar, no tie in sight, sleeves pushed up just enough to show the ink on his forearms. His dark hair was freshly styled, and the sharp lines of his neatly trimmed box beard framed his jaw perfectly. The edges were lined, precise enough to make it clear he'd shaved for the occasion — but not enough to dull the rugged edge that would fool the unsuspecting viewer into thinking he was a bad boy instead of an absolute teddy bear.

He looked every bit the professional athlete in business mode — sharp, commanding, and sexy.

I wouldn't admit that to him, though.

Instead, I offered a slight arch of my brow as I opened my door to let him inside. "Dolce and Gabbana?" I mused.

"You said this was a business meeting," he reminded me.

"Color me surprised that you listened."

"Oh, I'm an excellent listener. Especially when I'm trying to impress my new teacher. Some might call me Teacher's Pet, even."

He punctuated the flirtation with a wink. I answered with a performative bored blink and a sweep of my hand toward the glass dining table, where two crisp stacks of paper waited — each topped with a black pen.

But instead of heading straight over, Carter slid his hands into his pockets and took in the view of my condo. I noted the silver ring on his pinky just before his hands disappeared from view, and something about that man confidently wearing jewelry had my intrigue spiking.

His gaze swept the space with idle curiosity until it caught on the diamond and pearl necklace displayed beside the fireplace — draped elegantly over a slender black velvet bust. His eyes widened.

"Whoa," he said, gesturing to the glittering piece. "That looks pricey. Are you a jewelry collector or something?"

"Crafter."

His brows shot up. "Wait... you *made* that?"

I nodded, folding my hands behind my back as I came to stand beside him. "It's one of my favorite pieces. Usually, I make them and donate to charity auctions or gift them to friends. But that one..." I smiled, stepping forward to run my fingers lightly over the gemstones. "I just couldn't part with it."

"Saving it for a special occasion?"

Something sharp and unwelcome flared in my chest at the question — because though I'd never admit it, a small, stubborn part of me still dreamed of wearing that necklace on my wedding day.

As if I could ever trust a man enough to pick the right restaurant for dinner, let alone put a ring on my finger.

I buried the thought and the ache it brought, sliding my mask of indifference neatly back into place.

"Certainly, something more special than teaching a boy how to play," I said, arching a brow at him with the tease.

Carter clutched his chest like I'd shot an arrow through it. "I'm twenty-six. Doesn't that qualify me as a man?"

"Not if you've never sucked a clit."

"You wound me," he groaned, staggering back a step for dramatic flair. But then he slid his hands into his pockets again, shrugging. "But you're not wrong. We are here for a reason, aren't we?"

"Speaking of which." I gestured toward the table again.

I refilled my wine and poured a glass for Carter, placing each beside its corresponding contract. He watched me with an amused smile before unfastening the button of his suit jacket and finally taking his seat.

"Let's get down to business, shall we?" I asked.

"Please."

I had to fight against a smirk when I read the eagerness in that word, in his body language as Carter leaned toward the contracts with eyes wide and hopeful.

Sometimes he made me feel like a kid again, like the carefree girl I had been before innocence was ripped from me like a rug from beneath my feet. The way he so easily smiled and laughed, the way he could take a joke from anyone, no matter how cruel, and still bounce around so happy and nonchalant...

I envied that.

I loved that some of it rubbed off on me.

And I sometimes wondered if there was more to this man than the joyous ball of sunshine he presented to the world.

Carter reached for the first stack of papers, brow furrowing as he flipped through them. I took my time settling into my seat across from him, crossing my legs and sipping from my glass as I watched his eyes flick over the contents.

"That one's the business contract," I said smoothly. "It's a legitimate consulting agreement between you and LY Performance Coaching, LLC."

Carter blinked at me. "You have an LLC?"

"I do now." I smiled around the rim of my glass, nodding to the inked paper in his hands. "You're paying me two-million dollars over the next three months, split into four, clean wire transfers, each with a lovely little invoice to match. In exchange, I provide one-on-one performance enhancement coaching, mentorship, and confidence training."

"So, it's legal, then."

"As a marriage. Or should I say divorce, since I'm taking your money?" I swirled my wine with a teasing grin at that.

"Won't Uncle Sam take his cut, then?"

I shrugged. "Of course. But that's fine. There will still be plenty enough for me to jet off to the Exumas."

And to freeze my eggs, parent a child solo, set my kid up with private childcare and schooling for life, make sure we never have to want for anything...

Carter's smile climbed as he flipped through the pages. "It says here that early termination results in forfeiture — unless it's initiated by you."

"Correct. That means I can walk away at any time, for any reason, and still keep the full payment. But if you're the one who ends it? You don't get a refund."

"That doesn't seem fair, Doctor Young."

"I never said I play fair, *Rookie*."

He frowned at that. "Hey, I'm not a rookie. This is my fourth season."

"And your first playing completely in the National League and not in the minors, if I'm not mistaken?"

His jaw clamped shut at that. "If we're going by the league's standards, I'm not a rookie. I've played more than twenty-five games at the national level."

"Well, technicalities aside, you *are* a rookie in the bedroom. Otherwise, we wouldn't be here, would we?"

"Why do I like when you talk down to me like that?"

"Oh, honey," I said, leaning forward with a salacious grin. "This is nothing. Let's get through these contracts and you'll see just how degrading I can be — and just how much you'll love it."

I knew without testing the theory that his cock was hard now. I saw it in the way his breath shallowed, in the way his pupils dilated, in the bob of his Adam's apple. It was confirmation of what I'd suspected after all these years of teasing him.

He liked a little abasement.

He was excited to play.

But we had business to settle, first.

After a few minutes of perusing the fine print of the first contract, Carter seemed satisfied. We signed three copies — one for each of us, and one that would eventually be the legally binding, notarized version.

"And where exactly is our notary?" Carter asked, finally trying his wine. He hummed his approval, and I internally smiled. The man clearly had good taste — in wine *and* women.

"I have one on standby who works with discretion."

"And one who doesn't mind bending the rules, I gather, since I'm pretty sure they're supposed to witness us signing. And there should be disinterested witnesses, too, no?"

"Leave the how of it all to Mommy, mmkay?" I purred, twirling the pen around my knuckles. "The rich have been signing shady deals in penthouses for centuries. We're just keeping tradition alive."

Carter snorted, but he let it go. He moved on to the second contract — slimmer, more intimate in nature. And when he saw the title at the top, his brows shot up.

"Personal Performance Improvement Plan or (P-PIP)," he read aloud, voice skeptical. I had to fight back a laugh as he frowned, and then his eyes floated up to meet mine. "This doesn't seem legal, despite your clever title here."

"It's not," I said. "Well, not entirely. Parts of it are legally binding — like the NDA, the exclusivity clause, the termination terms, and the financial agreements. But the rest?" I shrugged. "It's symbolic. It sets the tone."

"Symbolic," he echoed.

"It creates structure. Anticipation. Power exchange. You follow it because you agreed to, not because I'll sue you if you safe word out when you see a nipple clamp."

He gaped at me.

"Kidding," I said, leaning back and crossing my legs as I lifted my wine glass to my lips. "Or am I?"

Carter flipped through the pages, his gaze narrowed at me like he was really trying to decide if I'd bring out my nipple clamps.

Jury was still out on that one.

"There's a safe word?"

"Words, actually. High stick." I smirked at the irony. "You say those words, everything stops — play ends just like it would on the ice, and we have a clean slate. You say Offside, it's a sign that I've crossed a line, but you're still okay to keep playing. In that case, I ease up. You say nothing..." I shrugged, tilting my glass to my lips. "And I assume you're enjoying yourself."

"Hockey terms," he said, not as a question but more as a humored assessment.

"Didn't want to confuse you too much. Figured it was best to speak your language."

"Do you think they'll really be necessary?"

"My goal is to teach *you* how to take charge with the woman of your choosing eventually. But first, you will relinquish control to me. I teach by example. So... it's possible." I said with a shrug. "If you want to be not just adequate in bed but *incredible*? Then we're going to be exploring a lot more than just how to find the hole."

Carter bit his bottom lip on a laugh, nodding to the papers in his hand. "And this part — the 'try before you deny' clause?"

"You attempt everything once before you're allowed to turn it down. I get full creative control. You get full use of your voice and boundaries." I tilted my head. "It's meant to be a fun, educational experience, not a hostage situation."

"Why do I have a feeling that your version of *fun* will be much different than mine?"

"Scared already? There's still time to back out."

"No," Carter said immediately, shaking his head. "No way in hell I'm backing out of this. I'm still shocked I got you to agree at all."

"Trust me — that makes two of us. And don't be so sure to say there's no way in hell. You haven't read the next clause."

Carter frowned, returning his attention to the contract. I continued sipping my wine and watching him. Already, my wheels were turning with all the ways I could make him bend and squirm, all the ways I could bring him pleasure that he didn't even know he liked yet.

"This part that says I'm obligated to come when you call?"

"Any time, for any reason. I will, of course, respect your obligations to the team. But past that, if I want you? You're mine. And that isn't the part I think you may take issue with."

Carter continued reading, and then smirked, tapping the back of his pen to the page. "Ah. Participant agrees to remain monogamous for the duration of this agreement, unless otherwise authorized by Doctor Young." He tongued his cheek, eyes sparkling a bit when they met mine. "So, I need your permission to sleep with anyone else?"

"If you want to keep this arrangement, yes. I don't share my toys unless I choose to."

The flush of his cheeks was so goddamn pretty. It had the blood in my veins sizzling, the desire to top him nearly too much to contain now. I may have never seen this agreement coming, I may have never imagined I'd give Carter Fabri the chance to warm my sheets, and I may have still had reservations about whether he could handle what I planned to give him.

But fuck if I wasn't excited to find out.

He was hot — even if he felt like a stone in my shoe half the time. I knew he had a body sculpted by years of playing professional hockey under that suit of his, and any hetero woman — me included — would be excited to have all-access to peruse it.

This was the buzz being in control gave me. The wine paled in comparison to the kind of high that came from knowing I could do whatever I wanted to this willing man sitting across from me.

"It's not about possessiveness," I clarified. "I have no intention of having any sort of relationship with you past being your professor. This is about teaching you how to pleasure a woman — and how to get her in the position where she would even agree to let you try. But that clause is for health reasons. Which brings us to the next point."

Carter flipped the page, then read aloud again. "All physical contact and training activities are contingent on the completion of a full STD panel, updated within the past fourteen days, as well as a physical exam to ensure the participant is cleared for rigorous activity."

He barked out a laugh, his grin wide as he looked up at me.

When I didn't mirror the sentiment, his smile fell.

"You're serious?" He blinked. "I mean, I get the STD part, but I play professional hockey. I think I'm more than cleared for rigorous activity."

"I think you'll find that some of our scenes will vastly outpace three periods of skating around on the ice, Rookie."

I smirked, tapping the next part of the contract.

"And you'll see here that I am on birth control, but just to be extra cautious, we will avoid sexual intercourse whenever I am near my ovulation window."

"You really thought of everything." Carter shook his head, but he dragged his teeth over his bottom lip at the same time, his eyes alight with curiosity. "Fine. I'll get into the doctor first thing."

"Good boy," I praised.

His nostrils flared, and this time, I couldn't help myself.

I leaned forward, abandoning my wine glass on the table before my hand snaked beneath its surface. I found his knee, sliding my index finger over the smooth, luxurious fabric of his slacks before I walked my fingertips up along the seam.

Carter kept his gaze on mine, feigning that he wasn't aroused or scared or interested in the slightest, but his body betrayed him in every way. He slouched a little in his chair, his thick thighs widening to allow me better access as I slowly trailed my touch higher.

"You like when I call you a good boy," I whispered. "Don't you, Rookie?"

He wet his lips, refusing to answer. I slid my palm over his hard cock with a firm pressure, enough to make him groan and rock into my touch, his head falling back and eyes fluttering shut.

"Say it."

"I like it," he breathed.

He was big. Even through his slacks, I could tell. I wouldn't have cared either way — it was more about what he could do with his cock rather than the size of it. But it'd be more fun for me to play with a well-endowed student, and inside, I was salivating at the thought.

On the outside, I was a cold, level-faced Domme.

"You like *what*?"

I wrapped my hand around his shaft.

And then I squeezed, hard, tight enough to make Carter transition from a panting moan into a wince and hiss.

"I like when you call me a good boy."

"What's that?" I squeezed a bit harder.

"I like when you call me a good boy!"

I grinned, releasing him, but not before I rewarded him with a soothing stroke. He was still panting as I sat back in my chair, reaching for my wine glass.

"Then let's finish this, and perhaps I'll consider bending that doctor-approval rule in order to have a little fun tonight."

Carter looked as desperate as I wanted him to be as he quickly scanned the rest of the pages, and then he scribbled his signature fast and messy before sliding the pages to me.

"No more questions?" I asked.

"Not at the moment."

I carefully scrawled my own signature. "Well then, Mr. Fabri," I said. "Are you ready for your first lesson?"

He swallowed, voice cracking when he asked, "Now?"

I shrugged, standing slowly and noting how his gaze followed the gold chain that disappeared under my blouse. "Unless you need a week to prepare," I teased, tilting my head. "Do you want to carb load? Watch video? Get a pep talk from Coach?"

Carter stood a little too fast, knocking his thigh against the edge of the table. "No! *Shit*, that hurt," he said, rubbing the spot. His cock was still hard, pitching a tent against his slacks.

Why did I find it so fucking endearing that he wasn't the least bit embarrassed to be so eager?

"No," he repeated, schooling his expression. "I'm ready."

I grinned.

"Oh, Rook," I said, circling the table slowly, heels clicking with each predatory step I took. "You have no *idea* how not ready you are."

Chapter 3

Earn It

Carter

I was embarrassingly hard before she even laid a finger on me. Okay, so that was a bit harsh. Technically, she *did* lay a finger on me. In fact, she laid her whole damn hand on me and rubbed my cock before squeezing it so hard I didn't know if I wanted to scream and shove her away, or groan and beg for more.

I was so out of my element, but *fuck,* was I enjoying it. I still could barely believe Livia had agreed to the whole thing, so any time she shot me a look or rewarded me with a little piece of praise, it was enough to have me panting and howling for more.

It wasn't just that I was excited to touch her — though *Jesus*, that alone was enough to short-circuit my entire nervous system. It was that for the first time in my life, I felt like I was taking control of the part of myself I'd always been too ashamed to own.

I'd spent years trying to scrub off the voice of my OHL coach who'd broken me down. He'd told me I was too soft, too easily rattled, too emotional to lead. And I'd believed him. My parents had watched me turn from a confident, happy kid who loved to play hockey, into an anxiety-riddled mess who couldn't perform.

That pressure had haunted me for years — on the ice, in the locker room, in bed. Eventually, I was able to work with Coach McCabe, with our goalie, Will Perry, and with other players to figure out how to be better for the team. I'd painstakingly slowly figured my shit out, and I finally felt like a reliable teammate who could show up, play the puck, pass and score, and contribute to a winning season.

This was my opportunity to do the same thing for my personal life — this time, with Livia as my coach.

And I knew before we even got started that she wasn't just going to teach me — she was going to give me the tools to make the changes on my own. I could see it in her predatory gaze already, how she wanted me to crave the power of knowing exactly what I was doing and exactly how to make someone else feel good.

I'd fought tooth and nail to find confidence on the ice, building it brick by brick with every game, every season, every brutal loss and hard-earned win. Now, I had a chance to do the same thing here: to torch the fear, rewrite the narrative, and become the kind of man who didn't just score, but dominated.

I was tuned in to her every move now that the contracts were signed and the caps were back on our pens. Livia made me pull my chair to the middle of the room, and now, she circled me like a lioness sizing up her prey.

She told me she planned to teach by example.

So, I buckled in for the presentation.

I clocked every click of her heels, every brush of the fabric of her suit against the chair, and when she dragged her fingernail from one shoulder to the next as she passed behind me, I visibly trembled.

I really was like an eager schoolboy, early to class and sitting in the front row. I wanted to learn. I was fucking *excited*.

And if I thought her little touches and looks were undoing me, it was nothing compared to when she lowered her mouth to my ear and whispered her first command.

"Unbutton your shirt," she said, pausing to lick along the shell of my ear before she added, "Let me see what I'm working with."

Immediately, my hands flew to the button on my dress shirt. I shoved my suit jacket out of the way and hastily made work of each button until my chest and abdomen were exposed.

Livia circled me slowly, grinning as she watched me obey her.

"Are you ready to give up control tonight?"

She purred the words, her voice low and sure and amused. It lit me up like a goddamn firework, and I shot back my response without hesitation.

"Yes."

I was pathetic.

But apparently, that was exactly how she wanted me, because Livia's lips curled higher.

In a feat of balance, she effortlessly lifted one leg, dragging her heel up the inside of my calf before she planted the pointy toe of it right between my thighs. Half an inch higher and she would have stepped right on my balls — and I had a feeling that was the whole point of the move.

"It's a shame you don't have a tie with this ensemble," she mused, eyes dragging the length of me. "But your jacket should work."

When I didn't automatically move, she arched a brow at me.

"Strip."

The word popped off her red-stained lips, and I did as she asked, shrugging out of my suit jacket and handing it to her.

She smiled when it was in her hands, admiring the fabric for a moment before dropping her heel back to the ground. "Good boy. Now take out your cock."

That little spark I'd felt from her praise before ignited again, my next breaths coming wilder as she circled behind me once more. But I hesitated at her last request — mostly from the shock of hearing those words roll out of her beautiful lips.

Suddenly, nails dug into my chin, yanking until I looked up at the woman I'd dreamed of touching for so long this all felt a little unreal.

"Believe me when I say you don't want me to have to repeat myself."

Swallowing, I kept my eyes on hers, watching as they flared when I reached down and unfastened my belt. I slid the button through the slit next, tore the zipper down, and then shoved my pants and briefs down to my mid-thighs. I had to wiggle to get them down — even with custom-made pants, hockey had given me thighs and an ass big enough to make it a difficult task to accomplish.

When my cock sprang free of my briefs, the tip already coated with precum, Livia finally broke eye contact with me long enough to look down.

I thought I saw a hint of appreciation in those gleaming eyes of hers, but wasn't sure if it was because of my cock, the two-million-dollar paycheck she had coming, or because she was excited to toy with me.

Either way, she released my chin, patting my chest before she walked around the chair.

I took the momentary break from her intense glare to try to lock into student mode. I mentally noted the words she'd said so far, how they'd made me feel, how I'd love to make a woman feel that way, too.

Livia was beaming with assurance. Not even a full five minutes in and she'd already made me feel both safe and desperate for her. That was my goal, too — I wanted to emulate that.

But when she bent at the waist, pulling my arms behind me, and began to tie my wrists together — I slipped out of student mode as my heart picked up its pace.

Our first lesson, and this woman was already binding me.

"You're not allowed to touch me unless I say so. Understood?" She tightened the fabric around my wrists as I responded.

"Understood."

"What are our safe words?"

I smiled. "High stick and offside."

She stroked my hair, rounding the chair until she was in front of me again. Just because I was curious, I tested the knot she'd tied, attempting to pull my hands apart.

They barely budged, and the thick fabric somehow cut deep into my wrists, threatening me not to try that again.

Livia's eyes flashed like she anticipated that move, like she bet on it — and she was satisfied with how it all played out.

"If we're focusing on how to pleasure a woman, then there's no better place to start than with that pretty mouth of yours," she started, reaching out to slide her thumb across my bottom lip. The first deliberate touch of her skin against mine had me closing my eyes and leaning into her. "And you will use *only* your mouth tonight."

I chased the ghost of her touch with my tongue as soon as she pulled back, breath knocking hard against my chest when I looked up at her.

"You will not come until I allow you to," she said. "*If* I allow you to at all."

Fuck me.

My cock jumped, and Livia noted the movement with a teasing smirk. "Look at you," she crooned, her eyes skating over every inch of me like a blade. "So eager. So desperate. Just how I want you."

I swallowed, the lump in my throat making me gulp loud enough for Livia to hear. Her grin widened before she slowly unbuttoned her blazer, peeling it off one shoulder and then the other. She hung the expensive thing carefully on the back of a chair across the room, at the dining table we'd abandoned, and she took her time on her way back to me, rolling up the sleeves of her blouse as she took each leisurely step.

She stopped in front of me, the low bass and melodic beat of unfamiliar music serving as the soundtrack as she offered up her forearm like it was dessert. The velvety brown skin there was smooth and inviting, and she angled her arm until it was just inches from my mouth.

"Kiss me."

I dropped my gaze, heart racing like she had her pussy in my face instead of her arm. This already felt like a test I was ill-prepared for.

But the only way out was through.

It was impossible not to overthink, impossible to quiet the thoughts tripping over themselves in my mind as I leaned forward and lowered my lips to her arm.

Don't fuck up, loser.
God, you have no idea what you're doing.
She's bored with you already.
She can't wait for this to be over.
You're going to fail.
You already have.

I couldn't erase them, but I did my best to ignore them. I'd learned how to do that during a game, learned how to override those thoughts and lean into my intuition.

I only hoped I could do the same here.

Tentatively, I pressed a kiss to the soft skin of her forearm. I wasn't sure exactly what I was supposed to be doing, so I just... kissed her. Then, I inched back and looked up for my next direction.

"Again. And this time, don't kiss me like I'm your fucking grandmother."

The corners of my lips twitched, but then I stared at the spot where I'd kissed her arm before and furrowed my brows with determination. I leaned forward once more, but this time, I didn't just press my lips to the skin. I tried to tease her, kissing once, twice, three times, trailing each one across her delicate arm.

"Mmm... now we're getting somewhere," she cooed. "Where do you want to kiss me next?"

"Between your thighs."

Livia's brows shot straight up, and she wet her lips as a delicious, low, raspy laugh left her chest. "While I appreciate the enthusiasm, you have to earn that privilege." She dragged her nail down the line of my jaw, tilting my chin up higher. "Try again."

I swallowed. Again, it felt like a test, and I knew I'd already answered incorrectly once. "Your stomach," I said, and I tried to say it with certainty, but it came out more like a question.

"Ask for permission."

My cock twitched at the command, and Livia smirked at the sight.

"May I kiss your stomach?" I asked, my eyes locked on hers.

"You may," she answered. Livia held my gaze as she unfastened the buttons of her blouse, taking her time with each one. She didn't shrug out of it once it was open. Instead, she let the silk hang over her breasts, her nipples hard beneath the fabric, navel barely exposed by the slit she'd created.

I wanted to reach for her so badly I couldn't help but try. My suit jacket grew tighter around my wrists as I bucked against the restraint.

"Mouth only," Livia reminded me, and then she slid up between my thighs, knocking each of my knees open wider so she could position herself just right. It made my briefs and pants ride a bit higher where they were half-discarded down my thighs, and I groaned when her pant leg brushed against my balls.

She threaded her hands through my hair, pulling me to her stomach and sliding the fabric of her blouse open just enough for me to have access.

"Kiss me," she said again. "Let it linger. Show me you deserve to kiss me where you really want to."

My heart was thundering in my chest, eyes appreciating the lean, toned stomach now serving as my next assignment. I used my nose to widen her shirt, running the tip of it along her skin before I pressed my first kiss right above her belly button.

She didn't react to the first touch, not the way I did. I hummed in my throat, and then repeated what I'd done to her arm. I trailed kisses in a line up to her chest bone and back down, slow with my perusal.

"If you want to kiss my pussy, you better show me you can use that tongue."

Her words clipped out impatiently, and shame heated my neck that I hadn't thought to add tongue before she asked for it. But rather than fixate on the misfire, I put my focus on meeting her demand.

If I could just hold her, if I could wrap my arms around her waist and pull her to me as I licked along her abdomen... but my hands were bound. I felt inept, having only my mouth at my disposal.

And that was the whole point.

She was teaching me to get creative, to use each piece of my body individually instead of relying on multiple parts at once. It was a challenge I was desperate to rise to.

I kissed her beneath her belly button, lips lingering there before I opened my mouth and let myself taste her for the first time. I ran my tongue long and flat up the middle of her torso like I was licking an ice cream cone and didn't want to waste a single drop.

When I reached her rib cage, I kissed my way back down — slower this time, using my tongue and lips in tandem. I took the curl of her fingers in my hair as permission to get sloppier, licking and sucking her stomach the way I wanted to taste her pussy.

"That's it," she rasped, raking her nails over my scalp. "That's a good boy."

I groaned, increasing my efforts as my cock grew painfully hard. The cool air of her condo only heightened my senses, the fireplace doing nothing to provide relief.

I wanted her warm hand around my shaft. I *needed* that warmth, that pressure.

But I hadn't earned it yet, and I knew it.

"May I kiss your breasts?"

Livia smirked at the question, and it lit me up to think I might have impressed her by asking without being told.

"You may," she said. "But I want you to ask again. And this time, let me know what you're really thinking. Give me those dirty thoughts I know are swirling inside your head."

I swallowed, eyes flicking between hers. "Let me kiss those perfect tits of yours, Liv. I need to see them. I *have* to taste them next."

A spark of electricity shot between my thighs as she smirked and gave me a simple nod of approval.

You're doing it.
Don't fuck up now.
Relax, you've got this.
But you'll probably blow it.

I nosed her blouse out of the way with my thoughts still racing, revealing one beautifully perfect, dark nipple. I wanted so badly to suck it between my teeth, but I stopped myself, trying to think ahead to what Livia would expect me to do. I wanted to surprise her again.

So, I ran my tongue along the chain between her breasts first, toying with the metal before I slowly trailed my way over to her breast. I licked and sucked along the soft swell, relishing the weight of it against my mouth. I teased and played for as long as I could stand.

Then, I took her nipple in my mouth, swirling my tongue around the peak before I covered it completely and sucked.

Livia let out the softest moan, letting her head fall back, and I swore I could have come right there just from that little noise I'd earned.

"Is that okay?" I asked, unable to stop myself. I wanted to know. I *needed* to hear it. "Did I do it right?"

"That's it," she breathed, hands fisting in my hair and moving my mouth back to her nipple. I swirled my tongue again before flicking her bud with the tip. "*Yes.* You're doing so well."

The praise spurred me on, and I kissed my way over to her other breast, giving it the same treatment. Finally, Livia was softening, her breaths beginning to catch up to the labored ones coming from me.

I was turning her on.

And *goddamn*, I'd never felt prouder of myself.

After savoring each breast, I trailed my gaze up to meet hers. "May I kiss the inside of your sweet thighs next?"

"You may," Livia answered, eyes gleaming as she stepped back.

I missed her warmth immediately. I craved *more* of it. I wanted her in my lap, seated on my cock, riding me until I called out her name. I had a feeling that wouldn't be happening at all tonight, but I couldn't help but lust for it, for all of her.

My chest heaved as I watched her slip out of her slacks. She took her sweet time with it, making a show of unfastening her belt, unzipping the pants, and letting them fall into a puddle at her feet. She stepped out of them, leaving her heels on.

Along with a black lace thong and garter set.

My mouth watered as Livia strutted back to me — blouse hanging open, tits wet from my mouth, pussy hidden behind that decadent lace. She straddled my thigh before placing a hand on my shoulder to help her balance and hiking one leg up and over. Her heel hit the back of the chair, propping her ankle just beside my ear.

And I couldn't help it.

I leaned forward instinctively, breathing in deep to take in her scent.

"Naughty boy," she reprimanded, smacking my cheek lightly before she took my chin in her hand and forced me to look up at her. "Did I say you could do that?"

I shook my head.

"No, I didn't. Now, let's focus on our lesson." She tilted my face toward her inner thigh, forcing me closer. "If you want to pleasure me, to pleasure *any* woman, you're going to need to learn to read the signs. Pay attention to what makes me tremble, what makes my breath catch, what makes me moan."

She released my chin, letting me take over.

"I'll provide guidance when needed, but I want you to show me you can learn from observation." She paused, hands finding the back of the chair to help her balance. "You may begin."

Just like before, I started slowly, perusing the soft skin of her inner thigh with gentle kisses and swipes of my tongue. But when she didn't react, I changed pace, kissing harder, sucking the skin.

She flexed her hips forward, just a little, just enough to let me know I was onto something.

I made the kisses sloppier, harder, applying pressure and sucking the skin hard enough I could leave a hickey if I wanted to. Then, I used my teeth, sinking them into her flesh enough to make her jolt.

She rewarded me with a panting sigh.

"Eyes on me," she said, and when I flicked my gaze up to hers, I vibrated from the power she was transferring to me with that heated gaze. Her lids were hooded, mouth parted, chest swelling with the rise and fall of each breath.

I kissed and sucked and licked and bit all along her thigh, crawling down to her knee before I went the other way. And this time, I didn't stop mid-thigh. I climbed higher, nosing the line of her garter before I forced my tongue beneath the fabric. I licked along the band before biting it and releasing it against her skin with a pop that earned me a moan.

"Fuck, I want to make you feel good," I breathed, licking her again.

"You are. Keep going."

Encouraged, I kissed my way higher, until I was nosing the edge of her lace panties. I smelled her again, the scent like my own personal pheromone perfume meant to drive me into madness. When I ran my tongue along the dip of her thigh there, tracing the hills and valleys where her leg met her hip, Livia bucked.

And it emboldened me to ask again.

I looked up at her, nipping at her flesh. "May I taste your pussy now? Have I earned the pleasure?"

Livia wet her lips slowly, teeth dragging along her bottom lip. She didn't approve my request verbally. Instead, she reached down and pulled her panties to the side, wedging them in the crease of her lower thigh.

I groaned.

Her cunt was absolutely perfect — swollen and wet, dark curtains inviting me to dive my tongue inside. My heart tripped, but before I could lean in and feast, Livia yanked on my hair to stop me.

"If you want to be good at this, you need to listen — both to my verbal and nonverbal commands. Understand?"

I nodded.

She nodded in return, releasing my hair and re-gripping the back of the chair. "Good. Now make me come."

Chapter 4

A Little Teeth

Livia

Never in a million years would I have ever guessed I'd have Carter Fabri's face between my thighs.

But here we were, well into our first lesson, and he'd earned the chance.

I sensed his nervousness from the moment I told him to unbutton his shirt, but I also picked up on his anticipation. It was different from the excitement of the submissives I'd had in the past. His body reacted to my praise, sure. I had a feeling he'd like the humiliation even more, once we broke into that kind of play.

But he was more excited to *learn*.

From the first correction I gave him, he was listening. He was tuned in, asking if he was doing it right, watching my face for a reaction, smiling when I gave him something as small as an open-mouthed pant of approval.

My hesitation over this whole agreement was dissipating the more the lesson went on.

Because, apparently, my new kink was an eager-to-please student.

Carter's nostrils flared as he dragged his eyes down the length of me to where I had my legs spread for him. One heel was hiked up onto the back of the chair he sat in, the other one working to keep me steady. I held onto the chair with both hands at first, too, and bucked my hips to his mouth.

"I said *eat*."

He obeyed immediately, but when he dove straight into tonguing between my lips, I pulled away.

"Have you learned nothing? That's not how you kissed my breasts or my thighs, is it?"

Carter swallowed, his eyes searching mine before he leaned in to try again.

If he were my true submissive, I would have made him answer me. I would have made him call me mistress and I would have punished him for not knowing how to properly eat me out.

But this was a teacher and student, a moment of education.

I was almost as out of my wheelhouse as Carter was.

Still, I held the power I always craved, the control I would never be okay sharing. It was still him at my command and me calling the shots. It was just with a new twist.

I noted the way his arms shook against the restraints I had him in as he began again. This time, he toyed with me, nosing my clit before he teased it with a single slash of his tongue.

Better, I thought. But I didn't reward him yet.

I waited, watching, assessing what his first moves were. I was learning just the same as he was, except I was learning about the man I was working with, how he ticked, how to coach him, what areas would need coaching in the first place. I had no idea where he was on the scale of adept intimacy, but I was figuring it out.

He clearly wasn't brand new to eating a woman out. I knew that from how quickly he went from teasing and kissing my cunt to paying attention to my clit. Good. He knew where it was, at least.

But I could also tell he wasn't confident in his performance. His eyes kept darting up to mine, brows pinching just enough to let me know he wondered what was going on in my mind. He'd never stay with one motion too long before changing — sucking and then licking, kissing and then a nip of his teeth.

"If you want a woman to fall apart for you, you have to make her feel safe to do so," I told him, petting his hair. "She needs to know she doesn't need to be shy or worried about being selfish. So, how do you communicate that to me? How do you let me know that you like being there, between my legs, tasting me? How do you let me know you're not in a rush, that I can relax and take my time, and you won't feel burdened?"

That seemed to sink in for my student, his brows furrowing in determination now instead of concern. He closed his eyes, taking a deep breath before he slowed everything down — the kisses against the inside of my thighs, the drags of his tongue from my opening up to my clit, the swirl of it once he reached that detonator. Without further instruction, he began to make out with my pussy, his kisses long and sloppy and open-mouthed.

"Yes," I breathed. "Just like that. It feels so good."

His efforts doubled, and I knew from how his shoulders flexed that he ached to touch me. I also knew he could probably get me there faster if I let him. But this was a lesson in oral — and true oral meant only using his mouth.

Still, maybe I could help him out a bit.

Without warning, I pulled back, carefully removing my heel from where it was balanced on the back of the chair. I took a step away from Carter and beamed at the sight it left me with.

Fuck, it was sexy, the way he was bound in my chair, shirt open, hair mussed, cock dripping. Every breath rocked his chest, and the rhythm of it combined with the trip hop playing set my blood buzzing.

I loved to see him at my mercy.

I loved to know he was desperate to please me.

"Stand up," I commanded.

It wasn't an easy feat. I watched him struggle a bit to stand and get his bound arms up and over the back of the chair at the same time. Combined with his pants and briefs restricting his legs, it wasn't exactly graceful.

But he managed, and once he was standing, it was an even more gorgeous sight. His cock was heavy between his legs, jutting out over his pants, the tip of it slick and inviting.

I wanted to taste him.

The thought surprised me. This was *Carter* we were talking about. This was the kid who'd been tossing shameless lines at me since the day we met — all performative swagger, no follow-through. I'd always seen him as more of a harmless flirt, someone I dismissed with a sarcastic quip and an arched brow. I'd brushed him off with a smirk and a roll of my eyes, playing the part of unimpressed more times than I could count.

But right now, he was following my direction.

He was obeying.

And it turned me on.

"Sit," I said, nodding to the plush rug in front of my fireplace.

This maneuver was more graceful, Carter somehow making it look easy when he sat without the use of his hands. I wordlessly bent to untie his wrists, then ordered him to lay back. Once he did, I bound him again — this time, his hands above his head.

"The same rules apply, Rook," I said. "No touching. Mouth only. Your hands stay here. Understand?"

He nodded.

I stood, stripping out of my panties and garters.

And then I straddled his face backward so I could have a view of that beautiful cock.

Carter groaned at the first taste of my pussy in this position, and because I knew it'd be tempting for him, I rested my shins over the top of his biceps and hooked my heels over his forearms to keep his hands in place above his head.

Then, slowly, I began to ride.

"Follow my lead," I told him. "Can you figure out what I want without me having to ask?"

His need to do well wafted off him like smoke, each stroke of his tongue purposeful and seeking. I rolled my clit against that tongue when he extended it, moaning at the friction, and then I stilled, seeing if Carter would catch the hint.

And like a good boy, he repeated the motion, tongue flat and lapping at my clit as he hummed deep in this throat. The sound was delicious, and the only regret I had from sitting backward was that I couldn't watch his eyes as he tasted me.

But I had a view of his hard cock, now so erect it didn't even rest against his stomach like it did in the chair. I was tempted to reach for him and give him one pump just to fuck with him, but I resisted.

Tonight was about him learning to make me come.

He'd be lucky if I let him do the same.

Pushing up onto my knees, I toyed with my breasts, riding Carter's face as I continued to coach him through it.

"Softer, slow it down."

"Now pick it up."

"Use a little teeth."

"There you go."

"Circle my clit with your tongue."

"Now suck."

"That's it."

"Harder."

"Faster."

"Yes."

"Don't stop."

He moaned and panted with every command, every praise, his body growing more and more rigid under mine the closer he got me to release. And when I felt like he'd taken the lesson I'd provided, I gave him what he'd worked so hard for.

I let my eyes flutter shut, let my head fall back and my mind turn off. I was no longer teacher. I was *taker*. My lips parted, a low moan rumbling out of me as I plucked at my nipples and let myself sink lower onto Carter's face.

He groaned, the sound vibrating through me, and I ground my hips harder.

"Suck my clit," I breathed. "Little pulses. Don't fucking stop."

When he surrounded my clit with his lips and did as I asked, my orgasm began to crest. Tingles started in my toes and slowly raced up my legs, body buzzing, blood humming. Carter sucked in rhythmic pulses just like I'd asked, and I fucked his face hard, reminding him who was in control.

And this was the part I loved most.

When a sub was working hard for me, when my pleasure was at the forefront of their mind, when I was revered and cherished.

"Such a good boy," I purred. "You want me to come?"

No answer but for him to suck harder, meeting my urgency. I smiled and rolled my hips harder, faster, chasing my release.

And that's when I noticed it.

I wasn't the only one tensing.

Carter's abs were strung tight, flexing in labored twitches. His work between my legs was just as good as before, but I could tell it was harder for him now. His thighs were taut. His toes were curling.

He was trying not to come.

His breath caught, a groan vibrating my cunt again. It felt delicious, and the way he was sucking my clit, the sight of him nearly losing control just from tasting me.

It was all I needed.

"Hold it," I warned him as I found my release, but as I let go, as I fucked his face harder and moaned and let the wave take me under, he broke.

My first moan had him drawn tight, his hot breath choking out of him against my pussy. He didn't let up, didn't stop pleasuring me, but when I moaned again and fully succumbed to my orgasm, he followed right behind me.

The sight of his cock jumping, cum spurting over his abdomen, made me come harder. I smiled at the view, rocking against his mouth as fire licked at my nerves. It felt so fucking good to orgasm, but what felt even *better* was to watch Carter come without so much as a single fucking touch.

I got off on the power, on the fact that he couldn't fucking help himself even though he'd tried. I watched each spray of cum paint his abs and chest with a wicked grin, and I didn't let up, didn't stop using him until the last of my release had faded.

All the sound in the room came back slowly — first, our labored breaths, and then the trip hop, the crackling of the fire. I was still riding his face, softer now, more leisurely, my smile impossible to contain as I rasped out a low laugh.

"You've made a mess."

When I felt satisfied, I slowly crawled off of Carter, maneuvering until I was on my knees next to him.

The second I saw his face, my smile faded.

He couldn't look at me. Shame colored his cheeks, his jaw ticcing as he stared up at the ceiling. His stomach swelled up and down, covered with his seed, and he looked like he wanted to sink into the plush rug and disappear forever.

Carter shook his head, not an exaggerated movement, but a quick one, one riddled with embarrassment. "I'm sorry."

I smiled, leaning until I was sitting with my legs in stag and my hip against his ribcage. I reached out tentatively to stroke the side of his face. His eyes closed as soon as I touched him, a long sigh of a breath coming from his nose.

"You have nothing to be ashamed of."

He kept his eyes closed, answering with another shameful shake of his head.

"You couldn't help yourself, could you? You were so hungry for me," I cooed, my voice soft now that the scene was over. If this were a true Domme and submissive relationship, I'd lean into his shame. I'd tease him about it and punish him a bit before I soothed and cared for him after.

But Carter was my student, not my sub, and I took my role of teacher just as seriously as if I were his Domme. I needed him to know he did well, that he should be proud.

"I liked it."

Carter's eyelids peeled open then, his gaze questioning when it met mine. I let my fingers trail down to play with the cum on his stomach, and he shivered when I did, his eyelids fluttering with pleasure.

"Next time, we'll focus on control. But tonight? You made me come with nothing but your mouth. That deserves praise."

I could almost feel the relief that seeped out of him like it was my own.

"I actually find it quite hot that you got off just from tasting me," I told him, still playing with his cum. It made heat flash between my thighs, made me want to get him hard again and ride that slick cock of his. But I resisted.

He had to earn that privilege.

"Do I wish you would have waited until you had permission to come? Yes. But we'll work on that."

Carter swallowed, that blush shading his cheeks again.

I thumbed where the crimson bloomed with a grin. "You did well. Now, let me get you cleaned up."

With care, I loosened the bind of his suit jacket around his wrists, helping to lower them to his sides before

I stood. I massaged each wrist before I walked leisurely to my bathroom for a washcloth, running it under hot water. I let Carter have a moment to himself before I returned.

Then, I got on my knees and cleaned him.

A heavy, sated sigh left his chest when the warm washcloth swept across his skin. He trembled involuntarily as I wiped up every drop he'd spilled, saving his cock for last. I wrapped the cloth around him with gentle pressure, just enough to clean him up without giving too much attention to an area I knew was sensitive at the moment.

When he was clean, I helped him sit up and get himself somewhat dressed again. He left his shirt unfastened but pulled up his briefs and pants. When he was situated, I grabbed a blanket from where it was laid over the arm of my couch and draped it around his shoulders.

"You can sit here, or you can move to the couch if you'd be more comfortable. I'll be right back."

I took enough time to get myself dressed again — pulling on my panties but leaving the garter and my pants where they lay. Then, I kicked out of my heels and padded barefoot over to the kitchen, pouring Carter a tall glass of water.

I snatched the bottle of wine off the island for me.

Carter hadn't moved, so I sank down onto the floor next to him, leaning my back against the stone of the fireplace. I handed the glass of water to him before taking a swig of wine.

"Drink," I told him.

He maneuvered until he was sitting next to me, his back against the fireplace, too, and then he drained half the glass. We sat in silence for a long moment before I turned to him with a curious smile.

"Well?"

He shook his head, the corner of his lips quirking up as his head swiveled to face me. "Best two-million dollars I've ever spent."

I barked out a laugh. "That was nothing."

"I beg to differ."

"And did we learn something?"

He frowned at that, wrapping himself up a bit more in the blanket before he kicked back. "Tune into the nonverbal cues. Take my time, don't rush, let her know I enjoy it. Make her feel safe to let go."

"And?"

"Suck the clit like it's my sole purpose for walking this earth."

I laughed again, tilting the bottle to my lips. "We're off to a good start."

When Carter finished his water, I offered him the wine, and we sat for a while in comfortable quiet, passing the bottle between us. I imagined we were both a little in our heads, wondering how the hell we'd found ourselves here. We hadn't just crossed the line of our friendship, we'd bungee jumped over the damn thing.

Now that we'd both come and were floating down from the high, reality was sinking in.

Still, I didn't have regrets, and I didn't feel any rolling off of Carter. He looked... pleased — not just physically, but pleased with his performance. I liked the sated curl of his lips, the sleepiness in his gaze.

I liked that I'd given him that.

"So... have you been an actual Domme before?" he asked after a while. "Like..."

"With a submissive?" I angled my head toward him. "What do you think?"

"I think that contract seemed pretty fine-tuned."

"Then why are you asking?"

He shrugged. "I don't know. I guess I'm just... curious. How did you get into it?"

It was an unwanted and natural reaction, the way fear pricked my spine and sent chills racing over me. Carter wasn't doing anything to make me feel unsafe, but the very nature of what he'd asked did so, anyway.

I couldn't answer honestly without revealing a part of my past I preferred to keep buried.

So, I took a sip of wine to compose myself.

And I lied.

"I dated a guy when I was younger who was into it. He liked to be degraded and controlled, used. He asked me to try with him, to be his Domme." I shrugged. "And I liked it."

"Do you ever like to be the submissive?"

"Never," I answered immediately, but again, it was a lie.

There was a part of me that was curious what it would feel like to relinquish control in the bedroom, to switch and let a man use me and degrade me in a safe, consensual way.

I thought it would be hot.

But I also didn't think it was possible to achieve.

My trust for the opposite sex had been eviscerated.

"Now," I said, changing the subject as I tilted onto my hip and turned toward Carter. I leaned my chin on my palm, elbow propped on the stone ledge of the fireplace. "Tell me about this puck bunny who let you fuck her ass."

Carter nearly choked on the sip of wine he was in the process of taking, and when he saw my smile, he mirrored it, shaking his head.

"I don't know what more there is to tell."

"Was it like... a dare or something?"

"No," he said with a rueful laugh. "It was my first year in the league. Our rookie party. She was the one who invited us up to her hotel room — three of my teammates and me. Her name was Zina. She was gorgeous, confident, and... let's just say she knew exactly what she wanted. She told us straight up it was her fantasy to have multiple hockey players at once, and she was in charge from the second we walked in the room."

I raised my brows. "In charge?"

"Oh, yeah." He grinned at the memory, sheepish. "She set the rules, told each of us what she wanted, where she wanted it."

"You really do have a thing for Dommes, don't you, Rook?"

"She was so kinky, Liv," he said, sipping his wine with a grin like he was lost in the memory. "And honestly, I was kind of just enjoying watching. She was having the time of her life. But she saw me in the corner, probably sensed how nervous I was, and she crooked her finger at me and said, 'Come here, baby. This is your lucky night. You can put it anywhere you want.' So..." He shrugged. "I took her at her word."

"You chose ass."

He laughed, rubbing the back of his neck. "I figured opportunities like that don't come around every day."

That had a laugh bubbling out of me, too, as I stole the bottle of wine from him. "Well, I promise, with me? There will be plenty of ass opportunity..."

Carter paled when I sealed that promise with a wink. "Why do I feel like you're talking about ass in a completely different context."

"Oh, don't be scared," I cooed, rolling onto all fours before I stood. "I think you'll like it."

Carter scrambled up to meet me. "I think I need to revisit those safe words."

"So, you've really never had sex?" I asked. "I mean, in the traditional sense. You've never fucked a woman vaginally?"

He swallowed, that beautiful pink shade of embarrassment tingeing his cheeks again. "Never."

Something flared in my chest at the admission.

Maybe it wasn't just the payday that had me buzzing.

Maybe it wasn't just the fun of it all.

Maybe it was the promise of untouched territory — and the power that came with claiming it.

Chapter 5
Free to Explore
Carter

"Atta boy, Carter! Let's fucking go!"

The praise from Jaxson hit my ears as soon as I won the draw against the San Francisco Sea Dawgs's center. We were on the penalty kill, and I won the draw clean in our zone, snapping it back to Vince to start the breakout.

And we were off.

Up by one with three minutes left in the game, every single one of us was locked in.

It was always a toss-up in a game like this — either every minute flew by in the blink of an eye, or every second dragged like the game would never end.

It was the latter in this case, my muscles screaming, lungs aching as I struggled for breath. We were in battle mode, defense doing everything they could to keep that puck away from where Will Perry, also known as Daddy P, guarded the goal while the rest of us looked for a breakaway to seal the win.

The last three minutes of a matchup were ripe for surprises. Just because we'd played the stronger game didn't mean they couldn't come back and tie it, forcing us into overtime, or, worse — score twice in a row and send us into the locker room with our tails tucked.

We had to be focused, all of us, to see this through.

And in a time where it should have been the last thing I was thinking of, I couldn't help but channel what went down at Livia's condo last week.

I should have been focused on the puck, on getting it down the ice and into our opponent's net. Instead, I found myself thinking about those last couple of minutes of our first lesson, of how tightly strung I'd been, how hard I'd fought to focus enough to get her there before I let myself go.

I needed that energy right now.

I needed to channel that determination, that drive to fight against every bruised and battered part of my body begging me to stop skating and fall into a heap on the bench.

Finish strong, I chanted.

Don't fuck up, the voice of my old coach echoed.

I shook him off just as the puck went sliding down the ice toward our zone and the penalty kill ended.

Jaxson Brittain and Dimitri Volkov were ready, kicking into defense as Daddy P braced himself in the crease. And when Jaxson sliced the puck hard and fast to where I was at the center of the ice, I was ready, too.

I caught the pass, zipping toward the goal, but one of their wingers took advantage of a slight hesitation in which direction I was going to go and stole the puck away.

As soon as he crossed the blue line, their goalie bolted for the bench.

It was six on five, open net, less than two minutes to go.

It was all we could do then, working as a line to prevent San Francisco from scoring. We fought like we were *all* on defense, blades digging into the ice, bodies thrown against the glass, thighs screaming, lungs on fire. The stadium was roaring with noise, Sea Dawgs fans screaming for their team.

But when the final buzzer sounded and we'd managed to fend them off, all that noise died in an instant.

"Fuck yeah!" Vince toted his stick overhead as he skated around in a victory lap, Jaxson on his heels. They ended up in a tackle-hug as I bent at the waist next to Daddy P, gloved hands on my knees, wheezing like I had fucking asthma.

Will removed his helmet, squirting water into his mouth as he arched a brow at me. His long hair was dripping wet with sweat, but he was breathing normally, like those last few minutes hadn't fazed him at all. That was the mark of a true veteran. He wasn't even celebrating. This was just another game for him, and he wouldn't let himself hit a celly dance until we had the Cup in our hands.

"You good, Fabio?" he asked with a sly smirk. "Look like you might puke."

"I haven't ruled it out." I managed to stand on a wince, nodding at him. "How the fuck are you so calm?"

He shrugged. "I knew we had them."

A laugh burst from me then, making my stomach cramp more. "Cocky bastard."

"Take notes. We need you to have that same confidence," he said, clapping me on the shoulder with a gloved hand. Then, we were skating toward the bench to join the rest of our team.

And all I could think was that we were halfway through the season now. And with this win, we had solidified ourselves as a division leader.

We had a shot at the playoffs.

My nerve endings danced like I hadn't just played three periods of grueling hockey with just the notion that we might make it again, that we might find ourselves in position to play for the Cup. But on the tails of that buzz came the ever-present doubt.

Would I be an asset to the team, help us get to the playoffs?

Or would I hold us back?

I'd played decently in the game tonight — but that was just it. Decent. Not great, not terrible, just somewhere in-between. I'd won the majority of my face-offs, holding strong in key moments like when we were on the penalty kill. I'd set up Aleks Suter with a slick pass that led to a goal, our chemistry effortless, vision clear.

But I'd also tried to dangle through two defensemen and lost the puck in the process.

I'd whiffed a one-timer, a wide-open slot and great pass that should have equated to an easy goal. Instead, I'd straight up fanned on it.

It was those little mistakes that frustrated me most, the ones that could have been avoided if I held a bit more confidence, if I thought less and felt into the rhythm of the game more. When my adrenaline spiked and I felt the hum of an opportunity vibrating through me, it was tough to tune out the voice in my head telling me I was going to blow it.

And then, half the time, I would.

I tried to focus on what I'd done well as we made our way to the locker room, which quickly turned into a chamber of noise — equipment shuffling, pads hitting the floor, guys laughing and razzing one another.

The energy after a win was always palpable. It was impossible not to float on that cloud, not to feel unstoppable even if we all knew one bad period could have had the game swinging the other way. All that mattered right now was that we'd secured the win.

Coach McCabe stepped into the doorway, his hands shoved into the pockets of his quarter-zip, his sharp eyes scanning over us like a hawk surveying prey. The second we noticed him, the chatter dimmed — not completely, but enough to make the shift in energy obvious.

That was the effect Coach had.

He didn't yell often. He never had to. He was one of the youngest coaches in the league and had taken Tampa from a team barely considered competition to one of the best. The respect the team gave him was well-earned.

He'd always been a bit of an enigma to me, though. I understood him as a coach, as someone who loved hockey. But I had no idea who he was *off* the ice. Unlike most coaches in the league, he didn't have a wife and kids to go home to. And yet, he never went out with the players, never indulged in a way that landed him in any sort of limelight.

I had no idea who he was when he left the rink.

But I knew he was a damn good coach, one I trusted implicitly — one who was healing me from a coach who'd royally fucked me up years ago.

"You played like you wanted it tonight," he said simply, his voice cutting through the room like a skate blade over fresh ice. "That's the standard. That's who we are."

He paused, his gaze dragging from one end of the locker room to the other, resting on each of us in turn. And for a moment, there was a flicker in his eyes — something unreadable, something almost... tired. But then it was gone, replaced with the same unrelenting fire I'd seen since the day I joined the team.

"Celebrate the win. You earned it. But don't get comfortable," he finished, lifting his chin. "Shower up, ice baths if you need them, and bus leaves in forty-five."

With that, Coach stepped aside, the roar of the locker room returning as quickly as it had quieted. But I couldn't help watching him as he lingered in the hall for a second longer, jaw tight, like his mind was somewhere far away.

"Jesus, Fabio, you got magnets in your glove or what?" Aleks Suter asked, smirking at me as he stripped his base layer off. "Give the other centermen a fighting chance."

I couldn't help my goofy grin at the compliment, especially considering Aleks had given me a harder time than anyone else on the team. He was one of our newer players, a transfer from Seattle, and he had a reputation around the league — and the gossip magazines — for getting into trouble. He was absolutely deadly on the ice, though, which made it impossible not to want him on your team — even if he did end up in the penalty box more than on the bench.

He'd been downright mean to me last season — but that was before he and Mia got together. He'd turned as soft as a bunny then.

Okay maybe not *that* soft, but at least he wasn't riding my ass all the time now.

I had earned a fraction of his respect, proving to him that I could show up for him and the rest of the team the way the veteran center before me had.

The Ospreys paid a lot of money for my contract. With that deal, they said they believed in me, that they saw my potential to fill the shoes of the player retiring ahead of me.

It was an honor.

It was also an insane amount of pressure that felt like it could crush me at any minute if I stopped long enough to think about it all too hard.

"Yeah, you were on fire that first period, Fabri," Jaxson piped in. "That no-look pass to Suter was slick."

Jaxson Brittain was a defenseman and a close friend, one of the few who had given me pep talks and told me I could achieve what I wanted well before anyone else took the time. And it wasn't because he'd felt bad for me. I knew he genuinely wanted me to stay in The Show. He wanted me to play for the Ospreys and not be sent down to the AHL.

Unfortunately, that had been the case for me for a few years — but I got the hang of things in that last season. When I found out a veteran center was retiring and opening a space that needed to be filled, I saw my opportunity.

And I knew I couldn't blow it.

That was when I signed up to work with the team's sports psychologist, when I'd found a therapist, when I'd said *enough is enough.*

I was far from where I wanted to be, but I'd made progress.

If only that progress transferred to my sex life.

Before my mind could veer off into Livia Young territory, Daddy P clapped me on the shoulder. "Sure, you played alright in the first, but don't think we're going to let you live down that dangle."

It was Vince Tanev's turn to pipe in, his warm laugh rumbling through the locker room. "Oh, Carter went full highlight mode with that turnover. Did ESPN call and beg for blooper reel gold, or was it just that the Zamboni crew needed a little help sweeping the ice?"

The guys laughed, and I joined in — even if my chest stung a little. They weren't coming down on me. It was all playful, all love, and I didn't want anyone to think I couldn't take a little razzing.

But there was a little truth beneath those jokes, and it was so fucking hard sometimes for me not to take them personally, not to take those remarks home with me and let them beat me to a pulp.

"Yeah, yeah, yeah," I said. "Keep talking, Tanny Boy, and I'll pay the camera crew for footage of that failed attempt at a bar down shot you made in the third and put it on repeat in the team gym."

"Right next to the video of you fanning the puck when you had a wide-open net, right?" Aleks chimed in. "You need a GPS for that puck, bud?"

"Someone get the man an AirTag," Jaxson added.

Everyone laughed again, and I tongued my cheek against a smile before chasing them all into the ice baths with a snap of my towel.

Ten minutes later, I was in a meditative state — ice water up to my chin, eyes shut, brain muffling out the noise of the guys still chattering around me. Beneath those closed eyelids, a reel of everything I'd done right and wrong flashed on replay. I tried to do what our sports psychologist advised, taking what I could from each mistake before leaving them in the past, and making a moment to applaud myself for the achievements.

That last part was harder than the first.

Even when I did do something worth being proud of, I had to fight against my old coach's voice inside my head adding a negative spin.

Sure, you scored — but you could have scored twice if you wouldn't have missed that open net.

You won the draw. Big fucking deal. Never mind that you lost the puck in turnover a fucking youth player could have avoided.

Oh, patting yourself on the back for that pass, are you? If you were a better player, you would have shot the puck yourself. But you were too scared, weren't you?

I squeezed my eyes shut tighter as the thoughts battered me, and I tried to visualize me swatting them away with a stick like they were rogue pucks just like my therapist had taught me.

It did help.

But only temporarily.

I knew it wouldn't stop the barrage from coming in the future.

Once the reel highlights had died down and my brain was mush just like my body, I finally let my mind wander to Livia.

If I were listing out things I was proud of at the moment, then making that woman come would be at the top of the list.

Even a week later, just thinking about the sweet sounds she'd made had me eager for round two. The fact that I'd been the one responsible for those noises, that I'd made her fly apart with my mouth alone?

It was enough to make me feel like I deserved the MVP award.

Of course, my next thought was one that made me groan and shake my head. I still couldn't believe I'd blown my wad without her touching me, without her *permission*, as she'd said. I knew I wasn't her sub in the traditional sense of the word, but *fuck*, I loved when she went Domme on me. I loved the little bits of degradation, the control she exercised, the way she made it clear who was calling the shots.

It made me feel free to explore, to try new things, to fuck up and not have serious hell to pay. I'd been ashamed when I came, but she'd quickly made sure I knew I didn't need to feel that way.

She'd said it was hot.

She'd assured me she'd help me with that control.

She hadn't berated me or made me feel like shit, even playfully, and she could never know how much that meant to me.

My skin burned as I pulled my body from the tub when I couldn't take anymore, and I wrapped a towel around my waist before padding to my locker and pulling out my phone.

I texted Livia without a second thought.

> **Me:** Whiffed a goal and they won't let me live it down. Might need one of your "confidence building" sessions later. Preferably involving handcuffs.

It was late on the East Coast, so I was surprised when the gray letters spelled out *READ* under the text. Seconds later, she was typing back.

> **Doctor Pain:** Ouch. I'm with the girls and we had the game on. If it makes you feel any better, we only laughed a little bit. Like five solid minutes.

> **Me:** Laughing is the last thing I want to make you do right now.

> **Doctor Pain:** Oho. That line had a little growl in it. What is it you do want to make me do, Rookie?

Me: Moan the way you did last week.

The second I shot off the text, I regretted it. I hoped it sounded cocky and flirtatious but wondered if Livia could see right through it and would call me out. She'd laughed at me plenty of times in our friendship.

But now, I was desperate to show her I was a good student, that I was already learning.

Doctor Pain: I won't lie... that was a fantastic orgasm in the end. You took instructions so well.

I nearly passed out when the text came through, adrenaline spiking in my veins like I was being chased by a bear.

She'd liked it.
I'd made her feel good.

Doctor Pain: But no more play until you get your doctor's note, Rook.

Me: You mean this one?

I attached a picture I'd taken the day before of my STD test results and the clearance from my doctor for rigorous physical activity. The man had looked at me like I was crazy when I asked him to write it, considering I was a professional fucking hockey player, but thankfully, he didn't ask questions.

I'd meant to send the picture before we got on the team flight out to California, but it was always hectic on a travel day, and I'd never gotten around to it.

As soon as the photo went through, I sent another text.

Me: And if you'll check your bank account, I think you'll find that the first deposit cleared successfully today.

Doctor Pain: Such a good boy.

Me: You're going to give me a boner in the middle of this locker room full of sweaty dudes.

Doctor Pain: Sounds like a teachable moment. Maybe one of them can give you the next lesson?

Me: *flat face emoji*

Doctor Pain: You're off on Sunday, yes?

My heart kicked, anticipation flowing like a river through my chest.

Me: I am.

Doctor Pain: Good. Clean your place. Stock up on electrolytes.

Me: Yes, Mommy.

Doctor Pain: And Rook?

Me: Yes, Mommy?

Doctor Pain: Edge twice a day until I get there. Then take care of yourself once more when I say I'm on my way. I want to feel every second of that restraint when I finally let you come.

Chapter 6
Little Nike Shoes
Livia

An evil smirk painted my lips as I tucked my phone away after firing that last text off to Carter, turning my focus to where Chloe was holding up a new outfit option for her elopement trip with Will. She'd called an emergency girls' night when she'd discovered Grace would be in town, and now here we were, gathered in her living room around various mountains of clothing.

"What about this one?" she asked, pinning the multi-colored dress to her hip with one hand and her shoulder with the other.

The bright hues of fabric clashed a bit with her red hair, but her creamy pale skin and the curves that girl had made her a knockout in anything she wore.

She turned to look at herself in the full-length mirror. "I made it with leftover fabric from a craft I did with my class for Easter."

"Well, nothing says *fuck me brainless* like an Easter dress," I teased, sipping my white wine with a grin before

I picked up the bracelet I was crafting. I'd brought over my travel jewelry kit so I had something to do with my hands during this little girls' night other than drink myself into oblivion. Currently, my project was a delicate tennis bracelet peppered with round briolette cut moonstones. I planned to give it to Chloe as a wedding gift, but she didn't know that yet.

Chloe Knott was a kindergarten teacher and fiancée to our grumpy goalie, Will Perry. We'd been bugging them since he popped the question for wedding details, only to find out recently that they planned to elope. And though we all were bummed that we wouldn't be there to sob all over them as they exchanged vows, it made perfect sense.

I couldn't imagine a world where Will Perry would be excited to share something so intimate with a crowd of two-hundred people watching.

They *were* indulging us with a little close friends and family party when they returned, at least. That was the only reason we all hadn't rioted.

"I mean, if we're talking pagan origins, Easter *is* the goddess of fertility, so..." Grace shrugged, tilting her bottle of beer toward Chloe. "I guess it depends on what your goals are for this wedding trip."

Grace Tanev was our little adventurer in the group, a Coppertone tan ball of sunshine with platinum blonde hair who was always on the go. She was only in Tampa for a week before she was bolting off to do a cruise to Antarctica, stopping by long enough to give Chloe fashion advice and steal a few nights with her beloved Jaxson Brittain — who just so happened to be her brother's best friend and teammate.

That hadn't been at *all* scandalous.

Chloe's phone rang before anyone could tease her further, and she lit up at the name on the screen before running to her laptop to answer. She set it up to face all of us before accepting the call.

Mia Love's smile filled the screen in a dazzling flash.

"There she is!" Chloe sang. "How was night two in Kansas City?"

"Incredible," she breathed, peeling off her fake eyelashes. Her bronze skin was glowing, long brown hair wavy and sweaty at the roots. "I surprised them all with a guest appearance from REX."

"The rapper?!"

"Who else?" She laughed. "I think they were all very confused when I started an acoustic version of 'Barbie Q', but when REX came out, they lost their minds. It was epic."

"*You're* epic," I shot back.

She blushed, like she didn't already know it, like she wasn't the biggest pop star in the world.

Mia was the newest addition to our group, married in a flash to our stubborn asshat winger, Aleks Suter. It had been a surprise to all of us, how quickly they'd started dating, got engaged, and then married — but they'd been friends since they were kids, and apparently crushed on one another that long, too.

Whatever miscommunication kept them apart, I was glad they figured it out — because I already loved her fiercely. She was a girl's girl, through and through. The fact that she was rushing to her hotel to video chat her girlfriends after playing a sold-out stadium show was the perfect example of that.

"Well, you're just in time," Chloe said. "We've picked two outfits so far, nixed about seventeen, and now we're debating this dress."

Chloe stepped back so Mia could take in the full view of it, and when Mia's smile took on an awkward tilt and she blinked a little too much, I couldn't contain my laugh.

"It's... colorful!" she said, too much teeth in her grin.

Chloe deflated but was smirking when she started to hang the dress back on the hanger. "Not exactly the vibe I'm going for."

"Is the vibe you're aiming for more like *rip this thing off me and rail me into next year?* Because I might have a few things you could borrow, if that's the case," I said.

"Oh, God. If we take this party to Liv's place and dive into her closet, I have a feeling we'll send you off to the Seychelles in nothing more than fishnet," Maven teased.

I shrugged. "And this is a problem... how?"

"To be fair, I'm pretty sure Daddy P would rail you even if you wore a burlap sack," Grace said to Chloe. "Never seen that man turn to putty until he met you."

Mia offered up her closet next, but I missed out on the glitter and sequin jokes when Maven pinched me just above my elbow.

"Ouch!"

"Who were you texting just a minute ago?"

"That hurt," I said, rubbing the spot she'd assaulted.

She sucked her teeth. "Please. You don't fool me. I've seen your top dresser drawer, and that pinch probably felt like a tickle in comparison to the contraptions you've got in there."

"Touché."

"Who were you texting?"

"No one."

My best friend leveled me with a glare then. She was so beautiful I sometimes wondered if she could have been a model, had she not chosen the life of plant lady and community do-gooder. Her hair was natural at the moment — tight coils that framed her face like a crown, soft and full of life. Her skin was a rich, glowing brown that seemed to drink in the sunlight, radiant in a way that made you stop and stare. She wore a wrap skirt and a loose, off-the-shoulder blouse like she'd just wandered out of a bohemian dream barefoot, grounded, and completely at ease. Maven didn't ever have to try to be gorgeous. She simply was. Earthy. Ethereal. Unshakably herself.

Before she started dating Vince Tanev, she'd been quite prickly, too. She still had that edge about her, but her now-husband had given her warm, strong arms to relax in. He'd made her feel safe enough to put down her sword.

I envied what they had, even if I pretended like it was the last thing I wanted for myself.

"You are such a little shit," she whisper-yelled, pinching my elbow again.

"*Ow-ah-chuh!*"

"You had a goofy grin on your face and if there's anything to make me suspicious, it's that. So, who were you texting? Tell me right now."

"It was Carter! You sadist." I rubbed my arm. "Now stop assaulting me so we can help our friend pick her wedding wardrobe."

"Carter Fabri?" She scrunched her nose.

"Do we know another Carter?"

"Why is he texting you?"

"Why else but to be an annoying fly buzzing around my face?" I feigned indifference and nonchalance, shrugging as I looped another moonstone onto the delicate fourteen-karat chain with my pliers. "You know him and his corny pickup lines. Apparently, I'm his favorite victim to test them on."

Maven relaxed a bit at that, all the suspicion leaving her eyes as she settled her back against the couch again. She knew as well as anyone else in this room that Carter had been a flirt toward me since we met. It wasn't out of the ordinary for him to text me or trip over himself whenever we were all together.

And it wasn't a lie — he *had* been texting me lines, although the one about wanting to make me moan again had been anything but corny.

Still, my best friend didn't need to know that I'd taken on the role of *Sex Professor*. At least, not right now. She also didn't need to know that I had an impenetrable grin on my face not just from the glorious deposit that hit my account earlier today, but because I was excited to see Carter this weekend, to give him another lesson.

That part surprised *me* — so I knew it would make Maven fall out on the floor.

I was remiss to admit it, but I'd gone into that first night with Carter thinking this whole arrangement would be like a second job to me, something that took my time and energy in exchange for a paycheck.

What had surprised me was that *fun* was included in that exchange, too.

I'd thoroughly enjoyed it — bossing Carter around, discovering his muscled body and thick cock, coaching him through all the ways to please me with that mouth of his.

I was just as eager for round two as he was, even if I'd never admit it.

Maven smirked. "Ah, well — that tracks. Did you tell him he may want to make an appointment with an eye doctor after that shot he missed?"

I barked out a laugh. "You chirp almost as well as your husband now."

"Who do you think taught him?"

We turned our attention back to Chloe as Maven slid her arm under mine with a smile, cuddling me as we voted yes or no on the next round of outfits. When we transitioned from dresses to swimsuits, Grace brought the conversation full circle.

"I know we were joking about the whole goddess of fertility thing earlier, but on a serious note... where do you and Will stand on the whole baby thing?" She drained the last of her beer before setting the empty bottle on the coffee table. "You can totally tell me to fuck off, too. It's none of my business, and I know it's an invasive question. But also... I'm nosy, and you two are hot as fuck, and I think you'd make really cute babies. If you want to, of course."

Chloe's skin turned a lovely shade of pink as she held up a white one-piece that we all immediately vetoed.

"Too virginal," I said.

When she held up an emerald-green two piece with strappy hip bottoms and a triangle top we *knew* would show off her cleavage gloriously, we applauded like she'd just sung in an opera.

"We haven't talked at length about it yet, but... yes," Chloe said, carefully folding the green suit and putting it on top of the pile cleared to pack. "I would love to have a child. And I think Ava would make the best big sister."

"She would," Maven agreed with a soft, knowing gaze. "And *you* would make an incredible mother."

It felt like a corset was being pulled tight over my ribs as I smiled and nodded in agreement.

Chloe shrugged, looking at where her fingers were coiling in the silky fabric of a black swimsuit now. "I'd certainly try to be."

She held up the suit for us to see, and when we took in the one-piece with a set of three gold rings lining the chest and stomach area, it was an easy yes.

"What about you babes?" Chloe asked. "Any of you want to hop on the mom train?"

Stand *your* Ground

Grace laughed so loudly it startled Nacho, one of Chloe's cats who'd been happily snoozing on the back of the couch. He skittered off as Grace hopped up and grabbed a fresh beer from the cooler she'd packed and dragged into the living room so she wouldn't miss the fashion show going to the kitchen for a refill.

"Not me," she declared. "I'll happily play best auntie in the world to all of your kids, but mom life is not in the cards for this gal. I love to travel too much."

"You can still travel with a baby," Maven said. "It's not like they take your passport away when you give birth."

"It's hard enough to travel with Jaxson sometimes, and he doesn't wear a diaper." Grace popped the lid off the fresh bottle of beer. "Child-free life for me, lovers. What about you, Mave?"

"On the fence in a major way," my best friend replied, and I squeezed her arm where it was still threaded through mine. "I mean, I could see a happy life with just me and Vince, but I could also see a happy life with a house full of kids."

"Plural?" Grace asked, eyes wide.

Maven shrugged. "I can't explain it, but I feel like I'll either have zero or four."

Grace nearly spit out her beer.

"I'm a definite yes," Mia chimed in from the laptop screen. She had a glass of champagne in hand now and had changed into an oversized t-shirt, her free hand working on removing her makeup with a washcloth. "Not *now*, obviously, but... one day." She smiled. "What about you, Liv?"

Everyone went dead silent for a beat.

And then they all burst out laughing.

"Liv? With a baby?" Grace wheezed, setting her beer on the table so she wouldn't spill it. "Please. She's more likely to surprise us with a vow of celibacy than a pregnancy."

"Oh my God," Chloe gasped, laughing so hard she was crossing her legs like she was two seconds from pissing herself. "Could you imagine? 'Sweetie, no chewing on Mommy's leather whip, okay? Let's go get your teething ring.'"

"'No, no, that's a *cock* ring, honey,'" Maven continued the joke, and that earned her a new fit of giggles from everyone. "'Now drop it. *Drooop* it."

"Aww, I could see it, actually," Mia said when her laughter subsided. "You'd have the poshest baby ever, Liv. Full cashmere wardrobe. Custom stroller. Little Nike shoes."

"I think Liv would rather surrender her impressive collection of butt plugs than push a baby out of her precious vagina," Maven said.

"Entrance only — no exiting allowed," Grace managed as her face turned red.

The whole room howled.

And I willed myself to join them.

Smile, a voice inside me tried. *Roll with it. Play the part. Make a joke. Toss them a wink and a little ass shimmy for good measure.*

That was the gig, right?

That was what they all expected.

But for the first time, I couldn't do it.

My jaw was clenched so tight it ached, and I could feel my fingers curling tighter around my wine glass, so tight I was afraid it might shatter. My heart thudded once, then again, loud in my ears. I stared at the floor, then at my friends, each of them smiling, not a clue what they were stomping on with their jokes.

"Liv will join me in the cool auntie club," Grace said with finality. "We'll be here to spoil all your kids with sugar and then send them home to you."

And though it didn't make a single bit of sense, it was that comment that made me snap.

"Have any of you considered letting me answer the fucking question," I said, voice low and sharp, "since it was me she asked?"

What remained of the laughter immediately halted, a cold silence dropping over us like a cloudy night.

Mia's eyes grew wide. Grace paused with her beer bottle halfway to her lips and Chloe swallowed, her face turning beet red.

Maven turned to me slowly, brows drawing together. "Sorry, Liv, we were just—"

"Assuming there's no way in hell I could ever manage a pregnancy, let alone the task of being a mother?"

Her expression was horrified then. "That's not—"

"I'll have you all know the I'm actually in the process of freezing my eggs right now."

The words were out of my mouth before I could think better of saying them, my defensive instinct too strong to fight. The news landed like a bomb, and I tilted my chin higher like they all should have seen it coming when I *knew* they had every right to make the assumptions they had.

Technically, I hadn't officially started the process — but I had the plan in place. I had this agreement with Carter, cash to stash away, and finally, the security I'd needed to feel confident to take the next steps.

I hadn't made the appointment with my doctor yet, but I would.

And now, the cat was out of the bag.

I turned my attention back to where my hands were crafting the bracelet as the aftershocks of that truth settled over the room like dust after an explosion. I didn't want to look at any of them when I knew they were all looking at each other with expressions of *what the fuck just happened?*

"Liv..." Grace finally broke the silence, her tone apologetic. "We didn't know."

"No one did. And I'd appreciate it if it stayed in this circle until I'm ready to tell anyone else."

"Of course," Chloe said automatically. She ditched the swimsuit in her hand and rushed over to me, forcing me to drop the bracelet as she took my hands in hers. I had to resist the instinct to rip away from her touch.

I hated being vulnerable.

And I really despised being touched in the rare instance that I let myself be.

"I... I think that's amazing, Livia. I really do," she said, smiling.

"Me, too," Mia chimed in. "I think you'd make a great mom."

"We all do," Maven said from beside me, but I saw the hurt in her eyes, the betrayal of not knowing something she felt like she had a right to know as my best friend. Fortunately, she was *such* a good friend that she didn't make it about her. "Does this mean you want to start... dating?"

I snorted. "Oh, *hell* no. We all know men are incompetent of anything past providing an orgasm, and most of them struggle even with that." I paused. "Your lovely men excluded, of course."

Grace chuckled. "So... on your own then?"

I held my chin higher with a sharp nod. "On my own. When I'm ready." I pointed a finger at Mia. "And you can bet your sparkly little ass that she'll wear designer clothes just like you said."

"Little Nike shoes!" Mia squeaked.

The tension in the room melted with the next wave of laughter, and then we were back to helping Chloe sort through clothes, the attention off me at least for the moment.

Although I didn't miss the way Maven held me tighter, how she laid her head on my shoulder and rubbed my arm when I picked up the bracelet to work again. She was comforting me now, letting me know she was there for me — but I knew she'd want more details soon.

When my stomach settled, I took a sip of my wine, happy to return to our task of getting Chloe packed and ready to go.

But that happiness didn't get the chance to dip more than its toes before a text message on my phone was tearing it away again.

"Shit," I muttered when I looked at it, ice sliding down the back of my neck.

Maven bolted upright, brows pinched together. "What? Who is it?"

I swallowed, holding up the screen to the only person in the world who would understand my reaction when I answered her question.

"My sister."

Chapter 7

Giddy Up

Carter

Zamboni stared at me like I'd lost my goddamn mind.

Which, to be fair, maybe I had.

"Does this shirt make me look like I'm trying too hard?"

The golden retriever pup I'd adopted in November just tilted his head, tongue lolling out like the himbo he was, tail thumping against the kitchen cabinets with a rhythmic *thud-thud-thud*. I'd changed shirts three times already, finally landing on a plain black tee that hugged my arms just enough to show the toned muscles from wielding a stick on the ice without screaming *look at me, I lift weights*. I'd paired it with some light gray joggers, and since it was my house Livia was coming to, I didn't put on shoes, just acted like it was a normal Sunday evening at home.

I was aiming for casual. Cool. Collected.

Totally not sweating bullets over the fact that Livia-fucking-Young was on her way over to boss me around again, and I'd jerked off about ten times in the past few days preparing for it.

I ran a hand through my hair and turned in a slow circle, checking the living room for anything out of place. The vacuum lines on the rug were still visible, which felt like a win. Candles were lit. The lights were low, music soft in the background — not the beat-heavy music that Livia had on in her condo, but a jazzy, chill playlist I usually saved for post-practice decompression.

Zamboni let out a low woof and pawed at his water bowl.

"Don't worry, Zambo. You've got nothing to worry about." I refilled his water before patting his butt. "You only *almost* chewed her shoe to bits at Aleks and Mia's wedding. It's not like you actually did. And how could she not love you? She has to. Look at you." I crouched to scratch behind his ears, his whole body wiggling with joy. "But just in case, maybe try to avoid jumping up and slobbering all over her, okay?" I stood, smoothing my hands over my shirt. "That's my job."

I took a breath, scanning the place one more time like Livia might show up with a white glove and a clipboard to inspect it.

My house was small by pro athlete standards, but it was all I needed. It had a modern coastal vibe and was tucked away at the edge of a canal that fed into the Hillsborough River. It was quiet, peaceful, and just ten minutes from the arena.

Perfect.

The whole back wall was floor-to-ceiling glass, opening up to a deck with string lights, a pair of well-worn Adirondack chairs, my paddleboard, and the boat I barely used enough to justify owning. Inside, the colors were light and clean — white walls, pale wood floors, navy blue and gray accents. A few framed jerseys lined one hallway, along with a shelf of game pucks and photos from my rookie season. My bag of golf clubs rested in the corner, serving as décor as much as any vase would.

I didn't pretend to be an interior designer. Everything was minimal and masculine. Lived-in, but not messy.

I'd never once given a single shit about my place and how it would appear to anyone other than me until this very moment.

Something about knowing Livia would be inside these walls any minute now had me on edge. She'd seen me naked. She'd quite literally sat on my face. She knew about my insecurities, about all the ways I fell short and needed her help.

But somehow, this felt more vulnerable than any of that.

It was nerve-wracking, letting her into my space and hoping she would like what she saw, that she'd feel something other than amusement for the man who called it home.

I heard the purr of her car when it pulled into my driveway — and even if I hadn't, Zamboni barking his head off would have given away her arrival. I put him in his crate, promising him I'd let him out quickly if he was a good boy, and then I made my way toward the door at the sound of three punctuated knocks.

I tried to play it cool, but I was triple checking everything in my head.

Wine decanted and ready to pour? Check.

A board of meat, cheese, fruits and olives on my kitchen island just in case she's hungry? Check.

Electrolyte drinks in the fridge? Check.

Heart pounding like a fucking war drum in my chest? Checkity-check-check.

With one last deep breath, I plastered on my best relaxed smile and opened the door.

Livia stood on the other side like an award-winning photograph, everything about her so sexy and put-together, it almost seemed impossible to be real. Her hair was down tonight, straight and silky, falling like a glossy curtain over her shoulders and brushing the tops of her arms. A brown cowboy hat sat snug on her head, the brim casting the perfect shadow across her face and only adding to the drama of her entrance.

Her makeup was soft but striking — long lashes framed those sharp eyes, her skin was glowing with a golden warmth, and her lips shimmered with a nude gloss that made my gaze drop to her mouth instantly.

I knew she clocked that little slip when the edges of her lips quirked up.

She wore a sheer black dress that tied just beneath her chest, the fabric fluttering open to reveal the high-cut leopard shorts underneath, and a statement belt that gleamed at her waist like a warning sign.

Or an invitation.

Chunky silver jewelry glinted at her wrist and collarbone, and the whole look was tied together with a pair of worn-in brown cowboy boots. She looked like the kind of trouble that shows up on your doorstep after you told her to stay away, unbothered and breathtaking, just to see if you'll break and let her in.

And I just couldn't help myself.

I whistled low as I leaned against the doorframe, letting my gaze rake down and back up again.

"Well butter my biscuits," I said, shaking my head with a grin. "I didn't realize it was country night, but you can ride me any time, cowgirl."

Livia hit me with the slowest blink of all time.

Undeterred, I doubled down. "If I had a nickel for every time you've taken my breath away, I'd be able to buy the whole damn rodeo for you, sweetheart."

I was pretty proud of the country accent I managed with that one, but Livia just pressed her lips together in a tight line, hand finding her hip as she cocked one eyebrow up.

Fine. Time to bring out the big guns.

"I'm pretty sure it's outlaw behavior, looking that good in cowboy boots," I said, lifting my hands like I was just the messenger. "And I'm afraid I'll have to make a citizen's arrest."

That did it.

She fought it, her lips tightening as she tried to keep her poker face, but a laugh snuck through before she could stop it, her head dipping for a beat. When she looked back up at me, there was a smile pulling at her lips.

"You done?"

I pushed off the doorframe and gave a little shrug. "Honestly, I could go all night. But I think the plans you have in mind for us would be a lot more fun for all involved."

Then I stepped aside, gesturing her in with all the cowboy charm I could muster.

"Come on in, cowgirl."

It was impossible not to ogle that woman's ass as she passed me, but I kept the *yee-haw* I wanted to holler out loud at the sight of it tucked securely between my teeth.

She set her oversized leather purse on the table just inside, taking a quick glance around my place with a look

I couldn't decipher before she turned to face me just as I closed the door behind us.

"In the spirit of our agreement, since you are a paying customer, I feel like I should take this opportunity to teach you that every single one of those lines made you seem eager and inexperienced."

"Should I bend over for this lashing or?"

"Is that *really* how you act around other women, or is it only me who gets the unfortunate blunders?"

"I'm afraid my one-of-a-kind charm is a gift I must share with the world," I said, pressing a hand to my chest. "But don't be jealous, cowgirl. I save my best ones for you."

"Clearly." She sighed, but that smile was playing at the edge of her lips again. "You don't have to try so hard. You don't have to make it some cute, on-theme compliment. What a woman really wants is to get your guttural, instinctual reaction."

"So, she *does* want me to drool on her!" I snapped my fingers at the crate where Zamboni was patiently waiting for his release, his tail wagging, tongue flopped out of his mouth. "You were right, buddy. I owe you a bully stick."

Livia eyed the pup over her shoulder before turning back to me. "What I want, and what most other women want, is for you to show me that one look has already driven you out of your mind. I want to see how badly you want me, but I don't want you to make a joke of it. I want to feel your desire, your restraint. We don't need clever. We need *real*."

She took three, slow, purposeful steps toward me then, the heels of her boots tapping against my floor in a way that scratched an itch in my brain. She was an inch taller than me at the moment, with me barefoot and her wearing those boots, and she tilted her head at me, tongue toying with the corner of her lip as she sized me up.

"Try again," she purred.

And I knew without asking that it was a demand — not a request.

Livia walked past me, opened and shut my door, and then knocked again.

Poor Zamboni lost his mind, and I assured him he'd be free as soon as I passed this test. I waited until he calmed before I opened the door.

Livia stood there just like before, and this time, I tried to lean into her instruction, to do what she'd asked. I let my eyes trail the length of her as my brain whirred to catch up, and I thought I might have actually won the lottery in this *lesson*, since it meant I got to unabashedly check her out again.

Focus.

Listen to your gut.

Say what you really feel.

Be real.

Don't choke.

That last internal thought was one all too familiar, one that stung like a snake bite. It was impossible to escape its teeth that sank into me, but I did my best not to show it on the outside.

I leaned into the doorframe, lifting one arm to rest above me, the other hanging loose at my side. She was so close I could smell the sweet warmth of her perfume — something woodsy and dark, with a hint of citrus that made my mouth water.

"Damn, baby," I murmured, letting the words roll out low and gruff.

I paused, eyes dragging over every inch of her again before I met her gaze, dead-on.

"You walk up lookin' like that and the only thought in my head is how the hell I'm supposed to survive you."

It took every ounce of willpower I had not to smirk in victory when I heard her breath hitch, when I saw her lips part just a centimeter as her eyes flicked between mine. When her gaze fell to my mouth, I knew I'd won.

"Better," she breathed, and then tilted her head higher in defiance. "But try again. Less poetic. More... *man*."

I leaned in just a breath closer, jaw tight, voice rough.

"*Fuck*, Liv," I muttered, voice as raw as I felt inside. I shook my head, reaching out and hooking my finger through the belt loop of her shorts. "Look at you."

She wet her lips. "Good."

"Get in here. I need my hands on you."

I punctuated that request with a slight tug on her belt loop, enough to have her leaning forward and into my space, to have my lips just barely brushing hers.

"Much better," she breathed.

And then she shoved me away, making me stumble backward as she marched back inside and shut the door behind us.

I was still reeling from the electricity of the moment, blinking repeatedly as a laugh barreled out of me. But Livia was all the way inside now, making herself right at home as she poured us two glasses of wine and nodded toward Zamboni in his crate.

"Let him out," she said.

"You sure?" I asked, hesitant as I made my way to the crate. "He's just a pup still, pretty energetic. I've got him in a training school, but to be honest, he doesn't listen worth a crap."

Livia was completely unfazed, swirling her wine as she leaned a hand on the counter. "Open it."

"Alright," I said, grimacing internally at how I was fairly certain the next five minutes would go. I was picturing the chaos as I unlatched the door — the screaming, the jumping and scratching, the demand for me to put the damn dog in a bedroom somewhere as she half-crawled onto the countertop.

Zamboni bolted for her as soon as the latch was back.

"Zambo! No! Zambo, paws on the ground. *Paws on the ground!*"

I yelled after him as he darted for the kitchen.

But Livia didn't budge.

She stood there with her wine in hand, hip cocked, expression schooled. And when Zamboni was a few feet away from her, bracing to pounce, she held up her palm.

"Stop."

She said the word sharply, her voice low and firm.

And I'll be fucking damned if that dog didn't do exactly as she said.

He skidded to a stop, looking up at her with his tongue lolling out.

"Stay," she said next, her fingers curling into a fist.

And he did.

"What in the witchcraft..." I muttered.

"Sit," Livia commanded, and if I hadn't seen Zamboni's butt hit the ground with my own eyes, I wouldn't have believed it.

Livia nodded her approval, then slowly walked toward the dog with her hand still rolled into that fist that meant *stay*. She held her hand out to his nose next, letting him sniff her, and then she smoothed her hand over his glossy coat in two long, gentle, rewarding strokes, scratching under his neck after the last one.

"Good boy," she said. "Free."

That seemed to release him, and instead of jumping up on her the way he had *every other guest* I'd had over since I adopted him, he turned and bounded into the living room, snatching one of his toys before plopping down in his dog bed and chewing away.

I blinked at her. "What the fuck was that?"

"You said he was in training," she said with a shrug. "Do you not work with him here at home? Those are all the basic commands."

"And you know this because you've had so many dogs in your life?"

"Just one," she clipped. "My mother's dog. And trust me, that asshole was all I needed to learn to assert dominance from the get-go with any animal."

"Me included," I said with a wink.

That earned me a chuckle that felt hard-won, and I slid up at the island next to her, grabbing the glass she'd poured for me before tilting it toward hers.

"To you, cowgirl."

"Stop calling me that," she said, even as she clinked her glass to mine and drank.

"If the hat fits," I said, gesturing to her outfit.

"I was at a festival at Curtis Hixon Park with Maven," she said in way of explanation.

"Ah, so it's *me* who should be jealous of all the other poor saps who got to ogle you before I did."

The corners of her lips lifted again, but fell quickly as she sipped from her glass, eyes scanning my place.

I'd meant every line I'd tried to reel her in with when she stood on the other side of my door — she looked absolutely stunning tonight. But she also looked... different. Tired. Worn. Stressed.

Like something was on her mind.

"You alright?"

I asked before I could think better of it, and Livia blinked, looking at me like I was crazy. "Of course. I'm fine. Why?"

"You just look... I don't know. Not yourself."

"Because of the outfit?"

"Because of your eyes."

Her head snapped back a little with the comment, mouth shutting as those warm brown eyes searched mine. I internally grimaced as she repeated, "My... eyes?"

Well, might as well own it now.

I nodded. "They're usually playful and sultry, like a jungle cat's."

She scoffed a laugh at that.

"I'm serious," I said, but I laughed a little, too. "I know it sounds dumb, but it's true. Don't act like you don't know it when you do that little black line thing at the edge of your eyes, too." I waved my finger at her. "But right now, they seem... distant. Cold." I swallowed, debating if I should leave it there, but I couldn't help but add, "It's like you put that makeup on to cover something up."

Livia didn't show even a hint of emotion, but she paused for a long moment before answering. "You seem very confident about that assessment."

I shrugged. "We've been friends for years. I pay attention."

Livia hummed, sipping her wine. "Well, I don't know what you mean."

"So, everything is fine?"

She opened her mouth, shut it again, sighed, and sat her glass down. "No. But it kind of freaks me out that you can tell."

"What's going on?"

"If I give you the abbreviated version, do you promise not to ask questions so we can get down to business?"

For once, I wasn't keen to what she was offering, but I nodded my agreement.

Livia sighed. "My parents cut me off when I was eighteen, right after high school graduation. I haven't seen them since. The only tie I still have to them is my baby sister." She paused, a sad smile as she looked down at her nails. "Their pride and joy." Her eyes met mine then. "And I just found out that she's getting married and wants me at the wedding."

I was so pissed at myself for agreeing not to ask questions, because about a hundred of them were beating at the back of my throat and begging to get out.

Why did they cut her off?

What did that mean?

Why did she say her sister was their pride and joy as if she wasn't?

What happened between them?

Was she still close to her sister?

Why was the wedding upsetting news?

Was it because she didn't want to see her sister, or because she didn't want to see her parents?

Or was it because she didn't feel welcome, even though her sister invited her?

I longed to know the full story and all the dynamics, yearned to peel back the layer Livia had so graciously lifted the corner of so I could see more of her.

I wanted to know *everything* about this woman.

But just as quickly as she'd let me in, her guard snapped back in place.

She drank her wine on a shrug. "Now, let's start."

Livia wrapped her hand around my wrist then, dragging me toward the living room. I barely got another sip of my wine and set the glass down before I was stumbling after her.

She pressed her hands into my chest when we made it to the couch, sending me back into the cushions with a *whoosh*.

"Pretend I'm a girl you invited over and now you want to fuck me."

"Trust me," I breathed, eyes skating over her. "No pretending required."

Chapter 8

Get to Work

Livia

My heart was racing as I took back the reins and shoved Carter onto his couch. It was only a moment that I'd lost control, but it was enough to have me shaken.

How the hell could this man tell that something was off with me within minutes of me walking into his home?

It was difficult for *Maven* to figure out when I was in a mood. It usually took her at least an hour to see through my mask.

But Carter had picked up on it immediately.

And even more surprising, I'd told him what was wrong.

I could have easily said nothing when he asked. I could have told him he was crazy, he was seeing things, and he didn't have a fucking clue about me the way he thought he did.

But the fact that he'd seen me so clearly, so quickly, had completely fucking thrown me.

It's your eyes.

I guess it shouldn't have surprised me that my eyes were giving me away, considering how my sister's phone call had plagued me the last few days. I hadn't seen her in years, mostly because I always had an excuse — *work is too crazy, I don't have enough vacation time, I'm out of town when you want to visit, you know I can't come to Christmas.*

The truth rested in the fact that it was too painful to be with my sister, and so I just avoided it at all costs. We texted and talked on the phone every now and then, but even those interactions typically sent me into a spiral of sorts.

Now, my baby sister was getting married.

And I had to decide what to do with her invitation.

It would be one of the biggest days of her life, one I always imagined I'd be a part of. I wanted to be there for her. I wanted to celebrate her union.

But I couldn't stomach the thought of being back in Long Island, or even in the same *state* as my parents.

I didn't want to think about it — especially not right now.

I took a breath that would have seemed normal to anyone on the outside, but for me, it was all I could do to calm myself down and get back to focusing on the task at hand.

"Now that we've gone over what *not* to say when she shows up at your door," I said to Carter, asserting my dominance over him as I stood and stared down at him on the couch. "Let's talk about what to do once she's inside."

I sat down next to him then, crossing my legs, the heel of my boot sliding up his shin. The way he reacted to me with a little shiver already had my mind clearing.

"The wine and music and lights are a great start," I said. "But it's body language from here. You can't be tripping all over yourself. Relax. Let her know *she* can relax."

I waited until he took the cue, leaning back on the couch and tossing one arm around the back of it so it was draped around me, too. He leaned in a little closer, shifting his weight so he was angled toward me. Then, he crossed one ankle over the opposite knee.

"Good," I said. I felt the tension in my shoulders release now that I was back in control. "Now touch me."

"With pleasure," he muttered, hand shooting out for the tie of the sheer dress I wore. It rested just between my breasts, but before he could tug on it, I swatted his hand away.

"Pacing, Rook." I smirked, and just like that, I was the teacher, and he was the student, and my family drama didn't exist — at least for the moment. "Touch my hair, my neck. Toy with the straps of my top. Run your knuckles down my arm. And when you can't stand it anymore, when I'm leaning in and giving you all the signs that I'm with you..." I shrugged. "Kiss me."

His eyes shot wide at that.

"What?" I asked. "Don't tell me I have to teach you how to *kiss*. For fuck's sake, Rookie."

"No, no," he said hurriedly, shaking his head. "I just... I didn't expect you to let me kiss you."

"It's only for educational purposes," I clipped. "Don't think this is an open invitation for you to kiss me any time you want."

"I'll take whatever you give me, Mommy."

Again, he won himself an unbidden laugh with that, and I turned it into a growl before flicking his nose like a dog.

"Focus," I said. "Or I'm walking right back out that door."

"Okay, okay." Carter threw his hands up in surrender before settling back into his relaxed, cocky, laid-back posture. He hit me with a lazy smirk, and the hand he had draped around the couch, and therefore me, began to gently rub my neck.

He wore his nerves like an article of clothing, his brows pinching together a bit like he was thinking really hard about his next move. He winced before taking his next breath, his eyes fluttering shut as a long inhale and exhale left him.

When he opened his eyes again, it was with a sense of calm.

He was quiet for a moment, his eyes watching where he touched me before they started to hike the rest of me like I was a trail in the Appalachian Forest. His touch grew softer, fingertips swirling in soft circles that made goosebumps erupt over my arms.

"I like this," he muttered, fingertips sliding under the thin strap of my dress. He ran it slowly beneath the fabric, toying with it suggestively. Then, his hand trailed down, knuckles grazing my arm, rib cage, and oblique before he followed the line of my belt to the buckle that sat squarely between my hips. "I *really* like this."

He slid his hand under the belt and tugged with the words.

And white-hot electricity shot between my thighs.

I arched a brow and smiled, amused by how well that had worked. "Oh yeah?" I teased, still letting him lead.

He nodded, his hand finding its way back up to curl around my neck. He played with my hair at the back of it, making me close my eyes and let out a sigh at the way it felt.

"You're so beautiful."

I nearly gagged, eyes rolling open so I could pinpoint him with an unimpressed glare.

He chuckled. "Wow. You'd have thought I said you have warts."

"That line is tired," I said. "Try again."

He frowned. "But you are beautiful."

Why did it feel like he poured a bucket of roaches on me when he said that?

Maybe it was because those words made me flash back to the most horrid night of my life, to the time a man older than me, a man I trusted, said the same two words before completely destroying me.

"You're beautiful."

Panic was playing at the edges of my calm façade, but I must have still had a look of disgust on my face, because Carter full-on laughed and shook his head. "Alright, alright, no comments about beauty. Hmm..."

He wiggled his shoulders, sitting up taller as his brows folded together in concentration. I let that action bring me back to the present, shutting the door on the past and leaving it right where it belonged.

Carter continued playing with my hair, careful not to toy with it too much, just enough to give me the sensation. Then, he leaned in closer, taking my hat off and trailing the rim of it down my arm before he sat it behind me. His other hand came up to frame my jaw, and he tilted my head toward him.

"You are fucking remarkable, Liv. You know that?"

He slid his fingers to curl around the back of my neck, thumbs framing my jaw, grip strong as he guided me into him.

"Ever since you walked through that door, all I've been able to think about is touching you... *tasting* you."

His nostrils flared, his eyes on my lips. He shook his head like restraining himself was torture. "Please don't make me wait any longer."

That worked.

My mind was clear again, that hint of panic replaced by another jolt between my legs, another parting of my lips as I leaned into those words, into the heat that swept over me from the power of them.

And just like I'd given him permission to, Carter read the signs — and he kissed me.

He was tentative for only second, just a *beat* of insecurity when our lips first touched. I almost pulled back to scold him, but as if he sensed it, his grip on my neck tightened and he deepened the kiss.

After that, it was like he was pulling out all the stops to impress me.

His lips were warm and firm, seeking as he inhaled a deep breath like just kissing me was enough to give him all the pleasure he'd ever need in life. I loved the way his large hands spanned my jaw and neck as he held me to him, as he tilted me *just* slightly so he could fit our lips together perfectly.

He opened his mouth, and I followed, both of us moaning when he slid his tongue inside and met mine.

"Fuck," he groaned, and then he was pulling me into his lap.

One hand slid between us and tugged on my belt buckle so hard he lifted me, and I followed the cue, slinging one leg up and over until I was straddling him like a saddle. He wrapped me up then, large arms fully encompassing my frame as he kissed me harder, deeper, with more longing.

And I almost lost myself.

I almost forgot it was all a lesson as his hands slid down to cup my ass and squeeze.

I almost gave into the temptation to rock against him when he slid his hands into the back pockets of my shorts and flexed his hips up to meet mine.

I almost let out the whimper I was fighting to hold back when he nipped at my bottom lip with his teeth before capturing me in another hot, bruising kiss.

Carter Fabri.

A damn good kisser.

Who would have thought?

"Oho, so he *does* have a little game hiding up his sleeve," I teased, pulling back from the kiss with a press of my nails into his chest. I smiled when he opened his eyes as if he were drugged, his lids heavy, lips swelling. "That wasn't so bad, Rookie."

"Give me another five minutes and I think I can earn an A plus."

He breathed the words before he was hooking me behind the neck and pulling me into him again, his mouth capturing mine as he rocked his hips up against me.

"Did I say you could kiss me again?" I asked, still teasing, but with more of an edge to my voice as I bit down hard on his bottom lip.

Carter winced and groaned, but I knew the pain turned him on more than it warned him to stop. His hands gripped my hips hard, holding me in place like he wanted to fuck me right through all the layers of clothes still between us.

"Next lesson," I said against his lips, teasing him with little brushes of my own that weren't quite kisses. "Strip me out of these shorts. Slowly. Make everything count. Make me drip for you."

"Fuck," he rasped.

"And then use your mouth *and* these big hands of yours to make me come."

I barely got the words out before Carter flipped me onto my back.

I couldn't help but smile, and I dragged my teeth across my lip as I watched him hike one of my legs up onto his shoulder. He kissed along my calf as he tugged one boot off, then switched legs to take care of the other.

"Slow," I reminded him, and I felt him take a breath against my skin as he brought the pace down.

His mouth stayed on me as his hands traveled up. He planted a long, lingering kiss just below my knee, and then his fingers hooked onto my belt buckle, yanking it open. He thumbed my belt open next, unfastened the button of my shorts, and peeled the zipper down.

All the while, his mouth was working. He licked and sucked his way up my thighs as his hands hooked into the waistband of my shorts and started pulling them down. It was only the act of peeling them off me that made his kisses stop, and he sat back on his heels so he could maneuver better.

"Tell me what to do," I coached. "A woman wants you to take control."

"That's not what you want," he threw back with a mischievous grin.

"Well, we're not talking about me. Now, tell. Me. What. To. Do."

Carter licked his lip, curling his fingers inside the band of my shorts.

"Lift your ass, baby. Let me get these off you."

I smirked, lifting my hips as he asked me to. I worked with his guidance until my shorts were off along with the black cotton thong I had beneath it. Carter tossed both somewhere behind him before he was on me again.

And I let out a sigh, closed my eyes, and focused on how to make him a pussy-eating machine.

"Show me how well you listened during our first lesson," I told him. "Show me what you learned."

I peeked one eye open just long enough to see the determination settle in on Carter's face. It lit me up like nothing had before, enough to have me wondering what the hell it was that I found so fucking hot about teaching this man how to touch me. I didn't let myself overthink it before I was dragging my nails through his hair and guiding him right where I wanted.

Just like I asked, he proved to me that he'd paid attention during our first lesson. He took his time, his kisses wet and longing as he worshipped my thighs and toyed with me enough to make me squirm. When I thought I couldn't stand it any longer, he rewarded me with a long lap of his tongue from my opening all the way up to my clit.

"Mmm," he moaned against me, and I arched my back, body reacting without my permission to how badly he wanted me.

Carter pressed on both of my thighs, opening me like he couldn't get me wide enough to do everything he wanted to. He licked me again, slower this time, and then two fast licks in quick succession that had my clit buzzing to life.

"Talk to me," I managed, licking my lips as a panting breath slipped through them. "Make it dirty."

Carter licked around my opening and up to my clit, flicking the tip of his tongue over it with just the right pressure to make my legs quake. When he covered my clit with his whole mouth, kissing it sloppily and swirling his tongue in a figure eight, I moaned and bucked up to meet his touch.

He smiled against me, winding his arms up and under each thigh so he could hold me still. "Look at you, filthy girl," he purred, swirling his tongue around my clit before he teased the inside of my thighs again. "You're so fucking pretty when you squirm for me like this."

"Yes," I managed, rolling my lips together. "Good. Now, get to work."

Carter smiled against my thigh again before he was dragging his mouth where I wanted.

And I was so glad he had use of his hands this lesson.

I loved the way his fingertips dug into my thighs, the way his palm spanned the length of my abdomen as he slid one hand up and roughly shoved it under the bralette beneath my sheer dress. I fucking *loved* the way he toyed with my nipple, the way his other hand slid beneath me, fingertips dancing in the wetness there.

"God, I can't wait to fuck this pussy," Carter breathed, circling my opening with one slick finger. "I can't wait to feel you stretching for me, to feel you hugging every inch as I break you wide open."

I didn't even fake the moan that got out of me, but I did quickly realize I was losing myself again.

Hold the reins, an inner voice warned me.

"That's it," I encouraged him. "Just like that."

Carter sucked my clit with conviction then, my praise spurring him on. And when he slid his finger inside me, I rewarded him with a bucking of my hips, with my hands twisting in his hair and holding him to me.

Until he started jamming that finger in and out of me.

I laughed a little, reaching down to slow his assault.

"You're listening so well," I breathed, chest heaving as my orgasm began to play at my nerve endings. "Now, do exactly what you did last time with your mouth, and use your hand. But be easy. Curl your finger inside me. Wiggle it until you find the spot that makes me tremble. Then read my body language, figure out the combination to make me come."

Carter hummed his understanding, and when I released my grip on his wrist, he started to move his finger inside me again.

This time, it was exactly what I needed.

He curled the digit slowly, hooking until he found that sensitive area that made me moan. When he did, he slipped another finger inside to join the first, and I felt every ounce of his concentration as he sucked my clit and moved his fingers like he was a thief, and I was the combination to the safe he had to unlock.

"Yes," I breathed, hips rocking, hands gripping his hair. "*Fuck*, yes, yes, right there. Don't stop."

Carter doubled down, fingering me faster, his tongue swirling over my clit before he closed his lips over it and sucked in the perfect little pulses I needed.

And when his other hand started plucking my nipple in the same rhythm, it was just what the doctor ordered.

I came with a cry, legs shaking, ribcage constricting, every muscle in my body coiling tight. Wave after wave of pleasure rolled over me, and Carter didn't let up until I was completely spent, until I was tapping his arm and wincing from the sensitivity of so much attention on my clit.

Slowly, Carter relented, pressing soft kisses against my vulva as he slowed his fingers inside me. When he withdrew them altogether, I shivered again, letting out a low string of curse words that made him smile as he kissed my thigh and sat back on his heels.

"Jesus, that was sexy," he said, wiping the edges of his smirking lips with his thumb. "And much more fun when hands are involved."

"You just say that because you got to feel up my tits."

"Oh, I'm not denying the facts."

I chuckled, stretching my arms up overhead as my body hummed with the delicious energy of the orgasm that had just rocked me.

"That was nice," I said. "I love how you listened."

"Are you saying I'm a good boy?"

"I am," I said, leaning up on my palms. "Now, go reach into my purse and pull out your reward."

Carter jumped off the couch like I'd just told him the key to the Stanley Cup was in my bag, and I laughed a little when Zamboni startled from where he'd been passed out on his dog bed. But he lifted his head only a moment, decided whatever Carter and I were doing was too boring for him to care, and then he laid back down.

My smirk was permanent as I watched Carter dig inside my purse. I sat up all the way, slowly stripping out of my dress and bralette while his back was turned to me.

By the time he turned around, I was completely naked.

And he was holding up his reward with a shocked, slightly scared expression.

My smile grew wider.

Because in his hand he held a Fleshlight.

It was modeled to look like me, from the dark silicone lips down to the faintest hint of my trimmed landing strip. It was impossibly realistic, complete with a tight, ribbed tunnel hidden inside that I knew would make him see stars.

He blinked down at it, then up at me, then back again like he wasn't sure whether to drop to his knees and thank me or run screaming from the room.

I patted the couch cushion next to me with a grin. "Bring it to me. You're going to learn how to fuck *this* before you earn the real thing."

Chapter 9
It's Called Edging, Rook
Carter

It took all of sixty seconds for Livia to have me sitting wide legged and butt ass naked on my couch.

Unsurprisingly, I was hard as fucking granite as she slowly dripped lube into her hand, her kohl-lined eyes sparking with excitement. She was naked, too — and the lines and curves of her body played together in the low lighting of my house in a way that made her like a moving piece of art. I was greedy with my perusal of her, letting my eyes linger on her plump lips, the slope of her neck, the subtle swells of her breasts, the lean dip of muscle that ran between her rib cage all the way down to the top of her belly button. I hummed in my throat as my sight dipped lower, to her perfect cunt, my mind racing with the memory of feeling her walls squeeze around my fingers, of hearing her moan when I made her come.

"Someone's excited," Livia teased, rolling her hands together to coat her palms with the lube.

"I'd be more excited if you were about to sit that sweet pussy in my lap."

"Mmm, nice line," she said, her lips curling. "But like I said... you've got to earn that privilege, just like you earned the right to taste me."

"Just tell me what to do, and I'll do it."

"We'll see about that." She smiled wider with the words, and then she slid off the edge of the couch and onto her knees between my legs.

"Fuck, Liv..." My voice was low and husky, the sight nearly breaking me. My cock jumped at just the thought of her touching me with this as my view.

"Tonight, we're going to get you that control you were lacking in our first lesson," she said, slipping right into teacher mode as she smoothed her hands together. Then, she reached forward, one hand wrapping around my shaft as the other cupped my balls.

I saw stars and planets and a whole goddamn universe when she did.

"*Fuck*," I cursed again, letting my head fall back.

Livia squeezed hard enough to make my head jerk right back up.

It was just on the edge of pain, and I hissed before she loosened her grip and slid her hand up and over my tip before slicking it back down. Her other hand rolled my balls softly, and when she repeated the motion altogether, I knew I was seconds away from coming.

She must have known it, too, because she instantly pulled her hands away.

"Sorry," I grunted, pinching the bridge of my nose as I squeezed my eyes shut and shook my head. "I just... it feels so fucking good."

"You don't need to be sorry," she said, her fingertips resting on my knees. She squeezed gently until I looked down at her. "This is what the lesson is for. Honestly, I find it very arousing that you want me so badly, that just me touching you like that has you so affected. But..." she continued, tilting her head. "If you come within two seconds of fucking a woman, she's going to leave unsatisfied — and probably never grace your doorstep again."

I nodded. "I know, I know. I'm such a fucking—"

"Don't finish that sentence."

The words clipped out of her with more menace, her expression serious. She pressed up onto her knees enough to dig her fingernails into my chin as she grabbed it and forced me to look at her.

"*I* am the only one who gets to punish or reward you, understand?"

I swallowed. "Yes."

"Good." She released my chin like I'd disgusted her, and for some reason, that made my cock jump again.

I had no idea why I fucking loved that, why I instantly reacted to the glimpses of humiliation she gave me, but I chose not to question it as she lowered back down to her knees...

And reached for the toy she'd brought.

The Fleshlight was large in her delicate hands, and she twisted it one way and then the other as she assessed it with a smile.

Her eyes found mine with that wicked grin still in place. "Ready?"

"I hope so."

A warm chuckle left her lips, and then she lined the toy up with the tip of my cock, pressed a button that made the thing start humming softly, and slowly slid it down.

I groaned at the first sensation of it hugging my cock. Livia worked slowly, covering just my tip before she removed it and then worked it down another inch. She kept that pace until it covered me completely, until the ribbed toy was hugging and sucking my cock in a way I'd never experienced.

When I'd fucked Zina's ass as a rookie, it had been in a room with my teammates and I'd lasted all of six seconds. I didn't have enough time to even think about what it felt like to be inside her before I was busting — a fact she was quick to poke fun of, which did nothing for my confidence.

But this...

The toy hugged me like a glove, the ribbing testing my ability to hold myself together as the rhythmic pulsing teased and tempted me. I moaned when Livia slowly slid it off me and then lowered it all the way back down.

And I knew it was the sight of *her* that would do me in — the way she was balanced on her knees, her lips parted, eyes on my cock as she used the toy to fuck me.

"This is a special kind of Fleshlight," she said, slowly pulling it off me and lowering it again. "It's a stamina-training stroker."

I could barely focus on a fucking word she was saying. My orgasm was cresting as I watched Livia, as I watched my cock disappear inside the toy and then reappear again.

"So, here's your assignment. When you feel like you're about to come, you're going to tell me."

"Now," I managed with a grunt.

Livia's eyes widened, and she hesitated only a second before she pulled the toy off me.

I groaned at the loss of sensation, my body protesting in a violent tremble. Cold rushed over me like I'd just opened the door of an industrial freezer, and I winced against the pain.

"Mmm, naughty boy," Livia teased, but she soothed the bit of pain still lingering with a slow stroke of her hand over my shaft. "Did you fuck your hand every day like I told you to?"

"Multiple times."

"Tell me what's making you lose control."

I laughed. I couldn't help it.

Was she serious?

I waved a hand over her, eyebrows lifting. "You're kidding, right?"

"Words, Rook," she purred, and the way her lips curled, I knew she already understood what I wasn't saying, but she delighted in hearing it.

"You're fucking sexy, Liv," I rasped, wetting my lips and shaking my head. "Your body, your mind, just… everything about you. And you're on your knees for me, fucking me with a toy. How am I supposed to keep it together?"

The corner of her lips tilted, and she lubed up her hand again before slicking it over me. I didn't know if it felt good or hurt this time, my cock sensitive yet aching.

"With patience and practice," she answered simply. "Now, we're going to go again, and I want you to do the same thing. When you feel like you're about to come, tell me."

"Why do I feel like I'm going to fail this lesson?"

"There's no pass or fail. It's just learning, okay?" A softness washed over her when she noted my uncertainty. "Listen, take a deep breath…" She waited until I did so before she continued. "Let go of whatever pressure you're feeling to *do* anything, okay? I'm not expecting anything of you right now other than to tell me when it feels like you're going to come. And I think you can do that, can't you?"

I nodded, heart racing a little less with her permission to relax.

"Good. Now, let's have some fun, shall we?"

Livia stroked me with her hand a couple times before she lined the toy up again, and this time when she sank it down, I felt just marginally more in control.

I sighed, letting my head fall back against the couch.

"Does it feel good?" Livia asked.

"Fuck yes," I breathed. "Feels so fucking good."

"That's it. Imagine it's a woman you're sinking into right now, and she's feeling that same anxiety you are. What would you say to her? How would you let her know she can relax?"

It was nearly impossible to hold onto my title of student with how good it felt for her to fuck me with that toy, but I did my best to fight through the fog and deliver. "Goddamn, baby. You feel so good. Better than I imagined. Like you're meant for me."

I pulled my head up to see Livia's face, and she met me with a tilt of her head side to side. "The first part was good. The last part..."

"Too much?"

"A little. You don't have anything to prove. You don't need to be poetic. Just be honest."

She picked up her pace a little, her hand moving the toy up and down my shaft as it sucked and teased me.

"Oh, fuck," I breathed, flexing into it. "*Fuck,* baby, that feels so good. I love when you ride me like this."

"Yes," she praised. "Good."

The pace quickened again.

And it was too much.

"I'm going to—"

Livia pulled the toy off me before I could finish the sentence, my orgasm tingling up every nerve along my spine. But as soon as she removed the toy, it washed away, and my nerve endings were on fire as if I was coming, but I wasn't.

I shook and cursed and gripped the couch cushion beneath me, and Livia soothed me with her palm against the inside of my knee.

"Good. I'm so proud of you. You're doing so well."

"This is fucking torture."

"Is it?"

Instantly, I shook my head. "No. Yes. I don't fucking know. It feels like it *should* be, but it also feels..."

"Incredible?"

I nodded, wincing as the strange pleasure completely washed away and left me aching again. "Like blue balls mixed with the world's best orgasm."

Livia chuckled, the sound low and raspy in her throat. "It's called edging, Rook."

The moment she wrapped her hand around my shaft, I moaned, flexing into her hand with a desperation I was unable to control. I wanted to come so bad it was all I could think about.

"Believe it or not, this will actually make it even better when I finally *do* let you come," she said, stroking me softly. Her hand was loose around me, gliding over every sensitive inch without giving me the pressure I ached for. "But right now, I want you to *resist*."

I whimpered.

I fucking *whimpered* like a weak little boy because that was the absolute last thing I wanted to do right now.

"Imagine you're with the woman of your dreams."

Okay, so... picture you?

I bit down the words.

"And let's just say it takes her a while to warm up. Maybe she's shy. Maybe she's worried about how she looks."

"Why in the —*fuuuck,*" I groaned when Livia tightened her grip slightly, just enough to have that orgasm toying at the edges of my grasp again. I was panting my next words. "Why would she worry about that?"

"Are you kidding? So many women worry about that. Maybe it's because of a toxic ex or watching porn or reading magazines or hearing godawful sex advice from their mothers. Believe me, there is ample messaging about how women need to please men, and that sex is not about their own pleasure. So, yeah — a lot of women will be self-conscious. They'll worry if they look fat when they're riding you."

"Stop."

"Or if their tits are bouncing in the perfect pornographic way."

"Get the fuck out."

"Or if they're making the right face to make you come."

At that, I stopped where her hand was stroking me — much to my cock's chagrin. "You're being for real right now?"

"Do I look like I'd waste lesson time with anything *not* real?" Livia began stroking me again, and I sank farther into the couch cushions, my body on fire. "The truth is the majority of women you bring home are going to need your time and attention and encouragement to come. And *you* need to not come until you get her there. So," she said, placing the Fleshlight over my crown again. "Let's practice holding off."

"Jesus Christ," I muttered, but it was cut short with a moan ripping from my throat when Livia slid the toy over me.

She moaned when she sank it down. "Oh, yes, Carter. *God.* You're so big."

"Coming—"

I muttered the word, and Livia laughed as she pulled the toy off, and I fought through another strangely pleasurable, torturous withdrawal.

"Rude," I said, but it was with a smile of my own, because it *was* kind of funny.

"I'm sorry," she said around her laughter. "I just — that was fucking hilarious."

"I guess I do have a praise kink."

"I think you have more kinks than you even know exist, Rook." Livia slid the toy back onto me and I shuddered at the overwhelming sensation. "Now, focus. Do what you have to do to last. Think about something else — running drills or losing a playoff game or whatever works. If you can't distract your mind, then zero in on your goal. Imagine you're in a game and you *have* to score — or the team loses. Resist with everything you have. Last for her," she said, and then she squeezed my knee as she flexed the toy down farther. "Last for *me.*"

"Fuck," I groaned, loving those words from her lips enough to tell her I was about to fucking come again, but I did what she said and fought against it.

I tried to think about whatever I could to distract me from how good the toy felt. I thought about sand crabs and raccoons, about cooking and paddle boarding, about calm morning waves at the beach and the soft chirping of birds in the evening. I even tried using Livia's example of imagining the loss of a game, the shuffle of skates back into the locker room, heads hanging low.

But none of it worked.

Because Livia was fucking me with the Fleshlight, the ribbed gel of it hugging my cock perfectly as the little machine sucked and pulled. And she wasn't just silently fucking me, either. She was moaning, panting, whimpering, making all the sweet little sounds I imagined she'd make if I was fucking *her*.

"Oh, Carter. Yes. Just like that. Oh, it feels so *good*. I love when you fuck me like this. Yes. Harder. Faster. Fuck me deeper."

"*Christ*, Liv," I cursed, gritting my teeth against my climax.

When she started pumping faster, granting my silent wish, I knew I was screwed.

Switch gears, you idiot.

Don't fucking come.

Game time. Imagine it's game time.

Livia continued on with her moans and words of encouragement, but I did my best to ignore them. I kept pumping up into the toy but imagined I was on the ice, instead. I channeled that energy I felt when I was exhausted, when it was overtime and the next person who scored won the whole fucking game. I imagined it was all up to me, that my one job was to contain my climax.

It was the first time my body listened.

I found an almost Zen-like state of being, like Livia was muted under water. I felt what she was doing to me, but I willed my mind to focus on what *I* was doing. Every bit of my control went to holding back, to lasting just a little bit longer.

"God, yes, Carter, I'm coming. I'm coming!"

Livia started pumping the toy faster and I bit my lower lip so hard I released it with a hiss.

And then I broke.

"Fuck, I can't—"

Once again, I didn't finish the words before Livia removed the toy.

And this time was the worst.

I was *one fucking second* away from busting, but the moment she pulled off, my orgasm froze. It was like pouring soda into a glass too quickly, the foam rushing to the top — but stopping just before it toppled over the lip of the glass.

Every nerve in my body was alive, burning and tingling as I trembled and cursed and clutched the couch cushions. I was fucking the empty air like I could find relief there, but my orgasm slowly receded, like the tide drawing back out.

"Fucking hell," I panted, shaking my head. "I can't. I can't do it."

"You can."

"I can't."

Livia grabbed my chin until I looked at her. "Yes," she repeated, her gaze sincere. "You can. And you will. One more time. All you have to do is last long enough for me to come, and you can come, too. Understand?"

Something about how she referred to the toy as *her* had me willing to say yes to anything. I nodded, even though I was still unsure I could make it. I tried to hold onto her belief that I could as she lowered the toy back down.

I was so sensitive, so ready that just fucking the thing three more times had me groaning with the restraint not to let go.

"Carter... *ooohhhh*... God, yes. Yes. Yes!"

Livia dragged each little word out, moaning and making me wait, and then she pumped harder and faster like she was on top of me. She moaned the entire time, screaming out my name while I pinned my bottom lip between my teeth and pushed all my focus into holding back.

You can't do it, can you?

You weak little fuck.

You're going to lose it.

You're going to disappoint her just like you—

I shook my head against the noise, eyes squeezed shut, cock begging me for release, but I refused. I held on and rode out every tantalizing pump of the toy.

And then Livia slowed, her breaths evening out, and when I chanced peeling one eye open and then the next, I was met with a satisfied smirk of her lips.

"Such a good fucking boy," she praised. "You may come."

"Oh, thank fuck."

I panted the words, and then I released the restraint I'd been clinging to, but I didn't relax. I *couldn't* fucking relax. Every nerve inside me was strung tight, and the second Livia started pumping me again, I felt my orgasm rush to the surface.

And it wasn't like a normal climax. It wasn't slow and easy and familiar.

It was like a tsunami taking out an entire fucking city.

I barely had time to register that it was happening before my orgasm crashed into me like a wall of water, knocking my breath from my chest as it took me down. I thought I moaned, or maybe cried out, or maybe sucked in my last breath and stayed completely silent — I couldn't be sure. I just gripped the couch tight and held on for dear life.

"You're still fighting it," Livia soothed. "Let go. Come for me, Rook."

I panted, gripping tighter, thighs spreading, ass clenching as I reached and reached and—

"Oh, *God!* Oh fuck, fuck, *fuuuck.*" I cried out as my climax finally took me, and it was like having ten orgasms at once. The pleasure was indescribable, like witnessing a miracle or achieving a lifelong dream. It wasn't just surface level. It was bone deep, *soul* deep, and it whipped through me like a beautiful, punishing wind.

Every muscle was painfully tight until the second I came, and then I was spasming, panting, screaming, succumbing. It was heaven. It was euphoria. It was fucking deliverance.

I couldn't be sure how long I came for. It felt like hours, but it might have only been moments. Either way, I collapsed on the other side of it, bones going limp and muscles melting into the couch. I was suddenly so tired, I felt like I could fall asleep right then and there.

"That was so sexy," Livia praised, slowly working the toy off me.

I hissed and convulsed a little when she slid it over my tip, and then we both moaned at the sight of my cum dripping out of the toy and all over me.

"Look at you. You filled me up."

"Liv," I panted her name, because *fuck,* that was the hottest thing I'd ever heard. I wanted to fill her up. I wanted it to be her I got to fuck next time.

"You did so well. But... we aren't done yet."

My eyes shot open. "We're not?"

She shook her head, fingers crawling up my thigh until she was wrapping her hand around my softening cock. I didn't know whether to cry or moan at the sensation, but the sight of her playing with my cum had me leaning toward the latter.

"For learning purposes, let's pretend you *didn't* last. Let's pretend you came before she did, but she's still turned on and ready to go. What would you do?"

I held up my index and middle finger, wiggling them in the same motion that had made her come earlier.

She shook her head. "No, no."

I made a peace sign and wiggled my tongue between them next.

Livia sucked her teeth. "Come on, now. You will have already done that. If your line was playing in the third period and you were down by one, you wouldn't ask coach to bench you, would you? You wouldn't leave it to someone else to finish the job, would you?"

"Liv," I said, shaking my head. "I can't. I literally cannot—"

"Yes, you can," she assured me.

And she squeezed her hand around me, just the right kind of pressure, and started pumping.

"Please," I begged.

"If you want me to stop, you know the words to say."

She was asking me to use the safe words if I wanted out, and *God,* I was tempted. I was fucking spent.

But I was also insatiable when it came to this woman, and watching her play with my cum on her knees had my cock hardening again of its own free will.

Livia smirked at the sight. "That's it. Get hard for me again, baby. Get me off."

I groaned, head falling back as she worked me until I was hard as stone. Then, she slid the toy back on.

It was actually easier this time, that restraint I had to hold onto. My body wasn't wound as tight. I wasn't quite as desperate. But it was still work as she increased the pace, as she moaned and teased and drew it out until she knew I was actively fighting against coming.

When she said the word and allowed me my second orgasm, I sounded more like I was in pain than in ecstasy. The climax ripped through me swift and sweet, like a little exclamation point on the night.

And then I really did melt into the couch.

"I can't move," I mumbled like I was drunk. "I'll never move again. I live here now."

Livia just chuckled, and then I swore she pressed a slow, soft kiss against my cheek, but I couldn't trust my reality at the moment.

"You don't have to move. I'm going to take care of you. Just relax. You did well."

That praise was the final nail in the coffin, and the last thing I heard before darkness took me.

Chapter 10

If You Let Me

Livia

There is this euphoric kind of Zen that comes with jewelry making.

At first, everything requires focus and attention. I have to pick out all the jewels, chains, beads and fasteners. I have to lay everything out, plan, measure, get my tools set. My hands are shaking a bit as I get started, knowing one little mess up could mean starting all over again.

But somewhere in the middle, all that focus fades, and I find a rhythm.

It's like meditation, the methodical repetition of crafting a gold chain or linking beads or setting jewels. It's one of my favorite parts of the whole process, one of the reasons this craft became so much more to me than just a hobby.

I felt that kind of Zen now — post-orgasm high, a glass of wine in my hand and my feet kicked up on the couch next to Carter. Zamboni was curled up next to me, his head in my lap, and I stroked the fur behind his ears absentmindedly as he snoozed. I wore one of Carter's t-shirts that I'd stolen from his bedroom closet, and I savored the smell of it as I sipped the wine.

Cedar wood. Bergamot. Mint.

I told myself it was just a little observation. It definitely wasn't me pulling the fabric into my fist and closer to my nose. I most certainly didn't inhale it with a little smile, either. And it was just out of necessity that I also pulled on a pair of his boxer briefs.

I just wanted to be comfy.

A car backfired somewhere nearby, and Zamboni's head popped up, his ears alert before he let out a little bark. I soothed him with another pet, patting my leg for him to lay back down, but the bark was enough to make Carter stir.

He was right where I'd left him, on the other side of the couch with his legs spread wide. He was slumped into the cushions, his head resting against the back. I'd cleaned him up and covered him with the thickest blanket I could find, and there was a fresh glass of water on the table next to him, ready for when he woke.

Carter groaned a little as he came to, squeezing his eyes shut before he blinked repeatedly and maneuvered to sit up. He ran a hand through his hair and over his short beard before his eyes found mine, and a slow, sleepy smile spread on his face.

I ignored the way my heart jumped at the sight, at how my own lips curled up to mirror his.

"How long have I been out?"

"Just an hour."

"An *hour*?!" He shook his head. "Jesus, woman. You quite literally fucked me to sleep."

"Technically, a toy fucked you to sleep."

"You were the one driving."

I chuckled, still petting Zamboni as I nodded to the glass of water beside him. "Drink."

Carter followed my gaze before picking up the glass and downing half of it. It was then that his eyes took in the sight of me, and he groaned, setting the water back on the table before he turned to face me.

"Liv... you're wearing my shirt."

I hiked the hem of it up to show where the navy-blue fabric of his briefs hugged my thigh. "These, too."

He shook his head, hands reaching for me like he couldn't help himself. He slid one hand roughly up my leg all the way to my hip. "I didn't think it was possible to get turned on again tonight, but..."

A zip of something unfamiliar flittered through my stomach, but I laughed it off, laughed *him* off as I pressed a hand to his chest and pushed him back to where he was sitting before.

Carter sighed heavily, but then he started petting Zamboni's back legs, his lazy gaze on me. "That was fun."

"Was it?"

"I mean, it was absolute fucking torture, but it was also fun."

I smirked. "My favorite kind of play."

"I have no doubts."

"And what did we learn?"

Carter groaned. "A quiz already?"

I just sipped my wine and arched a brow, waiting.

He sat back farther, still petting his dog as his brows folded in concentration. "I need to be in control. I need to set the pace, give her permission to relax, and show her I want her in every possible way."

"Amen."

"And if all else fails, treat it like a game." He pointed at me. "That really worked for me. When I started thinking about it being overtime and everything riding on me holding it together, I could push through and resist."

I chuckled. "You are such a boy."

"And you are one hell of a woman."

I chewed the inside of my cheek against a smile, tapping my wine glass and nodding toward his water in a silent request to finish it.

When he did, he relaxed more into the couch, smiling at where I was still idly petting behind Zamboni's ear. "I can't believe how fast he took to you."

"Well, the little brat did owe me, since he ruined my shoes at Mia's wedding."

"I've just never seen him obey... well, *anyone*. Me included."

I smiled, running the back of my finger along the smooth bridge of the pup's nose. "We were only allowed to have one dog growing up — and it was my mother's dog. She was a poodle, stubborn and hyper as hell. But my mom trained her to be obedient and made sure my sister and I followed suit. She didn't want anyone undoing her hard work."

"Did you ever want a dog of your own?"

"Oh, all the time. But I was never deemed responsible enough."

Carter frowned a little at that. "What about when you moved out of your parents' house?"

I stilled, swallowing with a mouth that felt full of sand. "I had other things to focus on when that time came."

A heavy silence fell over us. I sipped my wine and stared at where we were both petting Zamboni, and just when I was ready to call it a night, Carter spoke.

"Are you going to go?"

I barked out a laugh. "Wow. Okay, I think the next thing we need to work on is post-sex etiquette."

"No, no," he said hurriedly, sitting up straight. He let out a laugh that mirrored mine before he shook his head again. "Sorry, I should have provided context. I don't want you to *go*, as in leave here. Hell, you can stay all night."

"I won't be staying."

"I make pretty amazing French toast, just saying. I could spoil you in the morning."

"I'm more of an omelet for breakfast girl. And the two mil you're paying me is spoiling me enough."

"Good thing I have eggs. And cheese. And veggies. Also, what exactly *are* you using that money for?"

"None of your business, Rook. And I'm not staying the night."

"Suit yourself," he said on a shrug. "But what I meant by my question was... are you going to go to your sister's wedding?"

All the playfulness slid out of me like grease down a drain, sticky and thick and out of place. I tilted my wine glass toward my lips before deciding I was done with it, the liquid suddenly too acidic now.

"I don't know," I answered honestly.

"Will she be mad if you don't?"

"She'll be heartbroken if I don't go," I said, lifting my eyes to meet his. "But *I'll* be gutted if I do."

Carter's brows tugged together. "I don't understand."

"No one does. No one but me."

I went to stand, but Carter caught me by the elbow, his grip gentle but commanding. He waited until I turned to look at him.

"That sounds lonely."

My nostrils flared. "Yeah, well... I like it that way."

"You said your family cut you off," he said carefully. "What does that mean, Liv? Is that part of why you agreed to this deal?"

"Alright," I said, smacking my hands on my thighs. "Share and tell is over."

"I don't think it ever started."

Carter's words made me pause before my body heard the cue from my brain to attempt to stand again. His eyes flicked between mine for a moment, and then with the balls of a man married to me, he slid his hand up my arm and into my hair, pulling me until I had no choice but to follow.

He tugged me toward him and bent until his forehead hit mine, and he took a deep breath, letting it out like he was exercising more restraint than when we'd been playing earlier.

"You don't have to do it alone... whatever this is," he said, wetting his lips. "I can go through it with you. If you let me."

I closed my eyes, tears stinging behind my lids like foreign predators. I didn't recognize them. They scared the shit out of me and yet I was also highly intrigued by them.

I was highly intrigued by a lot of things that came out of Carter Fabri's mouth.

It was tempting, to lean into his touch, into his promise, to lose myself and let someone else carry the weight with me for a while.

But it was like trying to get a fish to fly.

I just... couldn't.

I patted his chest with a forced smile, pulling back until there was a good foot between us. "I think it's time for me to go."

Carter deflated, but when I stood, he hopped up, too — along with Zamboni, who went from snoring to wide awake and alert, tail wagging like we were about to take him to the park.

"Wait," Carter said, wrapping the blanket around his waist. I arched a brow at the motion before smirking at him. He acted like I hadn't just been on my knees with a perfect view of every inch of what he was covering now.

His cheeks flamed a little, like he was remembering, too.

"I have a request for my next lesson."

"Oh?"

He nodded. "A date."

My brows crested into my hairline.

"Every step of a date," he clarified. "Getting you to agree to one and all the follow through."

I wrinkled my nose, gathering up my clothes and making my way to my purse. "I don't know, Rook. That's less my forte."

"Come on," he said, right on my heels. "You know what works and what doesn't. Just because you don't go on dates doesn't mean you don't understand them."

Ouch.

That hurt.

I didn't mean to pause when he said the words, but I did — hand hovering over the handle of my bag for just a split second before I lifted it and hooked it over my arm. I slipped my boots back on, and Carter stopped his pleading long enough to trail my ensemble with an appreciative gaze.

"This is some look you've got going on right now."

I ignored him. "Sure, whatever. We can practice a date." I held up one finger. "But it's on my terms, and this is the only time we do anything outside of the bedroom."

"Yes, Mommy."

Without warning, Carter swept me into his arms. He wrapped me up tight, his warmth enveloping me as he scooped and lifted until I was up on my toes.

And then he kissed me.

He inhaled at the touch of our lips, his smiling against mine, and I pressed my hands into his chest.

But I didn't push him away.

I kissed him back, a little unbidden moan breaking free when he slid his tongue inside to taste mine. My arms were around his neck before I gave them permission to be, and when I finally found sense to pull back, it was with both of us panting, our foreheads tilting together.

"Did I say you could kiss me?" I tried, but with my heart racing and breath labored like it was, it sounded like a kitten's meow more than the jaguar's growl I was aiming for.

Carter smirked, gently moving my hair from my face and sweeping it over my shoulder. "I was just reading the signs."

I swallowed, a sharp and violent reality slap ringing my ears.

I could feel it happening, my grip on control failing me like wet hands trying to hold fast to a pull-up bar.

Panic flared in my chest. My heart tripled its pace.

But I caught myself just before I teetered over the edge.

"Yeah, well, you read wrong," I said, shoving him back. "No kissing me unless I explicitly give you permission. Understand?"

Carter's expression was laced with concern now. "Liv, I didn't mean—"

"I'll wash your clothes and give them back to you at our next lesson. Goodnight."

I was out the door and shutting it firmly behind me before he could respond.

Chapter 11

Winning Combo

Carter

"So, it sounds like things have been a little tough."

Doctor Arman had a deep, somehow soothing voice — like a grandfather who'd worked years on a farm and had more wisdom than someone my age could grasp. He didn't dress like a grandpa working on a farm, though. No, he was more like a hipster businessman — olive skin, salt-and-pepper beard trimmed close to his jaw, dark-rimmed glasses perched low on his nose. Today he wore a rust-colored sweater layered over a button-up, the sleeves pushed to his forearms to show off an old-school leather watch that probably cost more than my first car. His boots were scuffed but expensive, one hooked over the opposite knee as he relaxed on the brown tweed sofa across from me.

His office matched the vibe: soft lighting, warm tones, exposed brick on one wall and a leafy fig tree in the corner. There were no motivational posters or degrees displayed, no certificates announcing his credibility. Just books. Shelves of them — philosophy, psychology, poetry. There were titles I'd never heard of and some I'd underlined back in my college psych electives and then promptly forgotten.

It felt more like a reading nook in a Brooklyn bookstore than a shrink's office. And maybe that's why I kept showing up.

I nodded, tossing a forest green hacky sack in the air a few times. Doctor Arman had learned from our third session that I opened up more when I had something to fidget with, and ever since then, he'd tossed me this little bean bag ball as soon as I walked in the door.

"It's just a lot of pressure," I said. "It doesn't really make sense but it's like... the better I do, the more insecure I feel. I've been outperforming my past seasons, but I'm second-guessing myself more than ever."

"What does Doctor Marsh say?"

Doctor Marsh was the team's sports psychologist, and I saw her once a month now that I felt like I was in a better place. I used to see her every week.

"She talks to me about the general pressure of being an athlete at the level I'm at, how that sort of second-guessing and pressure is normal to feel. She's working with me on how to live in the discomfort."

"Do you still hear Coach Leduc's voice in your head?"

I caught the hacky sack and held it for a beat. "Always."

"Can you quiet him?"

"Sometimes."

Arman nodded, scribbling in his notepad.

"It hasn't all been bad, though," I added, as if this was some sort of progress report card rather than a therapy session.

I knew I had nothing to prove, and yet I always yearned to come into this room and have nothing to talk about. I longed for the day I'd plop down and say, *"I don't know, Doc! Everything has been great. Not sure what to say!"*

"Like I said, I'm feeling good on the ice. More focused. Less in my head. Like I'm finally starting to play the game instead of overanalyzing every pass before I even make it."

"And off the ice?"

My thoughts immediately raced to Livia.

Not that they weren't always trained on her, but I was actively trying not to think about her during this session because I knew I couldn't talk about her — not with the NDA she'd had me sign.

Then again... maybe I could talk about her *without talking about her*.

I shifted, tapping the hacky sack against the sole of my shoe before I started rolling it in my fingers. "I've been spending time with someone," I said carefully. "A friend. Sort of a... mentor. She's been helping me work through some stuff."

Doc lifted one brow — not in a judgy way, just his usual "go on" expression — and I knew I'd walked right into it.

"She's... experienced," I said, already regretting the phrasing. "She has a lot to teach me, and I have a lot I can learn from her. And I'm trying to. She's working with me, and I think it's helping."

I cringed.

"Shit. I don't mean—she's not, like, a coach. Or a player. Or..." I rubbed the back of my neck. "She just... knows stuff. About people. Pressure. Control."

He didn't say anything. I hated when he didn't say anything, and yet it was very rare that I'd shut my trap long enough that he'd pose a question or offer an observation. He knew *just* the right amount of silence to leave me with that I would start yapping again and bury myself a little deeper.

"She's teaching me things I didn't even know I *needed* to learn," I said, blowing out a breath. "Like how to be present. How to listen. How to show up without trying to perform all the time."

"Have you talked to her about Leduc?"

I hesitated, stilling where I'd been shuffling the hacky sack from hand to hand.

"No."

"No?" Arman scribbled that down. "I find that surprising, if she's a mentor of sorts. Don't you think she should know about that history?"

Everything inside me shut down at the thought, but I fought through the ache and worked through it. That was the whole fucking point of being in this room, after all.

"It's weird. I trust her with stuff I've never told anyone, with *doing things* I've never done before. But also... I don't really trust her at all."

Doc tilted his head slightly. "I don't think I follow."

I leaned forward, elbows on my knees and hacky sack gripped between my hands as I tried to explain. "She's got this... shield. Like titanium-grade. She's composed all the time. Calm. Controlled. She doesn't do messy." I paused. "I don't think she *can* do messy."

I felt my chest tighten as I said it, like I was betraying her just by putting it into words.

"If I told her about Leduc — about the way his voice still echoes in my head every time I fuck up — I think she'd hear me. But I also think she'd laugh at me. I think she'd see it for what it is, for what *I* am." I swallowed, sitting up straight again with my eyes on the floor. "Weak."

Arman didn't flinch at the word or assure me I wasn't weak. He didn't *there, there* me, either. He just gave me one of those patient nods, leaving me space to explore that feeling.

When I didn't say anything else, he cleared his throat. "It kind of sounds like you've written an ending to this story in your head without any of it playing out in reality."

That shut me up.

I stared down at my hands. They looked too big in my lap. I found myself overanalyzing them for the first time in my life, like I'd just realized they were as awkward as the rest of me.

Then, I thought about how those hands had graced Livia's body, how she'd let me touch her, taste her. I looked at my dumb fingers and wondered again why she was wasting her time with me.

Because you're paying her, dumbass.

Still, I wondered if Doc was making a fair assessment. When I'd first asked Livia about what was wrong the night she came to my place, she'd brushed me off. But after our lesson, she'd opened up a bit more. Not too much — but enough for me to see that she had warmth beneath her cool exterior.

There were more layers to her than she presented to the world.

I just didn't think she was eager to let anyone, least of all me, peel them back.

But did that mean she would judge if I showed her my own vulnerability?

I thought about our first lesson, how ashamed I'd been when I'd busted like a fucking teenager without her touching me.

She'd soothed me. She'd assured me I had nothing to be ashamed of.

Why did it still feel fucking terrifying to consider telling her about Coach?

Another thought hit me like a brick after that one: would she feel more comfortable opening up to me if I let her in first?

"You think telling her would help?" I asked Doctor Arman, voice rougher than I meant.

"I think you might be surprised," he said. "Maybe don't decide who she is for her. I don't know much about her, but if she's been a mentor to you like you said, then I think this could unlock a missing piece of the puzzle for her. And in turn, help both of you."

Doctor Arman's words buzzed around in my head like a trapped fly as I left his office. I didn't know why it was easy to admit every sexual shortcoming I had to Liv, but the thought of confessing the origin of my insecurities made me want to run out in traffic.

I pulled my phone from my pocket when I exited the office building and headed toward my Range Rover Sport in the parking lot. The group chat with the guys had a dozen missed texts.

> **Daddy P:** Save the date, benchwarmers. Having a party at our house on February 21.
>
> **Tanny Boy:** ... to celebrate marrying the love of my life. There, I filled in the gaps for you, Daddy P.
>
> **Brittzy:** Lmao I was about to ask if Chef Patel was forcing this on you so she could try out a new grilling recipe. No way would you willingly host a party.
>
> **Daddy P:** It'll be outside. By the pool. Casual attire.
>
> **Tanny Boy:** Please, try to contain your excitement,

Goalie. We need all your energy for the playoff race.

Su Man: Who the fuck added me to this chat?

Daddy P: Like it or not, you're part of the group now, Aleks. Think your wife could make an appearance?

Su Man: She wouldn't miss a chance to dance with Ava.

Su Man: Date saved. I'm leaving this chat.

Brittzy: Aw, come on, Su Man! Don't act like you don't love it. Especially when we rope you into golfing and roast you.

Tanny Boy: Never misses on the ice. Only misses on the green.

Su Man has left the group.

Brittzy: What a pylon.

I chuckled, thumbing out a reply once I was in the Range. I rolled the windows down, thankful for the short reprieve the Florida winter brought us from the extreme heat. It rarely got *cold*, especially by Canadian standards, but it cooled enough to enjoy the outdoors without sweating your balls off, at least.

Me: Sorry, was in therapy. You know I'm there, Daddy P.

Tanny Boy: Did Doc fix your game yet?

Brittzy: You saw him try to make a breakout pass and hit the ref in the ass last week, right?

Tanny Boy: That wasn't a pass, that was a cry for help.

Daddy P: Therapy won't fix weak wrists and bad edgework.

Me: Joke's on you. I've got strong wrists AND unresolved childhood trauma. That's a winning combo, baby.

Brittzy: Maybe you should put "strong wrists" in your dating profile. Never heard anything that could drop panties faster than that.

Me: The panty dropping starts with my impeccable fashion sense. "Casual attire" means vintage college hoodie, socks with holes, and Crocs, right, Daddy P?

Tanny Boy: Is that what you wore to practice this morning?

Brittzy: Nah, that was the hoodie with the mysterious stain on the sleeve. Real versatile piece.

Me: It's not a stain, it's character. I'm cultivating layers, gentlemen.

Daddy P: Cultivate a shot on net.

A few more chirps rang out in the chat before Daddy P threatened to give us all wedgies if we didn't shut up. I wasn't normally scared of a teammate, but Will Perry was the exception to that rule, so I chuckled and tossed my phone onto the passenger seat before throwing the SUV in drive.

But before I let my foot off the brake, I eyed the little device again, Doc's words still playing in my ear.

"Fuck it," I finally said, and I put the car in park again to shoot off one more text.

Me: So… how about that date?

Chapter 12

Horny Little Witch

Livia

"Have you seen those memes that are like *girls be like 'I needed this'* and *it's just a beach vacation*?" Maven shook her head, relaxing back on my couch with her wine in hand. "Well, I be like *'I needed this'* and it's just time with you."

"Wow," I mused with an arched brow. "That was soft, even for you."

"I can't help it. I'm feeling all kinds of mushy lately. I blame work. Seeing these kids be so happy with just a bed to sleep in at night..." Her eyes welled a little at that. "It's amazing, to be able to do things like this, but it's also so sad sometimes, you know?"

"I can imagine," I said, reaching over to squeeze her knee in understanding. "But trust me, I needed this, too. Work has been absolute hell this week."

I scooted closer on the couch once I sank back again, pulling my current project into my lap. The bracelet I'd been designing for Chloe was on pause — something about the balance felt off — so tonight I'd laid out a scattering of metals and tiny gemstones for rings instead.

The little tray of gems sat on the coffee table beside my pliers, jeweler's saw, and a mandrel. Maven wrinkled her nose at the clutter, grinning when I handed her a pair of oversized safety goggles.

"You're joking."

"Nope. You drink wine near flying metal shards, you wear the goggles. Rules are rules."

She laughed, pushing them onto her face, the lenses magnifying her wide eyes as I put my own goggles on before I picked up a strip of gold.

This was the part I loved most — the dreamer's stage. Raw metal, loose gems, a sketchy idea in my mind's eye. All I had to do was imagine what it could be, and then coax it into reality — bend it, solder it, set it, polish it. I loved watching something as plain as a wire transform under my hands into a ring someone might treasure forever.

"So, it's going well, then?" I asked Maven before sliding down to the floor in front of my coffee table full of tools. "The Sweet Dreams Initiative?"

Maven nodded, accidentally hitting her goggles on her wine glass before she laughed and maneuvered them slightly so she could take a sip. "It is. We have a lot of work to do, but... so far, so good."

"I'm glad. You seem so happy," I said. "I like that. I like seeing you happy."

Maven stared at the wine in her glass, swirling it. "I am happy. But... there's something I wanted to talk to you about."

I arched a brow, though my fingers stilled where I'd been idly rolling a loose piece of gold wire between them. "Uh-oh."

She bit her lip, brows pinched together like she was unsure how to say what she needed to." I just... it hurt a little, finding out at the girls' night that you were freezing your eggs."

My heart broke. "Shit, Mave. I'm sorry."

She winced. "No, no, I don't need a big apology or anything. It's not about me. You don't owe me every detail of your life, Liv. I just... hope you know that you can tell me anything. If you want to."

I exhaled slowly, setting the wire back on the tray of gems and metals spread across the coffee table. "It wasn't that I didn't trust you." I plucked up a moonstone with my tweezers, holding it up to the light before setting it down again. "It's more... I wasn't even sure if I was going to do it at all."

Maven leaned back, eyes soft on me as I tucked my legs beneath me. "I didn't even know this was on your radar."

I shrugged. "I've always wanted to be a mother. I just kind of thought that was impossible for a while, given that I rarely have a sub for longer than a couple of months, let alone seriously date anyone."

"This is something that could be changed, you know," Maven challenged.

"Is it crazy that I feel more comfortable considering life as a single mom, doing it all on my own, than I do letting any man near my heart?"

Maven softened. "No. It's not crazy. I know the feeling."

And she did. Maven was there not too long ago when her ex broke her heart and nearly ruined her chance with Vince. Our experiences weren't the same, but I knew she understood better than anyone else.

"I'm sorry I didn't tell you sooner, but there was a lot to figure out. I promise I planned to."

"Now I can be a part of it all."

I smiled, reaching for the mandrel and sliding a half-shaped ring up its tapered length, checking the fit. "It's a long process. Expensive. Not to mention actually raising a kid afterward — childcare, school, the whole mountain." My pliers clicked softly as I tightened the curve. "And you already know I'm drowning in student loans."

"Yeah." Maven snorted, a sharp sound that cut through the quiet. "No thanks to your parents."

My hands stilled, brushing stray filings off the bench pad, the silence between us heavier than the little tools in my lap.

"Well, it doesn't matter because I've come into some money and it'll all be covered."

Maven blinked. "Now you've *come into money*? Woman. Are you in a mob or something? What's with all the secrets?"

I chuckled. "No secrets. I just wasn't sure how it was all going to go and didn't want to tell you before I knew the details. But yeah, I..." I paused, considering the lie. Carter and I had signed an NDA, so even if I *wanted* to tell Maven, I couldn't. "I inherited some cash from a long lost great-great-aunt on my father's side."

"Oh, I bet your parents were seething when they heard about that."

I reached for my own wine glass, taking a sip. "I don't even know if they know. It was all very secretive." I waved her off. "The details don't matter, only that now I have everything I need to get the ball rolling."

Maven hummed, watching me. I knew without her saying that she wasn't sold on my very unconvincing lie, but being the angel that she was, she didn't push me on it.

At least, not tonight.

I had a feeling she wouldn't let me get away with it for long.

"Speaking of your parents," she said, watching as I worked the ring in my hand. "How's it going with the whole wedding debacle?"

I sighed, polishing the band with a cloth, the circular motion slow and deliberate. "I haven't figured out what I'm going to do yet."

My phone lit up beside the gem tray, and it was like we'd summoned the devil. My stomach dropped at the name on the screen.

I froze, torch still in one hand, cloth in the other, eyes stuck on where my mom's full legal name spread out over the glass.

Maven didn't hesitate. She was off the couch in seconds, calling my name with concern. When she saw my phone screen, she cursed, set her wine on the table, and squeezed my knee.

"Answer it," she said softly. "I'll be right here with you."

My body was already revolting at the possibility of me answering, both feverish and plagued with chills at the same time. But Maven's reassuring eyes and her hand squeezing my arm gave me the strength I needed to get it over with.

I tapped the green phone button. "Hello, Mother."

"I hear you've been invited to Lacey's wedding."

I sighed, and Maven squeezed where she held me.

"Yes, she did tell me about it."

"She told *me* she wants you to be a bridesmaid."

"Well, I am her sister. Or have you forgotten that you have two daughters?"

"Don't snip at me when it was you who turned your back on this family."

I gaped at her audacity, running a hand over my open mouth before I clamped it shut and resisted my urge to scream. "Is there something you wanted? I'm actually busy at the moment."

"Too busy for your own mother, for your *sister* whom you never see. Typical. I suppose you'll be too busy to attend the wedding, then?"

I didn't miss that she said that last part with more hope in her voice. That was exactly what she wanted — for me not to show. Of course, she wouldn't tell my sister that. She would want me to be the one to take the blame. She wouldn't dare give anyone a reason to say a bad word about her.

I knew that better than I knew my own face in the mirror.

"I don't know what my plans are yet," I said without fanfare. "I told Lacey I would let her know."

"Well, it would be great if you could *let her know* sooner rather than later. Weddings take a lot of planning, not that you would know."

Maven growled at that, and I saw her open her mouth like she was about to let my mother have it. I shook my head once in warning, giving her the eyes to let her know I could handle it.

"While this first phone call in years has been such a delight," I said, voice level and void of emotion. "I really am busy. I will be in touch — with Lacey — and you can go back to pretending like I don't exist."

"If only it were that easy."

The click of the phone was swift, and then the screen went back to my normal background in an instant.

I rolled my eyes, but Maven was irate. She hopped up and started pacing the room with little grunts and growls escaping those beautiful lips of hers as I got right back to the task at hand.

"The nerve of that woman! How horrid can she be? She is your *mother*. She—I—I don't—" My best friend shook her head before dropping to her knees next to me, gathering me up in her arms and squeezing me tightly. "Liv, that was awful. I... I'm so fucking sorry."

"It's fine," I said numbly. "I'm used to it. Although, I do admit it's easier when she just leaves me alone."

"It's not fine. Nothing about any of that was fine."

"It's just how it is."

Maven hugged me for a long time, and I felt the sadness, the pity, radiating off her. I almost wished I felt as sad as she assumed I was. The truth lay more in the fact that I was just numb to it all now.

I'd taken back my power when I left that town. It took me a while, but I found my voice, my path, and my way to own control again.

I wouldn't relinquish it ever again — least of all to the woman who birthed me but only wanted a shiny little doll who did exactly as she said, not a daughter.

Maven sat back on her heels, her hands still framing my arms. "And Lacey still doesn't know, does she?"

I shrugged. "I haven't explicitly told her, no, but..."

Maven crumpled, then shook her head like she was determined to turn the night around. "What are you doing Sunday? Come to our house. Vince's parents will be in town and mine are coming over for dinner. We'd love to have you join."

I smiled at the sweetness, even if the gesture tasted a bit sour on my tongue. I loved Maven and I loved that her parents had always treated me like their own.

But that didn't make up for the fact that mine had abandoned me in my deepest time of need.

"I'd love to," I said, squeezing her knee. "But actually... I have a date."

I thought Maven was going to fall out on the floor. "A... date?"

I nodded, rolling my lips together. "Mm-hmm. And no, I'm not telling you about him."

"What?! Why not? Have I been removed from best friend status without my acknowledgment? First the eggs, now this?"

I chuckled, turning back to my rings. "Relax. It's just a first date, and you know me, it probably won't lead anywhere other than back to my bedroom for a night of fun."

"Who is he? How did you meet? Do I know him?"

"Tell you what. If he makes it to a second date, I'll tell you about him," I said carefully, stating that I'd tell her about him, but wouldn't exactly tell her *who* he was.

Maven huffed, picking her wine glass up so forcefully it nearly sloshed onto my rug. "Fine. But I want some kind of details even if he doesn't make it to date two."

I shot her the Cheshire Cat grin. "You sure about that?"

"You horny little witch."

"Guilty as charged."

Fortunately, the conversation shifted after that, away from my parents, my sister, and my nameless date. But while I worked on rings and Maven filled me in on how she and Vince were doing, my mind couldn't help but race.

But it wasn't my family drama I was consumed with.

It was the fact that I was going on a date with Carter Fabri...

And what the hell it meant that I was excited to see him again.

Chapter 13

Flying Colors

Livia

"...and that's why I can't ever show my face at a Chili's again."

I blinked at Carter over the rim of my cocktail glass, lips twitching. "Please tell me you're joking."

"Oh, but I only wish I was," he said. "Listen, I thought it was the smoothest line in the book at the time."

"To tell the waitress she had *jalapeño eyes*?! Carter, what does that even mean? Like her eyes were... spicy?"

"And green!"

"Oh, my God."

"It gets worse."

"Can it possibly?"

"As she stared at me with the very same blank stare you have right now, I followed up her silence with, 'So, this Triple Dipper, can I get it with the egg rolls, sliders, and your phone number?'"

"Carter..." I pinched the bridge of my nose and shook my head, shoulders bouncing as I tried to fight the laughter that was impossible to contain.

"Admit it... that's kind of slick."

"Like an oily car salesman."

Carter grinned, boyish and unguarded, the firelight dancing in the gold flecks of his eyes. Although our evening had started with him quite tense, he was relaxed now — loose in his seat, fingers curled casually around his whiskey glass, one ankle hooked over his knee like this was just another night out with the guys.

But it was a test, and another lesson — one I was finding myself enjoying more than I anticipated.

In the week since I'd last seen him, I'd been so busy with work I'd barely had time to think about anything else. We'd had two Osprey players in our chairs, a new set of veneers rush-ordered for a local newscaster whose wedding photoshoot got moved up, and one of my regulars decided mid-cleaning that she wanted to "just try" a full Invisalign consult — during my lunch hour. On top of that, my associate called out sick three days in a row, leaving me to juggle our packed schedule solo. I'd been running on caffeine and that post-orgasm high Carter had left me with.

But that hadn't been the only thing I'd taken home that night.

He'd also gotten under my skin with his whole comment about not taking on the world alone. Whenever I wasn't focused on work, it was hard not to let my thoughts drift to the sincerity in his eyes, to the careful caress of his hand against my jaw.

And when those thoughts did pop up, I smacked them down like a basketball I was guarding the net from.

Two-million dollars.
Eggs frozen.
Set up for life.

I control when I have a kid and how.
I control every lesson between me and Carter.
This is a means to an end.

By the time Carter picked me up for our date lesson, I had myself back in check.

We were each two drinks in now, tucked in the corner of a rooftop bar that overlooked the Hillsborough River, the Tampa skyline glittering like scattered sequins in front of us. String lights arched overhead. A firepit flickered at our feet, our chairs side by side and angled toward one another. Music thrummed softly from the indoor lounge, muffled by glass doors and cool January air.

It was cozy and intimate and the perfect setting for a date.

It was also supremely uncomfortable for me.

Carter didn't pick up on that — at least, not that I could tell. On the outside, I was the dominant instructor as usual. And yes, I *did* feel like I was back in control.

But I also felt like I was dancing around a room of eggshells.

I'd agreed to his request for this date lesson mostly out of my need to vacate his house after our last one. But I'd also been curious. He'd said he needed my help, and that was part of our agreement.

I just wasn't as confident when it came to this part of intimacy.

I typically skipped dates, which was why my best friend had been so shocked when I mentioned I was going on one. Why waste time pretending like I cared about what my future sub did for work, or making up some lie about my own background, knowing I'd never feel safe enough to share the truth, when all we both *really* wanted was to get naked?

But Carter was different. He wasn't like me. He was... *good*. Pure. Eager to please.

He'd make a great boyfriend to someone someday. A great husband.

And that was part of why I didn't love toying with the whole dating thing in our lessons. There were too many opportunities for pesky feelings to creep up — especially for him. And I didn't want to hurt him.

That was the whole reason I'd set up so many rules.

Still, so far, I'd called the shots all night. We'd started inside, where I'd perched on a barstool with my legs crossed and a smirk in place, watching him psych himself up from across the room like he was about to approach a total stranger. That was the exercise: act like we'd never met.

He flubbed the approach twice — once leading with a compliment that landed too sexual, once with a joke that didn't land at all. I coached him through both, reminding him not to come in too hot, not to make it about him. Ask questions. Be curious. Eye contact, but not too much. And for the love of God, don't open with *"So, do you come here often?"*

Eventually, he got me to laugh. That's when I let him sit beside me. We ordered drinks and kept the game going. I pretended to agree to letting him take me on a date, and then we met outside the bar and acted like it was date night some days later.

He was in stride once that next phase kicked in. He'd guided me to our table with a hand at my lower back. He'd ordered our second round without looking at the menu, remembering that I'd ordered a dirty martini with extra bleu cheese olives, and sticking with a classic Old Fashioned for himself. And he'd initiated conversation with ease, skipping over the shallow *so, what do you do?* bits and launching right into people watching that transitioned smoothly into us trading stories.

He was doing well. Really well.

And that was the problem.

Because somewhere between lesson and leisure, the lines started to blur. And I didn't like how that made me feel.

It wasn't that I didn't enjoy his company. I did.

That was the issue.

It made me feel out of control, like the structure I'd crafted was flimsy. The safety of the roles we'd defined from the start were written in black and underlined in red. Teacher and student. Dom and sub. Boss and rookie.

But this? Cuddling next to him, legs brushing, hearing him talk about college and his guinea pig and the time he pissed himself in a bounce house as a kid?

This felt real. This felt... soft.

And intimacy — *real* intimacy — had never been something I trusted. Not since I learned how quickly it could turn into a weapon.

The waitress bringing us a fresh round of drinks had me blinking out of my thoughts. Carter looked her right in the eyes as he thanked her, and of course he made some endearing joke that had her laughing and flushing and me thinking *you idiot, can't you see that you don't need me?*

Then his attention was back on me, his grin wide, eyes glassy. "If you think that was a disaster, you should hear about my time at Hooters."

"Oh, God, please, no."

He laughed, sipping his whiskey with his eyes dancing as they watched me. His demeanor shifted — just marginally, enough for me to notice him rubbing his hands down his slacks and scratching at the hair on his jaw.

Stand *your* Ground

"There is another story I want to tell you, actually. For real. Not a joke."

I finished off the last of the martini I'd had in hand, picking up my water next. "That sounds ominous."

He let out a soft breath, sitting forward slightly, his elbows resting on his knees. His gaze was on the firepit now and my stomach tightened at the shift in mood.

"I want to tell you why I am the way I am. Why I need your help the way I do." He paused, rolling his lips between his teeth before glancing at me. "I'm sure you've thought about it surface level. Like I'm just some guy who doesn't know how to flirt or fuck or talk to a woman without making her cringe." He smirked, but it didn't reach his eyes. "But it's more than that."

I tilted my head, softening. "Okay."

"I just... I need to get it all out, and I—can you just listen? And try not to judge?"

That made my brows furrow. "Why would I judge you?"

He gave a tiny shrug, looking at his hands before he found my gaze again. "Because what I'm about to tell you is going to tell you a lot about me, and it's not flattering."

My heart squeezed at the sight of him, his head hung like an abused animal expecting to be hit again. "I'm listening."

He was quiet for a beat before he started, voice lower than before.

"I grew up in Ontario. Middle-class, pretty standard childhood. Parents were sweet — strict, but loving. I started skating when I was three, playing hockey when I was four, and it became everything to me. I begged my parents to watch every Maple Leafs game, practiced year-round, and it just... it made me so fucking happy, Liv. My dad always says he never saw my real smile until I had a stick in my hand. As a kid, I played for hours in the street, on frozen ponds, in the kitchen when my mom wasn't looking. I'd pretend I was in the NHL, game on the line, last-second shot..."

A soft smile touched his lips, then faded.

"And then, when I was fifteen, I made it to the OHL. It was a big deal. That's where I met Coach Leduc."

He said the name like it was venom in his mouth.

"That man was the opposite of any adult I'd ever come into contact with. While my parents were docile and quiet, he was barking at me within minutes of meeting him. He towered over all of us — nearly seven-feet tall, absolute giant. He didn't smile when he met me. I discovered real quick that he never smiled at all.

"At first, it was fine. Tough love, sure, but I could handle that. But then the yelling started. The threats. The mind games. 'If you don't want it bad enough, there's ten other kids gearing for your spot on the team who do.' 'You think you're talented? You're soft. You'll never make it.' Every mistake was personal. Every missed pass, every bad shift — it was never just a mistake. It was proof I didn't belong."

My chest pulled tight. Carter was still staring into the fire, but I could see the tension in his jaw, the way his fingers twisted in his lap. I'd never seen him like that.

"It got worse the older we got," he continued. "Leduc loved to pick favorites. He'd pit us against each other. If you weren't his golden boy, you were nothing. He made me *feel* like nothing."

My stomach twisted.

I knew that feeling.

"And things just started changing. Where hockey was my happy place before, my safe place... it became like this weird, toxic relationship. I still loved the game, but I hated how I felt playing under Leduc. I stopped smiling at games, stopped celebrating wins. I'd go home and snap at my mom, lock myself in my room, skip dinner. I'd run drills tirelessly, sometimes until I injured myself, and then I'd punch myself in the face repeatedly and chant how weak I was. I became this... this fucking monster. This version of myself I didn't even recognize. And I stayed in it. For years. Because I thought that's what it took to be great."

His voice cracked on that word, and he looked away, blinking hard.

Oh, God.

If this man cries, I'm going to fucking lose it.

"And you know what? I did make it. I got drafted. I got the dream. But I didn't get it without those years of abuse still sticking to me like mud. That was why I bounced back and forth between the AHL and NHL for so long." He shook his head. "When I got drafted, Leduc looked me right in the eyes and scoffed with a nasty curl of his lip. He said they'd made a mistake and I'd be out before they could print my name on a jersey. He said I'd fail." Carter paled. "And I believed him."

I closed my eyes on a long exhale. "Carter..."

"Please, just... let me finish." He squeezed his eyes shut for a long moment before speaking again. "I knew — deep down — I was never playing free again. Every time I lace up my skates, he's still there. He's this loud and ever-present voice in my head telling me I'm not good enough. That I'm soft. Weak. A loser."

He drew in another long breath.

"And it didn't just stop on the ice. I learned early on that silence was safer. That keeping my head down, not taking up space, not making mistakes — that's how I stayed out of the line of fire. It bled into everything. Friendships. Dating. Sex."

He rubbed the back of his neck.

"I had *one* sexual experience before you. With Zina. And I was a fucking kid, Liv. I had no idea what I was doing. And I know I told you the story and joked about it and that's what I do. I joke about it with everyone. I joke about every fucking thing." He gritted his teeth, then shook it off like he was getting off topic. "But I choked that night. I didn't know what to do. What I left out of that story was that I didn't last long, and Zina laughed at me. All the guys there did, too, and it became this running joke. *'Don't put Fabri out in the third. We all know he can't last.'"*

I shook my head.

Hockey players could be real fucking asshole sometimes.

"I have this vivid memory of Zina saying I had no idea what I was doing. But it was *his* voice I heard when she said it." There was that soft not-smile on his lips again. "And yeah, after that, I just... I gave up. I throw out corny lines and jokes because I know no one will take me seriously, women included. I make fun of myself before anyone else has the chance. And that's easier, isn't it?"

Carter lifted his gaze, and when it crashed into mine, it was like we were the only two people in the world.

"To laugh first is easier than waiting to be humiliated. To pretend I don't care is easier than letting it matter. Because if it matters — if I actually try, actually want something — and I still fail?" He shook his head. "Then it means they were right about me all along."

My chest ached as I watched him, as I did my best to hold space for what he was trusting me to hold for him. Subtly, somewhere in the back of my mind, there was a voice whispering that I should shut this down, that I should tell him I don't need to know anything else.

But I threw a pillow over that voice and muffled it completely because I wanted to know. I felt honored that he was telling me.

And I felt a burning desire to help him more than ever.

That was something not many understood about The Lifestyle; how consensual, kinky sex could be freeing and could heal wounds so deep no amount of therapy can touch them. It's not just about getting off — it could be about facing fears and overcoming insecurities, or reclaiming power and control, or *releasing* control and learning to relax.

His final words hung there, fragile in the air between us.

When I didn't respond right away, he dropped his gaze to the fire again.

"You're not going to say anything?"

I swallowed. "I'm thinking."

His lips twitched, almost a smile. "Dangerous."

"Only when it's about contracts or cock rings," I teased gently, then let the moment settle. "Thank you. For telling me."

He gave a half nod, but I could see the tension still lived in his shoulders.

"You know," I added, reaching for my third martini, "there's a big difference between being bad at something and never being given the chance to be good at it."

He blinked, looking at me like he was trying to decide if he believed me.

"You're not broken, Carter. You're just untrained."

He smirked. "That supposed to be sexy?"

"It's supposed to be honest." I ate my olive, tapping the skewer against my lip a moment. "And while we're on that honesty kick, yes... it is sexy. I find it incredibly hot, actually."

"Okay," he said, sitting up with flat lips. "You don't have to patronize me now."

"I'm not. Your corny lines make me laugh, which is a rarity. I like corny. And I like teaching you. I like the thought of molding you to be my own little pleasure provider. I like how eager you are and how well you listen. And I can tell you that just by the first two times we've been together, that coach doesn't know shit about you. You're more than capable, Rook. And you're passing this class with flying colors already."

"Is this praise kink foreplay? Because it's working."

I smiled. "Do you have plans on Friday?"

"We travel home from the Winnipeg game that morning, but I should be free that night. Why?"

"Because I think it's time for your next lesson. And you better catch a nap on that plane ride home..." I tilted my martini to my lips with a wicked grin. "We're turning up the heat."

Chapter 14
Mistress Livia
Carter

Friday came faster than I imagined, my week jam packed with travel and games. We were still locked into the playoff race, fighting for our spot and for our lives, and every second counted. We took a loss at home against Columbus but managed to secure a win in Winnipeg. Back and forth, we teetered on the edge of clenching or having our season end before we were ready.

I had to be locked in, and I was.

I was quicker in the face-off circle, reading plays faster, keeping my head on a swivel. My minutes were up, my line was clicking, and I was finally playing like I belonged — not just as a role filler, but as a fucking problem for the other team. My teammates were trusting me more. Coach, too. Vince even tossed me a chirp after one game about how I'd been "possessed" on the forecheck. I took it as the highest form of praise.

But off the ice, I was still working through what I'd told Livia on our practice date.

Bringing up all the history with Coach Leduc had nearly made me throw up. It was like dragging a corpse out of a locked trunk in the back of my mind, one I'd shoved in there years ago and told myself I was fine leaving buried. Except the fucker still smelled and there was no ignoring him, no matter how I tried.

Doctor Arman was right. I shouldn't have assumed I'd know what Livia's reaction would be, which wasn't much at all. She'd just... listened. She'd heard me out and she hadn't tried to comfort me or tell me I had to let it all go.

"You're not broken, Carter. You're just untrained."

Those words had hit me harder than I braced for.

Because for once, I felt like someone understood.

And something about that — about being seen, being heard — quieted the noise. Coach Leduc's voice, usually so loud in my mind, barking critiques and shaking his head with that look that made me feel like I'd never be enough... it faded. It wasn't gone completely, but it was like someone had turned down the dial.

I had no idea how long that would last.

But it felt like the first breath after being underwater for years.

And now, with that breath still fresh in my lungs, I was pulling up to a mansion on Bayshore Boulevard — my pulse thudding and Livia smirking beside me — about to step into a place that made me feel as inexperienced and incompetent as ever.

"Don't look so scared," Livia purred from the passenger seat of my Range Rover. I had to admit, I loved seeing her there. I loved how her legs were crossed, how the coat she wore exposed the top of her knee and begged me to slide my hand over her smooth skin. I thought about it more than once on our drive over, but held back, remembering how she'd reacted when I'd kissed her without asking.

This was her game, her show, her rules. My job was to behave myself — even when it felt impossible to do.

"Can you blame me?" I asked, pausing at the large iron gate. "I had to sign an NDA and get a full background check for you to bring me here, and I have no idea what waits for me inside."

"Fun," she said easily. "That's what waits for you."

"I think we've established that our definitions of things like that differ a bit."

Livia smirked as the gate slid open with a slow, mechanical hum, revealing a driveway that looked like it had been ripped from the pages of *Architectural Digest* — all clean lines and softly glowing lanterns nestled among perfectly manicured hedges. The mansion at the end of it was massive but not gaudy. It sprawled out confidently along the bay, all sleek stone and glass, its silhouette lit with the soft, golden warmth of well-placed lighting.

I whistled low under my breath. "Damn."

The valet opened Livia's door the second we stopped at the front portico. She stepped out in tall, chocolate brown stilettos with red bottoms, that long brown coat cinched at her waist and hiding whatever wicked thing she was wearing underneath. I followed, adjusting the jacket of my own dark, low-profile suit — she'd told me to wear black and nothing else. I hadn't dared argue.

The front doors were wide open, spilling warm light and low music out into the night. A man stood just inside, tall and built like he doubled as a bouncer on the side. His black suit was crisp, his expression unreadable. Though we could hear the party inside, we couldn't see it. A tall black curtain hung from the ceiling all the way to the floor, puddling on the marble behind where the bouncer stood.

He held out a velvet-lined box without a word.

Livia unfastened just enough of her coat to reach her phone, revealing a sliver of sheer, dark brown fabric beneath before she slipped her phone into the box. I followed her lead, depositing my own phone, smart watch, and keys. The man gave a small nod, then gestured to a second, shorter man behind him with latex gloves and a scanning wand.

"Really?" I asked under my breath as the wand passed over my chest and down the inside of my thigh. "We getting frisked?"

"I told you," Livia said, amusement curling in her voice. "No cameras. No surprises. Everyone here knows the rules."

I arched a brow as the wand beeped at the button on my waistband.

"Yeah, yeah, NDA and all. Where exactly have you brought me, Mistress?"

A fire I'd never seen before flashed in Livia's eyes with that title, and she rewarded me by sliding a hand up the back of my neck, her fingers curling possessively. Her mouth was close to my ear when she whispered, "Welcome to The Manor."

Then she led me behind the curtain.

Instantly, the noise that had been a muffle from outside enveloped me. The music was low and rhythmic, something jazzy and seductive. Conversations murmured all around us, laughter blending with the clink of glasses and... moans?

Yeah. That was definitely moaning I was hearing.

The ceiling soared above us, modern chandeliers dripping crystals that refracted light into rainbows across the white marble floor. The windows were floor-to-ceiling, offering a glimmering view of the water beyond. Every inch of the place gleamed — silver trays, mirrored accents, glass sculpture installations — and yet, it still managed to feel intimate. Dark.

Sexy.

But as I scanned the room, I realized that though the house was impressive, it was the people inside it who demanded the most attention.

From one end of the massive room to the other, there were little groups of people gathered and stragglers wandering around taking it all in just as I was. There were couples, throuples, small groups, and larger ones lounging in an oversized corner sofa.

And they weren't wearing a suit the way I was.

Instead, they wore silk robes, corsets, collars. They wore lace and leather and nothing but high heels. Some wore masks. Others wore nothing at all. Most outfits looked like they'd cost more than my first car, and yet not a single one of them felt like a costume. They were all luxurious, made with the finest fabric and leather.

My heart kicked like a bass drum in my chest.

Livia trailed her fingers down my arm and along the inside of my wrist before she wrapped her grip around me like a leash, subtle but firm. "Take a breath," she said, her eyes watching me as I continued watching the room. "You're safe here."

She released me then, hands unfastening the large buttons of her coat. When she shrugged it off her shoulders and handed it to a woman waiting in the wings, all my attention snapped to her.

And if my heart was struggling before, it was ready to give out completely now.

Livia was wrapped in lace the color of luxury — rich, deep brown, just a shade darker than her skin, so close it blended and disappeared and teased. It was the kind of lingerie that didn't scream for attention but demanded it anyway, subtle and masterful, like art hung in a museum too expensive to ever step foot in.

The bodysuit hugged every curve, delicate straps crossing over her chest in a way that framed her breasts without caging them, the lace dipping into a plunging V that ended just above her belly button. Her thighs were bare save for a sliver of matching garters, each one clasped to sheer, silky stockings that shimmered slightly in the low light. And those heels I'd had a sneak peek of all night were the same warm tone, a perfect match, with glossy red bottoms that caught the light every time she shifted her weight.

She was the sexiest person in the room.

And tonight, she was mine.

Even if it was just a lesson. Even if it was just a game. She was with me tonight, and I wanted every fucker in this place to know it.

"Goddamn, Liv," I croaked, reaching out to stroke along the smooth, exposed skin at her hip with my knuckles. I teased the top of her garter, sliding my finger beneath the fabric and tracing along her thigh before I pulled back and let it snap against her skin. "You are always sexy, but seeing you like this... *fuck*, it makes me want to drop to my knees."

"Oh, don't worry," she said, gripping me by the lapels as she leaned in to whisper. "You will be."

I swallowed, looking around the room. "I'm a little nervous."

"That's perfectly normal. But I'm here with you, and this is a safe place for you to learn. I will take care of you. Understand?"

I nodded.

"Good. Now, before we go further, I need a few verbal agreements from you. First, do you agree to be more of a submissive tonight, to stay in your role as student, but also allow me to dive deeper into what I believe will bring you pleasure?"

"I think so."

"I need more than that."

"Well... what exactly are you referring to?"

She shrugged. "You not knowing is half the fun. I may praise you. I may degrade you. I may present you with toys you've never seen or heard of. The key here is trust. So... do you trust me?"

I swallowed thickly. "Yes. I trust you."

Her lips curled. "Excellent. Now, remind me what our safe words are?"

"High stick," I said with a laugh. "Which I already have, thanks to you dressed in this." I plucked at the lace over her stomach.

Livia rewarded me with a buttery laugh, and then she hooked her arm through mine and led me farther into the house.

For a while, we just circled the room, Livia whispering into my ear about each person or group we passed. She squeezed my arm when I witnessed a man pull another man's cock out and start rubbing him, and she chuckled with amusement when I full-on stopped to watch one of the women who'd been divvying out champagne glasses drop to her knees and start sucking a guest's cock.

As suspected, I was hard and curious and a little uncomfortable by the time we'd made a full pass around the room, and that's when we were approached by a couple who appeared to be in their mid- to late-fifties.

They were impossible to miss or overlook, both of them elegant and sexy and undeniably in charge.

"Look alive, Rook," Livia said low in my ear, squeezing my arm where she held it. "You're about to meet our hosts and the masterminds behind The Manor."

The couple smiled at us before chatting in hushed voices to one another, but they were still on track for us.

"Who are they?" I asked Livia, feeling a bit foolish that I hadn't thought to ask until this moment.

"Marcello and Evelyn Rovelli. He's a real estate tycoon and owns half the west coast of Florida. She's a retired ballerina and a philanthropist."

"She's wearing a dog collar."

Livia chuckled before straightening and offering a small wave to our approaching hosts.

Marcello Rovelli moved like a man who'd never once rushed in his life. He was tall and broad-shouldered, with perfectly groomed silver hair and espresso-toned skin. He wore tailored black slacks and a crisp, open-collar dress shirt with the sleeves rolled, his chest exposed, wrists dripping with gold. His hand held a thin, polished chain leash.

The leash was attached to the collar of his wife — who was stunning.

Evelyn's skin was deep bronze, her hair a cascade of black coils pinned up in a loose chignon that exposed the long, graceful line of her neck. Her makeup was dramatic — dark eyes, sharp cheekbones, deep plum lips — and her dress, if you could call it that, was sheer mesh embroidered with gold thread in ornate patterns that just barely shielded the curve of her breasts and the apex of her thighs. Beneath it, I saw nothing but a high-waisted thong and the glint of jewelry.

And at her throat, that thick leather collar that I couldn't take my eyes off.

"*Tesoro*," Evelyn purred, letting go of her husband's arms just long enough to sweep Livia into a hug once they reached us. I didn't miss how she seemed to know *just* how far she could stretch away from her husband without the leash catching. "You look edible, darling."

"Are you telling me I'm good enough to eat, Ev?"

"Always."

She winked as Marcello stepped in and took Liv's hand in his, planting a soft kiss to the back of it. "What a pleasure to have you with us tonight, Mistress Livia. It's been too long."

"I agree. But I've had a... *project* occupying my time." Livia slid her arm back through mine with those words, and our hosts swung their gaze to me.

Marcello's eyes swept over me from head to toe, not unkindly, but like a man assessing the quality of a rare bottle of scotch. He nodded once, satisfied. "Carter Fabri. We're honored."

His voice was drenched in power, just like everything else about him.

"Welcome to our home," Evelyn added, her gaze twinkling with mischief. "We've heard lovely things about you."

That alone made my stomach clench. I shifted on my feet, but Marcello lifted a hand, his tone softening just enough to reassure.

"She only means from Livia when she delighted us with her request to bring you as her guest. And let me ease your mind. You have our full discretion," he said. "No one here will utter a word about hockey, and no one outside these walls will know you were ever here."

"You're safe," Evelyn echoed, brushing her fingers over the chain that connected her to her husband once more. "Free to explore. To observe. To indulge. And if at any point, you'd prefer to disappear into one of the private rooms, Livia knows the way."

Their words settled over me like warm water, and somehow, I felt both more exposed and more at ease than I had all night.

Livia squeezed my hand. "We'll take it slow."

Marcello nodded. "That's always the best way to begin."

With a final wave, the couple left us, and then Livia turned to face me fully and slid her hands up over my chest before hooking them behind my neck.

"Alright, Rook. Keep those safe words handy." She grabbed my hands and started walking backward then, a wicked gleam in her eyes. "Time to play."

Chapter 15

watch and be watched

Livia

Carter was tense as I pulled him through the main play area and down the dark hall to one of the voyeur rooms.

I could feel it in the way his shoulders squared, the way his hand twitched at his side like he wasn't sure whether to reach for me or fold into himself. His eyes were hungry, gaze devouring everything before him, but his jaw was tight, breath shallow.

Once we were tucked behind the invisible side of the one-way mirror, I leaned in, brushing my lips near his ear, hoping my voice would anchor him.

"I brought you here to watch tonight," I murmured. "To learn. To feel."

His eyes flicked to mine, those golden flecks swimming in the dark brown as his pupils dilated.

"I want you to see what it looks like when people let go. When they play. When they ask for what they want without fear they'll be punished, or laughed at, or told they're wrong for wanting it."

I reached for his hand, threading our fingers together, grounding him in my touch. I wasn't usually one for a touch so intimate, but in this moment, I was not just his teacher — but his Domme in a way. I needed to make him feel safe before I brought him fully into the scene.

"You told me about Coach Leduc, about how you were made to feel like every mistake was the end of the world. You said every misstep was proof you weren't good enough."

His jaw twitched, but I held a long nail against his chin, not letting him look away from me.

"I want you to know that doesn't exist here," I whispered. "Here, you're safe to stumble. To be awkward. To not know the answer. To ask questions. To get hard at the wrong time. To say you're scared. To try something and change your mind."

I squeezed his hand.

"Here, you get to feel what it's like to fail without consequence."

He exhaled like he'd been holding his breath since we walked through the door.

I let silence stretch between us for a beat, then added, "And maybe if you're a good boy..." I pressed up on my toes, lips brushing his cheek as I smiled. "You'll get to play, too."

Carter angled his head toward my lips, and for a moment, I lost myself in how he stared at me, how his eyes were filled with an unspeakable gratitude.

I leaned in more, eyes flickering to where his lips were parted slightly.

And then I swallowed and pulled away, trailing my finger along his shoulder as I walked around to stand behind him.

"Let's watch, shall we?"

Inside the room we were secretly gazing into, a couple had just burst through the door, both giggling and clinging to each other as the man kissed the woman and backed her into the closest wall. They knew we were there, of course — or at least, they knew there was the possibility of someone watching. That's what the voyeur rooms were for.

Some liked to watch.

Some liked to *be* watched.

For a while, Carter seemed somewhat unfazed as we gazed in at the couple. The man was dressed in a suit while the woman wore a short dress with an apron over it. As he started to undress her, they played out their scene.

"We have to hurry, my husband will be home any minute," she panted against the man's lips as he tore open the buttons on her dress.

"I can't believe we're doing this. He's my best friend."

"He'll never know. And I've always wanted you. Haven't you wanted me?"

"Always. He doesn't deserve you. I'll fuck you better than he ever has."

The woman moaned, each word punctuating another article of clothing gone. But as if they were too desperate to wait, the man hiked the woman up against the wall with her dress still on, the fabric split open to expose her breasts. His pants were at his ankles, boxers caught at his knees as he pinned her to the wall and reached for his cock.

I knew the exact moment he thrust inside her because he groaned, and she gasped, and they stilled for a long moment before he started fucking her hard.

I slid my hand down Carter's chest and over his dress slacks, gripping his erection through the fabric.

He sighed, his head falling back as he flexed into my touch. The sound of the other couple fucking filled the small, dark room we were in, and when Carter lifted his eyes to watch them again, I felt his cock pulse in my hand.

The couple inside the viewing room was quick. The man came first, and then he dropped to his knees and ate the woman out until she came, too. They finished their scene with giggles and kisses before they redressed and exited.

Moments later, the room was occupied again — this time by a woman and two men.

"You want to be inside me?" I asked Carter, nipping at his earlobe from behind as I squeezed his cock. Inside the room, the woman was pretending to be scared, like she was cornered by the two men who were hungrily moving in on her. "Then you need to learn what it means to be open. To surrender."

Carter's breath was more labored now, his heart pounding loud enough I could hear it where I stood behind him.

"Ask questions. Observe. Learn. Use them as an experiment and me as your professor."

I began to unfasten his belt as the scene played out in front of us. The woman turned like she was going to run and escape, but before she could, one man snatched her by the waist and lifted her. The other grabbed her kicking feet and restrained her, and then they tossed her onto the bed.

Carter stilled. "Is she okay?"

"She is perfectly safe and okay. This is all consensual. Everyone here is vetted, and everyone has their safe words in order."

He relaxed a bit with that, and I continued to work his pants open enough that I could reach him.

"That's a friend of mine. Her name is Cami. She likes consensual non-consent play, or CNC. It's a safe way for her to play out a fantasy, and it's completely normal."

Carter nodded, and when the men inside the room started to roughly undress Cami and force her to touch and taste them, I pulled Carter's cock from his pants.

I stroked him lightly at first, using the precum gathered at the tip to lube him and play. When I tightened my grip a little, he flexed into the touch.

"Do you have a fantasy, Carter?"

"Fucking you in this room."

I chuckled in his ear. "What if I told you I plan to let you fuck me tonight?"

His cock jumped in my hands. "Liv..."

"But first, I want you to surrender. Tell me your fantasies, Carter."

His eyes creaked open again, locking on the people inside the room. One of the men was sliding his cock between Cami's feet while the other watched her give him head.

"I... I don't know," Carter panted.

"Sure, you do. What do you search when you watch porn?"

He wet his lips when I started stroking him in a smoother rhythm, his breath short. "Uh..."

"You don't have to be embarrassed. Name one thing."

"Deep throat."

I smirked against his shoulder. "Mmm... does it turn you on to think about fucking my throat, Rook?"

"Fuck yes."

"You want me to gag a little, to choke on it?"

I asked the words as I licked along his neck and pumped him faster, and Carter groaned, his hips moving to fuck my hand. "Liv..."

"Watch how they do it," I said softly, still stroking him. Any time I thought he might be close to coming, I slowed down to a torturous pace. "Do you like how he grabs her hair like that, how she relinquishes control to him? She likes it, too. She feels safe to let go. She doesn't have to think. He's leading."

Carter hummed and watched, his jaw tight.

"What else?"

He panted, licking his lips like he wasn't sure he could say. "Sex slave."

That made me pause.

"You... want one, or?"

"I want to be one."

Fuck.

I didn't expect that answer, and I *definitely* didn't expect the way I would react to hearing it. My nipples hardened beneath my lingerie, thighs clenching at the thought of Carter bound and gagged and at my service.

"I don't know. I just feel like it'd be really fucking hot to be completely at someone's mercy, but in a safe way, like I do any and everything they tell me to for a weekend, but obviously if I really want out, I can get out."

Inside the room, the men were fucking Cami now. She was seated in the lap of one while the other leaned over them and lined up to fuck her anally. Carter's eyes widened when the man slid inside, when Cami cried out and pretended like she wanted them to stop. She didn't utter a safe word, but rather played into the scene beautifully.

I started slowly stroking Carter again. "Is that why you like when I tell you what to do?" I murmured in his ear. "You like when I give you direction."

"Yes."

"You like when I use you to make me come."

"*God*, yes."

"Filthy fucking boy," I hissed, squeezing his cock a little harder. "My little pet. So hard for me, so desperate. I should make you get on your knees right now."

"Yes," he moaned.

"You like when I humiliate you, too, don't you? When I make you come fast."

He whimpered, flexing into my hand and begging me for more.

"Desperate little thing. You want to come right now, don't you?"

"Yes."

"Do it."

I released him, taking his hand and wrapping it around his cock, instead.

"Watch them, think of me, fuck your hand, and come."

Carter bit his bottom lip, his eyes on the room where Cami was getting double penetrated. I heard him groan when the first man came in her ass, when he slowed and pulled out and they all watched the cum leak out of her. But then they were right back to it, the man she was riding pulling out and rolling over until he could fuck her mouth. He did so until he found his release, and Cami played with herself the entire time, finding hers right as he finished.

Carter stroked himself, his large hand covering his cock and sliding from tip to base and back again. He worked slow at first, picking up his pace as he watched the scene unfold.

But he didn't come watching them.

Instead, right when I knew he was close, his gaze swung to me.

He kept those warm eyes on mine, his lids heavy, lips parted as he stroked and flexed. He let that gaze trail over the length of me before he caught my eyes once more. And then he shuddered and groaned and came, his release painting the two-way mirror, and his eyes locked on mine.

"Fuck," he panted when he was done, squeezing the last out of his cock as he trembled and shook his head.

"I love when you listen," I praised him, and then wordlessly, I used the supplies in the corner of the room to clean up his mess. There were hot, wet towels rolled and waiting in a cabinet warmer, and I wiped him up with one before helping him refasten his pants.

The scene was finishing in the room, and the two men and Cami slid carefully into the aftercare portion of their scene. The men doted on her in an instant, ensuring she was okay, pampering her with cleanup and comfort.

"This is private," I told Carter. "Come. Let's explore."

He looked like he was ready to sleep when I pulled him from the room, but he perked right back up as we continued roving through The Manor.

There was so much to see, and I wanted him to see it all.

We passed a couple in a candlelit corner, the woman restrained in an aerial rig, suspended from the ceiling like art. Her partner circled beneath her, alternating between light swats to her inner thighs and slow, reverent kisses to her calves. Carter stared, mouth slightly parted.

Next, a wax play demonstration, a topless woman writhing in bliss as drops of red and gold wax painted a canvas of sensation down her back. Her Dom stood tall beside her, steady and calm, watching her every movement with the kind of attentiveness most men reserved for sports scores and stocks.

Carter's hand was warm in mine, his eyes wide and dark and alive.

Each scene we happened upon, I encouraged Carter to stop and watch. I called attention to when he was embarrassed, to when he was hard, to when his heart was pounding. I let him know it was okay. I asked him questions and corrected him when he gave the wrong answers.

And I let him know that was okay, too.

"We're not looking for perfection. Perfection is a mirage, anyway. We like messy here. We want you hard and aching. We want you to stumble and be unsure. We want you to surrender to what it feels like to know nothing, and then allow us to properly teach you. No one is a master here," I told him. "Not even me. We are all learning together. We're exploring and having fun. And you have permission to do the same."

We circled back to the main playroom to give him a break. I led us to a quiet corner where he could catch his breath. He was buzzing — I could feel it in the way his knee bounced, the way his eyes flicked around the room like he didn't want to miss a thing now that he felt comfortable to take it all in.

"You okay?" I asked, brushing my hand along the back of his neck.

He nodded. "Yeah. Just a little... overwhelmed, maybe? Not in a bad way."

I smiled. "It's a lot to take in your first time."

"It's fucking hot," he admitted, adjusting his cock in his pants. "Kind of torturous, to be honest. Being turned on all night."

I laughed at that, but just as he leaned in to say something else — likely a joke, knowing him — a figure approached us.

It was a woman; one I didn't recognize. That didn't mean she was new, but rather that we hadn't crossed paths yet. It was possible she'd played in areas I hadn't or been here on nights I wasn't.

She was tall, striking, with honey-blonde hair and long, gloved arms. Her skin was pale as snow, her eyes a frosty blue. She walked up to us like a graceful doe, and then she sat down in the empty chair next to Carter.

"Hello," she said simply, her voice soft and pure.

Carter looked at me with a concerned brow raised before addressing her. "Um... hello."

"I don't think I've seen you here before," she mused, and then she looked up to me. "You have such a beautiful sub, Mistress."

"Thank you." I didn't mean to clip the words. She was being friendly. She was playing by all the respectful rules.

But I didn't like the way she was looking at Carter.

"May I touch him?" she asked next, and though I knew the words were coming, I still internally fumed at her audacity.

Carter's eyes widened, and he looked to me as if he wasn't sure what he was supposed to do.

Slowly, I stood, taking two steps until I could carefully lower myself into Carter's lap. I draped myself over him possessively, my eyes hard on our new friend's as my voice dropped an octave.

"No."

The woman nearly pouted but must have thought better of it when I tilted my head in warning. She nodded graciously. "Of course. Enjoy your evening."

As she turned to leave, I felt a low laugh rumble through Carter.

I turned my attention to him with my brow cocked. "Amused, are we?"

"A bit."

"You're mine tonight," I murmured. I was a bit surprised how fiercely that possessiveness had taken me by the throat but I chose not to dwell on it. "They can look, but they don't touch."

"Whatever you say, *Mistress*."

"Keep calling me that and I'm going to test that sex slave fantasy of yours."

"Promise?"

I smirked, pinching his ribs. "Behave."

"Yes, Mistress."

I rolled my eyes, but when my gaze settled on Carter again, he was looking at me with reverence. His eyes flitted between mine, his brows subtly folding together.

"I really want to kiss you right now."

My heart fluttered.

And then I surprised myself when I responded with, "Then ask."

Carter stilled beneath me, but he paused only a moment before he was pulling me into him, sweeping my hair back, sliding that hand in to cradle my neck.

"May I kiss you?"

A simple nod was his only answer, and then his lips were on mine.

It was a starved kiss, one of a man denied for too long. He inhaled at the contact, brows pinching together more as he pulled me into him like he couldn't get me close enough.

And I gave in, too. For one moment, I let myself not think about the consequences. I let myself play into the night and pretend it was all fun and games.

I let him kiss me.

And I kissed him back.

And *God*, it felt good.

"Come with me," I said, pulling back and pressing my forehead to his.

He snuck one more kiss before asking, "Where?"

I stood, taking his hand in mine and dragging him up out of his chair as I answered.

"To a private room."

Chapter 16

Universe Speaking

Carter

The only other time my heart beat this fast and hard was in a playoff game.

When everything was on the line, when every second counted, when I had no *choice* but to perform at my highest level — that was the only thing I had to compare this feeling to.

I felt that same adrenaline pumping through me as Livia led me through the house, her hand wrapped around mine, the perfect curves of her ass and the gorgeous muscles of her back guiding me.

We passed by plenty of sexual scenes that should have had my head turning. It seemed as the night progressed, the crowd surrendered more and more to their kinks. No one was shy or bashful anymore. Everyone was giving in to their deepest, darkest desires — or watching someone submit to theirs.

But none of it was alluring enough for me to take my eyes off Livia.

I studied every lean slope and smooth patch of skin on her body, marveling at the fact that she was holding onto my hand proudly as she dragged me through the house.

She'd told that other patron that she couldn't touch me. She'd practically fucking *growled*, had climbed into my lap like I was her property.

And I wanted to be.

God, I'd never wanted anything so fiercely in my life — not even the Cup.

I was turned on, yes. That was a fucking no-brainer. She'd already made me come once tonight, and the fact that we were on our way to a private room told me the night wasn't close to over.

But it wasn't that simple fact that made me want to let her own me in every way a man can be possessed.

It was that she saw me.

She fucking *saw* me, the real me, the version of me at his most vulnerable, and she didn't laugh. She didn't tease me. She... she fucking heard every word I couldn't even say.

She brought me here tonight to please me, but she also brought me to show me something not even my therapist could help me grasp.

That it was okay to fail.

That there was no shame in trying.

That there were no consequences for voicing what I wanted.

Right now, my brain was too hardwired on the way her body looked wrapped in lace to think too hard about what this night would unlock for me, but I knew it without even fully understanding it.

I could feel it, like a puzzle piece snapping into place in the depths of my being.

Stand *your* Ground

She'd healed a part of me tonight.

We wandered through the mansion and upstairs, twisting through dark hallways until Livia pushed through a large wooden door to an empty bedroom. She locked it behind us, releasing my hand to take in the scene.

The air was warm, heat spilling from a sleek, modern fireplace built into the far wall, its flames throwing soft, amber light across everything it touched. In that glow, the king-size bed dominated the center — draped in rich black sheets with a headboard padded in deep charcoal leather.

A play swing hung from a thick beam near the corner, the straps black and gleaming. Beside it sat a low, cushioned bench made of dark wood.

Against one wall, glass shelves displayed toys like an art installation. Polished metal, glossy silicone, braided leather — all shapes and sizes, some I recognized, and plenty I didn't. Their reflections winked in the firelight like they knew secrets I didn't yet, like they couldn't wait to be in on what we were about to do.

The whole space smelled faintly of leather and clean linen, with the faintest trace of spiced vanilla — which I knew was all Liv. I'd smelled it on her the first night in her condo, that warm and inviting scent. It was like a warm sugar cookie and a shot of bourbon.

I let out a low whistle as I turned to face Livia, sliding my hands into my pockets. "This looks like a room out of a Bond movie."

"Young. Livia Young."

I smirked. "Nice."

"This is our room for the night," she said. "It's completely private. No one is watching." She took calculated steps toward me with every word, her heels clicking on the marble until they hit the fur rug under my feet. "I can still taste your desperation from earlier... and I'm not done with you yet."

I swallowed, cock instantly growing hard beneath my slacks.

"You've been so good, listened so well... I want to reward you." She trailed her long fingernail down my chest, her heated eyes locked on mine before she dug the nail into the flesh enough to make me hiss. "But I want to use you first. And I want you begging for me."

She leaned in, swiftly kissing me and taking my bottom lip between her teeth.

I cursed as she bit down hard, but then she released me with a grin and my body was surging to life, already silently pleading for more.

"Take your clothes off," she commanded, gracefully taking a seat on the bench. "Slowly. I want to see what I get to play with."

Instantly, my hands moved to my jacket, unfastening the buttons at my waist before I shrugged it off and tossed it on the bed. I was already starting on my dress shirt when Livia leaned back on her palms and crossed her legs with a wide grin.

"So eager," she teased. "So desperate for me, aren't you?"

"Always," I panted, unfastening my belt next.

"You're pathetic."

I stilled, heart kicking hard in my chest at the word.

Instantly, Livia leaned forward. "Safe word check."

"High stick for stop, offside if I want to keep going but need to slow way down."

"Or if something went too far," she reminded me, her eyes sincere as they watched. "Do you need to use one now?"

I blinked, trying to sort through the emotions swirling through me. I was so fucking turned on, so ready for whatever she was about to do to me, but I was also triggered by that word.

But somehow... not in the same way I was used to.

It made me feel that familiar wash of shame, the heat behind my cheeks, but it also sent tingles through me. It had me vibrating and almost wanting... more?

I shook my head. "I... no, I don't think so."

"Good. Then listen to me carefully, Carter. When I call you pathetic, or desperate, or anything else tonight... it's not to cut you down. I'm not him. I'm not trying to make you smaller so I can feel bigger."

She rose from the bench, every step toward me slow and intentional until she was right in front of me, tilting her chin up so her eyes locked with mine.

"I say it because you want me to. Because it flips a switch in you when it comes from me. Here, you're in control of what I call you. Here, you can stop me with a single word. And when you don't? That means you're letting me own you in a way that's safe, in a way that feeds you instead of starves you."

Her hands slid up my chest, hooking my open shirt until I let her strip it off my arms. She threw it to join my jacket on the bed.

"When he said things like that, it was about breaking you. When I say them, it's about building you into something that turns us both on."

She smirked again, heat returning to her gaze.

"So, I'll ask again, pretty boy — are you still eager for me?"

I wet my lips, nodding. "Yes."

"Do you want to pull your cock out for me?"

"Yes," I groaned, already doing what she asked. My pants and briefs were gone in a flash, and when she dropped her gaze to watch me fist myself, I moaned.

"Is that the best you can do?" she asked, and the bite in her tone sent a zip of electricity through me. "God, I'm already bored."

I stroked my cock with my eyelids fluttering at the feel of it. "Tell me what to do."

"Always needing to be told. You're lucky I waste my time on you."

"I am. I'm so lucky."

What the actual fuck was happening?

She was right. Every word she said to me should have stung, but it lit me up, instead. Because I knew it was for her pleasure — and for mine.

"See that bench?" she asked, nodding toward where she'd just been seated. "Bend over it. Hands on the cushion. Spread your legs."

That had my eyes shooting open. "Uh..."

When Livia arched a brow in warning, I did my best to surrender and do as she told — but my heart was racing again, every nerve in my body on high alert.

I got in position — bent over, hands on the bench — and Livia took her time walking over to stand behind me. She smoothed a hand over my back with an appreciative moan.

"You do look so pretty like this."

Her heel tapped the inside of each of my ankles.

"Wider, Rook. Open for me. Let me see you."

I swallowed, doing as she said as my cock began to drip. I was so fucking turned on it almost hurt.

Livia hummed with approval again, and then her hands were on me, massaging my lower back, my ass, my thighs. Every touch was sensual and slow, purposeful. She was edging me, her hands coming so close to my balls that I felt the gentle brush of a knuckle or nail, but then she'd move away innocently.

"Fuck, Liv. I want you to touch me."

"Of course you do. But I get to have my way with you first."

She took away her touch completely then, and I groaned at the loss as I watched her cross to the wall of toys. She trailed her nail along the glass before carefully selecting something and making her way back to where I was bent over with a knowing smile.

An anal plug.

Fuck.

I expected to be scared. If I were afraid of judgment from her or from the guys or from anyone else, I would have stood immediately and shook my head. I would have thrown my hands up and said, "Absolutely not. High stick."

But there were no judges here.

I was safe to explore my desires, and if I was being honest with myself...

I was curious.

I *wanted* to play.

"Mmm... someone's excited," she mused, holding the plug up for me to see more clearly. It wasn't intimidating, just a small, shiny, silver plug. "Do you know what this is?"

I nodded.

Livia traced my spine with the cool metal, dragging it over one ass cheek and up the next before she stood next to me, so I had no choice but to look up at her.

"I'm going to use this on you. I'm going to plug your ass, Carter, and then I'm going to ride your cock and you're going to fuck me until I come. You will not come first. You will be a good boy and use restraint until I finish first. Do you understand?"

"Yes," I panted.

Fuck, she was going to let me inside her.

How the bloody hell was I going to last?

Livia bent down to smile right in my line of vision. "Such a good boy."

She circled me then, pausing at a table with different types of lubes until she found the one she wanted. She squirted it into her hands, covered the toy, and then walked out of my vision to stand behind me.

My pulse kicked up a notch, breath stuttering in my chest.

"You can't wait to be inside me, can you?" she mused, and the first touch I felt was soft, a tentative walk of her fingers around my hip. "Are you going to last for me when I finally let you?"

"Yes," I promised. I hoped I could keep that fucking promise when the time came.

Livia wrapped her hand around my cock, moaning when her lube-covered hand swathed me from tip to base and back up. I flexed into the touch, already tingling, already so keyed up I could come just like this.

"My big, thick boy," she praised, the words soothing the sting of her previous statements. "Dripping for me."

I moaned, and that's when I felt the cool metal slide between my cheeks.

It was impossible not to freeze up, not to tense as she toyed with my entrance. She teased and played, skating around the hole before she'd press against it with just enough pressure to have me gasping, but not enough to enter.

"You're going to need to breathe, Rook," she coached. "Big inhale in for me, and then let it out slowly, and when you do, I want you to push out."

She didn't have to tell me what she meant for me to understand. If I didn't breathe, if I didn't relax, this wasn't going to feel good.

I nodded, doing as she said and taking a deep inhale. I let it out slowly, pushing as I did, and she pressed the plug against my entrance with a moan of encouragement.

"Yes, my filthy little plaything. Just like that. Open up for me."

She squeezed my cock and pumped me with that praise, making me moan and flex and reach.

"You're ready," she assured me, though I wasn't sure I shared her confidence. "Breathe."

I sipped in air.

I held it for a long breath.

Then I did my best to relax, to let every drop of air out as I sent that message to my lower half.

And Livia worked the plug inside me.

There was so much lube, I was surprised how easily it popped in. There was one slight moment of discomfort when the largest part of it passed the rim, but as soon as it was in, the pain was gone, and in its place was just an unfamiliar and exciting feeling of *fullness*.

"Fuck, Carter," Livia breathed. "This is so hot, seeing you plugged for me."

She moved the plug then, tilting it until the smooth metal pushed against my prostate.

And I let out a moan so loud I wasn't sure it belonged to me.

"Oh, yes," Livia praised. I looked over my shoulder at her and nearly died at the satisfied curl of her lips, of how hungry her eyes were where they watched what she was doing to me. "You love it, don't you?"

"I... I don't know."

She pressed the toy down again, this time moving it side to side a bit as her other hand worked my cock in three long, smooth strokes.

I cried out, flexing into her hand, my legs trembling. It felt so fucking good.

"Yes," I amended. "I like it. I like it."

"That's right. You like when I plug your ass, don't you?"

"Yes."

"You like when I stroke your thick, heavy cock and play with your ass, don't you?"

"Yes," I cursed the word, holding back against every instinct in me that wanted to just let go and come.

"You'll let me peg you one day," she promised. "You'll beg for it. But tonight, you want to be inside me for the first time, don't you? You want me to ride your cock with this plug in your ass, don't you?"

"Oh, fuck. Yes. Yes."

Livia released my cock, and my body trembled violently at the loss. It was like the edging lesson all over again as she helped me stand, guiding me carefully over to the bed. Every step with the plug had it rubbing against my prostate, and I didn't know whether to moan and give in, or cry from how hard it was to resist chasing that friction.

"On your back, Rook."

I did as she said, lying down on the black sheets.

"Play with yourself while I undress for you."

Instantly, my hand was on my cock, and I shivered with relief at the first pump. Livia smiled as she watched me, her fingers deftly removing all the lace and nylon covering her body. I watched each piece come off and slide to the floor like I was hypnotized. It was so sensual, how the fabric revealed her in a way I'd never witnessed before, how the lace pattern disappeared and left only smooth, inviting skin behind.

The fire set her silhouette in a glow, her hair in long braids tonight that fell over her shoulders and shielded her breasts once she'd uncovered them. When she bent to take her garters off, I couldn't help it. I moaned and fucked my hand faster.

"I could watch you forever and it wouldn't be long enough," I breathed.

Livia paused, her eyes finding mine in the low light. I would have sworn I saw something of a shy dip of her chin, but this was Livia fucking Young we were talking about. As soon as I thought I saw it, the moment was gone, and she climbed onto the bed.

Onto me.

"I'd rather you taste me, instead."

She straddled my face then, and when I went to grab her hips, she swatted my hand away.

"Touch your cock. Taste my pussy."

Fuck.

Every dirty command had me closer to the edge, and when she sat her cunt on my mouth, I groaned, tongue darting out to taste her as soon as I could. I followed her lead, licking and sucking while she set the pace.

And when she was ready, when she was panting and moaning, she moved my hand away from my cock and started sliding down my body until she was sitting in my lap.

"Make me come, Carter," she said, her lids hooded as her eyes fastened to mine. She reached down and grabbed my wet cock, sliding it between her pussy lips and making me arch off the bed in a cry of ecstasy. "Don't let me down. Show me you can do it. Show me how well you listen."

Then she pressed up onto her knees, wedged the head of my cock into her pussy, and sank all the way down.

"*Fuuuuck.*"

The word dragged out of me like a smoker's rasp, all the air deprived of my lungs by the way it felt to have her take me inside. I felt every slick, tight press of her walls, felt her hug me like a glove, like she was made for me, like we were made for *this*.

And when she moaned with me before pressing up and sliding back down again, I had to clamp my hands onto her hips.

"I can't," I breathed, shaking my head. Already, my nerves were firing to life. The plug moved inside me every time she lifted and sat again, and the combination of that and the feel of *her* was too fucking much. "I can't."

"You *can*," she assured me, and she covered my hands with her own before lifting and lowering again.

"Liv, it feels too fucking good."

"I know. I feel it, too."

She panted the words, which did nothing to help my cresting orgasm.

I was making her feel good.

Nothing made me want to come more than that.

"Focus on me," she managed, her breaths heavy. "Play with me. Worship me. Don't think about anything but *me*. Get. Me. There," she said, bouncing on me with the words. "And then you can come, too."

"Fuck," I cursed again, but this time, I blew out a breath and did everything I could to follow her command.

Game time.

It's game time, motherfucker.

Like I did before an overtime period, I closed my eyes and found my Zen. I soothed my breathing. I slowed my heart. It was like mentally sinking myself to the bottom of a pool, breath held and body calming.

When I opened my eyes again, I saw Livia — breasts swollen and heaving, lips parted and wet, brows pinched together in pleasure as she pressed her hands to my chest and started to ride me in slow, methodical waves.

Please her.

Give her what she needs, what she deserves.

Give her what she's given you.

Determination slid into my veins, and just like that, I was locked in.

I ran my hands up her body, one palming her breast and playing with her nipple just the way I knew she liked while the other climbed higher still. I hooked it behind her neck, pulling her down until she was riding just above me, our foreheads together, breaths hot and labored in the space between us.

"You look so fucking pretty riding my cock," I breathed, planting a bruising kiss against her lips as she moaned and bucked her hips. "Hugging me so tight, letting me watch these perfect fucking tits bounce."

I earned another moan, and it spurred me on, my body momentarily letting me focus on getting those little noises out of her rather than seeking my own pleasure. I tried to remember everything she'd taught me.

Make her feel safe.

Make her feel wanted, desired.

Let her know how bad I want her.

"Good," Livia managed. "That's... that's really good, Rook."

"Don't call me Rook. Not right now. Not when I'm buried deep inside you and you're begging to come."

"Fuck." It was a little whimper of breath out of her, like I'd surprised her, and that only fueled me on.

"So long, I've wanted to fuck you. So long, I've waited and pined for you. And now look at you. Riding me. Letting me fill you up. You love it, too, don't you? You love taking my thick cock inside that tight pussy of yours."

"Yes," she whimpered. "Yes, I love it. I love it."

I moved the hand I had around the back of her neck down between us, seeking out her clit and pressing three finger pads to it before I began to circle.

"Oh, fuck," she cried out, pushing back until she was seated on me again. She stared down at me with heavy, seeking eyes.

And my body burned to life again.

It was so much better than that fucking Fleshlight she'd tried to prepare me with — as if *anything* could compare to how she would actually feel. She was so perfectly tight around me, so hot and wet and my cock was so deep, my ass so full. Combined with the view of watching her ride me, it was incomparable.

Livia Young was elite in every way, and I'd been ruined from the first sight of her.

"Fuck me, Carter," she rasped. "I need you to help me. Fuck me while I ride you."

I bucked up to meet her, matching her pace, and then my fingers were curling into the skin at her hips again as I did everything I could to hold on. Her tits bounced wildly. Her legs shook. Her head dropped back, and her hands moved to palm her breasts, to pluck at her nipples and drive her to the edge.

Somehow, I fought through my own want and moved my hand back to her clit, applying the pressure I knew she needed. She rewarded me with a whimpering moan, and then she was seeking that touch, her body giving out as she rocked instead of bouncing. She started rubbing her clit against my hand, and it was up to me to keep pace now.

I fucked her like it was my only shot. I fucked her like she was the only championship in the world worth winning, like I'd spent every waking hour of my life preparing for this exact moment.

And then I felt it.

Her breath caught, and she came.

Her moans grew louder and louder, her body movements erratic as I fucked her and rubbed her clit and helped her chase that high.

"Fuck, Liv, I can feel it. I feel you squeezing me." I panted out the words, and with them, it was like I'd woken up my cock to realize what was happening.

My orgasm swarmed me like an unstoppable tidal wave.

"Liv, I can't. I have to come. Please, *please*, let me come."

"Yes," she breathed. "Yes, *yes*."

I didn't know if those affirmations were because she was enjoying herself or if they were permission for me, but I hoped for the latter, because I'd reached my absolute limit.

I let go.

And I surrendered to the fiercest orgasm of my life.

The sounds that ripped from my throat were foreign and unhinged, and Livia took over, riding me as I spilled inside her. I gripped her tight, alternating between my eyes squeezing shut to soak it all in and flying open to take in the sight of her smiling as she pumped me.

It was fire and ice, the two battling for dominance and completely searing every nerve as I tried to fuck her deeper, harder, *more*. More. I needed more.

And when the last of my climax receded, I was completely fucking wrecked.

I collapsed into the bed, hands falling away from Livia and slapping into the sheets, knees flaying open. I was breathing like I'd done a fucking Ironman.

"Christ in the penalty box, Liv," I panted.

The sweet little giggle she let out when she carefully climbed off me and rolled over to lie next to me was so cute, so perfect I wanted to save it as my ringtone.

"Very nice, Rook," she said, rolling until she had her head propped on one hand and the other trailing over my chest. "A plus."

"Yeah?"

She nodded. "The dirty talk was a very pleasant surprise."

"I learn from the best."

"That you do." She smiled slyly. "Now roll over so I can get this plug out of your ass."

I laughed, doing as she said. She worked through the breath with me, and though I was ultra-sensitive now, there wasn't any pain with the removal. Livia got up from the bed long enough to clean the toy and put it in a basket in the corner of the room that, until now, I hadn't realized was even there.

"For used toys, I presume?" I asked.

She nodded, pulling two hot towels from a warming cabinet before crawling back into bed with me. "Everything is meticulously cleaned, sometimes just outright replaced. The Manor is known for safety and luxury, after all."

I let out a long groan of a sigh when she covered me with the hot towel. She laid down next to me and let out a sigh of her own when she pressed the other between her legs.

For a while, we just lay there, smiling and sighing and cleaning ourselves. Then, before I thought better to stop myself, I rolled over toward her and slid my hand behind her neck, pulling her lips to mine.

"Thank you, Liv," I breathed, and then I kissed her again. I didn't care if I didn't ask for permission, and maybe it was still granted under this roof because she let me do it. She may have even kissed me back a little. "Thank you."

"For an orgasm?" she teased.

"For tonight. For making me feel safe. For..." I swallowed. "For understanding."

I pulled back so I could look into her eyes when I said it, and the sincerity in my heart was reflected in her gaze.

Until suddenly, panic slid in to take its place.

I saw it the moment it crept in, saw how her brows pinched together, and her lips parted slightly.

I'd crossed a line. I knew I had. She didn't want to get too much into feels, into emotions.

So quickly, I recovered, flopping back into the bed with a happy sigh before she could latch onto it and question me.

And then I laughed.

I laughed a real, deep, baritone laugh that shook the whole bed.

"What?" she asked, leaning up on her elbow. "Oh, my God, *what*? Are you having a mental breakdown?"

"No," I said through the laughter. "No, no, it's just... my first time inside a pussy, and there's still ass play involved."

I arched a brow at her with a grin as wide as my face, and Livia closed her eyes before submitting to a laugh I knew she couldn't fight off.

"Maybe the universe is speaking, Rook," she said.

"Well," I grinned, propping my hands behind my head, "consider this my official notice that I'm listening."

We cleaned up, dressed, bid adieu to our hosts, and rode back to Livia's condo in comfortable silence, but my mind was anything but quiet. Every step of the night replayed in vivid detail as I drove with one hand on the steering wheel and the other resting on the center console, begging me to reach over and slide it over her leg. I couldn't stop thinking about the way she'd looked at me when I got it right, the way she looked when I brought her release, the way I felt both stripped bare and stronger than I'd ever been.

I didn't know how the hell I was supposed to go back to just being her student.

Her friend.

Not when she'd given me this.

Not when every cell in my body was already leaning toward her, begging for more.

I'd had a taste of her, and instead of it making me feel confident to chase other women, it only made me desperate to chase *her*.

Which was a real fucking problem, since she'd made it more than clear that she didn't want to be chased.

I dropped her off with a kiss on her cheek, hanging onto the little smile she gave me like a lifeline when she disappeared inside the high-rise building.

And I knew it. No questions asked.

I was well and truly fucked.

Chapter 17

Bananas

Livia

"LET'S GO, OSPREYS!"
Clap, clap, clap clap clap.
"LET'S GO, OSPREYS!"
Clap, clap, clap clap clap.

The cheer rang out around the stadium, and I had no choice but to join in — mostly due to an elbow to the ribs courtesy of my best friend. She winked at me, clapping and cheering until I joined in, and then she celebrated the victory with a little shimmy of her shoulders.

Ava — Will Perry's daughter — was next to her, snug as a bug between Maven and Chloe as we watched the final game before the team got some much-needed time off for the Four Nations Face Off. Grace was still in Antarctica and Mia was still on tour, so it was just the three of us tonight, along with our favorite kid.

Ava Perry was one hundred percent the biggest hockey fan I knew. She'd been into it ever since I'd met her — since she was born, I presumed — and now that Will and Chloe had her enrolled in a youth league, she was even more unhinged. Add in the fact that her favorite pop star had become one of the crew, thanks to Aleks wife-ing her up, and you could say our little nugget was in heaven.

I watched her with a soft smile as she chanted louder than any of us, small hands cupping around her mouth to serve as a megaphone. When the chant ended, Ava screamed wildly and added, "Come on, boys! Take it to the net!"

Maven and I shared a grin at that, and then all our attention turned to the ice.

And mine went straight to Carter.

Lord help me, the sight of that man in his element tapped into the most feral side of me.

There was something about watching him play his ass off, something about how focused he was, how well he performed, how he seemed more on his game than ever that had me wanting to get on my knees and crawl to him. He was different tonight. He'd been different in every game this week.

He was locked in, his game effortless, his confidence beaming.

And I knew why.

It had been nearly a week since our exploration at The Manor — a week since I'd taken his virginity, plugged his ass, and led him through every wicked corner of that sultry mansion. I'd watched him shed the weight of shame and perfection, seen the relief in his face when he realized he didn't have to get everything right, that he was allowed to explore, to stumble, to laugh at himself.

It had been freeing for him.

And for me.

I hadn't realized how much I'd needed that night until it was over — the rush of guiding him, the way he'd thanked me like I'd given him something more valuable than an opponents' playbook. After all the drama going on with my family trying to force me into attending my sister's wedding, it had been a reprieve for me just as much him.

It had also surprised me.

I knew what we were walking into. I knew the play we'd witness, knew the way everyone would dress, knew that by the end of the night, I'd claim Carter's virginity. But I hadn't known the way I'd feel when he swept my hair back before kissing me, slow and reverent one moment, playful and grinning the next. I didn't expect him to make me laugh when I didn't think I had it in me. I certainly hadn't foreseen how I'd feel jealous of the first person to ask to touch him, that I'd mark him as my territory like a fucking dog.

That night had been on my mind all week.

He'd been on my mind all week.

And I heard a smothered voice deep within my soul screaming how much of a problem that was.

I'd convinced myself it was nothing more than the second payment hitting my account. It had gone through on Monday, another large chunk of change for me to add to my savings, another part of our contract complete.

Surely, that was the reason I'd been so fixated on him. I saw that paycheck and zeroed in on our goal, on the job I still had to fulfill.

I was just making sure he got his money's worth.

That same voice within laughed at me as I found myself tracking him on the ice again. I did it without thinking, like he was metal, and I was a magnet helpless to resist.

He was crouched low in the face-off circle now, stick angled just right, eyes locked on the puck. The ref dropped it, and Carter snapped it back clean to Vince before exploding forward, skating hard into open ice. He cut across the neutral zone, dug an edge so sharp it sent a spray of ice into his opponent's shins, and put himself in the perfect spot for the return pass.

The puck hit his tape, and in one fluid motion he curled toward the slot, pulling the defenseman with him. At the last second, he threaded the puck through a narrow lane — a perfect feed across the crease.

Vince didn't waste it, hammering it past the goalie so fast the net barely rippled before the goal horn blared.

The crowd erupted, and Carter looked up toward our section in the stands. I couldn't see his eyes from here, but I didn't need to. I knew exactly how they'd look — bright and sharp, the edges of them crinkled with his signature smile as he prepared to land a joke.

I knew without needing confirmation.

He was looking for me.

A hot zing shot through me, butterflies fluttering low in my chest.

Thankfully, my best friend swatted them away just as quickly as they'd appeared.

"Come with me to get refills?" she asked, holding up her empty wine cup.

I nodded, and after we checked to see if Chloe or Ava wanted anything, we shimmied out of our seats and up to the suite.

We were sharing the suite with other wives and girlfriends of players — and me, who was somehow always included even though I was just the dentist. Then again,

I guess if I was a general manager, I'd play nice with the woman who fixed all my players' faces, too.

Maven was one of the favorites, the kind of woman every player and significant other wanted to be around. I took up her side proudly as she flitted from group to group saying hi on our way to the bar, chiming in with my own stories when it fit. This was the woman who had once felt unwelcome and out of place in a setting like this. Now, it was like she owned the place.

I loved to see that change play out in real time.

There was nothing better than watching a woman claim her power, especially when she was your best friend.

Eventually, we were able to refill our drinks — Maven a glass of red wine and me a gin and tonic. I went to fill a plate with chicken tenders and fries — Ava's request — when Maven placed her hand over my wrist to stop me.

"Let's pause. Ava can wait a second. I want to chat with you in private."

My brows shot up. "Should I be scared?"

"Only if you have secrets to hide, which I'm betting you do."

She gave me that sassy little whip of her head that always made me laugh as she dragged me to one of the high-top tables in the corner of the suite. Her eyes skirted up to the television as the crowd roared to a higher decibel, but when whatever was going on died down, she looked back at me.

"Alright. Here's the thing. I may not be as good at this as you are, but I know when my best friend is off. And you're off. So, I need an update on this whole wedding thing, and I also need to know what the hell is going on between you and Carter Fabri."

There was a crack of a stick against the puck, but it might as well have been my jaw hitting the table.

"Don't even try to tell me it's nothing," she said, holding up her hand before I could say a word. "Fill me in on wedding drama first, and then tell me what's going on with our Center, or I swear, Livia, I will feed that Tory Burch belt you let me borrow to the nearest garbage disposal."

"Rude!"

Maven just waved her finger in the air as she took the first sip of her wine, as if to tell me to get to yapping.

With a glare, I took a sip of my own glass before letting out a long sigh. "The wedding drama is... relentless. My sister is begging me to come. My mother keeps texting me to say that I better be there, that I better not let Lacey down, but then she makes all these passive-aggressive comments that give away her true wish."

"Which is?"

"Come on. You heard her when you were at my condo the night she called the first time." I paused, not wanting to say it. "She doesn't want me there, Mave."

I didn't know why my body reacted like this was shocking news, like there was any other wish my mother would have. I knew when she turned her back on me as a teenager that I didn't matter to her.

But I was still just a girl.

And I wanted my mother to love me.

My eyes fell to my nails. I needed a manicure. My brain chose to focus on that so I didn't slip too far into my emotions. "Of course, she doesn't want me there," I continued. "She can't hide me if I'm in the same room as her and all her friends."

Maven's brows shifted inward. "And what do *you* want?"

"To not be in this position," I answered honestly. "I love Lacey with all my heart. I'm so happy she's found love, and I want to be there to celebrate her. But I don't want to be anywhere near Mom and Dad. I don't want to have to make nice with them when they... when they..."

I couldn't say the words out loud. Fortunately, Maven already knew the story, so I didn't have to.

I don't want to have to make nice with my parents when they covered up their friend assaulting me.

I don't want to pretend everything is fine when they cut me off the minute I said I wouldn't stay quiet.

I don't want to be in the same room with the person who abused me, who my parents sided with over their own daughter to keep their perfect little world intact.

I never let my thoughts get too far down that road before I ripped them right back on track. I was not a victim. I was over playing that part by the time I turned twenty.

I was a survivor, a woman who took back the narrative and control in my life despite those closest to me who tried to stop me.

"Lacey still doesn't know everything that happened, does she?" Maven asked.

"You asked me that already," I reminded her. "At my condo."

"That's because I was trying to do the not-so-subtle best friend thing and plant the seed in your mind." She paused, her eyes softening. "Liv, you need to tell your sister."

I shrugged, though my stomach bottomed out at the thought. Maven was the only one I'd ever told the whole story to other than my parents.

And Maven was the only one who believed me.

I couldn't handle it if I told my sister and she reacted the same way my parents did.

"I find it hard to believe she hasn't put the pieces together," I said softly, chest aching with the truth in that confession. "But just like Mom, I think she's afraid to ask me about it. She knows if I tell her, if I confirm her suspicions, then she'll have to act on that discovery. And just like Mom, she doesn't want to lose access to their little slice of society."

Maven's lips curled. "God, and you wonder why I had such a thorn in my ass about rich people for so long."

"I never said you were *completely* wrong," I pointed out. "Only that the actions of your snooty ex were not indicative of the actions of the hot rookie you were being paid to follow around." I took a sip of my drink. "And I was right. So, you're welcome."

"I'm really sorry you have to deal with this," Mave said, reaching out to squeeze my arm. "It's not fair. How can I help?"

I sighed. "Just be there with a bottle of wine on the other side of their nuptials. And maybe save a night for me to curl up on your couch — emotional state to be determined."

"Consider the date saved."

"Thanks, bestie. Now," I said, grabbing her hand in mine. "Let's get back out there with some chicken nuggets in hand before Ava—"

"Oh, no you don't." The cute little brat flipped her hand up over my head and twirled me until I was right back at the table. "I am sorry to hear about your terribly misguided mother, but not sorry enough to let you get out of telling me what's going on with you and Carter."

"Nothing is going on between me and Fabio."

Maven smiled sweetly but picked up the nearest utensil. "Lie to me again, and I will stab you."

"That is a plastic spoon."

"They say the dullest knives are the most dangerous."

I laughed through my nose, but then covered my face with my hands and let out a long sigh. "Fine," I clipped when my hands dropped. I pointed a finger at her. "But you cannot tell a soul, and you need to keep your reaction in check to what I'm about to tell you."

"We listen and we don't judge," she promised. "Although, now I'm *very* intrigued."

"I'm serious about not telling anyone. We signed an NDA."

Her eyes shot wide as she sipped her wine. "An NDA? Jesus, Liv, what's going on?"

I chewed my lip. "I'm giving him lessons."

"In how to fill a cavity?"

"In how to pick up women and please them in the bedroom."

Maven nearly spit out her wine, and she winced with the effort not to before coughing once she finally swallowed it down. "I'm sorry, I think I just hallucinated. Did you just say—"

"That I'm teaching Carter Fabri to be a sex god in exchange for two-million dollars?" I picked up my cup and tilted it to my lips. "Indeed, I did."

Maven's jaw dropped, and she looked around before leaning over the table and whisper-yelling, "*What?!* Two-million *dollars?!*"

"We listen and we don't judge!"

"I'm not judging! I'm foaming at the mouth for details! SPILL."

Her eyes were wide as I listed out the full scenario. I told her everything, from when Carter first proposed the idea and I'd looked at him like a psychopath, to our most recent lesson.

And because Maven was my best friend and I'd never left her out of my kinky stories before, I told her *everything*.

By the end of it, she was both fanning herself and getting a refill of wine, like she needed to drink to process it all.

"Liv... this is absolutely bananas."

"No bananas have been involved. Yet."

She flattened her lips but couldn't help but smile. "You kinky bitch. I can't believe this. And he's already paid you?"

"One mil paid, one mil to go."

She frowned. "I understand you saying yes just for the fun of the challenge, but the money... I don't know that I get that part of it."

"No?" I waved a hand in the air as if the points were all popping up like a scoreboard next to my head. "No money from my family, drowning in student debt, trying to freeze my eggs and become a single mom on my own terms?"

Recognition illuminated her eyes. "The money you suddenly *came into*." She sucked her teeth. "I knew you didn't have no damn long lost great-great-aunt."

"Nope. Just an eager puppy dog of a hockey player willing to blow his money on my services."

Maven softened at that. "I didn't realize the loans were so bad. You know Vince and I—"

I held up a hand to stop her. "Don't you dare finish that sentence. I am your best friend, not a charity case. And I am certainly nowhere near destitute. I would be fine on my own. I *am* fine on my own. This little agreement with Carter just expedites my savings and sets me up in a more comfortable position." I sipped my gin. "Don't worry — I'll still let you pick up the bill for fancy girls' trips."

She smirked. "So, you're really doing it, huh? Freezing your eggs?"

I nodded, heart skipping a beat as it settled in. "Soon."

"I'm so proud of you. I'm... amazed by you, frankly. But..."

"Uh-oh."

"No, no, it's just..." She chewed the inside of her cheek, eyes dropping to her hands around her cup before she lifted them to me again. "I know you will be okay at the end of all this. Better than okay, it sounds like. But what about Carter?"

"What about him?" I didn't mean for it to sound so crude when I shot the words at her. "He'll be a pussy god drowning in women and still as rich as ever."

"Does he *want* to be drowning in pussy? Or does he only want to be drowning in *you*?"

Fuck.

I didn't need to hear those words from my best friend, not when I'd been convincing myself it was all going to be fine.

"He understood what he was getting into when we drew up the terms," I said, my voice softer than I would have liked. "And he's been enjoying himself. He knows what we are and what we will never be. Trust me — all he wants out of this is knowledge and confidence."

Maven tilted her head. "And you?"

"Hello, did you black out when we were discussing the bank wires?"

"So, you don't have *any* feelings for him after all this?"

The scoff that left me was instinctual. "Maven."

"Livia."

"You know me."

"You're right, I do." She stood and rounded the table until she was right in front of me. "Which is why I asked. Because I just saw my best friend doing goo-goo eyes out there, and I have a feeling it wasn't because you've suddenly fallen in love with hockey."

I clamped my mouth shut, eyes searching hers. When she arched a brow, I sighed.

"I... I'm not in danger of catching real feelings or anything. But yes, I do like him. I... I've enjoyed spending time with him. It's surprised me."

The corner of her lips lifted. "It's okay to catch feelings."

"No, it's not," I clipped. "And I'm not. I just like teaching him. I like being in control. I like making him beg. I like testing his boundaries and helping him see his potential. Shall I go on with the things I like, or would you like to keep a somewhat safe for work image of our dear Carter?"

Maven chuckled, and then she was sweeping me into a hug.

"Fine. We can drop it. But just know I'm here if anything changes. And for what it's worth... I think you two would be great together."

"We're certainly great together when sex toys are involved."

"Oh, my God, Liv."

We both laughed, but before Maven could drag me back out to the seats, my phone buzzed in my clutch.

When I saw who was calling, all the joy left my body in an instant.

"Damn it, Maven, are you like a smoke signal for my mother? Every time I'm with you, she decides to call."

"Maybe it's the universe knowing we're meant to handle the tough shit together," she said, nodding toward the phone. "Go on. Answer it."

I rolled my eyes but did as she said.

"Hello, Mother," I greeted, holding the phone to my ear. Maven stayed close, her hand on my arm in assurance that she was there.

"Livia," Mom answered, her voice already laced with that familiar blend of clipped formality and thinly veiled irritation. "I'm calling because your sister's wedding is twelve weeks away, and I still don't have your RSVP. She's asked me repeatedly if you'll be there, and quite frankly, your indecision is inconsiderate."

"I've told her *and* you, I'm working on figuring it out—"

"Well, figure faster. This is her wedding, not some last-minute cocktail party you can waltz into when it suits you. Honestly, I think we'd all be better off if you just decided now." A pause. "Though, between you and me, it might be... less complicated if you stayed away."

I closed my eyes, jaw tightening. "Is that so?"

A faint, airy laugh — the kind she used when pretending something wasn't cruel. "Well, darling, you've been so... withdrawn these last few years. People might not know what to say to you anymore. And showing up alone, as you so often do... it's just bound to make things awkward. You've pushed everyone away, and now..." She let out a sigh. "Now, you're alone."

Alone.

The word echoed between my ears. She knew what she was doing — she always knew. It was her favorite move, pressing that exact spot she'd left black and blue years ago, as if to remind me she could. Alone wasn't just a description when it came from her mouth; it was an accusation, a verdict, a label she'd sewn into the lining of my skin so tight I'd never be able to rip it out.

It was the word she wielded every time she wanted to shrink me back into the girl she thought I should be — compliant, apologetic, small enough to fit inside her perfect little world. It wasn't about my relationship status. It was about control. About punishment.

And still, my chest tightened like she'd reached right through the phone and put her thumb on the bruise she'd left, pressing down until I could feel the ache in my bones.

My pulse roared in my ears. "I didn't push my family away," I said, each word deliberate, clipped. "My family walked out on me when I refused to stay silent about one of your friends raping me."

The word hung there, jagged and heavy, like a giant boulder suspended over us by nothing more than a thread. The threat of it crushing me was always there. I wondered if my mother felt it, too, or if she was able to easily forget, if having me out of sight had put it all out of mind for her.

For a heartbeat, I thought she might acknowledge it.

And then I heard my father's voice.

"Darling, who is it? Who's on the phone?"

My heart cracked open like an egg, all the despair I'd locked away leaking out like a sticky yolk. Maven squeezed where she held me, and I held my eyes open wide so none of the tears I felt stinging my nose would fall.

Mom's voice breezed back in, cool and unaffected. She ignored my father. She ignored me. "Anyway, let me know by the end of the week so we can finalize the seating chart."

The line went dead, and so did my hope.

I stared at the phone for a moment, my throat tight, every nerve in my body buzzing. I felt like a little girl again, craving love and understanding and pride from my mother, wishing on a deceased star for my father to act like the superhero he used to emulate when we'd play and save me.

But as usual, I was empty-handed in all of those areas.

Maven reached for me wordlessly, wrapping her arms around me like she could shield me from the sharp pieces of myself my mother always managed to shatter.

But she couldn't protect me.

The only ones who ever *could* chose not to.

And so, even in the arms of my best friend, I only heard my mother's words ringing true.

I was alone.

Chapter 18

Extra Credit

Carter

Nothing felt better than walking out of the locker room after a win at home.

Nothing... except the fact that Livia would be waiting for me in the friends and family room.

I usually skipped that room when I left the stadium. It was where I'd wave goodbye to Vince or Will or whoever else as they veered left to greet their loved ones, and I headed right to the parking lot.

But tonight, Livia had been in the suite with Maven. And now, she was in that friends and family room.

And okay, so she wasn't really waiting *for me*. Technically, she was just there with her best friend. But it didn't change the fact that I'd played my ass off in an attempt to impress her, or that I'd looked up in the seats for her after every goal, or that I was practically skipping down the hallway on my way to find her now.

I'd been playing it cool all week. I'd text her, but not too much. I'd reply to her texts, but not too quickly. I checked in on how her days were going without hovering or acting like a boyfriend.

Because I was not her boyfriend — and she would be quick to remind me that if I ever forgot.

But it'd been torture, being away from her after what we'd shared on Friday night. And now, I'd just wrapped up our last game before we had a long break for the 4 Nations Face-Off. It was the league's new stand-in for what used to be the All-Star games, and though I hoped to play in the tournament one day for Team Canada, I was happy I wasn't invited this year.

Because I could think of many better ways to spend the next two weeks, and every single one of them involved Livia Young.

"Fabri."

The call of my name came from behind just as I was about to swing into the room, and I found Coach still dressed in his game suit with a grin on his face.

"Hell of a game tonight," he said, clapping his hand hard on my shoulder. "I saw something in you I've never seen before. You had grit. Stamina. Determination. You played like it was a playoff game. You left everything on the ice." He paused, assessing me. "I knew you had it in you, and I'm glad I got to witness me being right about that."

My throat was tight when I answered, "Thanks, Coach."

He nodded, squeezing my shoulder before he released it. "Enjoy your break, but don't lose this fire you've found. Yeah?"

I returned his nod, stomach flipping a bit at just how I'd keep that fire alive. Because I knew it had nothing to do with therapy or practice.

It was Liv who'd lit that flame.

"Hey," I said when Coach turned toward the parking lot. "What are you doing for break? Going to see family?"

The corner of his lips twitched, but the smile didn't spread. "Nah, just hanging around the Bay, I imagine. Rest a little. Probably still work most days."

"You need a break, too, Coach."

He shrugged. "Hockey is my life, Fabio."

"Might be time to try dating."

He full-on laughed at that, saluting me with two fingers before he left me without much of an acknowledgement to my statement.

I frowned, watching him go for a moment, and then Vince was sliding into me.

"Come on, Fabio," he said, ruffling my hair before slinging an arm around my shoulder. "Let's go get the girls. I'm dying to see what discount Hallmark line you try on Livvy tonight."

Will strolled past, tossing a grenade over his shoulder without slowing down. "Yeah, and I'm curious how many seconds it'll take before she makes you regret speaking."

A laugh fizzled out of Vince, and though it usually would have bothered me, I just smiled. Let them think what they want. Let them joke and tease.

They didn't know what happened between us behind closed doors, and I loved holding onto that little secret.

The friends and family room buzzed with post-game chatter, laughter, and the clink of plastic cups. I scanned for her instantly — and there she was.

Livia stood with Maven, Chloe, and Ava, one hand curled loosely around her drink, the other tucked into the pocket of her perfectly tailored slacks. She looked like she'd stepped straight out of a glossy magazine spread — sleek ponytail, blazer cinched at the waist, heels that made my brain short-circuit — but there was something... off. It was just a flicker, a faint dulling in the way her gaze tracked the room, the way her smile lagged behind the conversation.

The other guys made a beeline for their people, but I hung back. Watching her was like wading into seemingly calm water only to realize you've walked into a rip current — and I realized quickly there was no hope of fighting it. I'd been trying all week to keep my head above water, to keep my feelings in check. But the second I caught the edges of that dimness in her eyes, the game was over.

And when she looked at me, I surrendered to the tide.

Our eyes locked, and it was like someone yanked the air out of my lungs. My pulse spiked, heat shot down my spine, and the noise of the room dropped to a dull roar in my ears. Her lips tipped into that devastating smile that could stop me dead mid-stride — and I felt it, low and hard, right in my chest.

I was hers, even though she'd never be mine.

She excused herself from the group and crossed the room, heels clicking, gaze locked on me like I was the only person in the building, like we didn't have anything to hide. And maybe that was because she was confident in the fact that she could hide it so effortlessly, that she could tease me the way she always did, and no one would be the wiser.

I, on the other hand, suddenly felt like I had all our secrets written on my face like a billboard.

"Hey there, Rook."

"Hey, yourself," I said, my grin automatic, and without thinking, I swept her into a hug.

I wanted to hold her there, to bury my nose in her hair and inhale everything that she was. But I kept it as short and friendly as I could manage before pulling back. "Enjoy the game?"

"Surprisingly, yes. Although, my favorite part was listening to Ava roast all the players on the Seattle team."

"Spicy little thing, isn't she?"

"Can't imagine where she gets it from."

We shared a knowing smile, but Livia's was a bit forced at the edges.

"You were pretty good out there tonight," she said, her voice warm but threaded with that teasing lilt that always knocked me off balance.

"Does that mean you're giving me an A, Professor?"

"A solid B plus. But lucky for you, there's a chance to earn extra credit tonight. If you're up for it."

My pulse skyrocketed.

"Fuck yeah, I'm up for it."

Livia rewarded me with that smoky little laugh of hers, but it faded too quickly, that sadness in her eyes overtaking the expression.

I looked around, making sure everyone was preoccupied before I stepped into her space a little more. "Hey... you good?"

"I'm great."

"You don't look great."

"Gee, thanks. Now I really want to let you see me naked."

"No jokes right now," I said, surprising both Livia and myself. But I didn't appreciate the dodge when I could see something was wrong. "What's going on, Liv?"

She swallowed, her voice quiet when she tried to lie again. "Nothing."

I flattened my lips, and that earned me a frustrated sigh.

"I'm fine," she reiterated with a huff. "Really. Just... some stupid family shit I'd rather not talk about."

"Your sister's wedding?"

She nodded, her lips tight.

The ache that hit me was sharp and immediate, like her admission had stepped on an already cracked rib. I wanted to close the distance, to take whatever was twisting her up and carry it myself.

But I knew even before I tried that she wouldn't let me.

"It's not a big deal," she tried, but the lie was thinly veiled. "And if you really want to do something for me... I need a distraction tonight." She pinned me with her gaze. "I need control."

The word sparked against my nerves, lighting me up like I hadn't just played three grueling periods.

"Can you give that to me?"

Her voice was just a whisper now, and the way she was staring up at me through her lashes, the way she was fidgeting, her fingers wrapping around each other... it was the most vulnerable I'd ever seen her.

"Haven't you figured it out yet?" I leaned in, my voice low and steady. "I'll give you anything you ask for."

Her brows inched together, nostrils flaring a bit before she attempted a smile. "Meet me at mine in thirty."

And then she was walking away, heels clicking back toward Maven and Chloe, leaving me in the middle of the room with the weight of her request lodged deep in my chest.

If this was all I could give her, I'd give it willingly.

If this was all she'd let me have, I'd take it like a greedy thief.

Whatever lesson she wanted to teach me, I was ready to learn.

And if all she needed was to use me tonight, I'd crawl to her, heart bound, begging for the privilege.

Chapter 19

Drop the Armor

Livia

All was right in the world again when Carter was in my condo, naked and on his knees.

Power coursed through me as I circled him, wearing my favorite emerald green garter set, the decadent lace of the bodice combining with the high arch of my heels to make me feel invincible.

Some people needed to talk when they were feeling rundown by life. Some people needed to go for a run or take a long hot bath.

This was what I needed.

Control. Certainty. Release.

"Have you been using the plugs I gave you when you've played with yourself this week?" I asked, dragging one fingertip down the slope of his shoulder before continuing my slow orbit around him.

His eyes flicked up, a faint flush climbing his neck as he hit me with a smirk. "Yes, ma'am."

"Good." My heels clicked softly on the hardwood when I stopped in front of him. "Because tonight, I'm going to take you somewhere you can't get on your own."

His breath hitched, but he held my gaze. Brave boy.

"You've spent our lessons so far learning how to take control," I said, tracing his jaw with my knuckles. "How to read a woman's body. How to make her feel safe enough to relax and give herself over to you." My nails grazed lightly along his skin. "But there's another side to that coin. If you want to guide someone that way, you have to know what it feels like to be guided yourself."

I let that settle before continuing.

"Think of how we played at The Manor as a warmup, and tonight is game day. If you want to be the kind of lover who wrecks a woman in the best way, you have to understand surrender. You have to know how to let go, to stop trying to perform and just... receive." My lips curled in a slow smile. "Pegging flips the power."

He swallowed when I said the word, when I called my plans for tonight into the light. But his eyes didn't leave mine, and he didn't protest.

His silent consent made my pussy throb. He trusted me. He really was ready to let go, to give me all the power.

It was so fucking hot to witness that surrender.

"It puts you in a position where your only job is to feel everything," I continued. "And when you do that — when you drop the armor — you become dangerous in bed. You go from a proficient lover to an absolutely lethal one."

It wasn't lost on me how I was preaching about dropping control when it was the very thing I was desperate to hold onto. But that was precisely why I was a Domme.

And I had to admit it, even if only to myself.

Tonight was just as much about my needs as it was about his.

But God, if he only knew.

I was still shaking from that phone call — from hearing my father's voice in the background, my mother's clipped dismissal echoing in my head. It was like being seventeen again, screaming into the void, begging someone to take me seriously, to believe me.

I'd been numb the rest of the game, held together only by the gravity Maven could provide with her hand secure in mine, reminding me everything would be okay somehow.

I wasn't sure.

So, when Carter gave me this tonight — when I asked him to hand me the reins and he didn't question it, didn't probe for me to talk when I didn't want to, didn't make me feel ridiculous for running from my past — it allowed me my first deep breath of the night.

He trusted me. He believed I knew what I needed.

He gave me the one thing my family never had: validation.

I wanted to tell myself this was just sex. Just control. Just the catharsis I craved.

But my heart knew better.

My heart was terrified, because the way I leaned into him, the way I trusted that he'd be there if I let go...

It felt a lot like falling.

I stepped behind him, nails skimming down his back, my voice dipping into his ear as I ignored the whisper of those terrifying truths and chose to focus on the gift he'd given me, instead. I didn't want to think tonight. I just wanted to feel.

"This isn't about making you less of a man," I said. "It's about rewriting what manhood means for you. It's about trusting someone enough to let them push past your boundaries with only your pleasure in mind."

I moved back to face him, drinking in his flushed cheeks, the tension buzzing off him.

"You've always been afraid of being a joke. Of not knowing what to do. But this..." I gestured between us. "This is you learning. This is you building confidence in a place where you've always second-guessed yourself."

His breathing was heavier now, but his gaze never wavered.

"You want to lead in bed one day? To make a woman feel safe enough to hand herself over to you completely?"

"Yes," he said, low and certain.

"Then you need to know what it's like to be led. To feel good direction. To be so present in your body that the rest of the world disappears. To understand consent. Attunement. Aftercare." I tilted my head, letting my gaze drag over him slowly. "You want to be a menace in bed? Learn what it's like to be on the other side of yes."

I crouched until we were eye to eye, resting my hands lightly on his thighs.

"I realize this kind of trust isn't easy, the kind that requires you to let me see you at your most vulnerable and believe I'll still be here when it's over."

His jaw flexed, and I could see the battle in him — years of conditioning telling him to hold the line while every nerve in his body screamed for him to drop the shield.

"I will still be here," I promised softly. "I will still see you as strong. I will still laugh with you. I will still want you."

That last declaration came out a little breathier than the rest, my heart squeezing tight with the admission.

Because it was true.

I did want him. I wanted him more than I should.

I stood again, walking toward the dresser where my toys were neatly laid out. My hand closed around the strap-on harness, the cool leather warming instantly in my grip. "This isn't just for me, Carter. It's for you. I want to make you *feel* instead of overthink, to show you your partner's power — and your own — when you surrender."

I glanced over my shoulder, catching the way he was watching me like I was both his salvation and his executioner.

"So tonight, you don't think. You don't try. You don't perform." I stroked the length of the strap-on before laying it neatly across the bedspread — positioned so he'd see it every time his eyes strayed in that direction. "The game is over now. You've already won, remember? So now... you feel. You speak your needs. And you let me lead."

His lids were heavy as he stared at the toy on my bed, and then his eyes were back on mine.

There wasn't an ounce of fear to be found.

"You sure that thing's regulation size?" he quipped.

I fought against a smile.

That's my Rook.

"Up," I commanded.

Carter rose instantly, unfolding from his knees with that natural athlete's grace — all muscle and height, completely naked and completely mine for the taking. I stepped into his space, running my palms up his chest, feeling the heat of his skin seep into my hands.

"Hands behind your head," I instructed.

He obeyed, the motion stretching him out, baring him to me. I circled him slowly, my fingertips grazing his ribs, his hips, the line of his spine — a soft touch that belied the command simmering under it.

I stopped in front of him again, close enough that the heat of him licked against my skin. "Before we start the lesson, I think I'll give you something you've been wanting."

His brows furrowed in confusion, but the second I let my gaze drop down his body, realization flickered in his eyes.

"At the club," I reminded him, taking a small step forward, "you told me how much blow jobs turn you on."

"*Fuck*, Liv."

I gave him a slow, knowing smile, but then cocked my head to the side. "Oh, did I remember that incorrectly?"

"No," he said instantly. "I just... Christ, Liv, if you get on your knees for me, this is all going to be over well before it starts."

I pulled my ponytail behind my shoulder, bracing my hands on his shoulders and leaning in until my breath was against his lips. "Not all of it. Just round one," I said with a wink.

And then I kissed a slow, fiery trail down his chest, his abdomen, until I was seated on my knees with his big, beautiful, heavy cock in my face.

"You may touch me," I said, sliding my hands up his thighs with my nails playfully digging in. "Fist my hair. Set the pace. Make me take you deep."

Carter groaned when I said those words, when I punctuated them with the first lash of my tongue against his shaft. I ran it from base to tip, slowly, my eyes locked on his.

"To be clear, you are not the one in control. I will stop when I want. You will only come if I allow it. But you may show me what you like. You may beg for what you want."

His nostrils flared as he stared down at me, and I kept his gaze as I let saliva gather in my mouth and then spit on him, coating him with wetness that my hand could play with.

His moan was deep and throaty when I slid my fist over him, my touch feather-light and teasing. I coated him, and then I squeezed a little tighter, giving him two full pumps before I lowered my lips to his crown.

When I sucked the first inch of him inside, he shuddered, his hands moving toward my hair. But he hesitated, unsure, his brows folding together as he watched me withdraw and then push down farther.

"I won't give permission again," I warned.

Determination settled in on his face, and he grabbed me with force — one hand sliding around to grip my ponytail and the other fisting at the base of his cock. "Open," he rasped.

I smiled as I did.

"Stick your tongue out."

Oh, Rookie came to play.

I did as he asked, and then moaned when Carter ran his crown and shaft along my tongue. He inhaled a hot breath at the sound, at the vibration, and then began to slowly fuck my mouth.

He guided himself in the beginning, hand on his cock as he flexed in and out. But when I challenged his pace, when I took more of him than he was pushing and gagged a bit, he cursed, both hands coming to cradle my face.

And he surrendered to his need.

His cock slid inside my throat, deep, enough to make my eyes water when he flexed and held it there.

"Yes, Liv. Fuck, you look so pretty with my cock in your mouth."

I hummed my approval of the dirty talk, opening my throat and working with my breath as best I could. He was big, and though I'd put myself through deep throat training, it was always a little difficult for me to settle in at first. I had to remind myself I was safe, that I could breathe, that I could take a break any time I needed to.

With that reminder, I relaxed, and used my hands to grab Carter's ass and help him fuck my throat.

He was tentative at first, slow and reverent from where he watched me above. But the more I swirled my tongue and took him deep, the more I kept my gaze on his, the more erratic he became. He pumped harder, faster, flexing in so deep that I would gag and choke.

And he loved it.

"God, yes. You love choking on my cock, don't you?"

I moaned and nodded, and Carter's head fell back, all his muscles coiling.

I knew he was close.

And that was the exact moment I pulled back.

"Fuck," he cursed, his cock jumping when I left it completely untouched. I loved the sight of it, how he trembled and fisted my ponytail tight. "Fuck, fuck, fuck, Liv."

I pinned him with a wicked grin, wiping the corner of my mouth with my thumb before I held up my hands in a silent plea for him to help me stand.

He swallowed hard as he did, his breath fiery and shallow.

"I hope you enjoyed your treat for being a good boy," I purred, and then I nodded toward my bed. "Now, lie down, lube your ass, and keep fucking that perfect hand of yours while I get ready."

The storm swirling inside him was so apparent in his wide eyes. There was a little fear there, a little hesitance — but it was overridden by curiosity, by desire, by trust.

"May I kiss you first?"

The question surprised me so much I couldn't hide my shock. I blinked, lips parting, the words throwing me out of the scene.

Carter didn't back down. His eyes searched mine, patient.

"Um... yes," I answered on a whisper. "Yes. You may kiss me."

I wasn't sure I understood the relief that washed over him then, but I didn't have time to process it before his hands were sliding in to frame my face and he was pulling my mouth to his.

The kiss was tender and sweet, longing, like he was trying to speak to me through it. He kissed me once, twice, before opening his mouth and asking me to do the same. His tongue swept in to dance with mine, and electricity sparked between my thighs with the touch.

"Whatever is going on, just know I'm here with you," he whispered.

And then the sweetness was gone.

The kiss turned hungrier, more frantic, laced with passion and arousal. I wove my hands through his hair and arched into it, and Carter wrapped me up fully, making me feel so safe and protected in his arms.

"I love tasting myself on you," he rasped against my lips.

I moaned, kissing him harder, all while my heart beat with a very unsteady, very unfamiliar rhythm in my chest.

When he pulled back, my lids were heavier, my hands clinging to his shoulders like I'd fall if he didn't hold me steady.

Wordlessly, he lifted my hand to his lips to kiss the back of it with a mischievous smirk, and then he did as I commanded, walking to the bed and crawling into it before reaching for the lube.

My pulse ticked up, anticipation thrumming through me like a river.

I stepped into the harness, buckling it tight around my hips as I watched him recline against my pillows. His hand was already between his legs, slick fingers working over himself with slow, deliberate circles.

The sight alone made my breath hitch.

"Such a good boy," I murmured, adjusting the strap-on, testing the weight of it in my hand. "You take directions so well."

His eyes darted to mine, heat sparking there. I marked all the proof of his anxiety, from the pinch of his brows to the thick swallow that constricted his throat. But under that surface-level emotion was what I loved to see most.

Excitement.

I crawled up the bed, the mattress dipping under my knees as I came between his spread thighs. My palm slid up his shin, over his knee, tracing the thick muscle of his quad until I rested my hand on his wrist. "Don't stop," I instructed. "I want you touching yourself while I'm inside you."

He swallowed and nodded, his hand returning to his cock as I slicked the toy with lube. Then I reached for the lube bottle again, pouring more into my palm before stroking it along his entrance, my fingers pressing just enough to feel him shiver.

"Breathe for me, Rookie."

I lined the toy up, my free hand braced beside his ribs, holding his gaze. The moment I began to push in, his lips parted in a quiet gasp.

"That's it," I whispered. "Let me in... nice and slow. You're doing so fucking well."

He nodded, but his hand on his cock sped up instinctively. I smiled at the unconscious honesty of it, working myself in inch by blissful inch.

I wanted him to feel every single one.

We kept our eyes locked. The air between us thickened, heavy with the sound of our breathing, the faint squeak of the harness shifting, the wet slide of his hand. And when I was finally seated all the way in, Carter whimpered.

"Fucking hell, Liv." He gasped the words, his hand moving over his cock with more intensity as he looked where I was nestled between his legs.

I withdrew just an inch before thrusting inside again, this time tilting my aim up to brush along his prostate.

The moan he let out was intense and unashamed, a higher pitch than normal, his eyes squeezing shut as he flexed his hips into his hand.

"That's it," I coaxed, picking up the rhythm to mirror the way he stroked himself. "Feel me. Let go."

It didn't take long — I could see the heat climbing his cheeks, the tension gathering in his abs. His breathing quickened, his fist working faster, and I matched him, hips rocking in time with his strokes until his whole body went taut.

"Liv—"

"Tell me."

"I'm coming. I'm—"

I pushed in hard, deep, and that was all it took. He came with a shuddering cry, spilling over his abdomen and chest, his entire body shaking and his free hand gripping my thigh tight.

Power hummed through my veins as I watched him,

as I fucked him to ecstasy and bore witness to the way he completely gave in to the moment, to *me*.

"Wow. Look at you," I praised when he squeezed out the last of his release, his hand falling slack as aftershocks rolled through him.

I slowed instantly, easing out with care so I didn't pull too quickly. I savored the way Carter looked now — dazed, flushed, gorgeous.

"Incredible, Rook," I praised, my voice soft now. I removed the strap before slowly climbing up his body, pressing a kiss to his hip, then to the trail of his abdomen, tasting the salt of his release as I worked my way up to his chest. "No one turns me on like you do. You know that? No one does this for me the way you do."

His breathing was still uneven as I showered him with praises, but his arm wrapped around my shoulders, pulling me close. I let him, settling into the space we'd just made together, my hand smoothing over his sternum in slow circles.

"You're safe," I reminded him. "You listened so well. I'll be dreaming about this."

He blew out a long breath, looking down at me with a sleepy, sated grin. "*You'll* be dreaming about it? I just had my whole world blown up."

I chuckled, pressing up to kiss his jaw. "How did it feel?"

"It was more intense than the plugs, a little painful at first but... not for long. I felt like I was instantly overwhelmed, but in a hot way. Like I felt like I could come as soon as you were inside me."

"Because it feels forbidden. It's new and exciting and out of the norm."

He nodded. "And then there was the sight of you on top of me in this," he said, plucking at the lace around my breast. "You look good enough to eat, Liv. And I'd very much like to do just that."

"Tonight was about you," I half-heartedly argued as he started to kiss his way down my body. "I need to get you cleaned up."

"We can take a shower after," he said, nipping at my thigh. "And don't lie to me, Mistress. We both know you needed tonight."

I leaned up on my elbows, watching him navigate my garters and silk thong until he had me exposed for him.

"It's okay to have needs, too," he said before I could argue, spreading my legs wide. He tossed my thighs on top of his shoulders. "You can be in control and still receive."

"So, it's you giving the lessons now?" I breathed in a challenge.

"If my student will shut up and let me," he shot right back.

And then his mouth was on me, and all other thoughts were lost.

Chapter 20

The Weight of the World

Carter

It was a funny thing, being on break in the middle of the season.

I knew how to relax in the summer. I knew how to go on a vacation, golf with the guys, or spend an entire day on the water without a care in the world. When it was offseason, I could easily turn things... *off* — my brain, my body, my routine.

But in the middle of a season where we were in a race for the playoffs, I found it impossible.

I decided to stick to as much of a routine as possible. Instead of practice in the mornings, I woke up around six to jog or hit the bike. I got soft tissue work done and worked through any physical therapy I needed. Once a week, I went to Doctor Arman.

But every day there was this gap — the place where practice or travel or a game would typically go.

There was no practicing on break — league's orders — and so I filled that time as best I could.

I did go for a round of golf with the guys, which was fun, especially since Aleks still *really* sucked and we all got to make fun of him for a few hours.

One day, I cleaned my house top to bottom. I had a housekeeper, but I *really* dug in, organizing and decluttering and all the things that usually went ignored during the season.

I took Zamboni on long walks around the Bay, everywhere from the Riverwalk to the Fort De Soto dog beach.

But most of the time those first five days of break?

I thought of Livia.

She was the first thing that popped into my head in the morning, and the last on my mind before I drifted off to sleep each night. I saw her sultry eyes in the shower, felt her any time I wrapped up in a towel or blanket, smelled her when I lit a candle — vanilla and jasmine. I heard her smoky voice on replay without trying, all the words she'd said to me the night I surrendered to her in a way I never thought I could.

"No one turns me on like you do. You know that? No one does this for me the way you do."

I tortured myself wondering if it had just been talk; if she'd just been praising me as part of the play, or if she'd meant it.

Because if she did...

It lit me on fire to think so, to think that I could be something more to that woman than just a project and a paycheck.

Her sporadic texts had fed me in the days of not seeing her, though I wished for more. But two nights ago, the texts had stopped, all the banter gone and my patience along with it.

I had to see her.

And so, I found myself "coincidently nearby" her dental practice on Wednesday afternoon, about ten minutes before I knew she'd be done for the day. She'd mentioned in an offhand comment during our date night that she took a half day in the middle of the week, letting her partner take over while she got caught up on admin or just fucked off for the day.

I hoped with everything I had in me that she was in the mood to do the latter.

The glass doors whispered shut behind me as I entered, the cool blast of air-conditioning cutting the humid sting of the afternoon. The faint smell of mint and something floral floated in the air, a perfect mask for the tang of antiseptic underneath.

Soft piano music played over hidden speakers, barely loud enough to compete with the gentle hum of a water feature in the corner. The reception desk gleamed white and gold, like it belonged in a luxury hotel lobby, and every chair in the waiting area looked too nice to actually sit in.

"Mr. Fabri," Tasha said with a warm smile that morphed into a polite frown as she glanced at her monitor. She wore her usual fitted blazer over a silk blouse, nails painted a pearly nude. "I don't see an appointment for you today..."

"I'm here to see Liv," I said easily, or at least I tried to. My tongue tripped on the next part. "As a... friend."

My heart rebelled at the use of that word, but I tamed it with a swallow and a straightening of my spine.

Tasha's brows ticked up, but she reached for the phone on her desk. "One moment." She murmured into the receiver, glancing at me with a knowing smirk I wasn't sure I liked, then set it back in its cradle. "She'll see you. Come on back."

The hallway was hushed except for the faint whir of something mechanical in one of the closed operatories we passed. The scent of mint got sharper the deeper we went. I couldn't help but look around the office with new eyes. It wasn't like I hadn't been there plenty of times before, but I knew the woman behind the name more now, and I felt invigorated being in the place she spent so much of her time, in the practice she dreamed of opening for so long.

Tasha led me to the far corner office with a glass wall, blinds half-drawn. Through the slats, I caught a glimpse of Livia at her desk.

Her bun was sleek and perfect, every strand locked into place.

And that was the only thing about her that looked composed.

Her white coat hung on the back of her chair; the satin rose sleeves of her blouse rolled to her elbows as she scribbled notes over a stack of patient charts. Her jaw was tight, her brows pinched together, shoulders hunched over like they carried the weight of the world.

She didn't look up right away when Tasha let me in and closed the door behind her as she exited. Livia appeared to be too focused on whatever was in front of her. And for a second, I just stood there in the doorway, feeling the knot in my chest tighten at the sight of her.

"Hello, Doctor."

And even though Tasha had called ahead of my entrance, Livia still jumped as if I'd knocked a stack of books to the ground rather than greeted her in a soft, even-keeled voice. She looked up at me and sighed like she was annoyed by my presence or her reaction to it or both. "What are you doing here?"

I crossed to the chair on the other side of her desk and took a seat, crossing one ankle over the opposite knee as I recited the words I'd acted out in my head a dozen times now. "Well, I was just in the area, and I remembered that you had a half day on Wednesdays. I thought I'd come by and say hi."

She blinked at me, eyes drifting to where I'd crossed my legs before they found my gaze again. "By all means, make yourself comfortable."

"I brought cookies," I said, holding up the brown box in my hand. "Bake'n Babes. You said they were your favorite, yeah?"

Livia softened, just marginally, like she was surprised I remembered. And then she shook her head, getting right back to the task in front of her. "I don't have time for this, Carter."

"You don't have time for a Fruity Pebbles cookie?" I mused, pulling one from the box. "Because I have sources that say it's impossible to be stressed with one of these in your mouth."

"Who says I'm stressed?"

It was my turn to blink at her. "Oh. Yeah. My apologies. You don't seem stressed at all."

She glared at me for half a second, and then her shoulders deflated, and she sank back in her chair, flicking her pen onto the desk and pinching the bridge of her nose. She sat like that for a moment before thrusting her other hand out toward me and gesturing for the cookie.

I grinned in victory as I handed it to her.

When she unwrapped the monstrous thing, she took a bite so large it didn't make sense biologically for her mouth, and then she moaned, sinking farther into her chair.

"Besh fuhgging cookiesh eveh."

I chuckled. "I'm sure I agree with whatever you just said." I paused, frowning at the exhaustion that settled in on her face as she took another bite. "Busy week, I take it?"

She shrugged. "Not busy, per se, but hectic. I had back-to-back complex crown or bridge cases that both needed unexpected adjustments. One of our VIP clients insisted on a same-day slot, despite how we insisted that it would be impossible."

"One of my teammate's wives, perhaps?"

She didn't answer, but the look she gave me told me I'd hit the nail on the head. I chuckled.

"And I've been avoiding my part of the end-of-year reporting, but now have no choice but to tackle it if we're going to file on time." She took another bite of the cookie, letting her head fall back against her chair. "And I'm just so... tired."

I tilted my head to the side. "Not sleeping well?"

"Not with my mother calling me every night."

I stiffened at the mention of her mother. We hadn't talked about her family much since the night of our date. She'd mentioned that the drama was still hanging around at the game before we went to her place last week, but she'd made it clear she didn't want to discuss it, that what she needed was a distraction.

Was her telling me this now an invitation to ask questions?

Because I had a billion of them.

"Your sister's wedding," I mused.

Livia nodded.

"Are you ever going to tell me why this is such an issue, you attending one of the biggest days of your sister's life?"

Livia strained with the effort to bring her head upright again. "It's a boring and tragic story."

"I like tragedies. Big *Romeo and Juliet* fan here. And I think it should be up to me to decide if it's boring or not."

She groaned, shaking her head as she wrapped up the rest of the cookie and set it on her desk. "I don't know, Carter. I'm not really the talking type."

"Maybe you could try it. For me," I added.

Stupidly.

Like this woman would be tempted to do anything for my sake alone.

For a moment, Livia seemed to consider it. But she shook her head again and picked up her pen. "Not today."

I couldn't fight the flood of disappointment that overtook me, but I battled through the rush of water, undeterred.

"That's fine," I said, standing. I rounded her desk and took her pen from her hand.

"Hey!"

"But I think you're done working for today."

She cocked a brow at my audacity, the Domme inside her firing up instantly. "Oh, is that so, *Rookie*? Since when do you call the shots?"

"Since I walked into this office and saw my girl stretched past her limits and drowning."

Livia opened her mouth, but her brows softened, and not a single word came out.

"Nothing has changed. You're still the one who leads when it comes to us. But..." I leaned a hip against her desk, close enough to catch the faint trace of her perfume. "Maybe you could let me take the wheel for a little while — just enough to get you out of your head."

Her eyes narrowed, but not in that sharp, cut-me-down way she had. This was softer. Cautious. "You want me to... give you control?"

"Not all of it," I said quickly, shaking my head. "Just a piece. Give me the part of your world that's weighing you down right now. Let me carry it for you for the rest of the day. I'm not here to boss you around. I just..." I trailed off, shrugging. "I just want to help you breathe again."

For a long moment, she studied me, her pen still laying where I'd set it down. I could see the war happening behind her eyes — one side all logic and walls, the other tempted by the promise of letting someone else hold the rope for once.

Finally, she tilted her head. "What do you have in mind?"

The way she asked it wasn't pure suspicion. There was a thread of curiosity in there, too.

I grinned. "I guess you'll have to say yes to find out."

Chapter 21
A Real Gem
Livia

The water was so clear it looked from another planet, like we were gliding over liquid diamond, the sunlight fracturing on the surface in flashes of silver and gold. Below, the sandy bottom rippled with light, fish darting between long ribbons of eelgrass that swayed in the gentle current.

It was warm up here, the late-afternoon sun soaking into my bare skin, but the air carried the kiss of the icy springs, cooling me just enough that my shorts and slouchy long sleeve felt perfect. The neckline had slipped off one shoulder, the fabric fluttering every time the wind shifted.

I trailed my fingers over the top of the water, letting it glide between them, cool and silken. Each breath I took seemed to carry a little more of my stress away — blown off on the breeze, dissolved into the glassy river. Being at Weeki Wachee Springs on a weekday afternoon like this meant the water was mostly ours, save for the occasional bird gliding overhead or the soft hum of insects hiding in the moss-draped trees. The branches swayed, their shadows stretching and dancing across the surface, dappling my skin in shifting patterns of light and dark

With every ripple, every chirp, every lazy push of the paddle, I felt my shoulders loosen. My mind, for the first time in weeks, was quiet.

"I see why you like this," I admitted softly, peeling my gaze from the water to Carter. He was floating on his own board next to mine, his muscular legs folded beneath him, abs gleaming in the sunlight.

"Peaceful, isn't it?" he asked, using his paddle to guide his board. We didn't really have to paddle much now that we'd turned downstream. The first half of our paddle was all upstream, and that had been the first relief of the trip — slipping into a quiet workout, arms pumping, abdomen fired up to stabilize me as we made our way.

My mind had still been racing at the beginning, but the farther we went, the quieter it became.

"It is," I mused. "Reminds me of the way I feel when I'm making jewelry."

"Really? I feel like I'd be too focused to relax, working with those tiny pieces of metal."

"I think that's why I can relax," I said with an easy smile, one that felt like I was shaking off rust. "I'm so zeroed in on crafting that I don't have room in my brain to think of anything else. I get lost in the movements, and before I know it... it's like meditation."

"I'd like to see more of what you've made," Carter offered. "If you'll show me."

"I noticed you wear a ring."

He held up his pinky, wiggling it. "I do, indeed. It's been passed down through the gentlemen in my family since my great-great-grandfather. Dad gave it to me when I got drafted."

I paddled away from the bank with that smile still in place. "What are they like? Your parents. I know your coach was a complete ass, but I can't imagine anyone other than two human-form teddy bears raising a man like you."

Carter laughed at that, tilting his head side to side. "That's actually a pretty great way to describe them. I grew up in a house filled with laughter. My dad is a comedian. Not famous, obviously, but he does stand up and improv at the club in Hamilton."

"Ah, so *that's* where you get it from."

"Fortunately, his jokes are much better than mine," Carter said with a grin. "And Mom used to be the manager at the bank, but she retired when I gave them a big portion of my signing bonus. She was never really in love with her job. I think she just wanted something stable since Dad's work was... not."

My heart ached. "That sounds really nice."

"Being a comedian's son?" Carter's brows popped into his hairline. "I feel like you don't know any comedians, then."

I chuckled. "I just mean your whole childhood. I... I have no concept of what any of that would be like, but I could picture it — the beauty of Canada, a mom and dad who work to make ends meet and spend time with their son, all your waking time spent thinking of hockey. It just sounds really nice."

Carter frowned, his paddle slicing through the water. He opened his mouth, and I knew he was going to ask about my family, so I dodged before he could.

"Do you do it often?" I asked. "Paddleboarding?"

He sighed like he didn't appreciate the subject change, but fortunately, he let me make it. "More so in the offseason, but yes. That's why I bought a house right on the water. I just launch into the canal and paddle out to the river any time I want. Mornings are the best," he added. "Or summer evenings, when you can be out there at nine o'clock and still have daylight. I love watching the birds fly across a pink sky. Or hanging out with the dolphins."

"Hanging out with dolphins?" I repeated incredulously.

He nodded, making a face like I had no idea what I was missing. "Oh, yeah. They love me. I may have no game when it comes to the ladies, but porpoises?" He scoffed, huffing on his nails before buffing them on his chest. "Can't keep them away."

"Pretty sure we have bottlenose dolphins, not porpoises."

"Technicalities."

I rolled my eyes. "You really need to stop saying that, you know."

"What? A man can't brag about being a dolphin magnet? Also pretty popular with the manatees. I bet one shows up any moment."

"I *mean* saying that you don't have game. It's not true." I paddled a bit closer to him. "It's not your game that's been stopping you. It's your lack of confidence."

"Obviously."

"But you don't lack it as much anymore, do you?"

I shot the challenge at him with an arch of my brow, and Carter smirked. I wished I could see his eyes under his sunglasses.

"I may be coming around," he conceded with that grin still locked in place. "I have a good teacher."

"Damn straight, you do."

Suddenly, Carter shot upright on his board, eyes wide as he pointed to the water beside mine. "Look!"

My natural reaction was to jump and scream a little, which highly annoyed me and highly amused Carter. He laughed, reaching out for my hand and pulling until our boards were side by side.

"Look," he repeated, and when I followed his finger to the water, I saw it.

A manatee.

"Told you." Carter smirked, waggling his brows at me. "The sea cows got it bad for Fabio."

I shook my head on a laugh, but then was lost in watching the magnificent creature. It was massive — easily ten feet long — and yet moved with a gentleness that didn't match its size. The nickname sea cow made sense, not just for the bulk of its body, but for the calm way it grazed its way through the river. At first, I thought there was only one, but then another drifted up beside it, their wide, gray backs gliding just beneath our boards like two slow-moving boulders.

"Oh, watch, they're coming up for air," Carter said, pointing again.

Sure enough, the pair surfaced in tandem, their whiskered snouts breaking the water. They lingered so close we could have reached out and touched them if we'd dared — but we didn't. We only watched, breath caught, as their dark eyes blinked back at us before they slipped beneath the surface again, weightless and unhurried.

I leaned back on my palms, soaking in the sunlight as the manatees continued upstream. Our boards drifted lazily in the current, the whole river humming with peace, like it, too, was in awe of the gentle giants passing through.

"Will you talk to me now?" Carter asked, his voice soft.

"What do you want me to say?"

"How about anything other than, 'I'm fine.'"

I let out a long sigh, staring up at the blue sky above us, at the white, puffy clouds floating by. A big part of me bucked like a bull. I felt the familiar resistance like a hand over my mouth preventing me from saying a word.

But there was a softer side to me that had suddenly grown teeth.

I heard her banging on my rib cage, felt her nails digging in as she attempted to scratch her way out.

For reasons I couldn't name and was too tired to try to figure out... I wanted to let Carter in.

"My mother has been on my ass about my sister's wedding," I said almost mechanically. It was like my body didn't know how to act now that I was choosing to speak to someone other than Maven. "During the game last week, she called me and said in not so many words that it would probably be better if I didn't show, since I'm not around much anymore and it might make people feel awkward." I paused, laughing a little. "And that I'd be alone, which would add to the discomfort."

"What the fuck?"

I smiled wider. "Oh, yes. My mother is a real gem."

"Why would she say that?"

"Because it's true," I said. "I am alone. Of course, she leaves out the part that she's one of the reasons I prefer it this way."

I swallowed the longer Carter stared at me. I could feel the more dominant side of me straining for the wheel, could sense the need burning through me to steer the conversation back to something safe.

"Anyway, she called me again the other night," I said, stomach tightening at the memory. "She was going on and on about how they needed to finalize bridesmaid dresses, and I needed to make up my mind. She wants me to commit one way or the other, and honestly, I can't blame her for being upset that I'm taking so long. I can blame her for a lot of things, but not that. I *should* have made up my mind by now... but I feel frozen."

Carter was quiet for a moment, both of us just using our paddles to straighten out our boards and then let the river take us.

"What happened with your mom?"

I shook my head, and in a panic, the softer side of me that had been trying to get out vanished. It was like the jerk of a car that was on track for an exit before getting yanked back on the highway. "Sorry, not ready to go there."

"Okay. Then... how about your sister? What's your relationship like with her?"

I blew out a breath. Lacey was safer territory, at least. "Complicated," I answered honestly. "I love Lacey. We were super close when we were younger, always sharing each other's clothes, playing in the yard, curling up in bed to read together at night." I smiled, the memory so far in my past it made my chest ache now. "She was always our parents' favorite. I know they're not supposed to have a favorite, but they did. We both knew it. Lacey was just more of what they wanted in a daughter. She was effortlessly poised, smart, beautiful."

"You are every single one of those things," Carter argued.

I pinned him with a look. "She's also docile, and agreeable, and happy to follow whatever path my parents lay out for her."

"Ah," Carter said in way of understanding. "I see the difference now."

I nodded. "It wasn't so bad when we were younger, because we had each other, so I didn't much care if Mom and Dad had a favorite. I was Lacey's favorite." I smiled. "She used to always want me to do her hair just like mine, used to ask me about boys and fashion." I paused. "But things changed in high school, right before I was set to graduate."

"How so?" Carter asked when I didn't automatically elaborate.

I shook my head. "I just went through something she couldn't understand, and it changed me in a way that complicated everything in my life — including my relationship with her."

To his credit, Carter didn't press on what the thing was that had happened to me. Maybe he already knew it was an off-limits topic.

"Anyway, we kind of grew apart when I graduated. I went one way; she went the other. We talk sometimes on the phone, text each other, send silly memes on Instagram, but..." I shrugged. "There's not much there anymore."

Carter nodded his understanding, and a comfortable quiet fell over us as we flowed into a narrower strip of the river. We both picked up our paddles to steer again.

"So, you don't want to go?" he asked after a moment.

"I want to support Lacey and be there for her. I want to celebrate her. But I don't want to be around my parents, or around their friends."

"Would you feel better if you had someone with you?"

I scrunched up my nose. "Doubtful."

"Take me."

I blinked, and then barked out a laugh. "To my sister's wedding?"

"Yeah. Why not?"

"Because then everyone would think we're dating?"

"And that would be the worst thing in the world," he shot back with sarcasm.

A strange noise came from my throat, something between a laugh and an incredulous scoff. I looked at him like he was crazy, but when he didn't back down, something inside me flared to life.

Panic.

I felt it in the shortness of my breath, in the way my hands suddenly went clammy, sweat gathering at the back of my neck.

What the fuck was I doing?

I'd let him in. I'd gone far past the outlines of our agreement and into a territory neither of us knew how to navigate. And this was exactly why it was a mistake to do so.

Because I told him a little about my past, and now he was trying to fix it all, to save me.

To be a part of my future.

I needed to take the reins. Immediately.

"Excuse me?" I asked, Domme voice taking over, all business. "I'll have to punish you for that."

Carter's grin was infectious. "Mm, is that so? What are you going to do to me, *Mistress*?"

"Drop the smile," I snapped, and then nodded toward an alcove in the river up ahead. "Paddle there. Fast. Find us somewhere no one can see."

He laughed a little, but when I only arched a brow in response, his smile fell. "You're serious?"

"Do I look *un*serious?"

He shook his head, tongue in cheek with a grin playing at the corners of his lips before he did as I said, paddling off in quick strokes. I followed, slower, taking my time until I paddled into the shady cove I'd directed him to.

It was a little pull off, no houses on the shore and thick trees creating a sort of grove. Carter waved me over to where he'd paddled under the protection of the trees, and once I was with him, somewhat blocked from the world...

I slipped off my board and mounted his.

"What are you doing?" he asked in a hushed whisper, but he was still smiling as he helped me climb into his lap, his hands playful on my waist. My ankle strap was still hooked to my board, keeping it from floating away.

"No talking," I clipped. "Take your cock out."

"Here?"

"Do not make me ask again."

"I don't think you *asked* me anything," he teased, but he was already moving for the strings on his swim shorts, and I felt control slowly slipping back into my bloodstream.

"I'm going to ride you until I come. You are not allowed to come with me. Do you understand?"

He let out a groan, like it both turned him on and tortured him to hear that. "Yes, ma'am."

The second the words were out of his mouth, I spit on my hand, coated him, slid my swimsuit bottoms to the side and sat all the way down on his beautiful cock.

We both shuddered when I was fully seated, Carter dropping his forehead to my chest and gripping my hips hard. "Christ, Liv. You feel so fucking good."

"Hush," I snapped, and then I started to ride him, my veins humming as control and power rushed through me.

Home.

This is home.

"Watch. Make sure no one sees us," I commanded.

And then I gave in.

It may not have felt like it to Carter, but even telling him as much as I had made me feel off-kilter, like I was hovering on the edge of a cliff with one foot in the air, losing strength and balance.

I'd given him all I could, and now I needed to take.

I closed my eyes and surrendered to the feel of him, to the knowledge that anyone could see us at any moment. Someone might be watching right now.

That thought turned me on even more, and I rode faster, rolling my hips to find the friction I needed against my clit.

I rocked and rode, holding fast to his shoulders, savoring all the groans of restraint that slipped from his perfect lips.

I came quickly, muffling my moans with my mouth around his trap, teeth sinking into the flesh just enough to satiate me and make him hiss with delight. And because I was a gracious Domme, I let him come when I was finished, let him pump himself inside me until he trembled and cursed and clutched me to him.

We didn't talk about my family after that.

And I found my balance again, the scales tipped neatly back in my favor.

But with Carter, balance never stayed put for long. He had a way of slipping past my defenses without even meaning to, loosening bricks I'd mortared in years ago.

I wondered if it would be his persistence that toppled the wall...

Or if I'd be the one handing him the sledgehammer.

Chapter 22

How Wrong You Are

Livia

Three days passed without seeing Carter in person, but he made sure I didn't forget him.

I threw myself into work for the rest of the week, burying my head in numbers, emails, and meetings until my eyes burned. Still, he had a way of slipping in. A text waiting for me every time I stepped out for a coffee run. A bag of Thai takeout delivered to my door after a twelve-hour day, no note except *Eat, Coach*. A late-night call when I was already in bed, his voice low and lazy as he complained about how bored he was on break, yapping about absolutely nothing until I finally told him to hang up and go to sleep.

But it was the third day that he really got under my skin.

First it was a smug selfie on the golf course, his arm slung around one of his teammates, the other holding up a gaudy little trophy like he'd just won the Masters instead of whatever beer-fueled scramble they'd been playing.

Something about his goofy, care-free grin, and the fact that he'd wanted to text me had an unbidden smile spreading on my face. It was like he was a proud cat with a mouse in his teeth prancing over to show his owner. I loved that he thought of me, that he wanted to brag to me, to show me how well he'd done.

And then I'd promptly scolded myself for feeling anything at all.

Then, hours later, when I thought I finally had a hold on my emotions, another photo came through — this one darker and grainier. It was him, Jaxson, and some rookies I wasn't too familiar with at a bar, drinks in hand, neon lights bleeding into the frame. The text beneath it read:

Carter: Alright, Coach. Think I'm ready for the big leagues? We're at Boomer's and there's a whole group of women trying to get behind the ropes of our VIP section. Should I try to land one and take her home?

The heat that flared in my chest was immediate and uninvited — sharp, hot, and blatantly territorial. He was acting in accordance with our contract, asking me for permission before he pursued anyone else.

But I was pissed he even wanted to.

I rolled my eyes and typed back with a fury I didn't know I possessed.

Me: Bold of you to think you're ready for that. Come here and I'll show you exactly how wrong you are.

He'd showed up an hour later.

I had him bound before he could get a word out, delivering a firm smack to his ass as punishment for even suggesting another woman could fill my role.

He'd only grinned, leaning forward to steal a quick kiss before murmuring words that tilted my whole world.

"Come on, now. You know I don't actually want anyone else. I just wanted your attention. And I got it."

I'd reacted with another sharp smack on his ass, this one more for me than him, because damned if I didn't smile.

Damned if I didn't like hearing that he only wanted me.

Now, it was Valentine's Day — my least favorite holiday in the fucking world. And since my best friend had a husband now, our tradition of ordering takeout and binge-watching Bravo shows had taken a backseat to her getting some real romantic action.

I wasn't mad at her for it, though. In fact, it'd been me who'd had to help her get her head out of her ass and move past her trauma to let Vince in. And I'd been happy to do it.

But it didn't change the fact that Valentine's Day sucked.

Which was why I'd entertained Carter's text this morning asking me what I was up to, if I wanted to hang out. *Let's have a lazy non-romantic bum day off*, he'd proposed.

And like an idiot, I'd said yes.

I played it off like I was just bored and had nothing better to do. The truth was I didn't want to be alone on this dumb holiday.

And I wanted to see him.

So here we were, both of us on Carter's couch, him kicked back on one end watching a golf documentary, and me with my feet in his lap, pliers in hand as I bent a stubborn jump ring into place. The delicate chain was cool against my fingertips, the gemstones clicking softly together every time I shifted them. A little pile of extra links and beads rested in a dish at my side, catching the lamplight as I worked on the bracelet I was set to give Chloe as a wedding gift when she and Will returned from their trip. Zamboni was snuggled between me and the back of the couch, snoozing away with his head on my stomach.

We'd had a lazy day just as Carter suggested. He'd arranged at-home massages for us, which I didn't realize I needed so terribly until I was a sated bag of bones afterward. There was a quick group FaceTime call after with Chloe and Will, long enough for them to show us their luxury hotel room right on the water before bidding us adieu until their elopement party once they were back. Then, Carter had made us a ridiculous snack board from all the random things in his pantry, from Zebra cakes and popcorn to aged cheddar cheese and garlic olives.

We'd laid in the sun, watching the boats drift by in the canal behind his house. I'd taken a nap while Carter played video games. When I woke up, we went for a long, slow walk with Zamboni, throwing a Frisbee at the park until he ran out all his energy. And now, the evening was winding down, the sun set, our bellies full of the Mexican food we'd had delivered — along with cookies from Bake'n Babes — and I was as happy as a royal pet as we did our own separate things, quietly, together.

"I'm glad we did this."

Carter's voice shook me out of my jewelry-making meditation, his hand squeezing my ankle in his lap. It was too intimate, the way I let him hold me like that, and yet I was powerless to fight against it tonight.

Because I was glad, too.

I was glad to not be alone. I was glad to feel so cozy and warm inside his little house on the water. I was glad to have my feet in his lap and his dog's head in mine.

I'd never had it like this with a man. I'd never let them get close enough to even try.

I smiled, eyes still on the delicate chain and stones in my hand. "It wasn't a terrible day."

"Whoa, easy there. I might think you actually like spending time with me."

I snorted, setting another bead on the chain. "Don't push your luck. But, speaking of people I actually *do* like spending time with, how was your day with Ava the other day? I have her tomorrow, and I'm thinking manis and pedis are in order."

"You know she'll love that. As long as you let her get hockey pucks painted on her nails, anyway," Carter said.

Will and Chloe were on their elopement trip, and as a group, we'd convinced them to leave Ava here with us. We knew how much they loved her and wanted her to be a part of their union, but we also knew the two of them needed some alone time to celebrate first. So, as a team, we'd planned to make sure Ava was cared for in their absence.

"My day with her was pretty low key. She wanted to get on the ice and practice, so I took her to the rink out in Wesley Chapel."

"Isn't that against the rules of the league? You're not supposed to practice right now, are you?"

"It wasn't *me* who was practicing. Besides, no one has to know — least of all Coach, who would probably pull me off the ice by the ear if he found out."

I chuckled. "Well, I'm sure she had fun, but I bet she's bouncing off the walls waiting for Chloe and Will to get home."

Carter snorted. "Or praying they don't. Mia Love has been her nanny all week and she's had the rest of us to entertain her twenty-four-seven — pretty sure that kid's living her best life."

"True. She's probably hoping her parents extend their trip another month."

Carter's grin softened. "She really is a good kid, though. If I ever had one, I'd want one just like her."

The comment startled me. My eyes flicked up, but Carter was watching the screen again now, like the statement was a flippant one, and not the kind that sank my stomach to the floor like an anchor.

"Do you...want kids?" I asked carefully.

I couldn't understand the feeling that swirled through me when I asked, the way my chest tightened and my fingers stilled where I was working on the bracelet.

But before I could digest any of it, Carter let out a short laugh — one of half amusement, half disbelief. "Me? God, no. I mean..." He rubbed the back of his neck, shaking his head as a bigger laugh tumbled out. "I can barely keep this one alive." He roughly scrubbed Zamboni's head then, who peeked one eye open before letting out a huff and closing it again. "I still forget to do laundry until I'm out of socks," Carter continued. "I feel like a kid myself most days. And I'm in therapy, still trying to figure my own shit out." He waved a hand over me. "Case in point, our little arrangement. The idea of being responsible for another human, of possibly *causing* the trauma that they have to go to therapy for one day? That's terrifying."

The sound of his laugh lingered, bright and easy, but it twisted like a rusty knife in my gut.

Carter didn't notice as he added, "Besides, it's not like I've even managed to land a girl for a date. Dad material, I am not."

My stomach soured. I pressed my lips together, hiding the sting, tucking my truth safely away. It wasn't like I was really considering telling him my own plans, to freeze my eggs and have a kid on my own one day, but if the inkling had been there, it was eviscerated now.

If he only knew the real trauma I held onto from my own parents, he would surely think I was certifiably insane to want a child of my own.

He looked like he was ready to ask, the words right on the tip of his tongue, but I redirected us before he had the chance.

"I'm surprised you didn't take a vacation or something for your break," I said, guiding us back to solid ground.

Carter looked at me a long moment, like he didn't want to drop the previous conversation yet, but he must have read my cue, because he didn't press. Instead, his eyes floated back to the screen as he shrugged. "Nah, nowhere I really want to go. Besides, we're still in season. I didn't want to clock out too much."

"Is that why our *lazy bum day* had to wait to start until after you ran five miles and got in a workout?"

"Listen, I'm playing the best I ever have, in large part thanks to you," he added with a little wink, as if it was nothing, as if those words didn't light me up like a firework. "And I'm not about to lose that momentum. I want the playoffs. I want the Cup."

"Do you really mean that?"

"That I want to win it all?" He scoffed. "Hell yeah. I know a lot of people don't think we have it this year, that since we won a couple years ago, it's not our time. But even though we've had some players leave, I still feel like—"

"I meant the other part," I said, cutting him short. "That you think you're playing your best because of what we've been doing."

Carter's expression was strange, something between a frown and a smile like he couldn't believe I was even asking. He grabbed the remote to pause the documentary, turning to face me fully.

"You're seriously asking that?"

"I'm sure it's your therapist, and Coach, and all the drills—"

"Liv, I one hundred percent am playing at my best because of you."

Why was my throat constricting?

Why did my heart feel like it was going to fly away?

"But it's just been sex."

"To you, maybe," he said, another unreadable expression washing over his face. "But everything you've said, everything you've allowed me to feel... it's unlocked something in me. I'm not overthinking. I'm taking control when I need to, without hesitation, but also falling back and letting my other teammates lead when they have the momentum. I'm acting on instinct for the first time since I was a kid." He shook his head. "I can't put it into words, but I *know* it's from this. From us." He smiled, squeezing my ankle again. "From you."

There was no fighting my own smile that mirrored his. "Good. I'm glad to hear that."

"Best two mil I've ever spent."

"You spend two mil often?"

"Never before in my life, but I'm still certain."

I chuckled, but there was a question heavy in my heart after hearing him say all that, one that felt like sludge as I tried to speak. "Speaking of which... I feel like we should check in. How are you feeling? Do you think... maybe you're ready to graduate?"

Carter's smile fell, but he recovered quickly. "I mean, I don't think I'm the one who gets to decide that, Professor."

I rolled my eyes but couldn't ignore how my stomach flipped that he didn't say yes, that he still wanted to do whatever it was we were doing.

This is dangerous, a voice inside me warned. *Don't be stupid.*

Business transaction.

Means to an end.

Freeze eggs.

Set up life.

But it was Valentine's Day.

Who called off a kinky sex arrangement on the holiday of love?

"True," I finally said, heart picking up its pace as I set my jewelry to the side. "Then that leads me to my next question."

Carter cocked a brow, waiting.

"Is playtime included in this whole lazy day itinerary?"

My smirk was wicked, and instantly, I felt Carter harden under where my legs were in his lap. He hummed, hand traveling up the inside of my shin, my knee, my thigh.

"You can play with me anytime you want, Liv," he promised.

I leaned up, meeting him in the middle, my lips dangerously close to his. "Then take me to the biggest mirror you have and lose the clothes, Rook."

Chapter 23

Stand Your Ground

Carter

In what had to be the wildest emotional moment of my life, I was naked and on my knees in front of the large mirror in my bedroom, and I'd never felt stronger, sexier, or more powerful than I did then.

Which was insane — because I wasn't the one in charge.

Livia stood behind me, tall and composed, her hand tangled in my hair, her gaze locked with mine in the reflection. It was magical, how quickly she'd transformed. One moment, she's this cozy, comfortable woman wearing my t-shirt with her feet in my lap, and the next, she's wearing nudity like a ballgown and commanding my attention, my obedience.

"This," she said, her voice low and smooth and completely unhurried, "is where we see exactly what you've learned. Everything I've taught you — without fear, without hesitation. You're not hiding behind the game face, or a joke, or what you think people want from you.

You're owning it. You're claiming it. This is where you stop waiting for permission and start demanding what you want."

I swallowed, heat prickling the back of my neck.

Her grip tightened in my hair, tilting my chin up until I was looking directly into my own eyes.

"Look at yourself," she said. "Look how desperate you are for it. That's good. That's where we start."

And *God*, it wrecked me — seeing myself like that. Not just on my knees for her but wanting to be there. She was right. I was desperate. My knees were spread, cock hard, chest heaving with anticipation.

I didn't feel an ounce of shame about it.

All the fears I'd had when we'd first started, the embarrassment I'd felt... it no longer existed. Livia had snuffed it out with the structure she provided, with the way she made me feel safe to explore any want or need.

"Touch yourself," she ordered.

I curled my fist around myself, every nerve ending lit, my own reflection suddenly foreign and raw as I watched the man in the mirror act without hesitation.

"Slower," she soothed. "I want you to see what you look like when you can't stand it anymore."

Changing the pace took effort, my body crying out for me to keep going. I squirmed at the switch in sensation, looking up to Livia in the mirror for permission to make my next move.

"Don't look at me — look at you," she murmured. "Watch how you fall apart for me. That's the face I want. Desperate. Hungry. Mine."

Mine.

The word was like a nail to my coffin of hope.

She doesn't mean it like that, my common sense tried to argue, but my desire overpowered that logic. I wanted to believe it. Even if just for now, I wanted to believe that Livia wanted me, that she felt possessive over me, that I was hers and she was mine.

I thought briefly of the text I'd sent her last night, teasing her about using what she'd taught me so far to get another woman in my bed. Even if she'd granted permission, there was no way in hell I actually would have tried. What started as a deal between us had grown into something so much more, I couldn't see straight through the dizzying spinning of it all.

I didn't want another woman.

I just wanted her attention.

I wanted to hear her say no. I wanted to hear her deny another woman access to me the way she had at The Manor.

And when she did, when she told me to come to her place instead...

It felt like a win better than any I'd experienced, hockey, golf, or otherwise.

Heat crawled down my spine as I snapped back to the moment, Livia's nails stroking my hair. I obeyed, eyes locked on my own as I stroked and succumbed to the feeling of fucking my hand. When I groaned and let my head fall back, flexing into my grip, Livia sharply tugged on my hair.

"You don't get to look away," she said. "Face it. This is who you are when you're mine."

Again, the word punched through me.

It made it impossible not to move my hand faster.

Livia hummed as she moved to my side, kneeling, her fingers trailing down my jaw until I was leaning into her touch. "You're growing impatient," she mused. "You want to come."

"Yes," I breathed.

"Say it, then," she whispered. "Tell me what you want."

"I want to come."

"Louder. Own it."

"I want to come for you, Liv," I said, breaking contact with my gaze in the mirror to look directly at her. "I want *you* to make me come."

Her lips curled into a pleased smile. "There it is. Now, tell me how you want me. How do you want me to make you come?"

Fuck, the words were so obscene, and the way she stared right through my soul as she said them...

I hesitated, my lips parting without sound. Then I swallowed hard. "I want..." My voice caught. "I want you to... taste me."

Her brow lifted, and like an unsure little boy, I backpedaled.

"I mean—if you want to—"

"Stand your ground, Rook," she cut in, her voice slicing through me like a clean blade. "If you want it, own it."

My chest tightened, pulse thundering in my ears. "I want you to taste me," I said again, steadier this time.

"That's not what you want," she rasped, leaning closer, running the tip of her nose along my jaw. "You don't want me just to taste you."

I closed my eyes, letting out a long, slow, heated breath. In that moment of suspended time, I reached for my power, for the control Livia was offering me. It was so rare she shared it with me. I didn't want to waste the opportunity.

I didn't want to disappoint her.

With my next inhale, I gave in to the most wicked part of me, to the side that longed to bring Livia the pleasure she brought me.

I reached for her with the hand not still fastened to my cock, tilting her chin until she was looking at me. "I want you to stay right here on your knees, open this pretty mouth of yours, and suck my cock until I come in your throat."

"Fuck." The curse from her lips was just a whimpered whisper, like I'd drawn it from her unwittingly, and I couldn't help but smile at the victory.

In a flash, she regained composure, her lips snapping shut before her gaze was hot on mine. "Good boy. I love when you talk to me like that, when you tell me what you need."

"You'll love it even more when I'm making you gag," I shot back, encouraged. "I saw you when you went down on me last time — the way your hand floated between your legs, the moans you let me feel vibrating through me. You liked it."

The words were a challenge, one that made Livia's next blink stutter.

"You were wet from tasting me, and I may be asking for it right now, but you want it, too."

"So how long are you going to make me wait?"

She punctuated the words with another arch of her brow, and that was all I needed.

I didn't ask to kiss her.

I slid my hands into her hair, gripping behind her neck, and I pulled her into me like my next breath depended on that kiss. I inhaled the moment our lips met, breathing all of her in. My cock ached with need when her tongue found mine, heat spreading fast and untamed from that point of contact.

I wanted to lose myself in her. I wanted to pass this test and ask for another.

She made a comment about me graduating.

How could I tell her sincerely that the only next step I wanted to take was to be hers?

I snapped out of that spiral of thoughts before it could take me under, gripping Livia's chin roughly as I ended our kiss. Then, I stood, towering over her, and offered my cock like it was made of gold.

"Open your mouth," I said, fisting myself as I waited. When she did as I asked, I licked my lips, shaking my head at the perfect sight — the swell of her breasts, her parted thighs, that pink tongue out and begging for me.

I grabbed the back of her head and guided her to me, toying with her at first. I slid my crown over her tongue, in just an inch and back out. Over and over again, I teased and played until she was moaning, her hands reaching between her legs and spurring me on.

"That's right, baby," I said, voice husky and raw. "Play with your pussy while I fuck this perfect mouth of yours."

The moan that earned me was paradise, like cool blue water and warm sand beneath my feet. The urge to fuck her mouth was too strong to resist now, so I moved my hands into her hair and started to take.

I flexed in slowly, all the way, holding her there as her eyes watered — but she kept them locked on me.

"*Fuck*, yes, Livia. Yes. God, you're everything."

I slid out and back in, again, again, picking up the pace each time until I had a steady rhythm that was coaxing my climax to the surface. When I groaned and pinched my eyes shut, Livia smacked my ass and pulled back, making me tremble at the loss.

"Watch," she instructed, gesturing to the mirror. "And tell me what you want, Rook. Don't back down now. You want to come in my throat? Tell me how to get you there." I thought I saw just a split second of vulnerability when she added, "I'm handing you the control. You've earned it."

A switch.

It was a true switch, and I knew without her having to say it that this was a rare fucking gift.

Still, even in the role reversal, Livia drove. She made me ask. She made me say exactly what I wanted. Every time I hesitated, every time my gaze flicked away from the mirror, she stopped.

And so, I watched, the visceral grip of it all so tight I felt like I couldn't breathe. It was too much, the flex of my abdomen as I rocked in and out of her mouth, the perfect slope of her back to the beautiful swells of her ass. I watched her head bob, her hair in my hands, and I felt a roaring fire searing through me.

"Lick my balls," I said with more confidence than I knew I had.

Livia hummed her approval with a smile before she did exactly what I asked, her eyes floating up to mine.

And *fuck*, I wanted to come. I wanted to spill right then and there, all over her. I wanted to paint her and watch the masterpiece unravel in real time.

But there was a desire that burned deeper.

And if this was the only time she was going to relinquish full control to me, I wouldn't waste it.

"Stop," I said, pulling away from her touch.

Livia frowned up at me, her brows folded together. "Are you safe wording me?"

"Fuck no," I breathed on a laugh. I helped her stand, and wordlessly, guided her to the bed. "But I can't take it any longer. I need to be inside you."

With that, I bent her at the waist, her hands finding the edge of my bed as I lined up behind her.

"Carter— oh, *fuck.*"

My hands on her waist, I slid all the way inside her in one flex, both of us moaning together at the feeling.

"God, Liv," I murmured as I began to work in and out of her. "Your mouth is so fucking hot, but it's nothing compared to this, compared to the way you feel wrapped so tightly around me."

She whimpered, fingers curling in the comforter.

"I know tonight is about me," I said, nipping at her earlobe as I fucked her hard and steady. "But I won't come until you do. I refuse."

I hiked one of her legs up onto the bed so I could have easier access to reach around and find her clit.

"Nothing turns me on more than hearing you fall apart."

She pressed her head back against my shoulder, legs trembling as I found her clit and began to smooth circles over it with my fingertips. I knew now how fast to go, where not to touch, the exact right pressure to apply.

She'd taught me well, and it took only moments before she was gripping and bucking and seeking.

"Fuck," she cursed. "Oh, fuck. *Yes.*"

"That's it," I growled in her ear. "Look at how you take my cock," I told her, grabbing her chin and forcing her to look at where our reflections still touched the mirror. "You fucking love the way I fill you up, don't you? You say I'm yours. Well, you're mine, too, Livia. Tonight, I own you. Now give me what I asked for."

"Carter," she whispered, and then her eyes were shutting, her hips rocking wildly, and I matched her pace until I knew she was close.

Then I fucked her deeper, not as hard, just little pulses in and out so I brushed that sensitive spot inside her I knew would get here there. That combined with my attention to her clit sent her over the edge, and I basked in the glow of her flying apart at my hand.

Livia was a goddess, an absolute fucking vision as she moaned and squirmed and clawed at me like she'd die if I stopped. I felt her walls tightening around me, pulsing as her orgasm ripped through her, and it was all I needed to follow.

"You've fucking wrecked me, you know," I growled in her ear, thrusting harder, chills racing up my spine with how good it felt to watch myself fuck her. "How could I ever have another woman? How could I ever find anything better than this?"

I groaned when my release caught, thrusting inside her and holding as it shuddered through me. Livia held onto me like a lifeline, both of us panting and moaning together until I was spent.

For a moment, we stayed like that. I planted soft kisses along the back of her neck, flexing in slowly as I softened inside her. Her breaths heaved through her, breasts swelling and falling as her hands gripped me wherever she could — my thigh, my ass, the back of my neck.

When I could barely stand any longer, I reluctantly withdrew, but I held onto her. I pulled her into my bed without asking, curling around her, any inch of space too much.

"Jesus, Mary, and Gretzky, Liv," I said into her hair on a smile, kissing behind her ear. "That was..." I shook my head, unable to find a single word in the English language to convey it.

Livia was silent in my arms, my legs curled behind hers, arms around her middle and pulling her closer.

"The way you looked in the mirror..." I continued with a groan. "I'll never get that out of my head. Which is quite unfortunate for my professionalism because that likely means I'll have a hard-on for the rest of my life."

I chuckled into her hair with the joke, but when she didn't laugh or scoff or roll her eyes and shove me away, I was suddenly on high alert.

She was still just... silent.

"Liv?" I asked.

It was like speaking her name broke her restraint, because without warning, her shoulders shook, a little choke of a sob coming unbidden from her lips. She covered them in an instant, curling in tighter on herself.

I froze.

Was she... crying?

"Liv," I said again, carefully, and then I pressed up onto my elbow, shifting her in my arms until she had no choice but to roll up to face the ceiling. She resisted at first before she gave in, and then she covered her face as soon as I saw it, and her whole body shook with another cry.

My heart lurched into my throat, and I'd never felt a need to comfort someone in such an all-consuming way as I did in that moment.

"Fuck, Liv, what happened? Are you okay? Did I hurt you?"

She shook her head, growling in frustration before she swiped the tears away and let her hands flop into the bed. "I'm fine," she bit out.

"Don't do that."

She shook her head, nostrils flaring as more tears pooled in her eyes. They fell down her temples right onto the pillow and she let out another huff.

"Ugh, God. This is so annoying." She swiped at her face again.

"Hey," I said, tenderly, my eyes searching her as if whatever had bruised her would be something I could see physically. I reached up to thumb away the next tear before it could fall, holding her face in my hand. "You don't need to be ashamed of crying. Not ever, but especially not with me."

Livia swallowed, her eyes on the ceiling.

"Is it... is it something I said?" I paused, considering. "Is it because you gave me control?"

At the word, her eyes welled again, fast and furious, and she squeezed her lids shut and shook her head, her whole face warping.

"Oh, baby." The words were painful as I said them, like a rusty blade to the chest. I pulled her into me, wrapping her up again like I could shield her from the hurt. "Come here. I got you. I'm right here. You're safe. You're in control."

She cried harder at that, but instead of pushing me away like I expected her to...

She clung to me.

Her legs intertwined with mine, her head buried in my chest, nails clawing at my back like she was afraid I'd leave her.

As if I ever could.

For a long while, we stayed just like that. Livia cried in a way I didn't know she was capable of, this impossibly strong woman showing me a side of her I felt honored to witness. I felt even more so to be the one to hold her and help her through it.

I didn't dare say a word to rush her. I let her feel every wave of whatever was happening, my hands in her hair, holding her to my chest as I whispered, "*Shhhh*" and "*I got you. I'm here.*"

Slowly, her sobs faded into sniffles, and then to the most weighted silence I'd ever experienced. I held her through it all, planting gentle kisses to her forehead and breaking every rule between us by not asking permission first.

"I'm sorry," she whispered.

"Stop. Don't apologize for feeling, Liv."

She shook her head. "No. I'm sorry for not telling you what I'm about to sooner."

That got my attention.

I paused where I was stroking her hair for a moment, unsure what to do. But Livia curled into me tighter, like she wanted to burrow into me.

"Please, I can't look at you when I say any of this. Just… just hold me and keep touching me and let me get it out."

My pulse quickened, anxiety prickling my skin. "I'm not going anywhere," I promised, and I held her tighter, waiting.

Her voice was stone cold and steady when she spoke, and what she said ripped my soul in two.

"When I was seventeen, I was raped."

The words hit me like a puck to the temple — hard, dizzying, life-ending. It knocked the breath clean out of me, like I'd never draw air into my lungs again.

Rage rose fast and hot, burning me from the inside out. My arms tightened around her without me telling them to. My throat struggled against my next swallow. My jaw tightened so hard I swore I cracked a tooth. And one thought surpassed every other.

I'll kill him.

Whoever he is, wherever he is, no matter what it takes or what I lose in the process, I will fucking end his life.

"Whatever you're thinking, I need you to not," she said, like she could read my mind. Maybe she felt it in the coiled muscles of my body. "This is not some knight in shining armor moment for you, okay? This is me, a survivor, choosing to share what happened to me. I just need you to listen. That's all. Okay?"

It was the hardest thing I ever did, to nod my head and mean it. Because it felt impossible not to act on what she'd told me, and I didn't even have the whole story yet.

But she was right. This wasn't about me.

And whatever she needed from me in this moment, in this lifetime — it was hers.

I softened my grip on her a bit, and when she seemed to believe my conviction, she continued.

"It was a family friend." Her voice was rough, but mechanical — like she refused to let herself feel any emotion. "Someone who'd been around my whole life. He did business with my dad. Golfed with him. Came to every party we had. Every summer barbecue in Long Beach. I never... I never thought to not feel safe around him."

Her tone didn't change, but her nails dug into my side, clutching like she needed me to hold her tighter. I answered her wordless plea with my arms pulling her in more, surrounding her.

"I told my parents right after it happened," she went on. "At first, they didn't believe me. Then they... started making it sound like maybe it wasn't what I said it was. Like I was being dramatic. They told me to keep it between us. That they'd handle it. That they understood, but that matters like this needed to be handled with discretion."

Now I was adding the very humans who made this woman I cherished to my list of people I wanted to end.

Livia's breath hitched, the first crack in her evenness. "I can still feel it, the way my dad squeezed my hand in his and told me he'd never let anyone hurt me."

My gut twisted. I held her with everything I had.

It took a moment for her to regain her composure, but then she continued.

"I believed him. I did. I thought he and my mom would handle it. I didn't need it to go to court or anything. I mean, I didn't want to be the girl who was raped, either. I didn't want the attention. But I did need justice. I did need to know I was safe."

She shook her head, pressing back against my chest just enough that I could see her eyes. They were fixed on my chest where her fingers curled.

"Days passed. Then weeks. Months. And nothing happened. He was still around. My mother told me whatever happened wouldn't happen again. That they had his word." Her voice hardened like steel. "And that it would be best for business—and for our reputation—if I just... dropped it and moved on."

I had to grind my teeth together to keep from screaming that that was bullshit, to stop myself from calling into light how badly I wanted to hunt them all down and make them pay. Who the fuck even was I? Like the dog I owned, I was usually of the non-threatening variety.

But the knowledge of someone hurting Liv like this, of her own family turning their backs on her...

It unleashed a rabid beast inside me that was out for blood.

I held him at bay, forcing a deep inhale and exhale and reminding myself that she was a survivor, that she didn't need me to do anything other than listen.

"And you know what? At first, I tried," she continued, her voice quiet now. "I tried to play their game, to move on and pretend like everything was fine. But I was... different. I was fundamentally changed. I couldn't go back to who I was before. And I had no idea how to be whoever came next.

"It got to a point where I couldn't take it anymore. He was always around, just laughing and kissing his wife's cheek like he wasn't a monster. At a gala my mom was hosting, I—" She sucked in a sharp breath, like the memory itself was a blow. "I told everyone. I outed him in front of the entire room. It was chaos. People gasped and looked from me to him in horror, and then to my parents." She paused. "I'll never forget my mother's face..." She shook her head, eyes squeezing shut. "But it proved useless in the end, because somehow, for reasons I'll never understand... no one believed me. He denied it. My parents denied it. And then they cut me off. They told me — without actually saying it — that if I cared so little about this family, I wasn't part of it anymore."

I pressed my lips to her hair, trying to keep from shaking with rage. "They don't deserve to call themselves your family."

Livia curled into me, like I was her shelter, and I did my best to be just that in that moment.

"After that, I was on my own. I graduated, moved straight to college. Took out loans because they wouldn't help. Worked for everything. My parents shielded my sister from it, but..." Her voice broke, just barely. "I think she knows. And she still won't talk to me about it."

She pressed her face to my chest, shoulders shaking once, and I thought that was it — but then the sob came, sudden and raw, and she clung to me like she'd drown if she let go.

"That's the part that hurts the most," she managed, voice muffled. "We were so close, me and Lacey. She had to know that something happened. She saw me die right in front of her eyes, but she never questioned it. I don't know if my mom told her not to ask, or if she's just always been afraid to, but she *has* to know. She has to know. And that kills me."

I kissed her hair, my throat burning. "I've got you. I'm here."

I thought about the wedding, how it all suddenly made sense. Of course, she didn't want to fucking go be around these hideous people. But then again, there was a part of her, this young, innocent girl who still existed inside of her that wanted to be with her sister, that wanted to believe there was still a familial connection somewhere in her life.

My heart was fucking shattering in my chest.

Livia sniffed, drawing a shaky breath, and when she spoke again, the mechanical cadence returned, like she was forcing it.

"It took me a long time to reclaim my sexuality. At first, I was numb. Sex was just... something to be used for. It wasn't about me at all. Then one night my junior year of undergrad, I was with a guy I'd been seeing for a few months. He asked me to bind him. And when I did, I slipped into this sort of dominant persona without even thinking."

Her body shifted slightly, like she was more comfortable now that we were talking about when she reclaimed her power.

"He loved it," she said. "And so did I."

I nodded, understanding before she even said it.

"That's when I knew," she finished. "This was what I needed. Control. Always. In every aspect. Because it's what keeps me safe."

I tightened my arms around her, my hand in her hair, my mouth at her temple. "Then I'll never take that from you. Not ever."

And I meant it with every fucking cell in my body.

But Livia shook her head. "No, no, don't do that. I gave you control tonight. I wanted you to take it. And I feel safe with you."

Fuck, the way those words crushed my lungs and filled them with life all at once.

"I just... it's been a long time since I've reversed the roles that way. I didn't mean for it to make me emotional, but it just... did."

"I'm sorry. I'm so sorry."

"Please, don't apologize. I don't want you to be sorry. I liked it. I mean, clearly," she added with her first laugh. That sound was like a wind chime in my soul, so promising and lovely. "I came so hard I'm pretty sure I saw the maker of the universe."

I chuckled, running my knuckles along her arm.

And then she lifted her eyes to mine for the first time, and my chest locked.

"I trust you," she whispered. "But I have to admit, I think that's what scares me the most."

I nodded, over and over, before pulling her into me and holding her tight. I knew she didn't need another word in that moment. She just needed to be held, to know I wasn't going anywhere after what she'd told me, that she was safe with me.

"Thank you, Liv," I breathed. "For telling me. For letting me in."

She stayed pressed against me until her breathing slowed, until the weight of her body shifted just enough that I knew she'd finally slipped under.

I didn't move. I couldn't. I didn't care if my arm fell asleep and both of us needed to get cleaned up and eat. She was finally at peace, and I didn't dare ruin it.

Her words circled me like vultures though — the mechanical way she'd told me, the moments she'd broken, the way her nails had dug into my skin like she was trying to fuse herself to me. And underneath all of it, the thing I couldn't stop replaying — she'd given me control tonight.

Not because she was trying to test me. Not because she was bored.

Because she wanted to.

For someone like her — someone who clawed for control in every aspect of her life, who needed it to feel safe — giving that up, even for a second, had to cost her more than I could even comprehend. And she'd given it to me.

Christ.

What did that mean?

I stared at the ceiling, my hand splayed over her hip. I thought about her voice when she told me to "own it," how her eyes had flared when I did, how she'd let me bend her over and fuck her like I hadn't just earned the privilege, but like it'd always been mine to take. She hadn't just tolerated it — she'd asked for it.

Like she'd said... she trusted me.

And something in my chest tightened so sharply I actually froze, the air leaving my lungs like I'd taken a body check square to the sternum.

I love her.

The thought slammed into me without warning, without mercy.

I was gone for her. I'd passed every exit ramp without even realizing it. And now I was barreling down this road at full speed with no brakes, no map, no plan for what the hell I was supposed to do when we got to the end.

And just like that, my pulse went haywire.

Because I was sure, more than I was of anything, that love was the last thing Livia wanted from me.

But I was powerless to stop it from being true.

I glanced down at her — hair spilling over my arm, lips parted in sleep, her hand still clutching my chest like even unconscious she wasn't ready to let go. My chest ached.

I could already hear the echo of her voice telling me she didn't want this, that I'd ruined what we had, that I'd read into something that wasn't there.

But none of that stopped the truth from sitting heavy in my chest.

I was in love with Livia Young.

And I had no fucking clue how to survive it.

Chapter 24

What I'm Counting On

Livia

Chloe and Will's pool area had been completely transformed.

Edison bulbs stretched in strands above the water, their golden glow mirrored in soft ripples as the sun sank toward the horizon. In the pool, clusters of paper lanterns drifted lazily, casting shifting halos of light that made the whole place feel enchanted.

At the far corner of the yard, Chef Patel commanded her makeshift kitchen with a sharp voice that carried over the music, barking orders at her team of sous chefs. I caught Will's uncle watching her from across the patio, smirk tugging at his lips, pride shining in his eyes.

Near the pool house where Chloe once lived, a string quartet played a delicate, romantic piece that threaded through the air as effortlessly as a breeze. High-top tables dressed in crisp white linens dotted the space, each crowned with a petite vase of hydrangeas and eucalyptus and a few flickering candles.

Stand *your* Ground

It was breathtaking, like stepping into a modern-day fairy tale — and it was exactly what Chloe and Will deserved.

The bride and groom floated from guest to guest, weaving in and out of conversations with ease. There were only about thirty people gathered, but I knew even that small number stretched Will's tolerance for crowds. Brooding in solitaire was more his natural state. Still, he kept a gentle smile fixed in place, his hand anchored at Chloe's back, his gaze never once straying from her. On her wrist gleamed the bracelet I'd made her, one I'd given her in private before the party. It came out perfectly, the moonstones making Chloe gasp just the way I hoped, and now I watched her absentmindedly touch it any time she felt a little nervous.

My job was complete, and the newlyweds were in heaven.

They were sun-kissed and radiant, carrying their happiness so openly it seemed to spill out of them, impossible to contain.

Maven and I were at the bar, waiting on fresh martinis as Maven filled me in on her latest philanthropic updates. I scanned the party as I listened to her, my eyes catching on the different packs of our friends who felt more like family now.

Vince and Jaxson were locked into a heated champagne pong tournament against Mia and Grace, their hollers of excitement ringing out over the otherwise calm and romantic space. But no one seemed to mind. In fact, they'd gathered a small crowd around them who were cheering them on — Mia and Grace especially, who I wagered were winning, judging by the little dance they were presently doing. Vince yelled something about cheating while his partner stood stupefied beside him, completely under Grace's spell just like he had been since the summer they ran away on a secret road trip together.

Aleks had that same love-dumb drooling thing going on from where he chatted with Will and Chloe, his eyes on his wife even as he carried out a conversation. It was nice to see the bastard smile. He was pretty insufferable before Mia got her hands on him. I loved how Will was dressed casually in white linen pants and a sage-green collared shirt, like he'd just rolled up from the resort he and Chloe spent a week at. And Chloe was her incredible, colorful self — her dress like a tropical sunset, all bright pinks and oranges and yellows flowing together in an eclectic and somehow elegant design. The fabric was heavy silk, and it draped over her curves in ways that reminded me why I loved women so much.

And then there was Carter.

He was in the far corner of the yard with Ava, making Zamboni perform tricks while Ava clapped and giggled and begged for more. I watched as he handed Ava a treat and illustrated what to do to command Zamboni to roll over. Ava did as he said, and when Zamboni flopped onto his back and rolled quickly before snapping back up to attention, Ava squealed with delight.

Ava was an absolute doll, her dark curls pinned into the cutest updo and a darling white fluff of tulle making up the dress she wore. Zamboni was battling her for cutest thing at the party, though, the little fur ball donning a doggie suit complete with bow tie.

But it was Carter who held my eye the longest.

Gone was the awkward rookie who stumbled over his own feet the night I first met him. Tonight, he looked like he belonged here — like he owned the place. His outfit wasn't overly formal, just a perfectly tailored navy jacket and crisp white shirt with the collar undone, no tie in sight. The fabric stretched just enough over his broad chest and shoulders to remind me exactly what was underneath. His beige slacks cut a clean line down his long legs, hugging those thick thighs and that impossibly toned ass. Even playing with a dog and a kid, he exuded a swagger I wasn't sure when he'd picked up... or how he'd learned to wear it so damn well.

He looked devastatingly handsome, but it wasn't just the clothes. It was the way he carried himself, like he finally believed he deserved to stand tall, to be seen. Confidence dripped off him in a way that startled me, in a way that made me wonder if this transformation was my doing, or if he'd simply been waiting for the right moment to step into himself.

That confidence rattled me, too. Because every new layer of him I uncovered made it harder to pretend I wasn't peeling back my own defenses along the way. I didn't want to want this, the butterflies and the stuttering heartbeats — not with him, not with anyone. But my pulse apparently didn't care what my brain was trying to tell it.

I still felt a little raw as I watched him from across the yard, like all my nerves had been exposed the night I confessed everything to him, and even a slight breeze had me wincing. That man had held me reverently as I broke in his arms, and he'd been with me every day since — even if all I had to offer him were a couple hours after work. It was like he didn't want me to be alone after what I'd told him.

Or maybe like he never wanted me to be alone again.

And all of it was just too much. I was dressed to kill in a champagne-colored dress that fell like starlight over my slight curves, but inside, I was as uncomfortable as a nun in a strip club. Add in the fact that I couldn't help but think of Lacey, of how my sister would get married soon just like Will and Chloe, and I had yet to decide if I'd be a part of it or not...

I was sick over it.

I wanted to be there with her, to hold her bouquet if she wanted, or help her navigate a giant dress when she had to pee. I wanted to see her all blubbery as she professed her love to the man who'd stolen her heart.

He was a man I didn't even know, and somehow, that made the pain of it all worse.

And I knew I couldn't be there with her without facing my biggest demons, without being in the same room with a man who'd assaulted me and the two people who were supposed to protect me but didn't.

Inside, I was an emotional tornado.

And at the same time, standing there in that fairy-tale backyard, surrounded by friends and love and light, I couldn't remember the last time I'd felt so safe. It was the lingering feel of Carter's arms around me that had me feeling that way, despite how my mind raced.

That contradiction unsettled me. It was confusing and terrifying and dangerous.

I was still swimming in that discomfort when Carter looked up. His eyes found mine across the crowd as easily as if there was a tether between us, invisible but undeniable. He smiled, his warm, dark eyes dancing in the glow of the party, and I felt my own lips curve before I could stop them.

My stomach dropped like I'd stepped off the high dive, like there was no ground beneath me anymore and I didn't know if I was diving into the safety of water or the certain death of concrete.

"Earth to Liv," Maven said beside me, snapping my attention to her. She arched her brow with a knowing grin as she waved my fresh martini in front of my face until I took it. "You okay over there?"

"I'm great," I lied. Or was it a lie? I *did* feel great, but I also felt... nervous.

Of what, I had no clue.

"Mhm," she said, sipping her glass with her eyes still assessing me. "Then tell me what I just told you about the Sweet Dreams initiative and who signed on to help."

I cringed. "Um... Cardi B?"

Maven swatted my arm playfully. "Brat. I knew you weren't listening!"

When my eyes drifted back to Carter without permission, I wanted to smack myself. And Maven clocked it immediately.

"Oh, I see. We're a little distracted, are we?" She looped an arm through mine and led us away from the bar to one of the cocktail tables. "I have to say... he seems like a completely new man. How are those *lessons* going?"

I sighed, curling my fingers around the stem of my glass. "I think he's well past ready to graduate."

"So, that's it, then?" Maven asked. "Deal's done, debt paid, and you two just... go back to him being a bumbling fool around you and you pretending like it annoys you?"

My throat was tight when I nodded. "That's the plan."

Carter's gaze swept to mine, and this time, he sent me a wink that had my stomach fluttering like a jar full of fireflies.

"Huh," Maven mused, sipping her drink with her eyes sliding to me again. "I don't think your student agrees with this post-graduation procedure."

My ribs squeezed painfully tight around my lungs, but before I could laugh and wave her off with all the nonchalance I could muster, there was a clinking of glasses and a call of attention to the makeshift dance floor near the pool.

Mia and Ava stood there together, Mia tapping a fork against her champagne glass as Ava bounced excitedly on her toes next to her, eyes alight with mischief.

I silently thanked the universe for the excuse to run from my confusing, terrifying thoughts a while longer, dragging Maven closer to the action.

"Our esteemed guests," Mia began as everyone gathered around. "We are gathered this evening to celebrate the union of Chloe and Will Perry, our little ball of rainbow sunshine to our grumpy little rain cloud."

Ava giggled loudly at that, and the rest of us chimed in, Vince elbowing Will where he stood next to him.

"And what better way to celebrate than with... a dance?!" Ava twirled with the words, landing in a wide stance with one hand on her hip and the other pointing off beyond the pool. "Hit it, DJ!"

And who was the DJ but Carter Fabri?

Seemingly out of nowhere, a giant speaker on a tripod had appeared. Carter must have had his phone hooked up to it because he tapped something on his screen and then a catchy pop beat rang out over the space.

I recognized it instantly as Mia's song, "Perfect Storm."

Mia handed her glass and fork to Grace, and then she and Ava launched into a fully choreographed routine — one that had all of us in stitches by the second line of the song. The lyrics were about finding your person in a time you least expected it, about bracing for a storm to be greeted with sunshine, instead. It was playful and fun, a complete bop, while also being layered with profound sentiment. That was the magic of Mia Love's songwriting, and watching her and Ava dance around throwing confetti over Will and Chloe, it was impossible not to smile.

It was impossible not to get emotional.

I felt it as soon as Chloe's eyes watered, her laughter sweet like the sound of wind chimes as she watched the show. Will tugged her in closer, his smile the brightest it'd been all night, his eyes on his daughter.

It was a full-circle moment for them, and my heart burst at the sight.

"Oh, my God," Maven said beside me, swiping tears from under her eyes. "This is illegally cute."

No tears found my eyes when I nodded my agreement, but my heart was in a vise grip. It was impossible to be surrounded by that kind of love and not feel it permeating through you.

As the chorus repeated, Ava and Mia snagged Chloe and Will and shoved them onto the dance floor, forcing their hands together like dolls. The newlyweds laughed, awkwardly swaying at first before melting into their own rhythm. Then Mia and Ava kept grabbing whoever was closest—friends, strangers, teammates — and shoving them into pairs until the whole yard was moving.

We howled when they tossed Jaxson and Aleks together. Jaxson performed a ridiculous curtsy before yanking Aleks into some sort of chaotic waltz, Aleks muttering curses the whole way.

I was still laughing when Maven was dragged onto the floor with Vince.

And then my laugh died in my throat at the sight of Carter sliding in front of me.

His hand closed around mine before I could protest, and suddenly I was being pulled through the crowd, straight into the chaos.

"Carter—" I warned, heels digging in, but he spun me out before I could finish. The crowd whooped. I nearly toppled over, but Carter was there, steadier than ever.

"Relax, Professor," he teased, catching me by the waist and spinning me back in. "It's just a little dance."

I scowled, or tried to. It was hard to look menacing when he twirled me again, his grin wide, his body warm against mine each time he reeled me in.

"Carter," I hissed, though laughter cracked through my voice. "That's enough."

"Mm, I think not. Besides, what are you going to do? Punish me?"

"That's exactly what I'll do."

Carter's grin turned salacious, and he dipped me low enough I gasped before slowly, dramatically, pulling me upright once more.

"Don't you think that's exactly what I'm counting on?"

His wink was too smooth, too charming, and I couldn't fight the laughter that bubbled out of me even if I'd tried.

And I hadn't.

I'd let it consume me, that breathless, unguarded laughter.

For one wild, fizzy second, the lighthearted girl I used to be burst free. No fear. No past. Just the dizzy joy of music and motion, of him holding me steady as the world spun.

And for just a moment, I decided to let it stay.

Chapter 25

Impossibly Lost

Livia

The party stretched into the night, winding down somewhere near when Cinderella's carriage turns into a pumpkin.

The music had softened, the band gone and replaced by quiet classical music from Chloe's phone, and only the core of us remained. Aleks and Mia collected empty glasses from tabletops, laughing together as they bumped hips. Vince and Maven stacked plates at the bar, their bickering playfully punctuated by stolen kisses. Jaxson and Grace perched on the edge of a lounge chair, Jax whispering something in Grace's ear that made her cheeks pink even as she swatted him away.

From beside the pool, Ava squealed, hiking up the hem of her tulle dress before launching herself straight into the water. A chorus of gasps and laughter rang out — and seconds later, Will kicked off his loafers and jumped in after her, the splash enormous.

Chloe's jaw dropped, her delighted shriek carrying over the water. "William Perry!" she yelled, tossing off her heels and diving in, too. The three of them surfaced, sputtering and laughing, and the whole backyard echoed with joy.

I smiled to myself, warmth blooming in my chest at the sight of it. For a brief, fragile moment, it was enough to simply stand on the fringe, martini in hand, watching love ripple outward like rings in a pond.

Then a hand slid into the crook of my elbow.

I startled, turning — but Carter was already guiding me wordlessly away from the crowd. I abandoned my drink on a cocktail table as we passed, looking around to make sure no one had eyes on us.

The only one who did was Maven, and she made a motion like her lips were zipped shut.

Carter's grip was steady, his body close enough that his heat bled into mine, and before I could ask what he was doing, we rounded the house and my back hit the wall.

His mouth found mine with a hunger that stole every ounce of air from my lungs.

His hands braced the wall on either side of my head, caging me in, his chest pressed hard against my dress, his breath shaking like he'd sprinted from the ends of the earth to get to me.

"I couldn't wait another second to kiss you," he rasped against my lips. His hands moved from the wall to my hips, bunching the fabric there. "You in this dress..." He groaned, kissing me again, reverent, desperate. "You in anything. You existing, Liv — it's the very thing that undoes me."

My pulse thundered. I kissed him back because how could I not, because every ounce of me had wanted this, but my body trembled with confusion, with fear of what it meant. This wasn't a lesson. This wasn't something safely outlined in a contract. This was Carter's graduation, and for his final assignment, he was claiming me like there was no other option than for me to be his.

He finally broke our kiss, his forehead against mine as our breaths met in a panting rhythm between us. My hands clutched his jacket and his held fast to my waist.

I felt the heaviness of the emotions warring inside him before he spoke them into existence, but I still wasn't prepared for their impact.

"Livia, I... I can't do this anymore. I can't skate within the boundaries of the deal we made or the contract we signed."

My pulse was razor sharp and unsteady, and I didn't know if I was petrified of what he'd say next or filled with an unshakeable hope.

Carter wet his lips, shaking his head — not like he was unsure of what he wanted to say, but more that he was uncertain of my reaction to it.

"I want more," he finally spoke, his voice low and raspy. "God, Livia, I *need* more. I know I said I understood the terms and conditions when I signed. And maybe I meant it at the time, but fuck, honestly, I'm not sure I did. Even then, I knew you held a key to unlocking a part of me no one else had access to. And you have. You've... you've shown me all I'm capable of. You've made me the best version of myself. But more than anything, you've let me see the best version of *you*." He kissed me again, this time slower and more urgent all the same. "And I can't go back to just being your friend. I can't lie to myself any longer, and I refuse to lie to you. It's not about lessons anymore. It hasn't been for a while. I want more. And I'm asking you to stand up to every ghost of uncertainty coming alive inside you right now and give it to me."

As if he'd conjured them, I felt the spirits of my dark past rising within my chest, long fingers wrapping around my throat and squeezing tight.

"Okay, Rookie," I said on a breathy, frail laugh that betrayed me. "Is this your practice run for *Bachelor in Paradise*? Because you've got the dramatic declaration down pat."

The words left my mouth on autopilot, my go-to armor of sarcasm, but even as they hung between us, I heard how brittle they sounded. The joke didn't land — not with the pounding in my ears, not with the tremor in my voice that gave me away. My pulse was still thundering, my hands still fisted in his jacket like I was clinging to a cliff edge.

And Carter didn't smile.

His jaw flexed, eyes steady, unwavering.

"You always think I'm joking," he said, voice low and hard as steel, each word pressed with purpose. "That *I'm* a joke. And you know now, better than anyone, how much that hurts."

Instantly, any mask of indifference left me. I shook my head, concern for my negligence eating me alive. "Oh, shit. Carter, I didn't—"

"No," he said firmly, stepping in even closer somehow, like he wanted to crawl inside me to deliver his next hit. "Don't soften it. Don't take it back. You wanted me to stand my ground? Well, here I am." His breath shook, his chest rising against mine as if this cost him everything. "I mean what I say, Livia. I'm not joking."

His eyes burned, steady and sure.

"I love you."

The words detonated between us.

My world tilted, ears ringing, the dust from the blast clouding every thought that battled for dominance inside my mind.

I shook my head, panic rising like a flame in the aftermath. "No. No, you don't—"

"Yes." He caught my chin, his thumb gentle even as his eyes were fierce. The way he stared at me, so intently, cleared everything, the dust settling, my senses rushing back at once. "I do. I love you."

I didn't mean to break. I didn't mean for emotion to warp my face, for me to lean into his touch as tears welled in my eyes and fell in a silent stream down my cheek.

"You don't think I know you don't want to hear that? You think it doesn't kill me to know you don't feel the same?" His voice cracked, and still he never wavered. "But I can't keep doing this halfway, Liv. I am impossibly lost inside the notion that you could actually be mine, if only I can stand my ground and claim you."

And then I was kissing him.

It was hard and messy and unbridled, teeth meeting teeth, my nails clawing at his back to get him closer. I mounted him, lifting one leg until he took my weight before I wrapped the other around him and held fast.

Carter pinned me to the wall, meeting my desperation with a kiss so powerful I felt it like a prophecy in my soul, like it was destined to be, and we were at the mercy of a higher power.

I pushed at his chest even as my mouth devoured his, shaking my head against the truth of it, against the part of me that wanted to collapse into him completely.

Carter frowned, still kissing me, but his hands steadied. "Are you telling me no?"

I whimpered at the question, at the way my body revolted against my soul with the answer.

"You know the safe words," he murmured against my lips. His hands framed my face, patient and certain.

He waited.

The fucking gentleman that he was, he made sure. He wasn't going to let me get by without using my words.

I hated him for it almost as much as I...

"You're wrong," I finally croaked, still shaking my head even as I clawed at him and wordlessly begged for more. "I do want to hear it. And I do feel the same."

The words broke out of me like water from a shattered vase, and Carter's face lit up with disbelief at their existence. But it was only a moment, a pause in the turning of our planet before his hands were on me again, more insistent this time, his kisses heated with pure need.

It was all in flashes after that.

His hand at his buckle, unfastening, unzipping.

My dress hiked up, thong yanked to the side.

A rock and a gasp, a moan that vibrated through the very foundation of who I was and brought all my walls down in a thundering crash.

Carter sank inside me like an anchor, flexing hard and wrapping his hands around my shoulders to pull me down farther, as if there was an unreachable depth he was determined to find.

I didn't know when it happened. I didn't know if it was in the searing moments of teaching him, in the honest moments of him opening himself to me and me feeling safe to do the same, or in the inconsequential moments, the ones where we were floating on a board side by side or laughing at a bar or sneaking glances across a room crowded with our friends — but I had fallen for him.

It scared me more than anything, and yet I didn't have the will to fight the truth.

I could have pushed him away. I could have invoked the contract and reminded him what he signed up for, what he agreed to. I could have reinforced my walls and crawled back into my lonely hole of safety.

But I didn't want to.

Claiming me against that wall, Carter was no longer my student, no longer timid or unsure. He seared me with every thrust, marked me with every kiss, scarred me with every shuttered moan of my name.

And he was right. I did know the safe words.

But I didn't reach for them.

Instead, I leaned over the edge and into the free fall, into *him* and everything he was promising.

My past screamed the whole way down, begging me to reconsider.

But it was too late.

I was his.

I only hoped it was warm, welcoming water at the end of that dive and not cold, hard concrete.

Chapter 26

Spinning Out

Carter

It wasn't lost on me that the bike fan wasn't the only thing spinning out.

Like a cannon blast from a barrel, the season had shot back into action just two days after Will and Chloe's party. The 4 Nations Face-Off was complete, the season resumed, and like a break hadn't even happened at all, we were back in the race for the playoffs.

It was easy for the week to fly by, a blur of practice, travel, and games. What *wasn't* easy was keeping my mind on hockey when all I wanted was to get wrapped up in Livia Young.

She'd come home with me the night of the party, neither of us satiated by the quick, frenzied claiming of one another against the side of Will's house. I'd kept her up until well into the morning hours, and it still hadn't been enough. And when she was leaving the next day, her lips swollen from me and eyes a happy kind of tired, I hadn't wanted to let her go. I'd kept pulling her back into me for another kiss, like everything we'd whispered to each other would disappear the moment she walked out the door, the spell broken.

And it was beginning to feel that way.

Here we were a week later, and I hadn't seen her since that night.

It made sense. I'd jetted off to St. Louis and then to Jacksonville with the team, and as soon as we'd returned to Tampa, it was with just enough time to prepare for tonight's game — which we'd lost. It was brutal, to be within reach of the playoffs, but also teetering on the edge of not making it. Every loss felt dire, every win like just a Band-Aid trying to hold together a wound that clearly needed stitches.

And I knew I wasn't the only one busy.

Livia had been struggling to keep her head above water even before the party. It was the sole reason I'd taken her out to the springs, to clear her mind and give her a little rest. Even on our lazy day off together, she'd had to field calls from the office, as if they couldn't function without her for even twenty-four hours.

Now, here I was on a bike in the team gym trying to flush out my legs after a grueling three periods, but it was my head doing all the sweating.

Livia hadn't been at the game tonight.

It wasn't unusual for her not to attend. She had work, a life, responsibilities bigger than sitting in an arena watching me chase a puck. But still... a part of me hoped she'd want to see me after I'd been away for our travel games, that she'd take any excuse to be with me just like I would with her.

I felt her empty seat like a bruise.

When I texted her afterward, she answered immediately, and for all I could tell, nothing was off. She met my humor with her own and eased a bit of my worry with her use of a kiss emoji, but I still felt a chasm between us.

I asked if I could see her soon, and she'd hit me with: *Of course, Rook. Just give me a few days to get some things in order. I have some business to take care of.*

Business.

A few days.

My legs pumped harder, the flywheel whining under the pressure.

Was I supposed to read between the lines? Was she pulling away? Or was she actually just busy and I was being the neurotic asshole who couldn't handle space?

A few days wasn't that long, but it felt like a decade after already not seeing her for a week.

Could she honestly not find a spare moment to see me?

And then there was the third payment. It had hit her account this morning — just like we'd outlined in the paperwork we'd both signed. Except this time, it felt dirty.

Was I supposed to stop sending it now?

Would she have my balls in a chain if I dared?

I wanted her to have the money, to use it for whatever she needed, but God, I hated how it felt now. I didn't want her to think anything between us was transactional, that this was just some sort of business deal to me. It may have started that way, but it hadn't been like that for a while now.

Then again, this was what she'd agreed to. We hadn't technically said it was all over, but it was certainly implied. Therefore, she'd fulfilled her side of the agreement, and I was to fulfill mine.

She didn't seem upset about that third payment hitting. Then again, she hadn't said anything about it *at all*. And while it was perfectly acceptable that a grown woman with a demanding career would ask for a few days before she sees me, I couldn't help but wonder if a part of that delay in getting together was because of the payment and her sorting through her own feelings about it.

Jesus, Carter. You're a fucking lunatic.

Just shut your brain off and give the girl a few days.

I pedaled faster, sweat dripping from my hair and down my temples, and for a moment, I cleared my mind. It was all I could do to focus on my breathing, on the pumping of my legs, the oxygen burning my lungs.

But sixty seconds was about all I got before my asshole brain was at it again.

Because what were we now, anyway?

Was Livia my... girlfriend? Did I get to call her that? Or was that something only she was allowed to decide?

Fuck, did she even want that?

She called me Rookie like she had since we signed the contract, her little term of degrading endearment for me. Again, it was nothing I should read into, but I couldn't fucking help it — because I didn't want to be Rookie to her now. I wanted to be Carter, her boyfriend.

Do you seriously think a woman like that would let you claim her publicly?

You're a fucking joke. She's embarrassed of you.

She's trying to think of a way to get out of all of this.

I hated thinking it, but my brain wouldn't stop. The words came in Coach Leduc's voice, and I visually imagined socking him in the jaw to shut him up, but those thoughts still echoed.

Could I tell people about us?

Did she want me to?

Or were the worst thoughts in my head right? *Would* that embarrass her? Was I just another secret she had to compartmentalize, something she'd never claim out loud?

I swiped sweat from my brow with the towel hanging around my neck, shaking my head at the thought.

I knew it wasn't true. At least, I wanted to believe that part of my heart that swore it wasn't. I saw the look on her face when I told her I wanted more. I felt the way she trembled against me when she told me she felt the same.

Still, she deserved more than stolen moments in the shadows. She deserved something real. A date. No, a gesture.

Something deliberate.

Instead, what I had was a brain that wouldn't shut the hell up.

What if she woke up one day and realized I wasn't enough?

What if she wanted someone older, steadier, someone who had his shit together instead of a man who still needed her guidance to please her?

What if she regretted saying she loved me back?

Technically, she didn't ever really say it, did she?

She just said that she felt the same. But maybe it wasn't as deep as what I was feeling.

What if it was just sex-high honesty, words spilled in the moment, not the kind that carried weight in the light of day?

My legs burned. My chest burned worse.

I couldn't sit in this. I couldn't just wait. I needed to do something. I needed something to offer her that wasn't a groan against her lips in the dark or a confession ripped out of me while I had her pinned against the wall in feral need.

I needed to show her I meant it. That this wasn't a game. That she wasn't a joke to me.

Maybe if I could figure out the right way to do that, I'd stop spinning out like this.

In an instant, I hopped off the bike, sprinting for the locker room and praying I wasn't too late. Most of the guys would be on their way out by now if not already long gone. Vince had been up on the bike with me for a while, but had retreated half an hour ago, and I hadn't seen the other guys since Coach gave us his post-game speech and released us.

But I held onto hope as I jogged through the arena, and when I slid into the locker room and found all of them there, I took it as a sign from the universe.

Jaxson was fresh out of the shower, a towel around his waist as he padded over to his locker. Aleks and Will were locked in a conversation — likely about how Aleks got thrown into the penalty box when we really needed him on the ice — and Vince was on the phone, the device nestled between his ear and shoulder as he tugged on one sneaker and then the next.

"Damn, am I glad to see you're all still here," I said, wiping the sweat from my face before I hung the towel over my shoulder. "Boys — I need you."

Will didn't even look up from where he was packing up his bag. "We're not going to Boomer's."

"God, no," Aleks added with a scoff. "Especially after you shanked that shot in the third."

"That's rich coming from the guy who took a dumbass penalty with five minutes left," Vince chirped, finally ending his phone call — which presumably was with Maven, since he'd said he loved her and would see her soon.

"Yeah, at least Carter didn't put us on the kill when we needed him on the ice," Jaxson chimed in, dropping his towel unashamedly.

"True," Vince said, grinning. "Carter just managed to fan on a wide-open net instead."

Aleks barked a laugh. "Seems to be his signature move. Should we name it after you, bud?"

"*Oy, did you see number 41? He completely Fabio'd that shot!*" Jax added.

"Hey, leave my number out of this," Vince said with a snap and a point.

The chatter picked up, jokes flying, all of them wearing easy grins as they chirped me incessantly. And usually, I'd laugh with them. I'd dish it right back.

But right now, I was wound tight enough to snap, and that's exactly what I did.

I slammed my fist into the metal of my locker hard enough to make the whole row rattle. The sound cut the room cold, every head whipping toward me.

"Goddamn it, guys, I am not fucking around!" My voice cracked on the words, raw and loud, my chest heaving. "I am in love with Livia."

I panted in the silence that proclamation left in the locker room, the guys I was less close with giving each other weary looks before they excused themselves and left me with the core group.

"No, I'm not joking. And no, I'm not delusional either. She and I have been..." *How the fuck do I explain what we've been doing?* "Seeing each other. It was supposed to remain casual and just between us, but I told her the night of Chloe and Will's party that I wanted more. I told her I loved her." I swallowed. "And she said she loves me, too."

Vince's eyebrows bolted into his hairline, and Jaxson smirked, tugging on a pair of sweatpants as he mused to himself. "Well, I'll be damned."

"But now I haven't seen her in a week," I continued, my breath labored. "And I'm losing my fucking mind. I need to do something. I need to show her that I'm in this with her, *for* her, that I'm serious about us. I can't just sit here waiting for her to call me off the bench like some rookie desperate for scraps." My hands shook as I ran them back through my hair before letting them fall against my thighs. "And I need you to take me seriously right now. I need all the jokes to stop. I need my friends to help me figure out what the fuck to do. Okay? I need you."

The silence lasted only a second before Will stood, his brow in a hard line. "Of course, we'll help. We've got you."

"For sure," Jaxson added with a nod, stretching a long-sleeve t-shirt over his head before working into it arm by arm. "And hey... sorry for the jokes before. We were just chirping."

"I know, I know," I said, pinching the bridge of my nose. "I just... I'm really fucking spinning out here, guys, and I have no idea what I'm doing."

"I think we need you to catch us up a bit," Aleks said, arching a brow. "Because last I knew, you were like a buzzing fly around Livia's picnic."

"Yeah, well, not much has changed other than she's stopped swatting me away."

Will smirked. "Seriously. Tell us what's been going on, and then tell us what we can do to help."

I blew out a breath. "Alright."

But before I could launch into the whole story, Aleks nodded toward Vince, who looked green on the bench where he sat. "You okay over there, Tanny Boy?"

Jaxson answered for him with a bark of a laugh, clapping his hands hard on his best friend's shoulders before he gave him a little shake. "Oh, he's fine. Probably just hoping like hell Carter doesn't remember what he said during our golf game last summer."

I frowned, trying to remember.

And just as I did, Daddy P slapped his knee and let out his own baritone of a laugh. "Oh, how could any of us forget? How exactly was it that he phrased it?"

Aleks slid in, rubbing his chin like he had to think about it before he held up a finger and said, "I believe it went something like, *'If you ever bag Liv, I promise you, I will literally get on my hands and knees and kiss your feet.'*"

Vince shook his head, but I saw the smile spread on his lips before he buried his face in his hands as the rest of us threw him playful punches and chirps.

"It was just me razzing him!" he tried.

"Oh, no," I said, holding up a finger. "It was quite literally a promise. Don't worry, Tanny Boy — there will be plenty of time for you to act out your foot fetish…"

"I'd like to be there when this happens," Jaxson piped in.

"Oh, I'm not missing it," Aleks added.

Will nudged Vince. "I'll record it. You know, just in case."

"…but right now," I continued on a laugh, the fist around my chest already loosening. "I'm less concerned about cashing in that bet and more so about how I keep the girl now that I somehow managed to get her."

Will nodded at that, his usual serious demeanor sliding back into place. "Alright, Fabio," he said, catching the gaze of the other guys before he folded his arms and looked back to me. "We're with you. Tell us everything."

Chapter 27

Unbelievable

Livia

I stared at the text from Carter as if it'd just come through and hadn't been living on my device for days now.

> **Rook:** Save Sunday night for me. I want to take you somewhere.

I'd shot back a silly text about that being ominous and wondering if I should share my location with Maven, but Carter hadn't joked back at all. Instead, he'd simply replied:

> **Rook:** Be ready by five, okay? Wear whatever makes you feel good.

I wondered if he could sense it, me pulling away and retreating into my shell like I was so used to doing. I wondered if that was why he was insistent, why he wasn't leaving it up to me any longer. I'd kept telling him I'd love to see him, too, but that I had some things to take care of — which wasn't a lie, but wasn't the whole truth, either.

I wasn't taking back anything I'd said to him, and I wasn't regretting any feelings I'd confessed.

But I was reeling, and I needed some space to figure out why.

Part of it was that we were now in unfamiliar territory, I'd realized after a few days alone. When he was my student and I was his teacher, everything was in order. I knew where to place him in my mind, knew how to handle him.

But when he asked for more, when he told me he loved me...

He obliterated whatever box I had him in, smashing it straight to hell.

I didn't know where we went from here. The obvious next step would be for us to date each other publicly, but after all we'd been through together, it felt strange to just pretend we suddenly started going out. And to call each other boyfriend and girlfriend already would probably send our friends into shock.

How did we explain it?

Did we really need to?

And without those clear boundaries of the contract we'd signed, what exactly were we? Was I his Domme, or just his girl? Where did the power reside?

Not knowing the answer to that question was what made my skin crawl most.

Adding more confusion to the pot was the fact that the third payment from Carter hit my bank account a few days after we'd set fire to our little agreement. And it wasn't that I expected him to just take back his offer and not pay me the rest of what he promised, but now it felt... strange.

Tainted.

Like I was a part of some shady business instead of a clearly defined transaction like we'd had laid out before.

I wasn't typically one for anxiety, but I was definitely having anxious thoughts. I was usually able to quell them by throwing myself into work or losing hours making jewelry. But right now, I was alone in a sterile room with nothing but time to think.

The good thing was that no matter how my mind raced, I didn't feel unsure about Carter. I didn't have any uncertainty about how I felt for him or how he felt for me.

And I decided at the end of the day, that was all that really mattered.

The rest, we could work out together.

But there was something I needed to do for myself first.

Which was why I was here now, butt-ass naked under a paper gown, waiting for my doctor to return and tell me what our next steps were for freezing my eggs.

I loved Carter. And I believed he loved me. But that didn't stop the independence that had burned in me since my parents cut me off as a teenager. The truth of the matter was that I wouldn't feel safe unless I was always looking out for myself, even if someone else was there to help carry the load.

And this, freezing my eggs, having a child one day... this was for me.

Carter and I had flippantly discussed it on our day off together, and I knew from that conversation that he didn't want kids.

Maybe he would change his mind about that.

Maybe we'd have a kid together one day.

But I wasn't willing to leave my dreams to chance.

This was still something I wanted, something that I felt deep in my soul like a tattooed fortune. The money he paid me for our arrangement still mattered to me. I already had my financial advisor tuck most of it away, getting it out of my bank account so I could pretend like it didn't exist. I told her to invest it and put it in a high-yield savings, whatever she needed to do to protect it.

I *would* have a child one day.

And I would be able to provide for us, with or without the help of anyone else.

That was a promise I'd made to myself, and I was intent on keeping it.

Still, sitting there in the too-bright room, the crinkling paper beneath me loud with every nervous shift, I couldn't help the old familiar whispers creeping in.

What if I was already too late?

What if I didn't have as many eggs as I thought?

What if my body betrayed me the way people I loved had?

I tried to shake it off, even as my doctor's warning about low AMH levels echoed in my mind. I took a long, slow breath and reminded myself that this was why I was here.

To get answers. To take control. To make a plan.

The door clicked open before I could spiral any further.

"Livia," Doctor Stroud greeted warmly, clipboard tucked against her chest as she crossed the room. "Sorry for the wait. Fridays are notoriously hectic, no matter how we try to schedule them not to be." She was all sweet, warm smiles and calm authority. "I know you understand."

I nodded, trying to mirror her smile, though mine felt as stiff as the gown I wore.

Doctor Stroud seemed to clock that, her smile softening. "I know these appointments can be a little nerve-wracking, but you're doing the right thing coming in."

"Thanks," I said, my voice scratchy from sitting with my thoughts too long.

She pulled up the stool and sat across from me, scanning my chart. "So, before we get into next steps, I do need to ask a few routine questions — just to have the full picture. These might be a bit repetitive from the nurse who took your vitals, but I just like to double-check things myself."

Her smile was so comforting, and yet I still felt my stomach somersault the way it had all appointment. "Okay."

"Are you sexually active?"

"Yes."

"One partner? Multiple?"

"One," I answered quickly, then cleared my throat. "Just one."

"Any contraception being used?"

"I'm on birth control, but otherwise, no."

Doctor Stroud nodded, jotting a note, then glanced back at me. "And how long have you two been together?"

My cheeks heated. "It's... new," I admitted.

"Alright." She smiled, reassuring, and set her pen down. "So, typically, we'd start with a baseline scan of your ovaries, hormone testing, and a discussion about your timeline. We'd also talk about retrieval cycles and what medications you'd need to begin in order to stimulate production."

Relief fluttered through me that we were moving forward. "Okay. So... we can do that today?"

"Well," she said gently, still smiling, "usually, yes. But in this case... we can't."

My brow furrowed. "Why not?"

Doctor Stroud's eyes softened as she folded her hands. "Because... you're pregnant, Livia."

I blinked.

The words detonated inside me, ricocheting off every corner of my chest. I was sure I'd misheard them. I was sure there was no way in hell that could be—

But even as I thought to dismiss it, the reality crashed in. I'd been so busy, so stressed with work and my sister's wedding that I knew I'd been a little inconsistent in taking my birth control. But a few hours couldn't make that big of a difference, could it?

Or was there a time I'd skipped a day and didn't realize?

For a long moment, I could only blink repeatedly as my thoughts raced to catch up, my mouth opening and closing like a fish pulled from water. Then, instinctively, my hand flittered to my stomach.

"I'm—" I choked on the word, a laugh bubbling up as my eyes filled. "I'm pregnant?"

Doctor Stroud nodded, calm and certain, her smile still as lovely as ever.

A sob-laugh broke free from my chest as I slapped a hand over my mouth. My shoulders shook, tears spilling while joy surged through me so fast it felt like sunlight cracking through every seam. I couldn't stop laughing, couldn't stop crying, my palm pressing harder into the flat of my belly as if I'd feel something there already.

But then the joy tangled with something darker, confusion and horror rushing in just as quickly. My smile trembled.

Carter.

If I was pregnant, the baby was *undoubtedly* his.

"I... I don't understand," I sputtered, shaking my head. "I'm on birth control. We weren't... I wasn't tracking my cycle or anything like that. We weren't trying."

He doesn't even want *a child,* I reminded myself with panic slipping in like a mud slide, but I kept that part to myself.

Doctor Stroud reached out, touching my arm with a reassuring squeeze. "Your hormone levels from the labs came back clearly positive, which confirms the pregnancy."

My throat was so tight I was sure I couldn't swallow, but I tried anyway. "I haven't felt anything."

"You're only a few weeks along — early enough that symptoms can be subtle or even nonexistent." Her smile softened. "And I know you're on birth control, and that we've discussed your AMH levels being lower than average. Both of those factors can make this feel confusing, even impossible. But low AMH doesn't mean you can't get pregnant — it just means you may have fewer eggs overall. Fertility and contraception don't always line up as neatly as we'd like. Even women with diminished ovarian reserve can conceive." Her shoulders lifted. "Sometimes when they least expect it."

"This is... unbelievable."

She nodded in understanding. "It may seem that way, but this is why we always test before we move forward with anything. With birth control pills, even slight inconsistencies — missing a dose, taking one late, or interactions with other medications — can reduce their effectiveness. It's rare, but it happens. And it seems it happened here."

My next exhale was shaky, my hand floating back to my abdomen. It was like everything in my universe had been shaken in that instant, like a snow globe without the pieces nailed down. Now everything was floating and flying, settling in the wrong places — or maybe the right ones all along.

Doctor Stroud paused, her voice steady. "We'll do an ultrasound to confirm viability, but there's no mistake, Livia. You're pregnant."

I stared at her, my pulse pounding in my ears, my body torn in two.

Joy, radiant and fierce, because this was the dream I'd always promised myself.

And dread, sharp and suffocating, because Carter Fabri had no idea what was about to hit him.

Chapter 28

Barry White

Carter

"Fuck, I hope this isn't stupid."

I was bouncing on my toes, fidgeting, not feeling even the least bit cool as I waited for Livia to arrive. It didn't matter that it was the perfect night, warm and pleasant with a crisp breeze for reprieve, the sun slowly sinking over the bay in the distance. It didn't matter that we had the whole rooftop to ourselves, that I'd rented the thing out and wouldn't have anyone watching me while I bumbled through my idiotic speech to Liv. And it definitely didn't matter that she'd already told me she felt the same.

For some reason I couldn't explain, everything just felt volatile, like my world as I knew it was a triangular-shaped rock balanced on its peak. It was stable for now, everything meticulously placed.

But one wrong move could shatter the whole thing.

"It's going to be great, Fabio," Will said, smirking from where he stood beside me. "Look, the worst thing that could happen is she turns you down and tells you to get lost. Nothing you haven't endured before."

"Comforting," I said flatly, but the corners of my lips curled a bit. He wasn't wrong.

When the guys had helped me come up with a plan for the evening, I'd suckered all of them into being involved one way or another. I wanted every step of the night to feel luxurious, VIP treatment from beginning to end. And I didn't just want strangers doing all the pampering. I wanted it to be our friends.

Our family.

I wanted to remind Livia that no matter what, even when things got difficult between us — which they inevitably would — we were never alone. We'd always have love and support around us.

I didn't fill the girls in on the plan, though. For some reason, that didn't feel like my place. I knew Livia would want to tell them in her own way and in her own time. So, all the girlfriends and wives believed we were having a guys' night on the golf course, sneaking in a few rounds without Coach knowing.

In reality, Vince was playing limousine chauffeur. He'd picked Livia up at five from her condo and had her en route to us now. They were just a few minutes out, and it felt like the longest stretch of time in my life — more so than any period of hockey I'd ever played.

The rest of the guys were here with me, each committed to their role. Will was the bodyguard and gatekeeper. He'd go downstairs to receive Livia when she arrived, walking her through the lobby and into the elevator like she was a celebrity being ushered into a private dinner.

Aleks had been tasked with all the details, and while it had felt like the biggest mistake when I agreed to let him handle that side of things, he'd surprised the hell out of me. The rooftop was beautiful enough without embellishment, but Aleks had transformed it into something out of a dream. A long table was dressed in a sleek black runner, the surface scattered with dark roses, low bowls of floating tea lights, and candles in staggered heights that flickered like fireflies in the evening breeze. He'd hung string lights from the pergola in a way that made the whole place glow, cozy and intimate but still elegant. Soft linen napkins, polished silver, wine glasses that looked like they belonged in some five-star joint — he'd thought of everything.

And, because it was Aleks, he'd added the most ridiculous touch: place cards. He'd written my name and Livia's in elaborate cursive on thick cardstock and propped them up against the plates like we were at a gala instead of my half-baked attempt at romance. But when I saw the way the whole scene came together — romantic, intentional, and just a little over-the-top — I couldn't even be mad.

Jaxson was the DJ for the evening. He'd taken over playlist duty, ignoring every text suggestion I'd sent him. Now, a beat-heavy jazz song floated over the rooftop, the kind of music that felt sultry and alive, and it reminded me instantly of Liv. I supposed I could trust that he'd done the job well.

And then there was Zamboni, running around with his tail wagging and sniffer going nuts as he inspected every corner of the space. His job was gift-holder, the poor bastard, and he wore my little secret in a box strapped to his back by way of a doggie hiking vest, completely oblivious to the treasure inside.

It meant everything to me, having the guys there, having them participate. They were giving up their Sunday night to help me make a statement to a woman I loved more than anything in the world, and I would never forget that they showed up for me.

Will's phone buzzed in his hand.

"She's here," he said, glancing at me before heading for the elevator. "Try not to puke before she makes it upstairs."

Jaxson raised his glass in salute, already manning the speaker with a grin. "Don't worry, I've got Barry White queued if things get awkward. Nothing sets the mood like deep baritone and a saxophone solo."

"Christ," I muttered, scrubbing a hand down my face.

Aleks smirked from where he adjusted the lanterns strung across the railing. "Ignore him. Everything's ready. Just breathe, Fabio."

Easier said than done, I thought, but I did my best to force air in and out of my lungs. I cracked my neck, rolling my shoulders and swallowing what felt like sandpaper in my throat. My hands were too big suddenly, too awkward, and I couldn't figure out what the hell to do with them. I alternated between cracking my knuckles, smoothing my sports coat, and shoving them in my pockets.

The ding of the elevator snapped through the rooftop like the starting gun of a race.

My pulse lurched, stomach twisting violently like I was on a rollercoaster that just did a loop before dumping me into a nosedive.

Don't blow it, a familiar voice whispered in my mind.

Before he could get another word in, I snuffed him out, visualizing me shoving him into a box and kicking it off the edge of the Grand Canyon.

And then the doors slid open, and at just the sight of her, all my nerves were calmed.

Will stepped out first, all smug professionalism with dark sunglasses covering his eyes and Livia's arm tucked into his like she was royalty being escorted to a throne. But the second I saw her, the rest of the world dimmed.

I'd been bracing myself for her usual armor: a killer dress, heels sharp enough to slit a man's throat, that don't-mess-with-me confidence that made everyone in the room orbit her like she was the sun.

Instead, she padded out in gray sweatpants and a black cropped tee, socks shoved into slides, her textured hair pulled back in a low bun. She still wore her jewelry, of course, gold chains glimmering from around her neck and studs in her ears. But she was bare-faced, cozy, like she'd just walked out of her condo and right into my best dream.

And Jesus Christ, she was beautiful.

The nervous hammer in my chest slowed to a steady and strong beat, like my heart was a drummer cast with the task to keep pace for every other organ. The moment my eyes locked on hers, the pressure released.

My breath evened out.

My spine straightened.

I didn't just feel calmed by her presence, but confident — in what I would say, in how she would receive it, in *us*.

Why the fuck was I ever nervous to begin with?

Still, as I started walking to meet her, I could see her wearing the same worry and exhaustion I had been, like she, too, was suffering from the distance we'd put between us. She looked like she'd been carrying just as much weight as I had these last weeks. But she was here. She'd come. And I knew right then that this was my chance to bring her smile back.

I took my next steps with swagger, like she was mine already, like there was no other option than for the night to end with her in my arms and my heart in her hands.

Will smirked when we met in the middle, bowing like the Queen's guard before handing me Livia's hand. I chuckled a bit, giving him a mock nod of polite gratitude, and then as he slipped back into the elevator with Aleks joining him, I pulled Livia's arm through mine.

"Hello, gorgeous," I said, smile beaming out of me like a spotlight now that I had her. The press of her warm body against mine had me as giddy as a child.

I waited for her to roll her eyes or tell me not to call her that, the way she had when I'd called her beautiful. But for once, Livia didn't seem to have a single word of retort. She only smiled, the edges of it soft and tinted with sadness. "Hi."

"Matilda" by Harry Styles began to play, and when I looked over my shoulder, it was just in time to see Jaxson cast me a wink before he joined the other guys in the elevator. Will moved his hand where he'd been holding the door open, and they disappeared, leaving us alone.

Zamboni finally realized there was someone new on the rooftop, and he abandoned where he'd no doubt been sniffing out the crumbs not even the world's best waiter could have found and sprinted straight for Livia. Like usual, she commanded him with just a raised fist, my ornery pup sliding to a stop in front of her and plopping his furry butt right down on the ground. He whined as he looked up her, tail wagging hard enough to knock over a small child.

"Good boy," she said, bending to pet him. And she didn't just hinge at the waist, either. She released me so she could squat down to his eye level, giving him her full attention, rubbing his chest and then up behind his ears with that soft smile of hers locked in place.

And if I didn't already love her, seeing her love my dog like that would have done the trick.

"What's this your dad has wrangled you into?" she asked, plucking at the hiking vest. She stilled for some reason after the words left her mouth, like she'd said something she didn't mean to, but I couldn't read too much into it before she was standing, and the look was gone. "Are we hiking or having a fine dining experience, because the way you're dressed and the way Zambo is dressed are really contrasting here."

"We're going skiing. Isn't it obvious?"

Liv's smirk was a tired one, and I reached out, thumbing just under her eyes where her full smile would usually reach. "I'm really fucking happy to see you."

She leaned into the touch, surprising me with the way her face warped. Her hands covered mine, holding me to her. "I'm glad to see you, too."

I led her to the table, pulling out her chair before I sat across from her. And as soon as I did, two waitresses poured out of the back kitchen. One unfolded our napkins and explained who they were, that they'd be taking care of us, while the other filled our water and champagne glasses. When they were gone, Livia arched a brow at me.

"This is a very different experience from our first rooftop together."

"I hoped it would be," I said, reaching over for her hands. "I thought a lot about what I wanted to do tonight. After my game last week, I was crashing out. I was just thinking about how I told you I loved you for the first time while fucking you against the side of a house in the shadows."

"Pretty iconic," Livia mused with a grin.

I laughed. "Yeah, I mean, it fit us for sure, but... Livia, you deserve so much more than just that. I thought about how I could do this big gesture for you, take you in a hot air balloon maybe, or book a quick overnight trip to Key West to dive."

"Well, I'm afraid of heights, and the thought of breathing out of a tube makes me want to claw out of my skin, so thanks for not doing that."

I smoothed her hand in mine with a grin. "What I decided was that I just wanted to take you on a good old-fashioned date."

"By renting out an entire rooftop and having your teammates treat me like a celebrity."

"Precisely."

The low laugh in her throat was raspy and delicious. "You are something else, Carter Fabri."

But for some reason, I thought she still looked a bit sad when she said it.

Chapter 29

Another Galaxy

Livia

By the time dusk settled in around us on that rooftop, I'd lost count of how many times Carter had made me laugh.

I'd managed to discreetly tell one of our waitresses to bring me nonalcoholic champagne when Carter was discussing something hockey-related with the other, and she'd winked at me before taking my glass and replacing it with a new one on her next round out to the table. But even though the bubbles were nonalcoholic, they still left me feeling fizzy inside.

The sun had slipped below the bay as we lingered at that ridiculous table Aleks had dressed like it belonged in a *Vogue* spread, the string lights above us glowing brighter with each passing minute. Carter only let go of where he held my hand across the table when a new course left, and as soon as it was cleared, he was holding me again. And sweet Zamboni was there for all of it, the kitchen crew being so kind as to bring him a giant water bowl and a meal that rivaled ours.

We'd talked about everything — his parents' home in Hamilton that he wanted to take me to, my love of trip hop, the merits of different designer brands we both fancied, and whether mint chocolate chip ice cream should be a felony. He kept the conversation light and easy, like he knew my soul was too weary for anything heavier. He didn't bring up my parents or the past that clung to me like a cloak, and he didn't press about what I was going to do about my sister's wedding.

He delivered on his promise — it just felt like a run-of-the-mill first date.

Except nothing was run of the mill when it came to this man.

Every time I looked across the table at him — at his soft grin, at the way he leaned forward like every word out of my mouth was scripture — I felt the ground tilt beneath me. I wanted to bottle the sound of his laugh, wanted to press pause on the sight of him cracking pepper over my pasta with a flourish like he was a sous chef instead of a hockey player.

I wanted to live here, in this suspended moment where everything was perfect.

But beneath the sparkle of candlelight and the gentle buzz of champagne, I still felt like I was stranded on a raft at sea — adrift, nauseous, terrified of what waited when the storm brewing in the distance finally found me.

Because at some point tonight, I had to tell him that I was pregnant.

I had to ruin this.

Every bubble of laughter that passed between us felt bittersweet because I knew it was the last of him carefree.

He didn't know what I knew. He didn't feel the secret pounding inside me, the truth that would drop like an anvil on his shoulders the second it left my lips.

And maybe I was a coward, but I couldn't do it yet. Not while his eyes still gleamed, not while he was beaming at me like everything was right in his world again now that we were together. And I felt that, too. The moment I'd stepped off that elevator and saw him, my breaths came easier, even knowing the news I had to break.

The truth was Carter felt like home in a way I thought I'd never experience again.

So, I soaked it in. I savored every joke and smile, every brush of his thumb against the back of my hand as the night deepened around us.

And then, just when I was debating if I could push the truth down for another hour or if it was time to rip the tape off the mouth of the secret held prisoner inside me, Carter leaned back in his chair, eyes glinting with mischief.

"Before we get to dessert, I have something for you."

"If you really did book a hot air balloon, I'm serious — I'm out of here."

He smirked, shaking his head before calling Zamboni over to us with a whistle. The dog hadn't laid down since I'd arrived, either drinking water, lapping up his meal, or exploring the rooftop with his nose going a thousand miles a minute.

His tongue lolled out of his mouth as he bounded over, and Carter rewarded him with a good rub down and some words of affirmation before he nodded to me. "Go give Livvy her gift."

Livvy.

I loved that nickname. It was the one Maven used with me, the one my sister once called me when we were younger. My stomach pinched at the thought of her, too. The reminder that I'd have to tell my parents was right on the heel of that.

I could already hear my mother's voice telling me that I'd disappointed them yet again.

I tilted my chin defiantly against that, because what the fuck did I care what she thought of me? But no matter how thick my skin was, she was still my mother, and I was still her little girl.

I'd always want her approval, even if I knew I'd never get it.

"Come here, Zambo," I said, cooing at him when he wiggled under the table to get to me. He spun in a circle before plopping down, and Carter nodded to the box attached to his little vest.

"Open it."

I unclipped the box from Zambo's vest, the velvet warm from where it had been riding against his fur. My heart already ached before I even knew what was inside.

Lifting the lid, I found a delicate gold chain glinting in the candlelight. A dainty key dangled from it, small enough to wear against my collarbone, intricate but understated.

Just like the rest of my jewelry, it was gold and delicate, and it fit so well with my style that I could put it on right now, or with any other outfit I had, and it would work.

It was beautiful and thoughtful, and it nearly broke my heart seeing it.

My throat tightened as I lifted it out by the chain, letting it sway in the glow of string lights above us. "Let me guess," I said softly, forcing a teasing grin. "The key to your heart?"

Carter tilted his head side to side, smirking. "Something like that." He reached into his jacket, and when he pulled out what he had hidden there, my smile dissolved.

It was a collar, thick and gorgeous, made of sleek black leather with a small, shining ring at the center.

And where it fastened, there was a lock.

My eyes shot wide, breath stalling in my chest as I looked from it to him.

His smile faltered, nerves flickering across his features, but then he squared his shoulders and pushed forward. "Alright, full disclosure, I have prepared this speech I'm about to give and rehearsed it a dozen times, but I'm so fucking nervous now that I have this thing in my hands and you're looking at me like that and I might vomit before I get it all out."

I didn't know if it was a laugh or a cry that came from me. My heart was bursting, the emotion swelling in me too much to contain.

Carter set the collar gently on the table, resting his hands on either side of it like he was offering a sacred thing. His eyes locked on mine, bright and unflinching.

"These last couple of months, everything we've done together — the lessons, the dates, the nights at The Manor, the mornings in my bed — it's meant more to me than I can even explain. At first, it was selfish. I needed your help. I wanted your guidance. And I didn't expect you to ever have anything more to do with me outside of that deal." He swallowed, his voice dipping. "But the truth is, the more time I spent with you, the more I realized I was fucked. Well and truly fucked. Because I couldn't stop wanting more of you. I still can't. I don't think I ever will."

He paused, our eyes searching the other's, his expression so open and raw that it broke something inside me.

"You've changed me, Livia. You've taught me things about myself I didn't even know existed. But it's not just about sex. It's about you. I admire the way you never stop pushing. Your tenacity, your drive, the way you walk into a room and everyone just knows you're the one in charge. I admire the way you aspire to excellence, in everything you do. The way you carry yourself. The way you believe in me, even when I don't."

His voice wavered, and he reached forward, his hand wrapping around where mine held the chain.

"I meant what I said that night you came to my house for the first time. You're beautiful, Liv. But your looks?" He shook his head. "They're the least interesting thing about you."

My eyes burned, the sting too sharp to blink away.

"So yeah." He gestured to the collar. "I bought a fucking dog collar that I fully intend to wear for you any time you like. Because I love when you own me in the bedroom — but I also need you to know that you own me everywhere else, too. Completely. Body and soul. And I'm not just eager to give myself to you, I'm desperate for it. For as long as you'll have me." He squeezed my hand. "And I know it's a lot to ask of you. I know I have a long way to go to earn your trust when those you've loved most in the past have done nothing but hurt you. But I'm asking you to try. I'm asking you to give yourself to me, too, even if it scares the ever-living shit out of you."

My nostrils flared, tears welling in my eyes.

"I promise you," he said, leaning forward, his gaze sincere and never leaving mine. "I will not hurt you. I will not fumble this. I will cherish you the way you deserve to be cherished, and I will take whatever sordid route you need me to take to get there." He added that last part with a laugh. "You are, and always have been, in control, Liv. All I ask is that you take me along for the ride."

I held my sob in my throat, trying my best to hold strong even as tears slid down my cheeks, hot and unrelenting.

Carter smirked nervously, like he was trying to lighten it all with another squeeze of my hand. "Damn, yeah, I nailed that one, didn't I?"

But instead of a laugh, the sob I'd been holding at bay ripped free, and I broke.

My hands flew to my face, covering it as I shook my head and gave in to the current pulling me under. My shoulders shook, and I clutched that key necklace to me even in my despair, wishing every word he just said would hold true when I knew it never could.

Panic crashed over his features as Carter bolted around the table. "Shit—Liv, hey, I'm sorry. Too much, right? I—fuck, I shouldn't have—"

I shook my head furiously, unable to find words, choking on the tears as he crouched in front of me. I never fucking cried, and here I had twice with him in the last two weeks. Was it hormones? Or was it just the power this man had over me?

His hands were on my knees, his eyes frantic and searching while Zamboni barked and danced around us, pawing at me like he couldn't stand to see me cry, either.

"Tell me what's wrong," Carter begged, voice breaking. "Liv, talk to me."

My lips trembled as I sniffed and looked up at the sky, my vision blurred, hands falling into my lap but still holding fast to the necklace.

I took a deep breath.

And then I let the truth fly like the grenade it was.

"Carter..." My voice cracked as I dragged in another ragged breath. "I'm pregnant."

There it was.

My next breath seared like I was breathing in straight smoke and fire, and the waitresses came out with smiles and dessert in their hands only to take one look at me and immediately round right back into the kitchen.

I couldn't look at Carter for a full minute, my eyes losing focus on the lights strung in the distance. I couldn't bear to see the disappointment in his eyes, to have to witness his world crashing down by my hand.

The silence between us stretched, endless and suffocating, and when I finally felt like I had no other choice, I faced him.

The look on his face gutted me.

His eyes were wide and devoid of life, his lips parted, like the earth had just tilted off its axis and he was waiting for space to swallow him whole.

Panic clawed up my throat, stomach twisting so violently I curled in on myself.

"I know," I blurted, the words tumbling out fast, frantic. "I know we didn't expect this — trust me, I know."

He opened his mouth, but I steamrolled right over whatever he meant to say.

"You have to understand, I never told you... but this was always my plan. This was always it for me. I was going to freeze my eggs, to have a child one day, on my own. That's why I said yes to your offer so easily — it was going to set me up to pay for all the procedures, the freezing and storage, and then one day... I was going to take care of a baby on my own. I knew with that two-million dollars, we'd never want for anything. I could hire a nanny to help. I could afford a nice daycare when the time came. That was always the plan. *On my own,* Carter. No husband, no boyfriend, no one else. Just me and her — yes, her, because in my mind it was always going to be a girl — and a chance to give someone the mother I never had."

His brows furrowed, shoulders deflating. "Liv..."

"I went to the appointment this week." My voice cracked again, the memory slicing me open. "I knew you and I had... I knew you said you loved me and goddamnit, Carter," I choked, eyes colliding with his. "I love you, too."

His eyes watered, which only made my own emotions harder to contain.

"But I still had to do this for me," I whispered. "Just in case. I wanted to know that I still had this option, especially because I know you..."

I shook my head, not ready to go there yet.

"And then my doctor told me we couldn't move forward." My lips trembled. "Because I'm already pregnant."

Tears blurred my vision once more, spilling hot and fast down my cheeks. My heart hammered so loud I was sure all of Tampa Bay could hear it. I hadn't felt so raw and exposed since the night my innocence was stolen, but this cut deeper somehow.

"I'm so sorry," I whispered, words tripping over each other, tumbling into a mess. "I know this isn't what you want, Carter. I know it's not fair to you. And I need you to understand that you don't have to do anything. You don't owe me a damn thing. I can do this. I *will* do this."

I swallowed hard, choking on the lie that tasted like blood.

"But I don't need you."
Please stay.
Please, please don't leave me.

"I can handle it on my own."

I can't handle it on my own.

I don't want to do this on my own.

"And you don't—you don't have to—you don't—"

I was in his arms before I could croak out anything else, and the moment he pulled me into him, I succumbed to another round of sobs. I clung to him, literally and metaphorically, and willed every lie I'd just said to be true. I tried to reassure my breaking heart that we would be okay, that we'd survive this no matter what Carter decided, but it was a weak and futile argument.

"Shhh," he said against my hair, kissing my forehead and letting his lips linger there as he held me tight. "Oh, baby, please, *please*. You're breaking my fucking heart right now."

"I've ruined it all."

I sobbed the words, and then was promptly startled when Carter laughed at them. He shook his head, pulling back to frame my face with his hands, his brows folded together. "What do you mean you've ruined everything? Livia, this isn't your fault."

"I... I made you do all that testing and made you feel safe, but I've been so stressed, and I haven't been consistent taking my pill, and I *knew* I should have just had a freaking IUD put in!"

Carter laughed again, kissing my lips before I could register what was happening.

"Oh, you silly, maddening woman. It is not your fault. These things happen. And, uh, in case you have forgotten, I was more than a willing participant in our unprotected sex."

"I'm so sorry, Carter."

"For *what*?!" He grabbed my face again. "Livvy, I feel like I just won the fucking Cup."

"You..." I balked. "You what?"

"I'm thrilled. I'm over the moon. I'm so far over the moon I've hit another galaxy completely."

"But you told me you didn't want kids."

"Yeah, because at that moment in time, you were asking Carter, the no-game having bachelor hockey player. But that guy died. I buried him the night I told you I loved you and heard you say you feel the same."

"Carter, don't fuck with me right now."

"I'm as serious as a positive pregnancy test, Mistress."

I laughed, despite feeling like it was impossible, swatting at his chest. "Stop."

"No. I won't. I refuse to stop. I'm going to make you laugh when you feel like crying for the rest of your fucking life. And I call bullshit on everything you just said. You don't get to do this on your own. You don't get to tell me it's okay if I just pass on being a fucking father?" He shook his head and hearing it from his mouth made me realize how ridiculous it was. "No. Fuck that. I am going to be right here," he said, pointing to the earth between us. "Right by your side through every symptom, every doctor's appointment, and every fucking push. I'm going to be the best father I can be, and the best partner, and I will annoy the hell out of you with how much I make this whole thing my personality."

I choked on another cross between a sob and a laugh.

"And I will love you, Livia Young, until the blood in my veins runs cold. You're not doing this on your own. We're doing this together. And the only thing I want to hear you say right now is *yes, sir*."

He kissed me as soon as the words left his lips, hard and passionate and with every promise he'd just made reverberating through him and right into me.

I melted into that kiss, clinging to him with everything I had. My fingers curled in his shirt, my lips moving desperately against his as tears kept slipping free, this time from sheer relief.

When we finally broke apart, my chest was heaving, and I pressed my forehead to his, laughing through the tears. "I can't believe this."

"You better believe it," Carter said, brushing his thumbs over my cheeks. He pressed a softer kiss to my lips, then pulled back and reached for my water glass, sliding it into my hands. "Here. Drink."

I obeyed, though my hands were trembling so badly half the glass nearly sloshed onto my sweatpants. He steadied it for me, watching me like I might break in half if he let go.

"How are you feeling?" he asked gently.

I exhaled, holding my head in one hand as I set the water back down. "Honestly? I don't feel any different yet, other than, as you can tell, I don't feel like getting dressed." I waved a hand over my ensemble. "But I imagine that'll change soon enough."

"You're beautiful."

"A sweatpants goddess, for sure."

His grin spread wide and sure. "You *do* realize I'm going to spoil the shit out of you through this whole thing, don't you?"

A startled laugh burst from my chest. "Of course you are."

But then my eyes caught on the collar still sitting on the table, gleaming dark in the candlelight. I picked it up slowly, turning it over in my hands.

"You know," I said carefully, "in the BDSM community, giving someone this is… a lot more serious than I think you realize."

His brow arched, eyes narrowing with curiosity. "Oh?"

"Yeah," I said, amusement curling in my tone. "To some, it's essentially equivalent to a wedding ring. A collar means belonging. Commitment. It means... ownership, in the most sacred, consensual way." My fingers ran over the leather, the metal ring cool against my skin. "It isn't a casual gift."

For a second, I thought maybe he'd backpedal, that he'd laugh and say he didn't know, that he didn't mean it that way. But instead, Carter tapped his chin like he was lost in thought, then pulled me up long enough to sit in my chair and yank me right back down into his lap.

"You know what? Fuck it. No regrets." He kissed all over my neck as I laughed and squealed, his arms wrapping around me. Then, he smoothed my hair back, his eyes on mine. "Collar, ring, no jewelry at all — it doesn't matter. I meant every word I said. I'm yours, Liv."

The breath rushed out of me, and I sank against him, curling into his chest as he wrapped me up in his arms. For the first time since the news from Doctor Stroud had flipped my world upside down, I felt safe.

I felt steady.

I was home.

My lips brushed against his neck, my voice just a whisper against his skin. "And I'm yours."

Chapter 30

All the Little Things

Carter

I'm going to be a dad.

The laces bit into my palms as I pulled them tight, the way they always did, the ritual so ingrained it should have been muscle memory by now. But tonight, like every night since Livia told me her news, nothing felt automatic.

I'm going to be a dad.

A million other things should have been on my mind: the lineup sheet, the players I'd be matched against, the fact that this was a home game against a division rival with playoff seeding on the line. This was the kind of game that could make or break a season.

But none of that could rival the six words that continued to rattle around in my head, louder than the crowd warming up outside, louder than the squeak of skates cutting across the fresh sheet of ice.

I'm going to be a dad.

It had been a month since Livia told me, and the thought hadn't left me once. Not on the ice or at the gym or when I tried to sleep at night.

And I didn't want it to.

I was happy to be consumed by the thought, by a fact I wasn't sure would ever play out in my life.

That first week, I was a planet knocked out of orbit. I'd alternated between burying Liv in mountains of kisses because she was somehow even sexier knowing our baby was growing inside her and having full-on meltdowns at how ill-prepared I was to welcome a child into the world. It was an absolute tornado.

But soon after that, a serene peace I didn't know I could feel settled in — the calm after the storm, as they say.

It started when we told my parents. Their faces were smushed together on a video call, both of them grinning and talking over one another in their rush and excitement to get to know Livia. I'd never introduced them to a woman, and clearly, they had no idea how to act when I did.

And when we told them we were expecting, I'd braced for the worst, for them to instantly sour and lecture me about responsibility.

Instead, my father had burst into tears like the big softy he was, and my mother had gushed, both of them unable to contain their delight.

We'd ended the call with them making us promise to send them date options for when they could come visit, and no sooner had we hung up than my mom was asking me for Livia's number. She instantly asked how Livia was feeling and if she had any questions about pregnancy or birth.

My mom didn't even know about Livia's mom, but it was like she could tell, like she saw it in her eyes or something.

And it meant more to Livia than she could ever tell me. I knew it every time I saw her smiling when she and my mom were on another phone call talking about breastfeeding or wake windows.

I'm going to be a dad.

After that, Livia and I had slid into this new routine without ever saying we were doing it. She still lived at her condo, I still lived at my little house on the water, but most nights we ended up together. Sometimes I'd wake up tangled in her sheets, sunlight spilling through her skyscraper windows while she muttered about missing coffee as she buttoned up her white coat. Other mornings, it was her half-asleep groan when my alarm went off before practice, followed by her burrowing into my pillow the second I left for the rink.

The worst days were when I was on the road for the team. It wasn't because of the grind of travel, but because of the empty stretch of bed, the absence of her. I caught myself scrolling through my camera roll in hotel rooms more than I'd like to admit — replaying videos I'd taken of her sketching new jewelry designs, or smiling when I found the photo of her curled up in my hoodie, feet in my lap, chewing absentmindedly on a pencil as she listened to one of those new-parent podcasts she'd gotten us hooked on.

And for the first time in our relationship, sex wasn't the focus like it had been. She was tired, nauseous, sometimes just not in the mood — and I didn't give a damn. Because it turned out what I craved even more were all the little things we'd built in between.

It was the way she'd let me take care of her after she worked a long day when our schedules matched up, allowing me the privilege of undressing her and running her a bath before I'd cook whatever she felt like she could stomach. It was how she'd hum while she worked on a set of earrings and then look up with a sleepy grin that made my heart stop. It was the way she looked in the setting sun when we'd take the boards out on the water, how she thought I didn't notice when her hand would hover over her still-flat stomach. It was the moments like when she'd rest her hand absently on my thigh while we rotted on the couch, both of us trying not to get emotional any time there was a commercial with babies and parents.

I never won that battle, by the way.

Even chores that should have felt overwhelming, like figuring out what crib or stroller or car seat to buy, filled me with an inexplicable joy. I cherished the way it felt to have Livia's hand in mine as we each scrolled on our phones, showing each other the different review videos or brands of choice.

Moments like that made me feel more alive than any highlight reel goal.

I never thought I'd be the guy who got high off quiet nights at home. I was always the one who wanted to go out to Boomer's after a game or find the best night life when the team traveled to different cities. But the last month with Livia, knowing what I know now about our future… it had changed me.

I'm going to be a dad.

Livia was crawling out of her skin, though. She enjoyed the nights at home, but I knew she missed getting dolled up and going out. So, I vowed that as soon as she was feeling better, that was exactly what we'd do. I'd take her out and let her show off her baby bump in her skin-tight dresses, and I'd be there to rub her feet when we got back home, too. I'd keep my hands to myself as long as she wanted, and then gladly drop to my knees and bark like a dog as soon as she said the word.

Because I wanted it all with her — the quiet and the loud, the bright and the dim, going out and staying home, dressed up and in sweats, cuddles on the couch and burying myself deep inside her.

And I wanted to parent with her.

I'm going to be a dad.

My stomach still tumbled with the thought, even a month later, and I wondered if that would ever change. Part of me hoped it wouldn't.

I wondered if we'd have a boy or a girl, if they'd favor Livia or me or be a perfect little blend of us both. But one thing I knew for sure was that Livia would be a damn good mom, and just like she wanted, she'd write the story she wished played out for herself. She'd be the mother to our kid that hers should have been to her.

She hadn't told her parents yet. She wasn't sure she would at all. And I didn't blame her for not feeling like they deserved to know. In fact, I felt protective over our baby in a way that I didn't want them to know, either. They would soon enough — but I didn't feel the need for them to be involved now, and Livia didn't seem to, either.

Livia did decide to share the news with her sister — along with her answer about the wedding.

She wasn't going.

And I fully supported her in that decision, too.

The ache in my chest was strong when I thought about all she'd been through, about how callous her parents had been, how complicated things were between her and her sister. I couldn't change that, no matter how I wished differently, but I *could* be with her in this new chapter and make the future brighter than the past.

That was a goal I would score, no matter what challenges stood in my way.

"Fabri."

I glanced up, blinking out of my thoughts as Coach McCabe stopped in front of my stall. His expression was sharp, the way it always was before a game.

"Coach," I greeted.

He nodded for me to stand, and once I did, he folded his arms over his chest and looked around the room before back at me. "I'm starting you tonight. First line."

The words punched me right in the chest.

First line.

Me.

Coach clapped a hand on my shoulder pad with a wry grin. "Don't look so surprised."

"Is that what I look like? I was going for *shocked to death*."

"Hey, don't joke about this, alright? You know as well as I do that you've earned the chance. Don't cheapen that with self-deprecation."

I swallowed, pride swelling in my throat even at the lashing. Because he was right. I had earned it.

And it meant a hell of a lot to me to hear that he saw that, too.

With one final squeeze of my shoulder, he released me without further fanfare. "Show me you can land it home."

And then he was gone, moving on down the row.

I sank back down into the bench in front of my locker, staring at the white of my tape, hearing the blood rush in my ears. A year ago, the pressure of this opportunity would have crushed me. I would have heard Coach Leduc's voice, sneering, reminding me I'd never be enough, that if I slipped even once it proved him right.

But tonight, that voice was nonexistent.

I wasn't that kid anymore.

I'm going to be a dad.

Maybe it should have scared the piss out of me, the inescapable truth of that. I knew parenthood wasn't for the weak. But instead of terror, I only felt steadiness. I was like an old oak tree, rooted deep to something stronger than my own fear.

"Yo, Fabio," Vince called from across the room, snapping me out of it. "Try not to whiff it in front of the home crowd tonight, yeah?"

He must have overheard Coach telling me I was starting. Or maybe McCabe had talked to him before he even told me. Vince was first line, too, after all. And I saw it in my friend's playful smirk with the chirp.

He was trying to relax me; to let me know he believed in me, too.

Aleks snorted, tossing a roll of tape to Jaxson. "He's not you, Tanny Boy. Man's been hot as hell lately. You just pay attention to your own game."

"And *you* pay attention to your hands," Will cut in, scowling like always as he leaned back in his stall. "One wrong slash and you'll be cozying up in the penalty box before the first intermission."

"Please," Aleks scoffed. "The refs love me."

"Yeah, like they love root canals," Will shot back, earning a chorus of laughter from the guys.

"Don't act like those penalties I get don't get the crowd fired up," Aleks kept defending.

Jaxson smirked, snapping his gum as he waddled past us on his skates. "Yeah, fired up to see me score on the power play your dumb ass just handed 'em."

The chirps kept on, but I didn't miss Daddy P's nod of encouragement as he stood, like he wanted me to know everyone had faith in me taking that first line. And then we were filing out, one by one, the lights and roar from the crowd thundering almost as hard as my heart.

And for the first time in my career, I didn't feel the weight of the moment.

I felt ready.

Because I'm going to be a dad.

Chapter 31
No Better Way to Be
Livia

The suite smelled like hot pretzels and melted cheese, and the spread laid out across the counter was nothing short of obscene. Chicken fingers, nachos, charcuterie, sliders — basically everything you could possibly want to inhale during a hockey game.

And every aroma that was currently making me ill.

I subtly popped another ginger chew between my teeth, all my hopes and dreams wrapped up in me surviving the next four weeks until the second trimester. Everyone swore it got better then, and I was banking on it.

Still, it was worth it to face my nausea and be at the game with the girls. It wasn't often we were all in town and our schedules lined up perfectly to make it happen, and I was soaking it in.

The game had yet to start, so we were all huddled up in the food and beverage area of the suite — well, everyone except for Ava, who, of course, couldn't possibly miss warmups and the pregame fun. She was down in her seat in the front row of the box, foam finger at the ready, leaning forward to see all the action. Chloe kept a close eye on her from where we stood, and she still had that newlywed glow about her, her smile radiant.

Grace and Mia were arguing over which travel destination was more worth a fourteen-hour flight — Japan or Australia — while Maven and I gabbed with Chloe about the renovations she was doing on the house she now shared with Will.

Ten minutes before game time, Grace popped up like a Jack in the Box, nearly sloshing her wine out of the cup. "Oh! I forgot to tell you bitches! I'll be in Tampa through playoffs."

"Wait, really?!" Chloe lit up. "You never stick around here longer than a week!"

Grace shrugged. "I know. I mean look, I'll still be traveling. I plan to hit a few of the away games. But... I don't know. I've seen a lot of things, been a lot of places... but I always miss *this* place when I'm gone. I think maybe it's time to hang out for a while. Plant some roots."

"Careful," Maven warned with a rasp. "You sound a lot like a woman ready to settle down with a fine ass defenseman."

"I settle about as much as a stubborn corporation in a lawsuit," Grace shot back quickly. She sipped her wine, tucking a strand of hair behind her ear. "I just maybe want to travel a teeny tiny bit less."

"It's okay to want to stay in one place for a while," Chloe said softly. "Doesn't mean you have to get married or anything."

Grace sipped her wine again, apparently done with the subject, and the rest of us shared knowing smiles.

"Speaking of settling down, how's newlywed life treating you?" I asked Chloe.

She sighed dreamily, leaning against the high-top table we were gathered around. The light from the ice caught her ring just right, throwing diamonds everywhere. "I still can't believe I'm married. I feel like I blinked and Will and I went from sneaking kisses to promising forever."

"And *I* feel like that could be a song," Mia teased, lifting her champagne to her lips. She had a glow of her own — tour exhaustion softened by pure giddy anticipation of her summer ahead.

"I have a feeling you'll have lots of song inspiration in just a couple months," Maven said. "Tour over, honeymoon loading."

"Is it weird that I miss tour already, but simultaneously can't wait to fuck off and dive off the face of the planet for a summer?" Mia asked.

I squeezed her hand. "Your fans will be waiting eagerly when you return, whenever that is, and you should take your sweet time. You've earned it."

"I wish I had a relaxing summer to look forward to," Maven chimed in. "Looks like our initiative to make sure every kid in Tampa Bay has a place to rest their head at night has caught fire. We've had invitations to work with nonprofits all over Florida to do the same."

"Don't act like you'd want to relax even if it was an option," I said with a suck of my teeth. "We all know nothing makes you happier than being in the community like that."

"And we all want to help," Mia chimed in. "So, tell me where to send the check."

"And tell me where to show up for work. I love to get dirty." Grace said that last part with a wink and a shimmy of her hips that had us all giggling.

"So, Livia..." Chloe said next, about as subtle as a train horn. "You and Carter, huh?"

I sipped my water with a sly grin. "Do I win the prize for most shocking development of the group this year?"

"I definitely hold last year's title," Mia said, and no one argued.

"I mean, look," Grace said, holding out her hands. "We all knew he was obsessed with you. But I'll admit, I'm surprised to see it reciprocated."

I smiled wider then, warmth blooming in my chest. "If you knew Carter like I do, you'd be obsessed, too," I said simply.

That earned a chorus of soft *awws* and cheeky smirks.

"He really is a sweetheart," Maven said. "He always has been. I remember when I was assigned to follow Vince around and how... awkward it all felt at first. Carter was the first to crack a joke and make me feel comfortable."

"He does always bring the best energy to the function," Grace added, tilting her head side to side. "No matter what the function is."

"And he's worked so hard to be where he is now. He would literally call Will and ask him for advice after games when he was playing in the AHL," Chloe said.

"I didn't know that," Mia mused. "But I *do* know that while Aleks pretended Carter annoyed him earlier this season, he loves him. I think Carter is his favorite of the group."

My chest swelled with pride as they talked about him, and I nodded. "He's just... attentive in a way I didn't know men could be. He's always checking in on me, making sure I eat when I'm too busy at work, paying attention to the little things like my favorite cookie or the kind of jewelry I wear... and don't even get me started on how patient he is. I'm a maddening woman," I said on a laugh to no arguments. "But with him... I've never felt so cared for in my life."

They all melted at that.

I paused, sipping my water. "Plus, his dick is huge, and he hasn't said no to a single kinky thing I've suggested."

Maven elbowed me as the rest of the girls dissolved into a fit of laughter.

"Well," Grace said, raising her glass, "I just want to go on record that I called this ages ago. I swore I saw something between you two even at that charity golf tournament."

Chloe leaned forward, eyes mischievous. "Okay, but does this mean you're still freezing your eggs?"

I rolled my lips together, gaze falling to my hands that were wrapped around my cup of water. My eyes flitted to Maven, who looked ready to burst, and I decided it was time. "Well," I said. "Turns out... I won't be needing to do that."

Confusion flickered across their faces as I lifted that cup in my hands, drawing more attention to the fact that I wasn't drinking. And then I watched the realization dawn slowly — each pair of eyes narrowing, lips parting, a little head tilt from Chloe. Maven was chewing her lip so hard I thought she'd draw blood, but she didn't dare say a word. She already knew. She'd been the first I'd told.

"Oh my God," Mia gasped.

"No way," Chloe whispered, her hands flying up to cover her smile.

"Do not tell me you're pregnant?!" Grace squealed, practically climbing over the table.

"Okay," I said with a shrug. "I won't tell you."

I sipped my water with a smug wink, and then they all lost it.

The suite exploded into a fit of high-pitched screams.

They swarmed me with hugs, voices overlapping in a chorus of *no way* and *holy shit* and *this is going to be the cutest baby to ever live*! Immediately after that, it was a gazillion questions aimed at how I was feeling and if I had anything figured out.

Mia, of course, brought back her designer baby shoes joke, declaring she already had a few bookmarked for when the shower invites went out. Grace kissed my cheek and promised she'd be here every step of the way, that this was even more reason for her to stay local for a while. Chloe looked like she might actually cry. And Ava, sweet Ava, started chanting *"Baby Osprey"* like it was a team cheer as soon as she ran up to find what all the commotion was about and Chloe broke the news.

Of course, she ran right back down to the seats once the chaos had settled.

It was impossible not to feel the overwhelming love in that moment, and my smile was impenetrable. But underneath that smile, a tangle of nerves still lived in my chest.

I was excited, yes — I felt that more than anything, especially since Carter hadn't even blinked when I'd told him. He'd just pulled me into his arms and said we'd figure it out together, like it was the most natural thing in the world. And since then, he'd been all in.

The fear that had kept me up at night had faded more and more with every grocery run he made for ginger ale and crackers, every podcast he queued up, every kiss he laid against my temple, every time he said he couldn't wait to meet our baby.

Still... fear had a way of lingering, like smoke that clings to your clothes long after the fire's out. And sitting here surrounded by my best friends, I realized I wanted to say it out loud. I'd kept my friends in the dark on so many things in my life, so many feelings, but I needed them through this. I needed to be vulnerable, even if it was hard.

"I know we're all buzzing over this," I said, wiping the tears from laughing away with a swipe of my thumb. My smile waned a bit. "But... can I admit that I'm also a little scared?"

"Well, of fucking course you are," Grace said. "It's a baby. It's a whole ass *human* that you have growing inside you."

"I'd be more concerned if you weren't scared," Mia added.

I nodded. "It's not even really being pregnant or giving birth. My relationship with my mom is just so..."

"Fucked," Grace finished for me, and we all laughed at that.

I'd confided in all of them not too long ago about everything going on with my family. Maybe knowing I would be a mom soon had emboldened me, because suddenly I couldn't figure out why I'd felt the need to hide it from all of them save for Maven. Of course, they'd all listened and comforted me, vowing their support for me no matter what I decided to do about my sister's wedding. But more than that, they didn't pity me when I told them the reasons behind my family's detachment. They treated me like the survivor I was, helping me through a tough storm of emotions while also reminding me that none of what happened in my past defined who I was now.

And that's the thing about girlfriends — the real ones. They're soulmates, too. They're the ones who show up in ways no one else can, who remind you of your worth when you forget, who fight for you and laugh with you and refuse to let you go through the hardest parts of life alone.

"Exactly," I echoed Grace. "And I guess I just... I don't want to get this wrong. I don't want to hurt someone. I want this kid to have the best childhood possible, better than mine. And some days I worry about whether I'll be enough to give them that."

The suite was quiet for a beat before Grace leaned forward, her expression fierce in that way only she could manage. "Livia. You will be an incredible mother. The fact that you're even asking these questions proves it."

Chloe reached for my hand. "You've already broken the cycle. You know what you don't want to repeat, and you'll build something better. That's what matters."

Mia nodded, her eyes glossy. "And you're not doing this alone. You've got Carter. And you've got us. We're here for every step."

"Every contraction, every craving, every meltdown," Grace added. "We'll be right there with you."

The knot in my chest loosened. For the first time, I let myself believe them.

"Can I ask... has any of this impacted your decision with Lacey's wedding?" The question came from Chloe, who was flushing red like she wasn't sure she should have asked.

I let out a breath. "Yeah. It has. I finally put boundaries in place and told her the truth. The whole thing — about the abuse from..." I swallowed down bile the way I always did when I had to say his name. "From Robert. I told her how our parents covered it up, and how they disowned me when I refused to stay quiet."

"Oh my God," Grace whispered. "What did she say?"

I shrugged. "Honestly? I think she's always known. She just didn't want to admit it, because then she'd have to choose between me and our parents. And I don't think she knows how to do that yet. She told me she loved me. That she was sorry it happened. That it was awful. But she didn't denounce them, either. Maybe one day she'll call them on it. Maybe she'll keep living in denial. That's her path to walk."

My throat tightened, but I forced myself to keep going.

"She did say she understood my decision not to go to the wedding. Or any family function ever again. And..." I hesitated, then smiled faintly. "I told her I was pregnant. That if she wanted to, I'd love for her to be a part of her niece's life."

A beat of silence passed before Mia asked softly, "Will you tell your parents?"

I shook my head. "No. I don't have anything more to say to them."

The girls all stared at me with glossy eyes, the weight of what I'd said settling between us. Then Maven reached over and laced her fingers through mine, squeezing so tight it almost hurt.

"You're so strong, Liv," she said, her voice firm, steady. "We're proud of you. And you don't need them. You've got us. We're your family now."

I swallowed hard as the rest of them nodded, murmuring their agreement.

It was then that I realized Maven had been a little too quiet in the midst of all of this, and now that the heavier moment had passed, she was still bouncing on her toes like she had to hold the secret I'd just spilled to everyone.

"Easy, bestie," I told her, looping her arm through mine. "You can relax and yap about all the things you've been forced to keep inside for a month."

"Well, actually, I'm having a hard time relaxing at all the past few days."

I frowned. "Oh no. What's going on?"

But she didn't look sad. She looked like she'd just won the lottery. For a second, I thought maybe she had.

When she held up a little white stick in her hands, I didn't even have to look closely to understand why she was so giddy.

"SHUT UP!" I screamed, and damn my fucking hormones because tears instantly sprung to my eyes. "YOU SHUT UP RIGHT NOW, MAVEN TANEV!"

Maven just started crying with me, her smile so big it took up her whole face. "I just found out! I wanted to surprise you!"

I shook my head in disbelief before wrapping her in the tightest hug of my life. We cried and squealed and clutched each other close while the other girls slowly caught on and had their own freak outs.

"I can't believe this," I whispered in her ear, squeezing her tighter. "We get to do this together."

"Thank fucking God because I have no idea what I'm doing," Maven said with a laugh that sparked one of my own.

"Neither do I. We can be the hot mess express moms."

"No better way to be."

"I'm laughing even harder now at your comment about a *relaxing summer*," I said, giggling. "Bitch, we are going to be everything but relaxed."

"Pregnant as fuck."

"In Florida. God help us."

We laughed and cried and held each other for as long as we could, right up until the lights began to flash and the crowd noise rose from a murmur to a roar.

The game started, and despite the mountains of questions all the girls had now, we all scrambled down to our seats to watch the puck drop, and instantly, the adrenaline of the game swept us away.

When I saw Carter skate out in the first line, I screamed so loud even Ava called me a fangirl.

But in the middle of it all, I let myself think about the past month. I thought of Carter and how he'd been by my side through the nausea and exhaustion, how he'd kissed my forehead when I apologized for being too tired, how he'd held me on the couch while I dozed off against his chest. I thought about how much I missed the electricity of us in the bedroom, even knowing it would return soon enough — and how much I'd unexpectedly grown to love the quiet, tender side of him just as much. Maybe even more.

And that night, we all watched the man my child would call Dada soon skate out with fire in his eyes. We sat in awe as he crushed it shift after shift, as the Ospreys clinched the playoffs.

Just like Carter had clinched my heart.

Chapter 32

Choosing You

Livia

Two weeks before my sister's wedding, she showed up at my door.

Or rather, at Carter's door.

I was curled sideways on his couch, one hand on my belly like I might feel the flutter I knew wouldn't come for weeks, the other cradling a mug of peppermint tea Carter had brewed me.

He hovered nearby, as he did — big body, soft eyes, and that burly beard he had thanks to the Ospreys being firmly in the playoff race. He informed me he wasn't shaving until they lost, which had me questioning who I was rooting for each time he hit the ice.

"Anything else I can get you?" he asked, grabbing Zamboni's leash from where it hung by the door. The pup scurried out from where I'd been using him as a footrest on the couch with a little bark of excitement.

I lifted my mug. "You've already done enough."

A knock rattled the door.

Carter glanced at me, that mischief-light in his eyes that usually preceded him saying something designed to make me roll mine.

"Who is that?"

His grin twitched wider, but there was a nervous edge to it, too. "Either a really great surprise, or one that is going to land me in the dog house."

Zamboni huffed impatiently, waiting for Carter to let him out now that his harness was in place. But Carter only used it to wrangle him before opening the front door.

When he did, time collapsed.

My sister stood on the threshold in a sundress the color of lemon bars, her hair twisted back the way she wore it in high school when we used to share a bathroom and a secret stash of lip gloss, her eyes shining with both hope and uncertainty. Her hands were full, tote bag straps digging into her shoulder, and another paper grocery sack hugged to her chest.

The mug nearly slipped from my hand.

"Hi," she breathed, the word shaking.

I just blinked.

I couldn't believe she was there.

Carter moved quickly, helping Lacey with the bags and inviting her inside as he struggled to keep Zamboni in check. Of course, my sister commanded him with ease just like I did, which made Carter go slack jawed and me grin.

For a heartbeat I stayed seated, body glued to leather. Fight, flight, freeze. I tried to work through what I knew could help — naming five things I could see, breathing in for four and out for six, but my brain was a jumbled mess.

Because my sister was here.

My sister is here.

As if it just registered, I abandoned my mug on the coffee table and rolled off the couch, scurrying over to her.

And as soon as the bags were out of her hands, Lacey was rushing to me, too.

We collided, arms thrown tight, both of us giggling, or maybe trying not to cry. I didn't care in that moment about any of the weirdness between us. I hadn't seen her in years, and something about just her presence alone had me forgetting there was any bad blood between us.

She felt the same. She smelled like the same honeyed vanilla lotion we stole from Mom's vanity when we were twelve. My chest caved, and once again I found myself blaming hormones for how tears flooded my eyes.

"Oh, how I've missed you," she whispered into my neck.

"I didn't know if I still had you."

The truth shredded my throat on the way out.

"You do," she said. She squeezed harder, like she could anchor the words into flesh. "You always do."

I wanted to believe her, to revel in those words, but something in me stayed wary. We separated, and I wiped under my eyes with the pad of my thumb. Lacey did the same.

"Come on, Zambo," Carter said, leaning in to wrap his arm around me and press a kiss to my temple. "I'll be right down the road," he whispered. "I have my phone. Call if you need me. Okay?"

I nodded, pressing up to kiss his lips. "You did this?"

"I only helped facilitate," he said with a grin, and then with one last squeeze of my hip, he and Zambo were gone.

Lacey watched me, her fingers writhing together in front of her waist.

"You—" It took me a second to find my voice. "You're here."

Lacey exhaled. "I am. Hi."

"Hi." I huffed out a laugh that still felt like a sob. "You said that already."

Her mouth wobbled. "I panicked. I had a better opening line in the car." Her eyes fell to where I was absentmindedly rubbing my stomach. I couldn't help it. It didn't matter that I was just barely showing a little bump that looked more like I'd eaten too much than anything else. I felt our baby like a piece of me, one I had to constantly cradle and protect. "Oh, Liv."

"I know," I said, shaking my head as I looked down. "It's crazy, isn't it?"

"It's wonderful."

Her brows pinched together when I looked back at her, but then she clapped her hands together. "Oh! I brought you some things."

She ran to the counter where Carter had dropped the bags, digging through them and pulling out items one by one. Black-and-white cookies. A box from a bakery I recognized from Long Island — soft everything bagels wrapped in white paper, a pint of scallion cream cheese. Rainbow cookies in a little windowed box. A jar of deli pickles as big as my forearm. Entenmann's chocolate frosted donuts and a loaf-pan icebox cake with the unmistakable mark of chocolate wafers and whipped cream. Malt powder. A six-pack of cream soda. A carton of tart cherry juice. Ginger candies. Lemon drops. Saltines. Peppermint tea.

"I wasn't sure exactly what to get," she said frantically as she kept unloading. "But I knew I wanted to bring you a little bit of home. Did I remember the cream cheese correctly?" She held it up. "Scallion, right? I thought maybe it was the almond one, but then I was like no *way* my sister would sabotage a perfectly good bagel with a sweet cream cheese."

My smile was wobbly. "You're right. Scallion."

"I knew it."

But she wasn't done. She pulled out a plush robe next, and then fuzzy slippers, a maternity dress still on its hanger, the kind that draped rather than clung, in a green that would melt against my skin. There was a little toiletry bag jingling with prenatal vitamins, a belly oil I recognized from a boutique, and a silk scrunchie. On top of it all, a handwritten note folded into quarters and tied with a piece of raffia in the way only my sister would think to do.

My throat closed.

"I made a pregnancy package," she said, like she needed to explain the obvious. "For nausea and comfort and... and so you feel taken care of." She swallowed. "Like you should have felt back then."

There it was. The rift, the fault line we both stepped on the last time we spoke and the earth gave way.

"I'm sorry," Lacey said. She said it quick and sure, like pulling a bandage. "I should have said those words first. I should have said them weeks ago. It's not an excuse, but I need to tell you—when you told me about... Robert, and about Mom and Dad—" Her face crumpled. She steadied it with a breath. "It felt like my world tilted. I was blindsided, and that made me feel guilty, because another part of me wasn't. It was like hearing the end of a story I'd been reading with pages missing. I think I knew something awful had happened. I just... didn't know what."

I stared at her. The honesty of it was both a balm and a blade.

"I wasn't sure where you stood," I admitted. I kept my voice even, the way I did when I was telling a patient hard news. "I'm still not."

"I know." Lacey rolled her lips. "I kept thinking if I took a minute, took a breath, I'd come back with the right words. And the longer I took, the more wrong every word felt. Meanwhile, you were here. Alone. And I made it worse. I'm so, so sorry." She reached for my hand before she could second-guess herself. Our fingers linked. They still fit. "I'm getting married, Liv," she said, her voice wobbling but sure. "And of course, I grew up picturing our parents there. I imagined judging what Mom spent on the flower arrangements and Mom telling the band how to play a Motown set properly. I held on to that picture even when I didn't want to. I tried to force the world to make sense so the picture wouldn't have to change."

I squeezed her hand when her chin trembled. "I get it, it's—"

"I told them not to come."

Air left the room in a rush.

"You... *what?*"

"I told them if they weren't capable of protecting their daughter when it mattered, then they didn't get the honor of standing in the front row of my new life." Her jaw was set, eyes bright, shoulders squared. "I told them if they couldn't say your name without spitting, they could keep it out of their mouths and out of my day. They argued, and wheedled, and threatened me with a hundred different silences. Mom said she'd cut me off just like they did with you."

"She means that," I warned.

"I know. I don't care. I didn't waver."

My hands hovered over my lips. "Oh, Lace..."

"And if you'll reconsider," Lacey continued, her voice breaking, "I want you by my side."

The sentence knocked me back like a wave. For a second, everything was static. Then the softness returned, the smell of vanilla, the cooling air, the quiet insistence of my own heartbeat in my ears.

"I—" I started, eyes burning, rib cage pressing in. "You really want me there?"

"I have always wanted you there." She leaned forward, our foreheads almost touching, her hands tight in mine. "And I don't care if Mom and Dad never come around. I don't care if they want to live in denial for the rest of their lives to save face. I believe you."

It wasn't loud, the way she said it. It wasn't dramatic. It was simple. It was steady.

It was the exact key my rib cage was waiting on to unlock.

Everything in me gave way.

We fell into each other in a hug so healing I gasped at the pressure of it. For years, I'd wondered what it would be like to have my family back, wondered how my life could have differed if I'd have played by the rules my parents played out for me. I never regretted standing my ground, but I regretted losing Lacey in the process.

"I'm sorry I didn't tell you sooner," I choked out. "I should have. I just... I'm your big sister. I'm supposed to protect you. I didn't want to have to put you in the position to choose."

"The last thing I ever want you to do is apologize. *I* am sorry. I knew something had happened, but I was content living in my own blissful ignorance, and I didn't pry like a good sister should."

We held each other tighter.

When the worst of the shaking passed, Lacey sniffled and pulled back. "How are you feeling?" she asked.

"I feel... everything," I admitted. "Nauseous if I look at raw chicken. Hungry every hour like my stomach is a black hole. Tired like somebody filled my bones with wet sand. And also... full of life. Like there's this tiny lighthouse inside me I didn't know I needed." I shook my head. "I didn't think this would happen for me. Not like this."

"Well, I'm glad it did," she whispered.

We reached for napkins, for bagels, for familiarity. I watched Lacey split an everything with the practiced hand of someone who knew the right ratio of cream cheese to carb, and I swore for a moment we were teenagers again, the kitchen light yellow over our heads, Dad's shoes thumping down the hall, Mom fretting about crumbs.

It felt like theft and reclamation both.

I asked her how long she was in town, and she told me just for the weekend, just long enough to tell me everything she needed to in person. But she promised to be back for the baby shower Maven and I were having together.

I was halfway through the bagel when Lacey cleared her throat. "There's something else I want to tell you," she said. "I wasn't going to bring it up today. But it feels wrong not to, given... everything." She looked at me, then at the door like she wanted to make sure Carter wasn't going to interrupt. "It's about Robert."

The world narrowed to a pinpoint.

"What about him?"

"He works with Cole." She paused. "My fiancé."

I wasn't sure how to feel or what to say, but I settled on, "Who I haven't even met because I have been so self-absorbed."

"Stop that." Lacey shook her head. "You had every right to distance yourself, and I would have done the same."

"He works at the same firm?"

"They're not friends," she rushed to add. "They're colleagues. Same firm, yes, but different teams."

"Lacey." My name for her was a warning and a plea. "Please tell me you didn't tell Cole..."

"I did but hear me out." She wedged those words in quick, like she was putting a chair under a doorknob. "He believes you. He didn't even blink. And he's been... careful. I didn't ask him to go to war. In fact, I begged him to keep his cool." She smiled softly. "He's a little like your man, I think, from what I know about him so far, anyway. He's sweet, but he's also loyal — and he has a hard time not losing his shit when someone hurts me."

I smirked at that.

"Anyway, I just told him the truth and that I didn't want to see that man's face anywhere near my wedding. He said okay." She swallowed. "And then... well. He just sort of started talking."

"Lacey..."

"People trust him. He didn't start a rumor mill. He didn't say your name. But he told the truth where he could. He told people to look closer. And it turned out — this wasn't the first time."

Something cold and hot washed through me at once — the kind of heat that came from fury, the kind of cold that came from recognition.

"Accusations?" I asked. My voice was steady in that surgical way I hated.

She nodded. "Whispers. HR complaints that went nowhere because Robert's the kind of man who knows how to keep his hands clean. But that's shifting, Liv. Cole said everyone is distancing themselves. He's lost clients. People have stopped laughing at his stupid jokes. He doesn't get invited to happy hours anymore. The partners keep telling him he's not needed."

My heart was in my throat as I listened.

"It's small. It is not—" Lacey sighed. "It's not a courtroom. It's not a monster in cuffs. But it's something. And I need you to know that even if we never see him answer for what he did the way he should, the world is changing around him. Because it turns out the people he needs to maintain his perfect illusion can't stand him. And the man I'm marrying was all too happy to help take the fucker down."

I licked dry lips. "Does Robert know... it was me?"

"No." Her answer was immediate. "He won't. Not unless you tell him yourself. And if you want it handled differently, say the word." She paused. "I told Carter all of this, by the way. Pretty sure he wants to be best friends with Cole now."

"I might want the same," I said softly, and then I pulled her into me for another hug. I never wanted to let go. "Thank you."

She squeezed me tight in answer.

When I pulled back, I was shaking my head, taking in the beautiful creature bound to me by blood. "You don't have to torch your wedding day for me. I... I don't want you to have to lose our parents, too."

"I'm not torching anything." She squeezed my hands. "I'm choosing you."

It was such a simple sentence. It hit me in a place I'd barricaded behind credentials and jewelry and the right lipstick and control, control, control. Pain I'd had chained inside my heart for so long loosened, and it spilled out as tears I didn't bother to wipe.

"Okay," I whispered. I nodded, and the nod kept going, gathering steam like a train. "Okay."

"Okay you'll be there?" she asked, eyes wide and shining.

"Okay I'll be there," I said.

And I meant it. For her wedding, for her life, for everything.

I had my sister back.

Nothing mattered past that.

Chapter 33

Because I Said So

Carter

"Move in with me."

Livia paused, a forkful of beef-flavored Maruchan ramen noodles halfway to her mouth. She looked at the food, back at me, and then shoved it all in and chewed on it along with what I'd said.

And because that left some silence, I, of course, had to fill it.

"I know it seems fast," I said, rubbing her calves in my lap. "But to be fair, this whole thing has been a little expedited given your condition."

"Okay, Bridgerton."

"I know you love your condo. You're close to work, it's a luxury high rise, and I just live in this tiny little house on the water." I gestured around to said house.

Then, as if I'd paid him, Zamboni leapt onto the couch, burrowing himself between where we sat and the back cushions. He had to wiggle us a little out of the way to fit and we both chuckled.

"But look! It comes with a built-in dog!" I said, scratching Zambo's head. "And in exchange for the slightly longer commute, you get a blank slate of a house to do whatever you want with." I swallowed. "And me."

I had come to measure my life differently than before. I used to mark the passing of time by the months or years, perhaps the weeks of the season. Right now, we were dipping our toes into the playoffs, and all my focus when I wasn't with Livia was there with the team. Maybe that's what I should have been measuring my life by at the moment, how far we were into the playoff season, how many games we had to go, how many wins until we could fight for the Cup.

But I now marked the passing of time by the size of the tiny human growing inside Livia.

Today, they were the size of a grape. Livia was twelve weeks along.

She was feeling better and better every day, her nausea almost entirely gone and her headaches fewer and farther between. She was still tired a lot, though, which made sense. I'd learned a lot about pregnancy in the last two months, like that she was not only creating a life but also building a whole ass new organ to sustain it.

And maybe it was the fact that we were near the end of the first trimester, that the reality of our situation was hitting me more and more each day, that I couldn't keep those words trapped inside me any longer.

"If you hate this house," I continued. "We can buy another. We can live wherever you want, Liv. You can pick everything about it. But I want to hold you when I'm falling asleep at night and have you there in my arms when I wake up. I want to feed you and bring you ice water, rub your feet and make it so you don't have to lift a finger once you're home from work." I swallowed. "And I want to be there the first time our baby moves. I want to make a nursery together and fill a house, any house, with baby toys."

Livia set her bowl of pasta aside, now nearly empty, her eyes softening as she listened to me. I grabbed her hand in mine.

"Is it too much to ask if I ask for everything?"

Her smile knocked the air from my chest, just as much as the sight of her on my couch like that did. I loved her like this — sweatpants and one of my shirts, her hair in all its natural beauty, face clean of makeup. She was a fucking knockout, and I cherished when she got dressed up for me, but it was this that I felt most honored to witness.

"First a collar and now this," she mused, squeezing my hand playfully. She paused a moment, her eyes searching mine, and then answered with one simple word. "Yes."

"Yes?"

She nodded. "I want it, too, Carter. Besides... it would be a little strange for our baby to have to travel back and forth between two houses, wouldn't it? Not to mention pretty exhausting for us." She chuckled, maneuvering to sit up a bit more. She winced as she did. Her stomach was still just barely showing that she was pregnant, but she was feeling it more, and I reached out to help her get comfortable. "But that's not the only reason I want to do it. I love you, Rook," she said, looping her arms around my neck and giving me a swift peck on the lips. "I want to spend all the time I can with you."

The sigh I let out was filled with relief.

"You act like you were worried I'd say no."

"And you act like that's unreasonable."

She frowned, picking at her nails. "Well, that's fair. But I'm in this. I'm with you." She looked back at me.

"And... I was thinking... what if we use some of the money from our deal for this?"

I blinked. We hadn't talked about the money, not since that final payment hit her account. I was perfectly content to just leave it behind us. She'd more than fulfilled her part of the contract, and I was a happy customer.

"What do you mean?"

"I mean yes, I love your little home, but... let's buy a new one. Together. One that's ours."

"Yeah?"

She nodded, smiling. "Yeah. Listen, that money is still going to be used for what I intended it to be used for — to set our kid up for life." She rubbed her belly. "And this is step one of that."

"I don't know what I did in a past life to earn this one, but I really want to thank that motherfucker for doing it right." I kissed her as she giggled against my lips, and then I was pulling her into my lap.

Instantly, my body reacted to her. If I thought Livia was hot before, it was nothing compared to now. There was just something about knowing she had my baby inside her that made me absolutely fucking feral.

I didn't care how caveman that was of me, either.

I inhaled on a groan, deepening our kiss and wrapping my arms flush around her.

"You know," she said against my lips, nipping at the bottom one. "We still haven't broken that thing in yet."

I arched a brow in question.

"The collar."

Oh.

My cock twitched in my sweatpants, and Livia must have felt it, because her grin doubled, and the little vixen ground herself against me.

"Are you up for that?" I asked tentatively, though my body was screaming for me to run and grab that damn collar right now if it meant I got to be inside her tonight.

"I can't think of anything I'd like more right now than to hold tight to that collar while I ride you."

She hummed the words low in my ear before licking it from the lobe up, and I cursed, grip tightening on her hips.

And then I was up in a flash, spanking her ass playfully and sprinting to my bedroom for the collar. Zamboni scrambled at my urgency, giving us both a look before he huffed and waddled back to his dog bed in my room.

When I slid back into the living room on my socks, Livia was already naked, her sweats discarded, and she lay on her side like a Renaissance painting.

She was so beautiful it stopped me in my tracks.

I tracked every inch of her rich, velvety skin, from the slope of her nose to the small swell of her belly all the way down to the red polish on her toes.

"Fuck, Liv," I breathed, shaking my head. "Look at you."

"I'd rather look at you in that collar," she said, curling her finger.

I took my time walking to her, and when she reached for the key around her neck, I held the leather in my hand out for her to unlock. It unfastened with a soft *snick*, and then Livia ripped it from my hand.

I saw it happen in real time, her slipping into her dominance.

It had me rock hard and ready to beg.

"Take off your clothes," she commanded. "Slowly. Let me see my play toy for the evening."

God, I'd missed this.

I stripped as slowly as I could with all the eager energy roaring through my veins, and when I was fully bare, Livia smirked at my cock already erect and dripping for her.

"On your knees."

I dropped instantly, eyes on hers, practically panting as she fastened the leather around my throat. She pulled it tight, and when it was where she wanted it, she used the key on the chain around her neck to lock it in place.

Every nerve inside me sizzled to life at the sound.

Her smirk turned wicked as she tugged the D-ring, testing the collar, tugging my chin up to meet her eyes. "There he is," she purred. "My Rook. My good boy. You ready to serve your Queen tonight?"

"Yes, ma'am." The words tumbled out hoarse, desperate, automatic.

Her nails grazed down my chest, leaving goosebumps in their wake before she grabbed a fistful of my hair and shoved me onto my back. I landed with a grunt, staring up at her as she straddled me, every curve of her body silhouetted in low lamplight.

"Hands behind your head."

I obeyed instantly, fingers locking. The collar tugged at my throat as she leaned down and kissed me hard, deep, before pulling back with a sly grin. "You don't move them until I tell you to. Understood?"

"Yes, ma'am."

Her hips rolled once, deliberately slow, grinding against me until I was trembling beneath her. When I bucked my hips, unable to help it, she slapped my thigh with a sharp smack.

"I said still," she warned, tugging the collar again. My cock ached, straining so hard I thought I'd lose it right then.

The power thrummed between us, hot and familiar and perfect. And the way she looked at me — fierce, proud, hungry — it burned through me like I was nothing but tinder.

Livia licked her lips as she pressed up on her knees. She spit on my cock, letting the saliva drip from her lips as I groaned and watched it coat me. Then, she used her hands to tease and play, to pump me until I was nearly in pain from doing my best not to move.

"It kills you to stay still, doesn't it?" she teased, her grip tightening. "You want to bury yourself inside me. You want the pleasure of fucking my sweet pussy, don't you?"

"Fuck yes," I croaked.

"Beg for it, then." Livia released my cock in an instant, hooking the loop on the collar and jerking so I was in a crunch staring up at her. "I'll only give it to you if you want it bad enough."

"Please, Livia," I pleaded, my voice hoarse, cock aching as I tried to fuck the air like it could relieve me. "I need it. I need *you*. Please, let me fuck you. Please give me what I need."

She seemed satisfied, her lips curling as she released me. I had to engage my core to not let my head slam back against the ground, and I'd no sooner laid down than she was grabbing me and lining me up right where I wanted to be.

Livia sat in a slow, torturous decline, taking all of me and moaning as she did. The sight was too much, especially with the view of her slightly swollen belly. I groaned and rolled my eyes up to the ceiling to stop from coming instantly.

"So fucking big," she praised. "You fill me perfectly."

And then her hips were rocking, slow and steady, like she was savoring every centimeter of me. I finally felt locked in enough to look up and watch her, and then my hands were wandering, roving over her breasts and nipples, teasing and toying until I found my way down to her clit.

"Yes," she encouraged, rolling against the touch. "Fuck, that feels so good. I feel so fucking good right now, Carter."

I groaned at the sound of my name in that breathy voice of hers. Livia started moving wildly then, bucking against my hand as she fucked my cock and used me to get her release. When she shook and moaned and cried out, I felt her tightening around me, and I couldn't hold back.

She rode me hard as we both shattered, Livia leaning forward to clutch the collar and hold me there, owned and undone. I spilled beneath her with a ragged cry, her moans echoing mine until we collapsed in a heap of sweat and laughter.

But before I could even catch my breath, she leaned over me, eyes flashing. "We've got a lot of time to make up for," she whispered, dragging her lips along my jaw. "And apparently the new update of these pregnancy hormones is that I'm absolutely insatiable."

"Fuck," I whispered, not sure if I was excited or scared.

"So, you better get hard again for me, Rook. Round two starts now."

I tried to laugh, but it was cut short when she squeezed me in her hand, already coaxing me back to life. "Jesus, woman," I groaned, rolling us so she landed on her back with a gasp. I kissed her, deep and hungry, soaking up every sound she made. "Maybe I want to take the reins for this round. What do you think of that?"

She arched a brow as I hovered over her. "Don't push your luck."

"Oh, come on," I teased, kissing the corner of her smirk. "You know you like it. When I remind you I've got you. That you're safe with me. That you can let go and let me lead."

Her sigh turned into a moan as I punctuated each of those promises with slow, lingering kisses across her breasts. Her hips arched into mine, thighs spreading to let me in, and I knew I had her.

"I'm going to take care of you," I murmured against her neck. "You understand me? I'm going to cook you anything you crave. Run you a bath every night. Massage you until you're moaning for me the way I love to hear. You're going to let me dote on you, Livia Young, because I fucking said so."

Her laugh was breathless, sultry. "God, I've never found it so hot to be bossed around."

I smirked, pressing into her, voice rough with laughter and desire and a love so deep I thought it might break me.

"Funny," I said. "That seems to be the number one turn on for me."

And with the laugh I earned and cherished, I kissed her again — letting the night swallow us whole.

Epilogue

No Threats Necessary

Livia

June in Tampa tasted like salt and celebration, despite the fact that some might think we shouldn't be celebrating at all. The air was heavy with summer, the kind that curled my hair and made it even harder to breathe than the little body crowding my organs.

There was a faint hum of laughter rolling out from the back deck of the waterfront house that belonged to the Ospreys General Manager. It was decorated and fully catered for the endofseason party. Lights were strung across the railing, and they twinkled against the dark water, the downtown skyline barely visible off in the distance. Tampa felt like home more than ever in that moment.

We didn't get the ending Carter dreamed of. The Ospreys lost in Game Five of the Stanley Cup Finals, and the entire city felt the ache of it. But there was pride split right down the middle of that ache. The boys had played like men possessed, Carter most of all. He was incandescent on the ice— stronger on the puck, calmer in the face-off circle, feeding passes like a conductor. His name was on lips that had never said it before. Broadcasters said "what a season" about him with reverence.

He was a revelation to the league.

And a revelation in my life.

At twenty weeks, I'd popped past the point of ambiguity; there was no mistaking who I was carrying with me everywhere I went. Our little girl announced herself in everything I wore, from the soft white dress I'd chosen tonight to the big Ospreys t-shirt I slept in most nights, one I stole from Carter.

It was wild now that we were in the part of pregnancy where movement was a thing. I laid awake most nights struck with wonder, my hand on my belly, feeling my world flip along with her. And when Carter talked, she stretched and kicked, as if she already knew his voice, as if she already adored it.

He followed me around the party with one hand tethered to me, unable to help himself. It would have been ridiculous if it weren't so sweet. The man had been shameless in his advances with me since the day I met him, but he was full-on obsessed now.

I couldn't even pretend like I didn't love it.

"You good?" he murmured for the third time in ten minutes, palm warm against the small of my back, thumb sweeping idly. His hair was tousled, his jaw cleanshaven after he and the rest of the guys let their beards grow all through the playoff run. He'd put on a linen shirt for me and left the top few buttons undone because he knew I liked to kiss the notch of his throat.

"I'm perfect," I said, and it wasn't a lie. Considering I'd had two Fruity Pebbles cookies from Bake'n Babes, a delightful little mocktail, my feet were bare, my friends within arm's reach, and my man glued to me? Perfect was the only way to describe it.

On the other side of the deck, Aleks and Mia held court at the long picnic table, her laughter ringing out like a bell every time he leaned in to whisper something at her temple. They were leaving for their honeymoon at last, bags already packed and waiting at the door, and the way they couldn't stop touching each other told me they were both over the wait.

Chloe and Will had claimed the hammock like a pair of teenagers, swaying gently, a newly married glow radiating off them both. Will still looked at her like he couldn't believe she'd said yes. Ava wore an Ospreys cap backward and was making her rounds to anyone who would listen to her discuss why our loss in the fifth game had been complete bullshit and all due to mistakes by the refs.

Maven and Vince were on the stairs just inside, heads bent together, whispering and giggling like kids. Vince had one hand splayed over Maven's barely there bump and the other braced behind her on the step. Every few minutes, Maven shot me a look that said *can you believe this?* and I shot one back that said *not even a little.*

She'd just found out that she was having a girl, too.

We'd giggled all night together, dreaming about how our daughters would be best friends. They didn't have a say in it. It was just how it would be.

It was a good night. The kind of night I wanted to bottle for our daughter and say, *This. This is your family. This is what love feels like.*

Grace breezed onto the deck in a sundress and bare feet, cheeks sunkissed from a day on the water. She pressed a cold beer into Jaxson's palm and stole his snapback, tucking her platinum hair up under it with a grin. "You look sappy," she told him, tilting her head at him like she was suspicious. "Is this what retiring your bad boy era looks like? Concern and a wrinkled brow?"

"I'm just tired," Jaxson said in way of explanation, his hand floating to her hip like it always did. "And talked out. I lost my voice yelling at refs, that's all."

"You always lose your voice yelling at refs," she said, stealing a sip of his beer. "Even when we watch from a bar."

"Some of us are passionate, Little Nova."

"Lucky me," she murmured, bumping his shoulder with hers.

I watched Jaxson a beat after Grace had turned away, and the second she wasn't looking anymore, he paled like he was nervous, like he was about to play a game instead of go into the offseason.

I narrowed my eyes, the suspicion mine now.

Coach McCabe was at the party, too — the host of it all alongside Dick, the GM. He made his rounds, talking to each of the players with a little glint in his eye. I could tell he was disappointed they hadn't gone all the way, and simultaneously proud of all they'd accomplished. I couldn't imagine it, fighting that hard for months and getting so close only to fall a bit short.

But that was what I marveled at when it came to the professional athletes I worked with. They were resilient as hell, never feeling discouraged for long before they were on to the next game, the next season. It was inspiring.

I beamed with pride when Coach stopped by to talk to Carter, congratulating us on the upcoming birth before he told Carter that it had been a hell of a year for him. I loved the way my man stood straighter, not backing away from the praise but soaking in the fact that he'd earned it. He'd learned to take a compliment this season, to let it land instead of batting it away like a puck. I liked that growth almost as much as I liked watching him win a puck battle along the boards with a man twice his size.

But not nearly as much as I liked watching him writhe for me with that leather collar around his neck.

When the party had settled a bit, Carter tucked me under his arm and leaned down. "How's she doing?"

"Practicing her slapshot," I said, tapping my belly. "Either that or she's discovered tap-dancing."

He laughed, quiet and delighted. He did that a lot lately. "Of course she's got a good slapshot. It's genetic."

"I hope she gets your patience," I said. "And your incessant need to kill any stretch of silence with a joke, no matter the merit of it."

"You love my jokes," he murmured, pressing his mouth to my temple. "They're a gift. And I'm patient because you taught me to be."

"Because I didn't entertain your pickup lines for years?"

"And because I know better than to come before you say I can," he added salaciously in my ear.

I elbowed him with a grin, but slid under his arm next, hugging him tight.

In a couple months, our families would cross paths for the first time when his parents and my sister came to the baby shower the girls were throwing for me and Maven. I'd become close with Carter's mom, accepting her gracious advice and support through the pregnancy. I was grateful for her, especially since my mom was nowhere to be found.

She and my father found out about my pregnancy after Carter and I attended Lacey's wedding. Carter had let it slip when he was chatting with Cole and some of the guys from the firm, and it didn't take long for news to travel in that circle.

It didn't change anything, though.

My parents hadn't spoken to me or Lacey, and as much as it pained us both, we resisted the urge to reach out. They were the parents. They were the ones who had messed up. It was on them to make it right, and at this point, I was unsure if they ever could.

And so, me and my sister clung to each other for dear life, vowing to build a new family together.

Across the deck, Chloe waved me over with the urgency of someone who had discovered something vital on her phone. "Baby clothes," she announced, thrusting the screen toward me as I regretfully parted from Carter with a squeeze of my hand, his holding fast to mine until he had no choice but to drop it. "Tell me this isn't the cutest dress you've ever seen. I think I could make something like it, but I might cry in the process."

"Well, I'm pregnant," I said, taking her phone to see the bright rainbow dress more clearly once I reached her. "I cry at Subaru commercials. But yes, that is...something."

"Wait until you see the tiny Ospreys jersey Mia found," Chloe said, taking her phone back.

Mia popped up beside us as if summoned, her own phone out, a picture already loaded — a custom white infant jersey with FABRI printed across the back and a soft pink number 00. "I know she won't wear it for a while," she said sheepishly, "but I couldn't resist."

"I love you," I told her, and I meant it. I loved them all. I loved the way they'd woven themselves around me this year, the way they'd heard me when I told them the truth, the way they'd held me up without pity when I confessed the worst thing that ever happened to me and the second worst thing that followed. I loved the way they'd cheered for my boundaries, the way they'd offered to be my standin family at every milestone from now until forever.

"Can I get everyone's attention?" Jaxson announced suddenly, hopping up on the low retaining wall that framed the deck. He cupped his hands around his mouth and called, "Everybody! Ten seconds! I've got an announcement. Not a sad one. Don't groan, Vince. I can see you."

Vince lifted his hands in surrender. "I just don't want everyone here to have to endure you recounting the last car show you went to in vivid, unnecessary detail."

A few chuckles from his teammates and Jaxson was flipping them all the bird.

Then, he thrust his chin at Grace. "Come here, trouble."

Grace narrowed her eyes. "If you push me in the water, I'll go back to that snake charmer in Morocco and have him mesmerize one right into your bed while you're sleeping."

"No threats necessary," he said, holding out his hand as she stepped up beside him.

I saw it again, how nervous he was, and I think I realized what was happening right when Maven did. Because she'd slid up beside where I was standing with the other girls, and she wordlessly squeezed my forearm.

"I wrote a whole speech," Jaxson confessed, patting at his pockets. "But I realized I've given you enough speeches in our time together and I just wanted to speak from the heart tonight." His blue eyes were glued to Grace's, like we weren't even there. "I met you on a bus full of my smelly teammates on a night I least expected you, and you asked me the weirdest string of *would you rather* questions."

Laughter rippled at that, and Grace did a little curtsy at the mention of her signature party game.

"I learned a lot about you that night, but not nearly as much as I did when we took to the road that summer. It was then that I discovered you're a world champion in quarters, you can't hike without tripping, and the limit does not exist for you when it comes to road trip snacks."

Grace smiled, pressing on her tiptoes like she wanted to melt right into him.

"And I know you're not meant to be anchored to one place. I knew it the first time I said goodbye to you in an airport and you took my heart with you. You're a tide, Little Nova. You go out and you come back, and the shore is better for it. I don't want to change a single thing about that. I don't want to tame you. I don't want to cage you. I fall in love with you every time you throw a bag over your shoulder and leave, and I fall in love with you even more every time you walk back through my door."

Maven sniffed loudly. "It's the hormones," she declared.

I squeezed her hand.

"I'm not asking you to stay put," Jaxson said. He dug in his pocket, and without a box barrier to give any of us time to prepare, a ring emerged, the stone catching the light with a wink.

And even though it was mostly hockey player brutes at that party, there was still a collective gasp.

"I'm asking you to take me with you. I'm asking to be your home, wherever you go."

Grace's hand flew to her mouth, then to his chest, like she needed to feel his heart under her palm to believe him.

"Jaxson Brittain," she said, shaking her head. "You act like I would rather run the Earth than be with you. I don't need to see anything else to know that what I love most about this planet is that you're on it." She held up her hand. "Tie me down. Tie me up." Laughter surged at that, and she smirked. "Put that shiny ass ring on my finger and let's do this thing."

And then she was airborne, launching into his arms. The cheer we all let out rivaled those of the final game we'd played, and I shared looks with the girls, knowing what a big deal this was for our little adventurer.

Grace was sobbing and laughing when her feet touched the ground again. She shoved the brim of Jaxson's hat back so she could see his face as he slid the ring home.

Carter slid up behind me wordlessly, his hands cradling my belly as he leaned in and kissed the back of my neck.

"Maybe we're next," he murmured, and there was no pressure in it, just wonder.

"You did give me a collar," I said, unable to resist teasing him. He huffed a laugh against my hair, and I tipped my face to his. Then, I rubbed my belly with both our hands, and our daughter nudged against my palm like she had an opinion. "Let's wait for her. I think she'd like to be a part of it."

"I can't imagine it any other way," he said simply, and then he kissed me.

It should have been a chaste kiss, given the audience. It started that way — soft, sure, sweet enough that Chloe made a little sound before abandoning us to find Will. But Carter lost his cool halfway through like he always did with me, and the angle shifted, his hand slid, and someone whistled and someone else yelled, "Get a room!"

Carter broke away just enough to murmur, "We could."

"We could what?" I breathed, already smiling.

"Get a room," he said, eyes wicked, and there it was — that boyish grin, the one that made my knees feel like they'd been replaced with spaghetti. "Think they'd miss us for ten minutes?"

"Ten?" I repeated, arching a brow.

"Five?"

I barked out a laugh, but before I could tell him how ridiculous he was being, he was toting me through the crowd, greeting his teammates and staff members as he did like we were completely innocent.

We slipped inside through the sliding door like teenagers at a house party, and it was ridiculous how quickly the two of us could go from sweet to stupid. The hallway was dim, a runner soft under my bare feet. Carter checked doors with the exaggerated caution of a cartoon burglar until he found a quiet guest room with a lamp left on low and a pile of beach towels tossed on the loveseat. The window was cracked to the water and smelled like salt and laundry detergent.

"Romantic," I said.

"The romance is me," he said, and then his mouth was on mine again, eager and greedy, reverent and ridiculous. His hands learned my body all over again like they did every day — this new curve here, this stretch of skin that had gone extra sensitive. He knelt when he kissed my belly, and I carded my fingers through his hair and cursed softly because the sight of him would never not undo me.

He was gentle because I was his, and he was hungry because I was his, and I pulled him down with a hand knotted in his shirt because he was mine. My world narrowed to the feel of his mouth on my throat, his palm cradling my belly, the little hitch in his breath when I whispered something filthy in his ear because I could, because we were us.

And there were a million things we still needed to figure out — what we would name our daughter, what color we'd paint the nursery walls, whether we'd buy an old house on the water or build a new one of our own.

But one thing was certain.

I was a better woman for having that man's love, for letting him in when it felt impossible to do.

And I'd always be thankful that, even at his most insecure, he was never too afraid to shoot his shot when it came to me.

Epilogue 2

Bound

Shane
(AKA Coach McCabe)

If a heart was tied to a person, mine was bound to her — and it stopped beating the day I left her behind.

Ariana Ridley had tried desperately not to be noticed when we were in college, but one look at her and it was clear how impossible that mission was. She was like a diamond buried deep, and her beauty was the volcano that unearthed her. It wasn't only her piercing blue eyes or snow-white complexion. It wasn't just her heart shaped lips or her goddess-like curves.

It was the untold stories in her gaze, the way she wore her trauma like a cloak.

She called to me in a way I couldn't fight, because I saw what everyone else overlooked.

Ariana was a survivor.

She was just like me.

We fell in love too easily, too quickly, at a rate that should have foretold how bad it would be once we finally hit the ground.

Stand your Ground

I was young and stupid when I let her go, when I chose my dream of hockey over her because hockey was the only thing I'd ever been able to depend on and staying meant total life destruction for her. I told myself I was doing the right thing, that I was saving her from the problem of me, that I was making everything easier.

But I hated myself for the choice I made.

And I regretted it every day.

I only saw her once after that, six years later, when I got injured and watched my dream go up in smoke. Our paths crossed by chance. I begged for her forgiveness. She rightfully denied it.

I never thought I'd see her again.

Which was why I was grinding my teeth together to keep my jaw from dropping now, my heart kicking back to life in my chest with a force strong enough to take me to my knees.

Because here she was, in front of me again.

My Ari.

Standing next to my new General Manager.

As his wife.

What happens when the youngest, most successful coach in the NHL comes face-to-face with the woman he never got over — only to find out she's married to his new General Manager?

Find out in the explosive final installment of the Kings of the Ice series, *Right Your Wrongs* (https://geni.us/rightyourwrongs).

Can't get enough of Livia and Carter?
Catch up with them in this bonus scene
https://kandisteiner.com/bonus-content/

Fall in love with the other Kings of the Ice couples!

MEET YOUR MATCH
Book 1
TROPES:
Pro Hockey
Romance
Forced Proximity
Opposite Sides of the Track
Interracial/Multicultural Couple
Workplace Romance
Enemies-to-Lovers Vibes

WATCH YOUR MOUTH
Book 2
TROPES:
Pro Hockey
Romance
Teammate's Little Sister/Brother's Best Friend
Road Trip
Forced Proximity
One Bed
Age Gap
Opposites Attract
Forbidden

LEARN YOUR LESSON
Book 3
TROPES:
Pro Hockey Romance
Single Dad/Nanny
Forced Proximity
Spicy Lessons
Grumpy Sunshine
Age Gap
Opposites Attract
Found Family

SAVE YOUR BREATH
Book 4
TROPES:
Pro Hockey Romance
Fake Engagement
Athlete & Pop Star
Childhood Friends to Lovers
Forced Proximity
Unrequited Love (or so they think)
Opposites Attract
Slow Burn

More from Kandi Steiner

The Red Zone Rivals Series
Fair Catch
As if being the only girl on the college football team wasn't hard enough, Coach had to go and assign my brother's best friend — and *my* number one enemy — as my roommate.

Blind Side
The hottest college football safety in the nation just asked me to be his fake girlfriend.
And I just asked him to take my virginity.

Quarterback Sneak
Quarterback Holden Moore can have any girl he wants.
Except me: the coach's daughter.

Hail Mary (an Amazon #1 Bestseller!)
Leo F*cking Hernandez.
North Boston University's star running back, notorious bachelor, and number one on my people I would murder if I could get away with it list.
And now?
My new roommate.

The Becker Brothers Series
On the Rocks (book 1)
Neat (book 2)
Manhattan (book 3)
Old Fashioned (book 4)
Four brothers finding love in a small Tennessee town that

revolves around a whiskey distillery with a dark past — including the mysterious death of their father.

The Best Kept Secrets Series
(AN AMAZON TOP 10 BESTSELLER)
What He Doesn't Know (book 1)
What He Always Knew (book 2)
What He Never Knew (book 3)
Charlie's marriage is dying. She's perfectly content to go down in the flames, until her first love shows back up and reminds her the other way love can burn.

Close Quarters
A summer yachting the Mediterranean sounded like heaven to Jasmine after finishing her undergrad degree. But her boyfriend's billionaire boss always gets what he wants. And this time, he wants her.

Make Me Hate You
Jasmine has been avoiding her best friend's brother for years, but when they're both in the same house for a wedding, she can't resist him — no matter how she tries.

The Wrong Game
(AN AMAZON TOP 5 BESTSELLER)
Gemma's plan is simple: invite a new guy to each home game using her season tickets for the Chicago Bears. It's the perfect way to avoid getting emotionally attached and also get some action. But after Zach gets his chance to be her practice round, he decides one game just isn't enough. A sexy, fun sports romance.

The Right Player
She's avoiding love at all costs. He wants nothing more

than to lock her down. Sexy, hilarious and swoon-worthy, The Right Player is the perfect read for sports romance lovers.

On the Way to You
It was only supposed to be a road trip, but when Cooper discovers the journal of the boy driving the getaway car, everything changes. An emotional, angsty road trip romance.

A Love Letter to Whiskey
(AN AMAZON TOP 10 BESTSELLER)
An angsty, emotional romance between two lovers fighting the curse of bad timing.
Read Love, Whiskey – Jamie's side of the story and an extended epilogue – in the new Fifth Anniversary Edition!

Weightless
Young Natalie finds self-love and romance with her personal trainer, along with a slew of secrets that tie them together in ways she never thought possible.

Revelry
Recently divorced, Wren searches for clarity in a summer cabin outside of Seattle, where she makes an unforgettable connection with the broody, small town recluse next door.

Say Yes
Harley is studying art abroad in Florence, Italy. Trying to break free of her perfectionism, she steps outside one night determined to Say Yes to anything that comes her way. Of course, she didn't expect to run into Liam Benson...

Washed Up
Gregory Weston, the boy I once knew as my son's best friend, now a man I don't know at all. No, not just a man. A doctor. And he wants me...

The Christmas Blanket
Stuck in a cabin with my ex-husband waiting out a blizzard? Not exactly what I had pictured when I planned a surprise visit home for the holidays...

Black Number Four
A college, Greek-life romance of a hot young poker star and the boy sent to take her down.

The Palm South University Series
Rush (book 1) FREE if you sign up for my newsletter!
Anchor, PSU #2
Pledge, PSU #3
Legacy, PSU #4
Ritual, PSU #5
Hazed, PSU #6
Greek, PSU #7
#1 NYT Bestselling Author Rachel Van Dyken says, "If Gossip Girl and Riverdale had a love child, it would be PSU." This angsty college series will be your next guilty addiction.

Tag Chaser
She made a bet that she could stop chasing military men, which seemed easy — until her knight in shining armor and latest client at work showed up in Army ACUs.

Song Chaser

Tanner and Kellee are perfect for each other. They frequent the same bars, love the same music, and have the same desire to rip each other's clothes off. Only problem? Tanner is still in love with his best friend.

Acknowledgements

I have to start with Rhiannon Gwynne and her husband, Josh Brittain. This series wouldn't be possible without you. Thank you for allowing me an inside look at what it's like to play in the professional hockey circuit (and be the wife of a player!). Your constant help has made each book in this series shine.

To my husband and daughter, thank you for giving me a life so beautiful I sometimes tear up just thinking about my fortune. And thank you for your unwavering support, always.

To my mom, Lavon, and my best friend, Sasha — I swear, I'll never write a book without leaning on you both. Thank you for being my safe place, my sounding board, and my constant. I love you endlessly.

To Tina Stokes — my Executive Assistant, my friend, and my rock — thank you for carrying so much of the weight while I buried myself in the writing cave with this one. You not only kept everything running smoothly, you poured creativity into this series that directly shaped its success. I love you big, and I'm endlessly grateful.

To my writing sisters who were in the cave with me on this one — Laura Pavlov, Lena Hendrix, Catherine Cowles, Staci Hart, Brittainy Cherry — thank you for being the kind of women who make this industry brighter, kinder, and a whole lot more fun. I'm lucky to walk this path with you.

To the OSYS Studios crew — thank you for breathing life into these characters in audio. Audrey Obeyn and Aaron Donahue, thank you for embodying Carter and Livia and putting your all into these performances.

To my beta readers — thank you for your patience when I hit pause right at the good part... and for being down for my spiciest adventure yet! Thank you for celebrating all the exciting book releases and tours this summer and then cheering me back into this story. Your notes and encouragement mean the world. Huge thanks to Frances O'Brien, Elizabeth Turner, Allison Cheshire, Kellee Fabre, Janett Corona, Jayce Cruz, Gabriela Vivas, Carly Wilson, and Nicole Westmoreland. I couldn't do this without you.

To my sensitivity readers — thank you for helping me honor Livia's voice and story as a Black woman with honesty and respect. To my reader in the Lifestyle — your insight gave me the confidence to approach these scenes with care and accuracy. And to my dental associates — thank you for generously sharing your knowledge so I could get the details right. Tiffanie Shipp, Chelé Walker, Kasondra Farmer, Kelly Monson and Elizabeth Sherrell — your time and energy mean the world to me, and I cannot thank you enough.

To the dream team who turns my vision into something tangible: Elaine York at Allusion Graphics, Nicole McCurdy at Emerald Edits, Nina Grinstead, Kim Cermak, the entire Valentine PR squad, Shaye Lefkowitz and Lindsey Romero at Good Girls PR, Ren Saliba and Staci Hart at Quirky Bird Cover Design — thank you for every detail, every late-night brainstorm, and every ounce of care. You make the impossible possible.

To my agent, Ariele Fredman — thank you for championing me, for believing in me, and for pushing my books farther than I dreamed they could go. You are magic.

To Sophie, Ethan, and Elsa with UTA — thank you for the doors you open and the passion you bring to my work.

To Janelle and Bonnie — the Lyla June cards and character stickers you've made are pure joy. You bring these characters to life in such fun, whimsical ways, and I love you for it.

To Elizianna — your artwork continues to blow me away. Thank you for pouring your talent into this series and gifting me with images that feel like magic.

And finally, to you, the reader — thank you for everything. For reading, for sharing, for reviewing, for telling your friends, for showing up. You are the reason this dream is real, the reason these characters breathe. I never take it for granted. Thank you for being here and for choosing my books out of the millions of choices you have. I will forever cherish you.

Content Notes & Trigger Warnings

I always want you to feel safe when stepping into one of my stories. Below you'll find a list of sensitive or potentially triggering content included in this book. Please use it in whatever way serves you best — whether that's to prepare, to skip, or simply to know what's ahead.

This book contains:

Explicit sexual content – steamy scenes, explicit language, and high heat levels.

BDSM & kink – including bondage, spanking, pegging, safe words, degradation, and praise.

Erotic humiliation (consensual) – verbal degradation as part of play.

Voyeurism – watching other people engage in sexual scenes.

Consensual non-consent – witnessed at a club, not involving the main characters.

References to past emotional abuse – connected to a mentor/coach figure, impacting the male lead's confidence.

References to past sexual coercion/abuse – connected to a family friend of the main female lead and contributing to her current fallout with her family.

Alcohol use – social drinking and intoxication.

Strong language – frequent profanity.

Sexual banter about past experiences – including references to group sex.

Discussion of fertility & pregnancy – including medical considerations.

Power imbalance – older woman/younger man, transactional arrangement.

A note of clarity:

The group sexual experience Carter participates in as a rookie is entirely consensual among all adults involved. It is portrayed with care and does not depict coercion or assault.

Similarly, The Manor is presented as a private, consensual space for adults within the Lifestyle. All encounters there are between informed, willing participants.

About the Author

KANDI STEINER is a *USA Today* and #1 Amazon Bestselling Author living in Tennessee. Best known for writing "emotional rollercoaster" stories, she loves bringing flawed characters to life and writing about real, raw romance — in all its forms. No two Kandi Steiner books are the same, and if you're a lover of angsty, emotional, and inspirational reads, she's your gal.

An alumna of the University of Central Florida, Kandi graduated with a double major in Creative Writing and Advertising/PR with a minor in Women's Studies. Her love for writing started at the ripe age of 10, and in 6th grade, she wrote and edited her own newspaper and distributed to her classmates. Eventually, the principal caught on and the newspaper was quickly halted, though Kandi tried fighting for her "freedom of press."

She took particular interest in writing romance after college, as she has always been a hopeless romantic and found herself bursting at the seams with love stories she was eager to tell.

When Kandi isn't writing, you can find her reading books of all kinds, planning her next adventure, or pole dancing (yes, you read that right). She enjoys live music, traveling, hiking, yoga, spending quality time with her family (fur babies included) and soaking up the sweetness of life.

Connect with Kandi:
NEWSLETTER: kandisteiner.com/newsletter
FACEBOOK: @kandisteiner
FACEBOOK READER GROUP (Kandiland):
facebook.com/groups/kandilandks
INSTAGRAM: @kandisteiner
TIKTOK: @authorkandisteiner
WEBSITE: kandisteiner.com

Kandi Steiner may be coming to a city near you! Check out her "events" tab on her website to see all the signings she's attending in the near future.

www.ingramcontent.com/pod-product-compliance
Lightning Source LLC
Chambersburg PA
CBHW020119161025
34096CB00018B/84